Praise for *A Flicker in the Dark*

"A fast-paced read that foretells more coming from this budding author." —*Star Tribune*

"Willingham delivers in keeping us riveted as one time line intersects with another . . . This atmospheric psychological thriller will have you on the edge of your seat." —*B&N Reads*

"A tension-soaked stunner of a tale that never lets up or lets us down." —*Providence Sunday Journal*

"A book you won't want to put down." —*Red Carpet Crash*

"A homerun . . . Willingham may be a writer, but she paints wonderfully with words." —*Holy City Sinner*

"You won't be able to put this one down once you pick it up." —*Daily Hive*

A FLICKER IN THE DARK

STACY
WILLINGHAM

St. Martin's Paperbacks

Published in the United States by St. Martin's Paperbacks, an imprint of St. Martin's Publishing Group.

A FLICKER IN THE DARK

Copyright © 2021 by Stacy Willingham.
Excerpt from *All the Dangerous Things* copyright © 2022 by Stacy Willingham.

All rights reserved.

For information, address St. Martin's Publishing Group, 120 Broadway, New York, NY 10271.

www.stmartins.com

Library of Congress Catalog Card Number: 2021035261

ISBN: 978-1-250-89644-5

Our books may be purchased in bulk for promotional, educational, or business use. Please contact your local bookseller or the Macmillan Corporate and Premium Sales Department at 1-800-221-7945, ext. 5442, or by email at MacmillanSpecialMarkets@macmillan.com.

Printed in the United States of America

Minotaur hardcover edition published 2022
Minotaur trade paperback edition published 2023
St. Martin's Paperbacks edition / October 2023

10 9 8 7 6 5 4 3 2 1

For my parents, Kevin and Sue.
Thank you for everything.

Whoever fights monsters should see to it that, in the process, he does not become a monster. If you gaze long enough into an abyss, the abyss will gaze back into you.

—*Friedrich Nietzsche*

PROLOGUE

I thought I knew what monsters were.

As a little girl, I used to think of them as mysterious shadows lurking behind my hanging clothes, under my bed, in the woods. They were a presence I could physically feel behind me, moving in closer as I walked home from school in the glare of the setting sun. I didn't know how to describe the feeling, but I just *knew* they were there, somehow. My body could sense them, sense danger, the way your skin seems to prickle just before a hand is placed on an unsuspecting shoulder, the moment you realize that unshakable feeling you had was a set of eyes burrowing into the back of your skull, lurking behind the branches of an overgrown shrub.

But then you turn around, and the eyes are gone.

I remember the feeling of uneven ground twisting my skinny ankles as I walked faster and faster down the gravel roadway that led to my house, fumes from the retreating school bus billowing behind me. The shadows in the woods danced as the sun streamed through the tree branches, my own silhouette looming large like an animal prepared to pounce.

I would take deep breaths, count to ten. Close my eyes and squeeze my lids.

And then I would run.

Every day, I would run down that stretch of isolated roadway, my house in the distance seeming to move farther and farther away instead of closer within my reach. My sneakers would kick up clumps of grass and pebbles and dust as I raced against . . . something. Whatever was *in there,* watching. Waiting. Waiting for me. I would trip on my shoelaces, scramble up my front steps, and slam into the warmth of my father's outstretched arms, his breath hot in my ear, whispering: *I've got you, I've got you.* His fingers would grab fistfuls of my hair, and my lungs would sting from the influx of air. My heart would crash hard against my chest as a single word formed in my mind: *safety.*

Or so I thought.

Learning to fear should be a slow evolution—a gradual progression from the Santa Claus at a local strip mall to the boogeyman under the bed; from the rated-R movie a babysitter let you watch to the man idling in a car behind tinted windows, staring at you for just a second too long as you make your way down the sidewalk at dusk. Watching him inch closer in your peripheral vision, feeling your heartbeat rise from your chest to your neck to the backs of your eyes. It's a learning process, an ongoing progression from one perceived threat to the next, each subsequent *thing* more realistically dangerous than the last.

Not for me, though. For me, the concept of fear came crashing down with a force my adolescent body had never experienced. A force so suffocating it hurt to breathe. And in that moment, the moment of the crash, it made me realize that monsters don't hide in the woods; they aren't shadows in the trees or invisible things lurking in darkened corners.

No, the real monsters move in plain sight.

I was twelve years old when those shadows started to form a shape, a face. Started to become less of an apparition and more concrete. More real. When I began to realize that maybe the monsters lived among us.

And there was one monster, in particular, I learned to fear above all the rest.

MAY 2019

CHAPTER ONE

My throat tickles.

It's subtle, at first. The tip of a feather being trailed along the inside of my esophagus, top to bottom. I push my tongue back into my throat and attempt to scratch.

It doesn't work.

I hope I'm not getting sick. Have I been around a sick person lately? Someone with a cold? There's no way to be sure, really. I'm around people all day. None of them looked sick, but the common cold can be contagious before ever showing any symptoms.

I try to scratch again.

Or maybe it's allergies. Ragweed is higher than normal. Severe, actually. An 8 out of 10 on the allergy tracker. The little pinwheel on my weather app was solid red.

I reach for my glass of water, take a sip. Swish it around a bit before swallowing.

It still doesn't work. I clear my throat.

"Yeah?"

I look up at the patient before me, stiff as a wooden plank strapped to my oversized leather recliner. Her fingers are clenched in her lap, thin, shiny slits barely visible against the otherwise perfect skin of her hands. I notice a bracelet on her wrist, an attempt to cover the nastiest scar, a deep, jagged purple. Wooden beads with a silver charm in the shape of a cross, dangling like a rosary.

I look back at the girl, taking in her expression, her eyes. No tears, but it's still early.

"I'm sorry," I say, glancing down at the notes before me. "Lacey. I just have a little tickle in my throat. Please, continue."

"Oh," she says. "Okay. Well, anyway, like I was saying . . . I just get so mad sometimes, you know? And I don't really know why? It's like this anger just builds and builds and then, before I know it, I need to—"

She looks down at her arms, fans her hands. There are tiny cuts everywhere, like hairs of glass, hidden in the webby dips of skin between her fingers.

"It's a release," she says. "It helps me calm down."

I nod, trying to ignore the itch in my throat. It's getting worse. Maybe it's dust, I tell myself—it is dusty in here. I glance over to the windowsill, the bookshelf, the diplomas framed on my wall, all of them sporting a fine layer of gray, glinting in the sunlight.

Focus, Chloe.

I turn back toward the girl.

"And why do you think that is, Lacey?"

"I just told you. I don't know."

"If you had to speculate."

She sighs, glances to the side, and stares intently at nothing in particular. She's avoiding eye contact. The tears are coming shortly.

"I mean, it probably has something to do with my dad," she says, her lower lip trembling slightly. She pushes her blonde hair back from her forehead. "With him leaving and everything."

"When did your dad leave?"

"Two years ago," she says. As if on cue, a single tear

erupts from her tear duct and glides down her freckled cheek. She wipes it angrily. "He didn't even say goodbye. He didn't even give us a fucking reason why. He just *left*."

I nod, scribbling more notes.

"Do you think it's fair to say that you're still pretty angry with your dad over him leaving you like that?"

Her lip trembles again.

"And since he didn't say goodbye, you weren't able to tell him how his actions made you feel?"

She nods at the bookshelf in the corner, still avoiding me.

"Yeah," she says. "I guess that's fair."

"Are you angry with anyone else?"

"My mom, I guess. I don't really know why. I always figured that she drove him away."

"Okay," I say. "Anybody else?"

She's quiet, her fingernail picking at a chunk of raised skin.

"Myself," she whispers, not bothering to wipe the puddle of tears pooling in the corners of her eyes. "For not being good enough to make him want to stay."

"It's okay to be angry," I say. "We're all angry. And now that you're comfortable verbalizing *why* you're angry, we can work together to help you manage it a little better. To help you manage it in a way that doesn't hurt you. Does that sound like a plan?"

"It's so fucking stupid," she mutters.

"What is?"

"Everything. Him, this. Being here."

"What about being here is stupid, Lacey?"

"I shouldn't *have* to be here."

She's shouting now. I lean back, casually, and lace my fingers together. I let her yell.

"Yeah, I'm angry," she says. "So what? My dad fucking left me. He *left* me. Do you know what that feels like? Do you know what it feels like being a kid without a dad? Going to school and having everyone look at you? Talk about you behind your back?"

"I actually do," I say. "I do know what that's like. It's not fun."

She's quiet now, her hands shaking in her lap, the pads of her thumb and pointer finger rubbing the cross on her bracelet. Up and down, up and down.

"Did your dad leave you, too?"

"Something like that."

"How old were you?"

"Twelve," I say.

She nods. "I'm fifteen."

"My brother was fifteen."

"So you get it, then?"

This time, I nod, smile. Establishing trust—the hardest part.

"I get it," I say, leaning forward again, closing the distance between us. She turns toward me now, her tear-soaked eyes boring into mine, pleading. "I totally get it."

CHAPTER TWO

My industry thrives on clichés—I know it does. But there's a reason clichés exist.

It's because they're true.

A fifteen-year-old girl taking a razor to her skin probably has something to do with feelings of inadequacy, of needing to feel physical pain to drown out the emotional pain burning inside her. An eighteen-year-old boy with anger management issues definitely has something to do with an unresolved parental dispute, feelings of abandonment, needing to prove himself. Needing to seem strong when inside, he's breaking. A twenty-year-old college junior getting drunk and sleeping with every boy who buys her a two-dollar vodka tonic, then crying about it in the morning, reeks of low self-esteem, a yearning for attention because she had to fight for it at home. An inner conflict between the person she is and the person she thinks everyone wants her to be.

Daddy issues. Only child syndrome. A product of divorce.

They're clichés, but they're true. And it's okay for me to say that, because I'm a cliché, too.

I glance down at my smartwatch, the recording from today's session blinking on the screen: 1:01:52. I tap

Send to iPhone and watch the little timer fill from gray to green as the file shoots over to my phone, then simultaneously syncs to my laptop. *Technology.* When I was a girl, I remember each doctor grabbing my file, thumbing through page after page as I sat in some variation of the same weathered recliner, eying their file cabinets full of other people's problems. Full of people like me. Somehow, it made me feel less lonely, more normal. Those four-drawer metal lockboxes symbolized the possibility of me somehow being able to express my pain one day—verbalize it, scream about it, cry about it—then when the sixty-minute timer ticked down to zero, we could simply flip the folder closed and put it back in the drawer, locking it tight and forgetting about its contents until another day.

Five o'clock, closing time.

I look at my computer screen, at the forest of icons my patients have been reduced to. Now there is no *closing time.* They always have ways to find me— email, social media—at least before I finally gave in and deleted my profiles, tired of sifting through the panicked direct messages of clients in their lowest moments. I am always on, always ready, a twenty-four-hour convenience store with a neon *Open* sign flickering in the darkness, trying its hardest not to die.

The recording notification pops up on my screen, and I click on it, labeling the file—*Lacey Deckler, Session 1*—before glancing up from my computer and squinting at the dusty windowsill, the dirtiness of this place even more obvious with the glare of the setting sun. I clear my throat again, cough a few times. I lean to the side and grab a wooden knob, yanking the bottom drawer of my desk open and rifling through my own personal in-office pharmacy. I glance down at the pill bottles, ranging from run-of-the-mill Ibuprofen to more difficult to pronounce prescriptions: Alprazolam,

Chlordiazepoxide, Diazepam. I push them aside and grab a box of Emergen-C, dumping a packet into my water glass and stirring it with my finger.

I take a few swigs and start composing an email.

> *Shannon,*
> *Happy Friday! Just had a great first session with Lacey Deckler—thanks for the referral. Wanted to check in re: medication. I see you haven't prescribed anything. Based on our session today, I think she could benefit from starting a low dosage of Prozac—thoughts? Concerns?*
>
> **Chloe**

I hit *Send* and lean back in my chair, downing the rest of my tangerine-flavored water. The Emergen-C deposit trapped at the bottom of the glass goes down like glue, slow and heavy, coating my teeth and tongue in an orange grit. Within minutes, I get a response.

> *Chloe,*
> *You're always welcome! Good with me. Feel free to call it in.*
>
> *PS—Drinks soon? Need to get details on the upcoming BIG DAY!*
>
> **Shannon Tack, MD**

I pick up my office phone and dial into Lacey's pharmacy, the same CVS I frequent—convenient—and am taken straight to voice mail. I leave a message.

"Hi, yes, this is Doctor Chloe Davis—*C-h-l-o-e D-a-v-i-s*—calling in a prescription for Lacey Deckler—*L-a-c-e-y D-e-c-k-l-e-r*—date of birth January 16,

2004. I've recommended the patient start on 10 milli-grams of Prozac per day, eight-week supply. No auto-refills, please."

I pause, tap my fingers on the desk.

"I'd also like to call in a refill for another patient, Daniel Briggs—*D-a-n-i-e-l B-r-i-g-g-s*—date of birth May 2, 1982. Xanax, 4 milligrams daily. Again, this is Doctor Chloe Davis. Phone number 555-212-4524. Thank you so much."

I hang up, eying the phone, now dead on the receiver. My eyes dart back over to the window, the setting sun turning my mahogany office a shade of orange not too dissimilar to the gluey residue sitting stagnant in the bottom of my glass. I glance at my watch—seven thirty—and start to close my laptop, jumping when the phone screeches back to life. I glance at it—the office is closed now, and it's Friday. I continue packing up my things, ignoring the ringing, until I realize it may be the pharmacy with a question about the prescriptions I just called in. I let it ring one more time before I answer.

"Doctor Davis," I say.

"Chloe Davis?"

"Doctor Chloe Davis," I correct. "Yes, this is she. How can I help you?"

"Man, you are a tough woman to get ahold of."

The voice belongs to a man, and it laughs an exasperated kind of laugh, as if I've annoyed it somehow.

"I'm sorry, are you a patient?"

"I'm not a patient," the voice says, "but I've been calling all day. *All* day. Your receptionist refused to put me through, so I thought I'd try after hours, see if I could be directed straight to your voice mail. I wasn't expecting you to pick up."

I frown.

"Well, this is my office. I don't take personal calls here. Melissa only forwards my patients—" I stop, confused as to why I'm explaining myself and the inner workings of my business to a stranger. I harden my voice. "Can I ask why you're calling? Who is this?"

"My name is Aaron Jansen," he says. "I'm a reporter for *The New York Times*."

My breath catches in my throat. I cough, though it comes out more like a choke.

"Are you okay?" he asks.

"Yes, fine," I say. "I'm getting over a throat thing. I'm sorry—*New York Times*?"

I hate myself as soon as the question comes out. I know why this man is calling. To be honest, I had been expecting it. Expecting something. Maybe not the *Times,* but something.

"You know," he hesitates. "The newspaper?"

"Yeah, I know who you are."

"I'm writing a story about your father, and I'd love to sit down and talk. Can I buy you a coffee?"

"I'm sorry," I say again, cutting him off. *Fuck.* Why do I keep apologizing? I take a deep breath and try again. "I have nothing to say about that."

"Chloe," he says.

"Doctor Davis."

"Doctor Davis," he repeats, sighing. "The anniversary is coming up. Twenty years. I'm sure you know that."

"Of course I know that," I snap back. "It's been twenty years and nothing has changed. Those girls are still dead, and my father is still in prison. Why are you still interested?"

Aaron is silent on the other end; I've already given him too much, I know. I've already satisfied that sick journalistic urge that feeds on ripping open the wounds of others just before they're about to heal. I've satisfied it just enough for him to taste metallic and thirst for more, a shark gravitating toward blood in water.

"But you've changed," he says. "You and your brother. The public would love to know how you're doing—how you're coping."

I roll my eyes.

"And your father," he continues. "Maybe *he's* changed. Have you talked to him?"

"I have nothing to say to my father," I tell him. "And I have nothing to say to you. Please don't call here again."

I hang up, slamming the phone back into its base harder than I intend to. I look down and notice my fingers are shaking. I tuck my hair behind my ear in an attempt to busy them and glance back at the window, the sky morphing into a deep, inky blue, the sun a bubble on top of the horizon now, ready to burst.

Then I turn back to my desk and grab my bag, pushing my chair back as I stand. I glance at my desk lamp, exhaling slowly before clicking it off and taking a shaky step into the dark.

CHAPTER THREE

There are so many subtle ways we women subconsciously protect ourselves throughout the day; protect ourselves from shadows, from unseen predators. From cautionary tales and urban legends. So subtle, in fact, that we hardly even realize we're doing them.

Leave work before dark. Clutch our purses to our chest with one hand, hold our keys between our fingers in the other, like a weapon, as we shuffle toward our car, strategically parked beneath a streetlight in case we *weren't* able to leave work before dark. Approach our car, glance in the back seat before unlocking the front. Grip our phone tight, pointer finger just a swipe away from 9-1-1. Step inside. Lock it again. Do not idle. Drive away quickly.

I turn out of the parking lot adjacent to my office building and away from town. I stop at a red light and glance in my rearview mirror—habit, I suppose—wincing at the reflection. I look rough. It's muggy outside, so muggy that my skin is slick with grease; my usually limp brown hair has a bit of a curl at the tips, a frizziness that only the Louisiana summer can achieve.

Louisiana summer.

Such a loaded phrase. I grew up here. Well, not *here*. Not in Baton Rouge. In Louisiana, though. A tiny little town called Breaux Bridge—the Crawfish Capital of the World. It's a distinction we're proud of, for some reason. The same way Cawker City, Kansas, must be proud of their five-thousand-pound ball of twine. It brings superficial meaning to an otherwise meaningless place.

Breaux Bridge also has a population of less than ten thousand, which means that everybody knows everybody. And more specifically, everybody knows me.

When I was young, I used to live for the summer. The swampy memories are so abundant: spotting gators in Lake Martin, screaming when I caught a glimpse of their beady eyes lurking beneath a carpet of algae. My brother laughing as we sprinted in the opposite direction, screaming *See ya later, alligator!* Making wigs out of the Spanish moss hanging in our multi-acre backyard then picking chiggers out of my hair in the days that followed, dabbing clear nail polish on the itchy red welts. Twisting the tail off a freshly boiled crawfish and sucking the head dry.

But memories of summer also bring memories of fear.

I was twelve when the girls started to go missing. Girls not much older than me. It was July of 1999, and it was shaping up to be just another hot, humid Louisiana summer.

Until one day, it wasn't.

I remember walking into the kitchen one morning, early, rubbing the sleep from my eyes, dragging my mint-green blanket across the linoleum floor. I had slept with that blanket ever since I was a baby, loved the edges raw. I remember twisting the fabric between my fingers, a nervous tic, when I saw my parents huddled in front of the TV, worried. Whispering.

"What's going on?"

They turned around, their eyes wide at the sight of me, turning it off before I could see the screen.

Before they *thought* I could see the screen.

"Oh, honey," my father said, walking toward me, holding me tighter than normal. "It's nothing, sweetheart."

But it wasn't nothing. Even then, I knew it wasn't nothing. The way my father was holding me, the way my mother's lip quivered as she turned toward the window—the same way Lacey's lip quivered this afternoon as she forced herself to process the realization she had known all along. The realization she had been trying to push out, trying to pretend wasn't true. My eyes had caught a glimpse of that bright red headline stamped across the bottom of the screen; it had already been seared into my psyche, a collection of words that would forever alter life as I knew it.

LOCAL BREAUX BRIDGE GIRL GOES MISSING

At twelve years old, *GIRL GOES MISSING* doesn't have the same sinister implications as it does when you're older. Your mind doesn't automatically flicker to all those horrible places: kidnapping, rape, murder. I remember thinking: Missing *where*? I thought maybe she had gotten lost. My family's home was situated on more than ten acres of land; I had gotten lost plenty of times catching toads in the swamp or exploring uncharted patches of woods, scratching my name in the bark of an unmarked tree or constructing forts out of moss-soaked sticks. I had even gotten stuck in a small cave once, the home of some kind of animal, its puckered entrance somehow both frightening and enticing at the exact same time. I remember my brother tying a piece of old rope to my ankle as I lay flat on my belly, wriggling myself into the cold, dark void, holding a flashlight keychain tight between my lips. Letting the darkness swallow me whole as I crawled deeper and deeper—and, finally, the sheer terror that ensued once I realized that I couldn't pull myself back out. So when I saw clips of the search party scouring through overgrown foliage and wading through bogs, I couldn't help but wonder what would happen if I ever went "missing" myself, if people would come for me the same way they were coming for her.

She'll turn up, I thought. *And when she does, I bet she'll feel silly for causing such a fuss.*

But she didn't turn up. And three weeks later, another girl went missing.

Four weeks after that, another.

By the end of the summer, six girls had disappeared. One day they were there, and the next—gone. Vanished without a trace.

Now, six missing girls will always be six too many, but in a town like Breaux Bridge, a town so tiny that there's a noticeable gap in a classroom when one child drops out or a quietness to a neighborhood when a single family moves away, six girls was a weight almost too heavy to bear. Their goneness was impossible to ignore; it was an evil that had settled over the sky the way an impending storm can make your bones throb. You could feel it, taste it, see it in the eyes of every person you met. An inherent distrust had captivated a town that was once so trusting; a suspicion had taken hold that was impossible to shake. One single, unspoken question lingered among us all.

Who's next?

Curfews were put into place; stores and restaurants closed at dusk. I, like every other girl in town, was forbidden to be outside after dark. Even in the daytime, I felt the evil lurking just behind every corner.

The anticipation that it would be me—that *I* would be next—was always there, always present, always suffocating.

"You'll be fine, Chloe. You don't have anything to worry about."

I remember my brother hoisting on his backpack one morning before summer camp; I was crying, again, too afraid to leave the house.

"She does have something to worry about, Cooper. This is serious."

"She's too young," he said. "She's only twelve. He likes teenagers, remember?"

"Cooper, please."

My mother crouched down to the floor, positioned herself at eye level, tucked a strand of hair behind my ear.

"This is serious, honey, but just be careful. Be vigilant."

"Don't get into a car with strangers," Cooper said, sighing. "Don't walk down dark alleys alone. It's all pretty obvious, Chlo. Just don't be stupid."

"Those girls weren't stupid," my mother snapped, her voice quiet but sharp. "They were unlucky. In the wrong place at the wrong time."

I turn in to the CVS parking lot now and pull through the pharmacy drive-through. There's a man standing behind the sliding glass window, busying himself with stapling various bottles into paper bags. He slides the window open and doesn't bother to look up.

"Name?"

"Daniel Briggs."

He glances at me, clearly not a Daniel. He taps a few keys on the computer before him and speaks again.

"Date of birth?"

"May 2, 1982."

He turns around, shuffles through the *B* basket. I

watch him grab a paper bag and walk toward me again, my hands gripped tightly on the wheel to stop them from fidgeting. He aims his scanner at the bar code and I hear a beep.

"Do you have any questions about the prescription?"

"Nope," I say, smiling. "All good."

He pushes the bag through his window and into mine; I snatch it, push it deep into my purse, and roll the window up again, pulling away without so much as a goodbye.

I drive for a few more minutes, my purse on the passenger seat radiating from the mere presence of the pills inside. It used to baffle me how easy it was to pick up prescriptions for other people; as long as you know the birthday that matches the name on file, most pharmacists never even ask for a driver's license. And if they do, simple explanations usually work.

Oh, shoot, it's in my other purse.

I'm actually his fiancée—do you need me to provide the address on file?

I turn in to my Garden District neighborhood and start the journey down a mile-long stretch of road that always leaves me disoriented, the way I imagine scuba divers feel when they find themselves completely enveloped in darkness, a darkness so dark even their own hand placed inches from their face would get lost.

All sense of direction—gone. All sense of control—gone.

Without any houses to illuminate the roadway or floodlights to reveal the twisting arms of the trees that line the street, when the sun goes down, this road gives the illusion of driving straight into a pool of ink, disappearing into a vast nothingness, falling endlessly into a bottomless hole.

I hold my breath, push my foot down on the gas just a little bit harder.

Finally, I can sense my turn approaching. I flick on my blinker, even though there's nobody behind me, just more black, and veer right into our cul-de-sac, releasing my breath when I pass the first streetlight revealing the road toward home.

Home.

That, too, is a loaded phrase. A home isn't just a house, a collection of bricks and boards held together by concrete and nails. It's more emotional than that. A home is safety, security. The place you go back to when the curfew clock strikes nine.

But what if your home isn't safe? Isn't secure?

What if the outstretched arms you collapse into on your porch steps are the same arms you should be running from? The same arms that grabbed those girls, squeezed their necks, and buried their bodies before washing their own hands clean?

What if your home is where it all started: the epicenter of the earthquake that shook your town to the core? The eye of the hurricane that ripped apart families, lives, you? Everything you had ever known?

What then?

CHAPTER FOUR

My car idles in the driveway as I dig into my purse and fish out the pharmacy bag. I rip it open and pull the orange bottle from inside, twisting the cap and dumping a pill into my palm before crumpling the bag in a ball and shoving it, and the bottle, into my glove compartment.

I look at the Xanax in my hand, inspecting the little white tablet. I think back to that phone call in my office: Aaron Jansen. *Twenty years.* My chest constricts at the memory, and I pop the pill into my mouth before I can think twice, swallowing it dry. I exhale, close my eyes. Already, I feel the grip in my chest loosening, my airways opening wide. A calmness settles over me, the same sense of calm that follows every time my tongue touches a pill. I don't really know how to describe it, this feeling, other than pure and simple relief. The same relief you would feel after flinging open your closet door to find nothing but clothes hiding inside—the slowing of the heart rate, the euphoric sense of giddiness that creeps into the brain when you realize that you're safe. That nothing's going to lunge at you from the shadows.

I open my eyes.

There's a hint of spice in the air as I step out of my car and slam the door, clicking the lock button twice on my key fob. I turn my nose toward the sky and sniff, trying to place the scent. Seafood, maybe. Something fishy. Maybe the neighbors are having a barbecue, and for a second, I'm offended that I'm not invited.

I start the long walk up the cobblestones toward my front door, the darkness of the house looming before me. I make it halfway up the walkway before I stop and stare. Back when I bought this house, years ago, it was just that. A house. A shell of a thing ready to have life blown into it like a saggy balloon. It was a house prepared to become a home, all eager and excited like a kid on the first day of school. But I had no idea how to make a home. The only home I had ever known could hardly be called a home at all—not anymore, at least. Not in hindsight. I remember walking through the front door for the first time, keys in hand. My heels on the hardwood echoing through the vast emptiness, the bare white walls littered with nail marks from where pictures once hung, proof that it was possible. That memories could be formed here, a life could be made. I opened up my little tool kit, a tiny red Craftsman that Cooper had bought, walking me around Home Depot as I held the lips open while he dropped wrenches and hammers and pliers inside like he was filling up a bag of sweet-and-sour gummies at the local candy store. I didn't have anything to hang—no pictures, no decorations—so I hammered a single nail into the wall and hung the metal ring that held my house key. A single key, and nothing more. It felt like progress.

Now I look at all the things that I've done to it since to make it appear like I have my shit together from the outside, the superficial equivalent of slathering makeup over a marbling bruise or fastening a rosary on top of a scarred wrist. Why I care so much about the acceptance of my neighbors as they slink past my yard, leashes in hand, I don't really know. There's the swinging bench

bolted to the porch ceiling, the always-present layer of
buttery yellow pollen making it impossible to pretend
that anybody ever actually sits there. The landscaping
I had eagerly purchased and planted and then subse-
quently ignored to death, the skinny brown tendrils
of my twin hanging ferns resembling the regurgitated
bones of a small animal I once found while dissecting
an owl in eighth grade biology. The scratchy brown
welcome mat that says, *Welcome!* The bronze mailbox
shaped like an oversized envelope bolted to the siding,
maddeningly impractical, the slit too tiny to fit an entire hand, let alone more than a couple of postcards
mailed to me by former classmates-turned-Realtors after the promise of their degrees turned out to be not-so-
promising.

I start walking again, deciding in this moment that
I'm going to throw away the stupid envelope and just
use a regular mailbox like everybody else. It is also in
this moment when I realize that my house looks dead.
It's the only one on the block without lights illuminating the windows, the flicker of a television behind
closed blinds. The only one without any evidence of
life inside.

I walk closer, the Xanax cloaking my mind into
a forced calm. But still, something is nagging at me.
Something is wrong. Something is *different.* I look
around my yard: small, but well-kept. A mown lawn and
shrubs push against a raw wood fence, an oak tree's
mangled limbs casting shadows against a garage I've
never once pulled my car into. I glance up at the house,
now mere feet before me. I think I catch a glimpse of
movement behind a curtain from inside, but I shake my
head, force myself to keep walking.

Don't be ridiculous, Chloe. Be real.

My key is in the front door, already twisting, when I
realize what's wrong, what's different.

The porch light is off.

The porch light I always, *always* leave on—even when I'm sleeping, ignoring the beam of light it casts straight across my pillow through the gap in the blinds—is turned off. I never turn the porch light off. I don't think I've ever even touched the switch. That's why the house looks so lifeless, I realize. I've never seen it so dark before, so completely devoid of light. Even with the street lamps, it is *dark* out here. Someone could come up behind me and I'd never even—

"SURPRISE!"

I let out a scream and plunge my arm into my purse, searching for my pepper spray. The lights from inside flick on and I'm staring at a crowd of people in my living room—thirty, maybe forty—all staring back, smiling. My heart is slamming inside my chest now; I can barely speak.

"Oh my—"

I stutter, look around. I'm searching for a reason, an explanation. But I can't find one.

"Oh my *God*." I'm instantly aware of my hand in my purse, clutching the pepper spray with a strength that startles me. A wave of relief washes over me as I release it, wiping the sweat on my palm against the interior fabric. "What—what is this?"

"What does it look like?" A voice erupts to my left; I turn to the side and watch the crowd part as a man steps into the opening. "It's a party."

It's Daniel, dressed in dark-wash jeans and a snug blue blazer. He's beaming at me, his teeth a blinding white against his tanned skin, his sandy hair pushed to the side. I feel my heart start to slow again; my hand moves from my chest to my cheek, and I can feel it growing hot. I crack an embarrassed smile as he pushes a glass of wine toward me; I take it with my free hand.

"A party for us," he says, squeezing me tight. I can

smell his body wash, his spiced deodorant. "An engagement party."

"Daniel. What . . . what are you doing here?"

"Well, I live here."

A wave of laughter erupts in the crowd, and Daniel squeezes my shoulder, smiling.

"You're supposed to be out of town," I say. "I thought you weren't getting back until tomorrow."

"Yeah, about that. I lied," he says, eliciting more laughs. "Are you surprised?"

I scan the sea of people, fidgeting in their places. They're still looking at me, expectant. I wonder how loudly I screamed.

"Didn't I *sound* surprised?"

I throw my hands up and the crowd breaks into a laugh. Someone in the back starts to cheer, and the rest follow, whistling and clapping as Daniel pulls me fully into his arms and kisses me on the mouth.

"Get a room!" someone yells, and the crowd laughs again, this time dispersing into various parts of the house, refilling their drinks and mingling with the other guests, scooping heaps of food onto paper plates. The smell from outside finally registers: It's Old Bay. I glimpse a table of crawfish boil steaming on the picnic table on our back porch and am instantly embarrassed about feeling left out from the fictional party I had invented next door.

Daniel looks at me, grinning, holding back a laugh. I hit him on the shoulder.

"I hate you," I say, though I'm smiling back. "You scared the shit out of me."

He laughs now, that big, booming laugh that drew me in twelve months ago still proving to hold a trance over me. I pull him back in and kiss him again, properly this time, without the watching eyes of all of our friends. I feel the warmth of his tongue in my mouth, savoring the way his presence physically calms my body down. Slows my heart rate, my breathing, the same way the Xanax does.

"You didn't give me much choice," he says, sipping his wine. "I had to do it this way."

"Oh, you did?" I ask. "And why is that?"

"Because you refuse to plan anything for yourself," he says. "No bachelorette party, no bridal shower."

"I'm not in college, Daniel. I'm thirty-two. Doesn't that seem a little juvenile?"

He looks at me, cocking his eyebrow.

"No, it doesn't seem *juvenile*. It seems fun."

"Well, you know, I don't really have anyone to help me plan that kind of stuff," I say, staring into my wine, swirling it against the glass. "You know Cooper's not going to plan a shower, and my *mom*—"

"I know, Chlo. I'm teasing. You deserve a party, so I threw you a party. Simple as that."

My chest surges with warmth, and I squeeze his hand.

"Thank you," I say. "This is really something else. I almost had a heart attack . . ."

He laughs again, downing the rest of his wine.

". . . but it means a lot. I love you."

"I love you, too. Now go mingle. And drink your wine," he says, using his finger to tip the base of my untouched glass. "Relax a little."

I lift the glass to my lips and down it, too, pushing myself into the crowd in the living room. Someone grabs my drink and offers to refill it, while another person shoves a plate of cheese and crackers in my direction.

"You must be starving. Do you always work so late?"

"Of course she does. She's Chloe!"

"Is chardonnay okay, Chlo? I think you were drinking pinot before, but really, what's the difference?"

Minutes pass, or maybe hours. Every time I wander

into a new section of the house, someone else walks up with a *congratulations* and a fresh glass, a different combination of the same questions flowing faster than the bottles piling up in the corner.

"So, does this count as *drinks soon*?"

I turn around and see Shannon standing behind me, smiling wide. She laughs and pulls me in for a hug, planting a kiss on my cheek the way she always does, her lips sticking to my skin. I think back to the email she sent me this afternoon.

PS—Drinks soon? Need to get the details on the upcoming BIG DAY!

"You little liar," I say, trying to keep myself from wiping the lipstick residue I feel lingering on my cheek.

"Guilty," she says, smiling. "I had to make sure you didn't suspect anything."

"Well, mission accomplished. How's the family?"

"They're good," Shannon says, twirling the ring on her finger. "Bill is in the kitchen getting a refill. And Riley . . ."

She scans the room, her eyes flickering past the sea of bodies bobbing together like waves. She seems to find who she's looking for and smiles, shakes her head.

"Riley is in the corner, on her phone. *Shocking*."

I turn around and see a teenaged girl slumped in a chair, tapping furiously at her iPhone. She's wearing a short red sundress and white sneakers, her hair a mousey brown. She looks incredibly bored, and I can't help but laugh.

"Well, she is fifteen," Daniel says. I glance to my side and Daniel is standing there, smiling. He slides up to me and snakes his arm around my waist, kissing my forehead. I've always marveled at the way he glides into every conversation with such ease, dropping a perfectly placed line as if he'd been standing there all along.

"Tell me about it," Shannon says. "She's grounded at the moment, hence the reason why we dragged her along. She's not too happy with us, forcing her to hang out with a bunch of *old people*."

I smile, my eyes still glued to the girl, to the way she twirls her hair absentmindedly around her finger, the way she chews on the side of her lip as she analyzes whatever text just appeared on her phone.

"What's she grounded for?"

"Sneaking out," Shannon says, rolling her eyes. "We found her climbing out of her bedroom window at *midnight*. She did the whole rope-made-out-of-bedsheets thing, like you see in the freakin' movies. Lucky she didn't break her neck."

I laugh again, clasping my hand to my open mouth.

"I swear, when Bill and I were dating and he told me he had a ten-year-old girl, I didn't think much of it," Shannon says, her voice low, staring at her stepdaughter. "Honestly, I thought I lucked out. A kid-on-demand, skipping right through the whole dirty-diaper-screaming-at-all-hours-of-the-night part. She was such a sweetheart. But it is amazing how the second they become teenagers, it all changes. They turn into monsters."

"It won't be like this for long," Daniel says, smiling. "One day, they'll just be distant memories."

"God, I hope." Shannon laughs, taking another swig of her wine. "He really is an angel, you know."

She's speaking to me now, but she motions to Daniel, tapping him on the chest.

"Planning this whole thing. You wouldn't believe the time it took him to get everyone together in one place."

"Yeah, I know," I say. "I don't deserve him."

"Good thing you didn't quit a week earlier, huh?"

She nudges me and I smile, the memory of our first meeting as sharp as ever. It was one of those chance encounters that could have easily meant nothing. Bumping into an exposed shoulder on the bus, muttering a simple *excuse me* before parting ways. Borrowing a pen from the man at the bar when yours runs dry, or running a wallet left in the bottom of a shopping cart to the car outside before it drives away. Most of the time, these meetings lead to nothing more than a smile, a thank-you.

But sometimes, they lead to something. Or maybe even everything.

Daniel and I had met at Baton Rouge General Hospital; he was walking in, I was walking out. More like staggering out, really, the weight of the contents of my office threatening to tear through the bottom of a cardboard box. I would have walked right past him, the box obscuring my vision, my eyes downcast as I followed my own footsteps to the front door. I would have walked right past him had I not heard his voice.

"Do you need a hand?"

"No, no," I said, shifting the weight from one arm to the other, not even bothering to stop. The automatic door was a yard away, less. My car was idling outside. "I got it."

"Here, let me help you."

I heard footsteps running behind me; felt the weight lifted slightly as his arm snaked between mine.

"Good God," he grunted. "What do you have in here?"

"Books, mostly." I pushed a strand of sweaty hair from my forehead as he lifted the box from my grip. And that was the first glimpse I got of his face—blonde hair and lashes to match, teeth that were the product of expensive adolescent orthodontia and maybe a bleaching treatment or two. I could see his biceps bulging through his light blue button-up as he hoisted my life into the air and balanced it on his shoulder.

"You get fired?"

My neck snapped in his direction; I opened my mouth, ready to set him straight, until he glanced my way and I saw his expression. His tender eyes, the way they seemed to soften as he took in my face, scanning his way from top to bottom. He stared at me as though he were staring at an old friend, his pupils flickering over my skin, searching for a trace of familiarity in my features. His lips curled into a knowing grin.

"I'm just kidding," he said, turning his attention back to the box. "You look too happy to have been fired. Besides, wouldn't there be some guards escorting you out by the armpits before throwing you down on the pavement? Isn't that how it works?"

I smiled, let out a laugh. We were in the parking lot then, and he placed the box on the roof of my car before crossing his arms and turning toward me.

"I quit," I said, the words settling over me with a finality that, for a second, almost made me burst into tears. Baton Rouge General had been my first job; my only job. My coworker, Shannon, had become my closest friend. "Today was my last day."

"Well, congratulations," he said. "Where to next?"

"I'm starting my own practice. I'm a medical psychologist."

He whistled, poking his head into the box on my car. Something caught his eye and he twisted his head distractedly, leaning in to pick up one of the books.

"Got a thing for murder?" he asked, inspecting the cover.

My chest constricted as my eyes darted to the box. I remembered, in that moment, that situated next to all of my psychology textbooks were piles of true-crime titles: *The Devil in the White City, In Cold Blood, The Monster of Florence*. But unlike most people, I didn't read them for entertainment. I read them for study. I

read them to try to understand, to dissect all the different people who take lives for a living, devouring their
stories on the page almost as if they were my patients,
leaning back in that leather recliner, whispering their secrets into my ear.

"I guess you could say that."

"No judgment," he added, twisting the book in his
hands around so I could see the cover—*Midnight in the
Garden of Good and Evil*—before flipping it open and
starting to thumb the pages. "I love this book."

I smiled politely, unsure of how to respond.

"I really should be going," I said instead, motioning to
my car and offering my hand. "Thanks for your help."

"The pleasure was mine, Doctor . . . ?"

"Davis," I said. "Chloe Davis."

"Well, Doctor Chloe Davis, if you ever need to move
any more boxes . . ." He dug into his back pocket, fishing out his wallet before pulling out a business card
and pushing it into the open pages. He flipped the book
closed and thrust it in my direction. "You know where
to find me."

He smiled at me, winking in my direction before
turning around and walking back into the building.
When the automatic doors closed behind him, I looked
down at the book in my hands, running my fingers
against the glossy cover. There was a tiny gap in the
pages where his business card lay wedged and I stuck
my nail into the crack, flipping it back open. I looked
down, feeling a foreign twist in my chest as my eyes
scanned his name.

Somehow, I knew that wasn't the last time I would
be seeing Daniel Briggs.

CHAPTER FIVE

I excuse myself from Shannon and Daniel and slip outside through the sliding door. My mind is spinning by the time I make it to the back porch, my hand clutching my fourth variety of alcoholic beverage. The endless small talk is buzzing in my ears, the bottle of wine I've polished off buzzing in my brain. It's still muggy outside, but the breeze is refreshing. The house was getting stuffy with the drunken body heat of forty people bouncing off the walls.

I wander toward the picnic table, the heap of crawfish, corn, sausage, and potatoes somehow still steaming on the newspaper. I put down my wineglass, grab a crawfish, and twist it, letting the juice from the head drip down my wrist.

Then I hear movement behind me—footsteps. And a voice.

"Don't worry, it's just me."

I swing around, my eyes adjusting in the dark to the body before me. The cherry-red tip of a cigarette glowing between his fingers.

"I know you don't like to be surprised."

"Coop!"

I drop the crawfish on the table and walk toward my brother, wrapping my arms around his neck and inhaling his familiar scent. Nicotine and spearmint gum. I'm so shocked to see him, I let the jab about the surprise party slide.

"Hey, sis."

I pull back, inspecting his face. He looks older than he did the last time I saw him, but that's normal for Cooper. He seems to age years within months, his hair turning grayer at the temples, the worry lines in his forehead creasing deeper by the day. But still, Coop is one of those guys who seems to get more attractive with age. In college, my roommate had referred to him as a *silver fox* once when his neck started to grow patchy with salt-and-pepper stubble. For some reason, that stuck with me. It was a pretty accurate depiction, really. He looks mature, sleek, thoughtful, quiet. Like he's seen more of the world in thirty-five years than most people have seen in their lives. I let go of his neck.

"I didn't see you in there!" I say, louder than I intended.

"You got mobbed," he answers, laughing, taking a final drag before dropping his cigarette to the ground and stubbing it out with his foot. "How does it feel to have forty people swarm you all at once?"

I shrug. "Practice for the wedding, I guess."

His smile wavers a bit, but he recovers quickly. We both ignore it.

"Where's Laurel?" I ask.

He shoves his hands in his pockets and glances behind my shoulder, his eyes growing distant. I already know what's coming next.

"She's not in the picture anymore."

"I'm sorry to hear that," I say. "I liked her. She seemed nice."

"Yeah," he says, nodding. "She was. I liked her, too."

We're quiet for a while, listening to the murmur of voices inside. We both understand the complexities of forming relationships after going through what we've been through; we understand that, more often than not, they just don't work out.

"So, are you excited?" he asks, jerking his head in the direction of the house. "For the wedding and stuff?"

I laugh. "*And stuff*? You've got such a way with words, Coop."

"You know what I mean."

"Yeah, I know what you mean," I say. "And yes, I'm excited. You should give him a chance."

Cooper looks at me, his eyes narrowing. I sway a little.

"What are you talking about?" he asks.

"Daniel," I say. "I know you don't like him."

"What makes you say that?"

Now my eyes are the ones that narrow.

"Are we really going to do this again?"

"I like him!" he says, holding up his hands in surrender. "Remind me what he does again?"

"Pharm sales."

"*Farm* sales?" he scoffs. "Really? Doesn't strike me as that kind of guy."

"Pharmaceuticals," I say. "With a *p-h*."

Cooper laughs, digs the pack of cigarettes out of his pocket, and pops another one between his lips. He offers me the pack and I shake my head.

"That makes more sense," he says. "Those shoes are a little too shiny to be spending much time around farmers."

"Come on, Coop," I say, crossing my arms. "This is what I'm talking about."

"I just think it's fast," he says, flicking open his lighter. He lifts the flame to the cigarette and inhales. "You've known each other for, what—a couple months?"

"A year," I say. "We've been together for a year."

"You've *known* each other for a year."

"And?"

"And how can you really know someone that well in a year? Have you even met his family?"

"Well, no," I admit. "They're not close. But come on, Coop. Are you really going to judge him by his family? You of all people should know better than that. Families suck."

Cooper shrugs, takes another drag instead of answering. His hypocrisy is pissing me off. My brother has always had this nonchalant way of getting under my skin, burrowing deep like a scarab and eating me alive. Even worse, he acts like he's not even trying. Like he doesn't even realize how cutting his words are, how badly they hurt. I have the sudden urge to hurt him back.

"Look, I'm sorry things didn't work out with Laurel, or with anyone, for that matter, but that doesn't give you the right to be jealous," I say. "If you'd just allow yourself to open up to people instead of being a dick all the time, you'd be surprised at what you can learn."

Cooper is quiet, and I know I've gone too far. It's the wine, I think. It's making me unusually forward. Unusually mean. He sucks on his cigarette, hard, and exhales. I sigh.

"I didn't mean it like that."

"No, you're right," he says, walking toward the edge of the porch. He leans against the railing and crosses one leg in front of the other. "I can admit that. But the guy just threw you a surprise party, Chloe. You're afraid of the dark. Shit, you're afraid of everything."

I tap my fingers against my wineglass.

"He turned off all the lights in your house and asked forty people to scream when you walked in. He scared the living piss out of you. I saw your hand fly into your purse. I know what you were going for."

I'm quiet, embarrassed that he picked up on that.

"If he actually knew how fucking paranoid you are, do you really think he would have done that?"

"He meant well," I say. "You know he did."

"I'm sure he did, but that's not the point. He doesn't *know* you, Chloe. And you don't know him."

"Yes, he does," I snap. "He knows me, Cooper. He just won't let me be afraid of my own shadow all the time. And I'm grateful for that. That's healthy."

He sighs, sucks down the rest of his cigarette, and flicks it over the railing.

"All I'm saying is we're different from them, Chloe. You and I are different. We've been through some shit."

He gestures back to the house and I turn around, eying all the people inside. All the friends that have turned into family, laughing and mingling without a care in the world—and suddenly, instead of feeling the love that I had felt just minutes before, I feel a hollowness inside. Because Cooper is right. We are different.

"Does he know?" he asks gently. Quietly.

I turn around, glaring at him in the dark. I chew on the side of my cheek instead of answering.

"Chloe?"

"Yes," I say at last. "Yes, of course he knows, Cooper. Of course I told him."

"What have you told him?"

"Everything, okay? He knows everything."

I watch his eyes flicker back to the house, to the muffled sounds of the party going on without us, and I'm quiet again, the inside of my cheek raw from grinding between my teeth. I think I can taste blood.

"What is it with you two?" I ask at last, the energy drained from my voice. "What happened?"

"Nothing happened," he says. "It's just . . . I don't know. With you being who you are and all, and our family . . . I just hope he's around for the right reasons. That's all I'm gonna say."

"The *right reasons*?" I snap, more loudly than I should. "What the fuck does that mean?"

"Chloe, calm down."

"No," I say. "No, I won't. Because what you're telling me right now is that it can't be possible for him to *actually* love me, Cooper. For him to have *actually* fallen for someone as fucked up as me. As *damaged Chloe*."

"Oh, come on," he says. "Stop being dramatic."

"I'm not being dramatic," I snap. "I'm just asking *you* to stop being selfish for once. I'm asking you to give him a chance."

"Chloe—"

"I want you in this wedding," I interrupt. "Really, I do. But it's happening with or without you, Cooper. If you're going to make me choose—"

I hear the door glide open behind me and I swing around, my eyes landing on Daniel. He's smiling at me, though I can see his eyes darting back and forth between Cooper and me, an unspoken question lingering on his lips. I wonder how long he's been standing there, just behind the sliding glass door. I wonder what he's heard.

"Everything okay?" he asks, walking over to us. He winds his arm around my waist and I feel him pull me closer to him, away from Cooper.

"Yes," I say, trying to will myself to calm down. "Yes, everything's fine."

"Cooper," Daniel says, extending his free hand. "Good to see you, man."

Cooper smiles, giving my fiancé a firm handshake in response.

"I haven't had a chance to thank you, by the way. For all your help."

I look at Daniel and I feel my forehead scrunch.

"Help with what?" I ask.

"Help with this," Daniel smiles. "The party. He didn't tell you?"

I look back at my brother, my white-hot words to him flashing across my mind. I feel my heart sink.

"No," I say, still looking at Cooper. "He didn't tell me."

"Oh, yeah," Daniel says. "This guy's a lifesaver. Couldn't have pulled it off without him."

"It was nothing," Cooper says, looking at his feet. "Happy to help."

"No, it wasn't nothing," Daniel says. "He got here early, steamed all the crawfish. He was toiling over that thing for hours, seasoning them just right."

"Why didn't you say anything?" I ask.

Cooper shrugs, embarrassed. "It wasn't a big deal."

"Anyway, we should get back in there," Daniel says, pulling me toward the door. "There are a few people here that I'd like Chloe to meet."

"Five minutes," I say, planting my feet beneath me. I can't leave my brother on these terms, and I can't apologize in front of Daniel without revealing the conversation we were having just before he walked outside. "I'll meet you in there."

Daniel looks at me, then back at Cooper. It seems like he's going to object for a minute, his lips parting gently, but instead, he just smiles again, squeezing my shoulder.

"Sounds good," he says, giving my brother one last salute. "Five minutes."

The door slides shut and I wait until Daniel is out of sight before turning back around, facing my brother.

"Cooper," I say at last, my shoulders sinking. "I'm sorry. I didn't know."

"It's fine," he says. "Honestly."

"No, it's not fine," I say. "You should have said

something. Here I am, being such a bitch, calling you *selfish*—"

"It's fine," he says again, pushing himself up from the railing and walking toward me, closing the distance between us. Enveloping me in a hug. "I'd do anything for you, Chloe. You know that. You're my baby sister."

I sigh and snake my arms around him, too, letting my guilt and my anger melt away. This is our dance, Cooper's and mine. We disagree, we shout, we argue. We don't speak to each other for months on end, but when we finally do, it's like we're kids again, running through the sprinklers barefoot in the backyard, building forts out of moving boxes in the basement, talking for hours on end without even noticing the people around us evaporating into thin air. Sometimes, I think I blame Cooper for making me remember myself—who I am, who our parents are. His mere existence is a reminder that the image I project out into the world isn't actually real, but carefully crafted. That I'm one small stumble away from shattering into a million pieces, revealing who I really am.

It's a complicated relationship, but we're family. We're the only family we've got.

"I love you," I say, squeezing harder. "I can tell you're trying."

"I am trying," Cooper says. "I'm just protective."

"I know."

"I want the best for you."

"I know."

"I guess I'm just used to being the man in your life, you know? The one that looks after you. And now that's going to be someone else. It's hard to let go."

I smile, squeezing my eyes shut before a tear can escape. "Oh, so you do have a heart?"

"C'mon, Chlo," he whispers. "I'm being serious."

"I know," I say again. "I know you are. I'll be okay."

We stand there for a while in silence, hugging, the party that came to see me seemingly oblivious to the fact that I have vanished for God-knows-how-long. Holding my brother in my arms, I think back again to the phone call I received earlier—Aaron Jansen. *The New York Times.*

"But you've changed," the reporter had said. *"You and your brother. The public would love to know how you're doing—how you're coping."*

"Hey, Coop?" I ask, lifting my head. "Can I ask you something?"

"Sure."

"Did you get a phone call today?"

He looks at me, confused. "What kind of phone call?"

I hesitate.

"Chloe," he says, sensing me backing away. He grips my arms harder. "What kind of phone call?"

I start to open my mouth before he interrupts me.

"Oh, you know what, I did," he says. "From mom's place. They left me a message and I completely forgot. Did they call you, too?"

I exhale, nodding quickly. "Yeah," I lie. "I missed it, too."

"We're due for a visit," he says. "It's my turn. I'm sorry, I shouldn't have put it off."

"It's fine," I say. "Really, I can go if you're too busy."

"No," he says, shaking his head. "No, you've got enough going on. I'll go this weekend, I promise. Are you sure that's all?"

My mind flashes back to Aaron Jansen, to our conversation on my office line—not that you could really call what we had a conversation. *Twenty years.* It seems like something I should tell my brother—that *The New York Times* is snooping around in our past. That this Aaron Jansen guy is writing a story about Dad, about us. But then I realize: If Aaron had Cooper's information, he would have called him by now. He said so himself: He'd been trying to reach me all day. If he couldn't reach me, wouldn't he have tried to move on to my brother? To the other Davis kid? If he hasn't called Coop yet, that means he hasn't been able to dig up his number, his address, his anything.

"Yeah," I say. "That's all."

I decide not to burden him with this. At best, the news of a *Times* reporter calling me at work to get dirt on our family will piss him off enough to chain-smoke the rest of the pack of cigarettes stuffed in his back pocket; at worst, he'd call him up himself and tell him to fuck off. And then Jansen *would* have his number, and we'd both be screwed.

"Well hey, your groom is waiting," Cooper says, patting me twice on the back. He sidesteps me and starts walking down the porch stairs, toward the backyard. "You should get back inside."

"You're not gonna come in?" I ask, although I already know the answer.

"That's enough socializing for me for one night," he says. "See ya later, alligator."

I smile, picking up my wineglass again and raising it to my chin. It never gets old hearing that childhood phrase escape the lips of my nearly middle-aged brother—jarring, almost, hearing the words in his adolescent voice, taking me back to decades ago when life was simple and fun and free. But at the same time, it fits, because our world stopped spinning twenty years ago. We were left stranded in time, forever young. Just like those girls.

I down the rest of my wine and wave in his direction. The darkness has enveloped him now, but I know he's still there. Waiting.

"In a while, crocodile," I whisper, staring into the shadows.

The silence is broken then by the crunching of leaves beneath his feet, and within seconds, I know he's gone.

JUNE 2019

CHAPTER SIX

My eyes snap open. My head is pounding, a rhythmic beating like a tribal drum making the room vibrate. I roll over in bed and glance at my alarm clock. Ten forty-five. How the hell did I sleep this late?

I sit up in bed and rub my temples, squinting at the brightness of our bedroom. When I had moved in here—back when it was *my* bedroom, not *our* bedroom, a *house,* not a *home*—I had wanted everything to be white. Walls, carpet, bedspread, curtains. White is clean, pure, safe.

But now, white is bright. Way, way too bright. The linen curtains hanging in front of the floor-to-ceiling windows are pointless, I realize, because they do nothing to mask the blinding sun that's now beating down on my pillow. I groan.

"Daniel?" I yell, leaning over to my bedside table and pulling out a bottle of Advil. There's a cup of water sitting on a marble coaster—it's new. The ice is still frozen, the cubes bobbing on the surface like buoys on a calm day. I can see the cold sweat dripping down the side of the glass and pooling at the base. "Daniel, why am I dying?"

I hear my fiancé chuckle as he walks into our bedroom. He's carrying a tray of pancakes and turkey bacon and I immediately wonder what I did to deserve someone who actually brings me breakfast in bed. All that's missing is a handpicked wildflower propped inside a tiny vase and this scene could be torn from a Hallmark movie, minus my raging hangover.

Maybe this is karma, I wonder. *I got a shitty family, so now I get a perfect husband.*

"Two bottles of wine will do that," he says, kissing my forehead. "Especially when you don't stick to the same bottles."

"People just kept handing me things," I say, picking up a piece of bacon and biting down. "I don't even know what I drank."

Suddenly, I remember the Xanax. Popping that little white pill seconds before being shoved drink after drink. No wonder I feel so terrible; no wonder the edges of the night are so fuzzy, as if I'm rewatching the events of the evening through the bottom of a frosted glass. My cheeks burn red, but Daniel doesn't notice. Instead, he laughs, running his fingers through my tangled hair. His, in comparison, is perfect. I realize now that he's completely showered, his face clean-shaven and his sandy blonde hair combed and gelled, his part a razor-thin line. He smells like aftershave and cologne.

"Are you going somewhere?"

"New Orleans." He frowns. "Remember, I told you last week? The conference?"

"Oh, right," I say, shaking my head, although I don't actually remember. "Sorry, my brain's still foggy. But . . . it's Saturday. Is it over the weekend? You just got home."

I never knew much about pharmaceutical sales before I met Daniel. Really, the only thing I knew about it was the money; specifically, that the position made a lot of it. Or at least it could, if you did it well. But now I know more, like the constant travel the job requires.

Daniel's territory stretches halfway across Louisiana and into Mississippi, so during the week, he's almost always in the car. Early mornings, late nights, hours on end driving from one hospital to another. There are also a lot of conferences: sales and training development, digital marketing for medical devices, seminars about the future of pharmaceuticals. I know he misses me while he's away, but I know also that he likes it— the wining and dining, the fancy hotels, the schmoozing with doctors. He's good at it, too.

"There's a networking event at the hotel tonight," he says slowly. "And a golf tournament tomorrow before the conference begins on Monday. You don't remember any of this?"

My heart lurches in my chest. *No,* I think. *I don't remember any of this.* But instead, I smile, pushing the plate of breakfast aside and throwing my arms around his neck.

"I'm sorry," I say. "I remember. I think I'm still drunk."

Daniel laughs, like I knew he would, and tousles his hand through my hair like I'm a toddler up to bat during a game of peewee T-ball.

"Last night was fun," I say, diverting the conversation. I rest my head on his lap and close my eyes. "Thank you."

"Of course," he says, the tip of his finger now drawing shapes in my hair. A circle, a square, a heart. He's quiet for a second, the kind of quiet that hangs heavy in the air, until finally he speaks. "What was that conversation with your brother about? The one outside?"

"What do you mean?"

"You know what I mean," he says. "The one I walked in on."

"Oh, you know," I say, my eyelids feeling heavy again. "Just Cooper being Cooper. Nothing to worry about."

"Whatever you guys were talking about . . . it looked a little tense."

"He's worried you're not marrying me for *the right reasons*," I say, lifting my fingers up to make air quotes. "But like I said, it's just my brother. He's overprotective."

"He said that?"

I feel Daniel's back stiffen as he pulls his hand from my hair. I wish I could swallow the words back down as soon as I say them—again, it's the wine, still buzzing through my bloodstream. Making my thoughts spill over like an overpoured glass, staining the carpet.

"Forget I mentioned it," I say, opening my eyes. I'm expecting him to be looking down at me, but instead, he's staring ahead, straight at nothing. "He'll learn to love you like I do, I know he will. He's trying."

"Did he say why he thinks that?"

"Daniel, seriously," I say, sitting up in bed. "It's not even worth talking about. Cooper is protective. He always has been, ever since I was a kid. Our past, you know. He kind of assumes the worst in people. We're similar in that way."

"Yeah," Daniel says. He's still staring ahead, his eyes glassy. "Yeah, I guess so."

"I know you're marrying me for the right reasons," I say, placing my palm on his cheek. He flinches, the touch of my skin seeming to wake him from his trance. "Like, for example, for my tight Pilates ass and orgasmic coq au vin."

He turns to me, unable to keep his lips from cracking into a smile, then a laugh. He covers my hand with his own and squeezes my fingers before standing.

"Don't work all weekend," he says, patting down the creases in his ironed pants. "Get outside. Do something fun."

I roll my eyes and snatch another piece of bacon, folding it in half before sticking it in my mouth whole.

"Or get some wedding planning done," he continues. "It's the final countdown."

"Next month," I say, grinning. The fact that we booked our wedding in July—twenty years to the month from when the girls first went missing—is not lost on me. The thought flashed into my mind the moment we walked into Cypress Stables, the oak trees dripping over a gorgeous cobblestone aisle, white painted chairs perfectly aligned with four massive farmhouse columns. Acres and acres of untouched land spanning as far as the eye could see. I still remember setting my sights on the restored barn at the edge of the property that could be used for a reception space, giant wooden pillars decorated with string lights and greenery and milky magnolia flowers. A white picket fence corralling horses as they grazed across the pasture, the plane of green broken only by a bayou in the distance, winding gently across the horizon like a thick, blue vein.

"It's perfect," Daniel had said, his hand squeezing mine. "Chloe, isn't it perfect?"

I nodded, smiling. It was perfect, but the vastness of the place reminded me of home. Of my father, covered in mud, emerging from the trees with a shovel slouched over one shoulder. Of the swamp that surrounded our land like a moat, keeping people out but also confining us in. I glanced over to the farmhouse, tried to imagine myself walking across the giant wraparound porch in my wedding gown before descending the stairs toward Daniel. A flutter of movement caught my eye and I did a double take; there was a girl on the porch, a teenager slouched in a rocking chair, her leg outstretched as brown leather riding boots pushed gently against the porch columns, moving the chair in a lazy rhythm. She perked up when she noticed me staring at her, pulled her dress down and crossed her legs.

"That's my granddaughter," the woman before us

said. I peeled my eyes from the girl and looked in her direction. "This land has been in our family for generations. She likes to come here sometimes after school. Do her homework on the porch."

"Beats the hell out of a library," Daniel said, smiling. He lifted his arm and waved at the girl. She dipped her head slightly, embarrassed, before waving back. Daniel directed his attention back to the woman. "We'll take it. What's your availability?"

"Let's see," she said, glancing down at the iPad in her hands. She rotated it a few times until she could get the screen upright. "So far, for this year, we're almost completely booked. You guys are behind schedule!"

"We just got engaged," I said, twirling the fresh diamond around my finger, a new habit. The ring Daniel had given me was a family heirloom: a Victorian-era jewel handed down by his great-great-grandmother. It was visibly worn, but a true antique, old in a way that couldn't be replicated. Years of familial stories scratched into the oval-cut center stone surrounded by a halo of rose-cut diamonds, the band a buttery yet slightly cloudy 14-karat yellow gold. "We don't want to be one of those couples that waits around for years and just delays the inevitable."

"Yeah, we're old," Daniel said. "Clock's a-tickin'."

He patted my stomach and the woman smirked, swiping her finger across the screen as if flipping pages. I tried not to blush.

"Like I said, for this year, all my weekends are booked. We can do 2020 if you'd like."

Daniel shook his head.

"Every single weekend? I can't believe that. What about Fridays?"

"Most of our Fridays are booked as well, for rehearsals," she said. "But it looks like we do have one. July 26."

Daniel glanced at me, raised his eyebrows.

"Think you can pencil it in?"

He was joking, I knew, but the mention of *July* sent my heart into a flurry.

"July in Louisiana," I said, twisting my expression. "Think the guests can handle the heat? Especially outside."

"We can bring in outdoor air-conditioning," the woman said. "Tents, fans, you name it."

"I don't know," I said. "It gets pretty buggy, too."

"We spray the grounds every year," she said. "I can guarantee you bugs will not be a problem. We have summer weddings all the time!"

I noticed Daniel staring at me then, quizzically, his eyes burrowing into the side of my head as if, if he stared at it hard enough, he could untangle the thoughts tumbling around inside. But I refused to turn, refused to face him. Refused to admit the completely irrational reason why the month of July morphed my anxiety into something debilitating, a progressive disease that worsened as summer stretched on. Refused to acknowledge the rising sense of nausea in my throat or the way the sour smell of manure in the distance seemed to mix with the sweet magnolias or the suddenly deafening sound of flies I could hear buzzing around somewhere, circling something dead.

"Okay," I said, nodding. I glanced at the porch again but the girl was gone, her empty chair rocking slowly in the wind. "July it is."

CHAPTER SEVEN

I watch Daniel's car back out of the driveway, his head-lights flashing a goodbye as he waves at me through the windshield. I wave back, my silk robe clutched tightly around my chest, a steaming mug of coffee warm in my hands.

I shut the door behind me and take in the empty house: There are still cups resting on various tabletops from last night, empty wine bottles filling up recycling bins in the kitchen, and flies that were apparently born overnight circling over their sticky openings. I start to tidy up, clearing dishes and placing them in the empty farmhouse sink, trying to ignore the drug-and-wine fueled headache nagging at my brain.

I think back to the prescription in my car; the Xanax I filled for Daniel that he doesn't know about or need. I think about the drawer in my office housing the various painkillers that would almost certainly numb the throbbing in my skull. It's tempting, know-ing they're there. Part of me wants to get in the car and drive to them, outstretch my fingers, and take my pick. Curl up in the recliner meant for patients and fall back asleep.

Instead, I drink my coffee.

Access to drugs is not why I got into this line of work—besides, Louisiana is one of only three states where psychologists can actually prescribe drugs to their patients. Other than here, Illinois, and New Mexico, we typically have to rely on a referring physician or psychiatrist to fill a script. But not here. Here, we can write them ourselves. Here, nobody else has to know. Whether that's a happy coincidence or a stroke of dangerously bad luck, I haven't quite decided. But again, that's not why I do what I do. I didn't become a psychologist to take advantage of this loophole, to sidestep the drug dealers downtown for the safety of the drive-through window, trading in a plastic baggy for a logoed paper bag, complete with a receipt and coupons for half-off toothpaste and a gallon of 2 percent milk. I became a psychologist to help people—again with the clichés, but it's true. I became a psychologist because I understand trauma; I understand it in a way that no amount of schooling could ever teach. I understand the way the brain can fundamentally fuck with every other aspect of your body; the way your emotions can distort things—emotions you didn't even know you had. The way those emotions can make it impossible to see clearly, think clearly, do anything clearly. The way they can make you hurt from your head down to your fingertips, a dull, throbbing, constant pain that never goes away.

I saw plenty of doctors as a teenager—it was an endless cycle of therapists, psychiatrists, and psychologists, all of whom asked the same series of scripted questions, trying to fix the endless slideshow of anxiety disorders flipping through my psyche. Cooper and I were the stuff of textbooks back then, me with my panic attacks, hypochondria, insomnia, and nyctophobia, every year a new malady added to the list. Cooper, on the other hand, recoiled into himself. I was feeling too much, while he was feeling too little. His loud personality shrunk into a whisper; he practically disappeared.

The two of us together were childhood trauma wrapped in a bow and placed delicately on the doorsteps of every doctor in Louisiana. Everybody knew who we were; everybody knew what was wrong with us.

Everybody knew, but nobody could fix it. So I decided to fix it myself.

I shuffle through the living room and plop down on the sofa, my coffee sloshing over the side of the mug. I lift it to my mouth and lick the liquid from the side. The morning news is already droning in the background, Daniel's channel of choice, and I reach for my Mac-Book, repeatedly tapping *Return* as I wake it from a long, groggy sleep. I open my Gmail and scroll through the personal messages in my in-box, almost all of them wedding-related.

Two more months, Chloe! Let's get that cake finalized, shall we? Have you decided between your two options: caramel drizzle or lemon curd?

Chloe, hi. The florist needs to finalize the table arrangements. Can I tell her to invoice you for 20 tables or did you want to cut it back to 10?

A few months ago, I would have consulted Daniel on everything. Every little detail was a decision meant for the two of us, together. But as time goes by, the small, intimate wedding I had been envisioning—an outdoor ceremony followed by a private celebration for close friends; one long, slender table with Daniel and I seated at the head, picking at our favorite foods between sips of rosé and bursts of open-mouthed laughter—has turned into something else entirely. An exotic pet that neither of us knows how to tame. There's the constant decision-making, the endless emails about details that seem so trivial. Daniel has been looking to me to make the ruling on almost everything, a gesture that he probably thinks is the right one, given brides and their reputation for wanting control. But the responsibility has left me feeling more stressed out than ever, the weight of it all placed solely on my shoulders. His only firm opinions revolve around the fact that he hates fondant cake and that he refuses to send an invitation to his parents, two demands with which I am eager to comply.

I would never admit it to Daniel, but I'm ready for it to be over. The whole thing. I say a silent *thank you* for a quick engagement and tap out my replies.

Caramel is good, thanks!

Can we meet in the middle and do 15?

I scroll through a few more emails before I click on one from my wedding planner and freeze.

Hi, Chloe. I'm sorry to keep asking about this but we do need to get the ceremony details nailed down so I can finalize a seating chart. Have you decided who you'd like to walk you down the aisle? Let me know when you get a chance.

My mouse hovers over *Delete,* but that pesky psychologist voice—*my* voice—echoes around me.

Classic avoidance coping, Chloe. You know that never eliminates the problem—it only postpones it.

I roll my eyes at my own internal advice and drum

my fingers on the keyboard. The whole idea of a father walking his daughter down the aisle is so outdated, anyway. The thought of somebody *giving me away* makes my stomach lurch, like I'm a piece of property being sold to the highest bidder. We might as well bring back the dowry.

My mind flashes to Cooper, the closest thing to a father figure I've had since age twelve. I imagine his hand clutched around mine, his body guiding me down the aisle.

But then I think of his words last night. The disapproval in his eyes, his tone.

He doesn't know you, Chloe. And you don't know him.

I shut my computer and push it across the couch, my eyes flickering back to the television playing in the background. There's a bright red bar stretched across the bottom of the screen: *BREAKING NEWS*. I grab the remote and turn the volume up.

Authorities are still looking for tips in connection to the disappearance of Aubrey Gravino, a fifteen-year-old high school student from Baton Rouge, Louisiana. Aubrey was reported missing by her parents three days ago; she was last seen walking alone near a cemetery on her way home from school Wednesday afternoon.

A picture of Aubrey flashes across the screen, and I flinch at the image. When I was a girl, fifteen seemed so old. So mature, grown up. I dreamed about the things I would do when I was fifteen—but in the years that have followed, I've been forced to realize how painfully young it is. How young *she* is, they all were. Aubrey looks vaguely familiar, though I assume it's because she looks like every other high school girl I see slumped over in the chair in my office: skinny in a way only adolescent metabolism can achieve, eyes smudged with black pencil, hair untouched by color or heat or any of the other destructive things women do to themselves as they age in an effort to look young again. I force myself not to think about how she probably looks now: pale, stiff, cold. Death ages a body, turns the skin gray, the eyes dull. Humans aren't supposed to die that young. It's unnatural.

Aubrey disappears from the TV and a new image appears: an aerial view map of Baton Rouge. My eyes are immediately drawn toward where my home and office are located, downtown near the Mississippi. A red dot appears at Cypress Cemetery, Aubrey's last known location.

Search parties are combing through the cemetery today, although Aubrey's parents remain hopeful that their daughter can still be found alive.

The map disappears and a video starts playing—a man and a woman, both middle-aged and severely sleep deprived, stand at a podium, the caption identifying them as Aubrey's parents. The man stands quietly to the side while the woman, the mother, pleads into the camera.

"Aubrey," she says, "wherever you are, we are looking for you, baby. We are looking for you, and we are going to find you."

The man sniffles, wipes his eye with his shirtsleeve, smears the snot under his nose on the back of his hand. She pats his arm and continues.

"To whoever has her, or has any information about her whereabouts, we are begging you to come forward. We just want our daughter back."

The man starts crying now, heaving sobs. The

woman presses forward, never peeling her eyes from the lens. That's a tactic the police teach you, I've learned. Look into the camera. Talk to the camera. Talk to *him*.

"We want our baby back."

CHAPTER EIGHT

Lena Rhodes was the first girl. The *original*. The one that started it all.

I remember Lena well, and not in the way most people remember dead girls. Not in the way distant classmates make up stories to seem relevant, the way former friends post old pictures to Facebook, rehashing inside jokes and shared memories, omitting the fact that they haven't actually spoken in years.

Breaux Bridge remembers Lena solely by the picture chosen for the *MISSING* poster, as if that one moment frozen in time was the only moment she ever had. The only moment that mattered. How a family chooses one picture to encapsulate an entire life, an entire personality, I will never understand. It seems too daunting a task, too important and simultaneously too impossible. In choosing that picture, you are choosing her legacy. You are choosing the solitary moment that the world will remember—that moment, and nothing else.

But I remember Lena. Not superficially—I really remember her. I remember all her moments, the good and the bad. Her force and her flaws. I remember who she really was.

She was loud, vulgar, cussed in a way I had only ever witnessed when my father accidentally hacked the tip of his thumb off with a hatchet in his workshop. The filth that spewed out of her mouth was at odds with her appearance, which made her all the more mesmerizing. She was tall, slim, breasts disproportionately large compared with her otherwise boyish fifteen-year-old figure. She was outgoing, bubbly, her hair a sunflower yellow that she kept pulled back into two French braids. People watched her when she walked and she knew it; attention inflated her the way it had always deflated me, the eyes gazing in her direction making her glow even brighter, walk even taller.

Boys liked her. I liked her. I envied her, really. Every girl in Breaux Bridge envied her, until her face appeared on the television screen that awful Tuesday morning.

One moment sticks out in particular, though. One moment with Lena. A moment that I will never forget, no matter how hard I try.

After all, that was the moment that sent my father to prison.

I turn the TV off and stare at my reflection in the dead screen. Every one of those press conferences is the same. I've seen enough to know.

The mother always takes control. The mother always keeps her emotions in check. The mother always speaks evenly, steadily, while the father grovels in the background, unable to lift his head long enough for the man who took his daughter to look him in the eyes. Society would have us think it's the other way around—that the man in the family takes control, the woman cries silently—but it's not. And I know why.

It's because the fathers think in the past—Breaux Bridge taught me that. The fathers of the six missing girls taught me that. They're ashamed of themselves; they think *what if*. They were supposed to be the protectors, the men. They were supposed to keep their daughters safe, and they failed. But the mothers think in the present; they formulate a plan. They can't afford to think in the past because the past doesn't matter anymore—it's a distraction. A waste of time. They can't afford to think in the future because the future is too terrifying, too painful—if they let their minds wander there, they may never return. They may break.

So instead, they think only of today. And what they can do today to bring their babies back tomorrow.

Bert Rhodes had been an absolute wreck. I had never seen a man cry like that before, his entire body convulsing with each tormented moan. He used to be a relatively attractive man in that rugged, working-class way: toned arms that made his shirt seams bulge, clean-cut jawline, amber skin. I barely recognized him on that first televised interview, the way his eyes sunk into his skull, drowning in two pools of purple. The way his body slumped forward, like his own weight was physically too much to carry.

My father was arrested at the end of September, almost three full months after his reign of terror began. And on the night of his arrest, I thought of Bert Rhodes almost immediately—before I thought of Lena or Robin or Margaret or Carrie or any of the other girls who had vanished over the course of that summer. I remember the red and blue lights illuminating our living room, Cooper and I running to the window, peering outside as the armed men barged through the front door and yelled, *"Freeze!"* I remember my father in his recliner, that old leather La-Z-Boy that was so worn in the center it was soft like felt, not even bothering to lift his head and glance in their direction. Completely ignoring my mother in the corner, sobbing uncontrollably. I remember the shells of sunflower seeds, his snack of choice, stuck to his teeth, his lower lip, his fingernails. I remember how they dragged him, his walnut pipe tumbling from his lips and staining the floor black with ash as that slender sleeve of seeds cascaded across the carpet.

I remember how his eyes locked intently on mine, un-flinching and focused. Mine, then Cooper's.

"Be good," he said.

Then they dragged him through the door and out into the damp evening air, slamming his head against the cruiser, his thick glasses cracking in protest, the flash-ing lights turning his skin a sickening shade of crim-son. They ducked him inside and shut the door.

I watched him sit there, quietly, staring ahead at the mesh metal divider, his body completely still, the only decipherable movement the trickle of blood creeping down the bridge of his nose that he didn't bother to wipe away. I watched him, and I thought of Bert Rhodes. I wondered if knowing the identity of the man who took his daughter would make things better or worse for him. Easier or harder. It's an impossible choice to be faced with, but if he had to choose, would he rather his child be murdered by a complete stranger—an intruder in his town, in his life—or a familiar face, one he had wel-comed into his home? His neighbor, his friend?

In the following months, the only time I got to see my dad was on television, his framed glasses, now frac-tured, always cast down to the ground below him, his hands cuffed tightly behind his back, the skin on his wrists pinched and pink. I pressed my nose to the screen and watched as people would line the street that led to the courthouse with homemade signs scribbled with horrible, nasty words, hissing as he walked past.

Murderer. Pervert.

Monster.

Some of the signs featured the faces of the girls—the girls who had been on the news in a sad, steady stream over the course of that summer. Girls who weren't much older than me. I recognized all of them; I had memorized their features. I had seen their smiles, looked into their eyes, once promising and alive.

Lena, Robin, Margaret, Carrie, Susan, Jill.

Those faces were the reason I had a curfew at night. They were the reason I was never allowed to walk alone in the dark. My father had been the one to enact that rule, spanking me until my skin was raw when I stumbled home past dusk or forgot to close my window at night. He had injected pure fear into my heart—a debilitating dread of that unseen person who was the cause of their disappearances. That person who was the reason why those girls had been reduced to black-and-white pictures glued to old cardboard. That person who knew where they were when they took their last breaths; what their eyes looked like when death finally took them.

I knew it when he was arrested, of course. I knew it from the moment the police barged into our home, the moment my father looked into our eyes and whispered: *Be good.* I had known it before then, really, when I finally allowed the pieces to fall into place. When I forced myself to turn around and face the figure I could feel lurking behind me. But it was in that moment—alone in my living room, my face pressed against the television screen, my mother unraveling slowly in her bedroom, and Cooper shriveling into nothing out back—it was *that* moment, listening to my father's ankle chains rattle, watching his blank expression as he was moved from cop cars to prisons to courtrooms and back. It was that moment when the weight of it all came crashing down, burying me alive in the debris.

That person was him.

CHAPTER NINE

All at once, my house seems both too big and too small. It's claustrophobic, sitting here, these four walls confining me inside, trapping me with this recycled, stale air. But it's also impossibly lonely; too large to be filled with only the silent thoughts of a single soul. I have the sudden urge to move.

I get up from the couch and walk into my bedroom, exchanging my oversized robe for a pair of jeans and a gray T-shirt, pulling my hair into a topknot and forgoing all makeup that takes more effort than swiping my lips with a stick of Blistex. I'm out the door within five minutes, my hammering heart slowing considerably once my flats hit the pavement.

I get in the car and crank the engine, driving mechanically through my neighborhood and into town. I reach for the radio but my hand pauses in midair, instead recoiling back to the steering wheel.

"It's okay, Chloe," I say out loud, my voice painfully shrill in the otherwise silence of my car. "What's bothering you? Verbalize it."

I drum my fingers against the steering wheel, push down my turn signal, and decide to take a left. I'm talking to myself the way I talk to my clients.

"A girl is missing," I say. "A local girl has gone missing, and it's upsetting me."

If this were an appointment, next I would ask: *Why? Why is this upsetting you?*

The reasons are obvious, I know. A young girl is missing. Fifteen years old. Last seen within jogging distance from my house, my office, my life.

"You don't know her," I say out loud. "You don't know her, Chloe. She isn't Lena. She isn't any of those girls. This has nothing to do with you."

I exhale, slowing down at an impending red light as I glance across the road. I watch a mother escort her daughter across the street, hand-in-hand; a group of teenagers are Rollerblading to my left, a man and his dog jogging straight ahead. The light turns green.

"This has nothing to do with you," I repeat, pushing through the intersection and taking a right.

I've been driving without direction, but I realize I'm close to my office, mere blocks from the safe haven of pills tucked inside my desk drawer. I'm a swallowed capsule away from a decreased heart rate and steady breathing; a giant leather recliner with a locked door and blackout curtains.

I shake the thought from my head.

I don't have a problem. I'm not addicted or anything. I don't go out to bars and drink myself into a coma or break into clammy night sweats when I deny myself that nightly glass of merlot. I could go days, weeks, months without a pill or a glass of wine or any kind of chemical substance to numb the constant fear vibrating through my veins; it's like a plucked guitar string reverberating through my bones, making them rattle. But I have it handled. All of my disorders, all of those big words that I've been fighting for so long—*insomnia, nyctophobia, hypochondria*—they have one common trait, one significant quality that binds them all together, and that's control.

I fear all situations where I'm not in control. I imagine the things that can happen to me in my sleep, defenseless. I imagine the things that can happen to me in the dark, unaware. I imagine all the invisible killers that can strangle the life from my cells before I even know they're being suffocated; I imagine surviving what I survived, living through what I lived through, only to die from a case of unwashed hands, a tickle in my throat.

I imagine Lena, the total lack of control she must have felt as those hands latched around her neck, tightening. As her windpipe squeezed shut, her eyes started to throb, her vision began to brighten before taking a sudden turn in the opposite direction, getting dimmer and dimmer until, at last, she saw nothing.

My pharmacy is my lifeline. I know it's wrong to write prescriptions that don't need to be written; more than wrong, it's illegal. I could lose my license, maybe even go to jail. But everybody needs a lifeline, a raft in the distance when you feel yourself starting to sink. When I find myself losing control, I know they're there, ready to fix whatever it is inside me that needs fixing. More often than not, it's just the thought of them that calms my nerves. I once told a claustrophobic patient to carry a single Xanax in her purse every time she boards a plane, its mere presence strong enough to elicit a mental reaction, a physical response. She probably wouldn't even need to take it, I told her; just knowing there was an escape within reach would be enough to ease the suffocating weight from her chest.

And it was. Of course it was. I knew from experience.

I see my office in the distance now, that old brick building peeking out from behind moss-lined oaks. The cemetery is only a few blocks west; I make a decision and turn toward it, driving in the direction of the wrought-iron gate, a yawning mouth inviting me inside. I ease my car into a spot on the street and kill the ignition.

Cypress Cemetery. The last place Aubrey Gravino was seen alive. I hear a noise and glance out the window; there's a search party in the distance, scouring the place like ants ambushing a sliver of forgotten meat. They're pushing through the overgrown crabgrass, sidestepping the crumbling headstones, rubbing their sneakers against the dirt pathways that snake their way through the graves. This cemetery spans over twenty acres; it's an impossibly large piece of land. The prospect of finding whatever it is they're hoping to find seems bleak, at best.

I get out of the car and walk through the gates, edging closer to the party. The property is dotted with bald cypress trees—the Louisiana state tree, and therefore the cemetery's namesake—their trunks thick and red and ropey like tendons. Veils of Spanish moss dangle from their branches like cobwebs festering in a forgotten corner. I duck under a ribbon of police tape and do my best to blend in, trying to skirt away from the police officers and journalists with cameras hung from their necks, wandering aimlessly among the dozens of volunteers in their hunt to find Aubrey.

Or to *not* find Aubrey. Because the last thing you want to find in a search party is a body, or worse: pieces of one.

They hadn't found any bodies in the search parties of Breaux Bridge. No pieces, either. I had begged my mother to let me tag along; I saw the hordes of people gathering in town, distributing their flashlights and walkie-talkies and cartons of bottled water. Hollering out instructions before dissipating like gnats being swat at with a rolled-up newspaper. She hadn't let me, of course. I was forced to stay home, watching the flicker of lanterns in the distance as they swept their way across the seemingly endless abyss of tall, grassy pastures. It was the most helpless feeling, watching. Waiting. Not knowing what they'd find. It was even worse when the search party was in my own backyard, my eyes glued to the window as police scoured every inch of our ten acres after my father had been taken into custody. But that didn't yield anything, either.

No, those girls are still out there, somewhere, the layers of dirt concealing their bones growing thicker every year. The thought of them never being found is mind-numbing to me, even though I know, by this point, they probably never will be. It isn't the injustice of it, or the lack of closure for the families, or even the concept of those girls decaying in the same way as the dead field rat I once discovered under our back porch, their humanity being stripped away along with their skin and their hair and their tattered clothing. An entire life whittled down to a pile of bones that are no different from yours or mine or even that field rat's, really. No, it isn't any of those things that keep me up at night, that keep me from ever giving up hope that they might someday be found.

It's the realization of how many hidden bodies could be buried beneath my feet at any point in time, the world above them completely oblivious to their existence.

Of course, there are bodies buried beneath my feet at this very moment. Lots of bodies. But cemeteries are different. These bodies were placed here, not dropped. They're here to be remembered, not forgotten.

"I think I found something!"

I glance to my left at a middle-aged woman dressed in white sneakers, khaki cargo pants, and an oversized polo shirt, the unofficial uniform of a search party concerned citizen. She's kneeling in the dirt, her eyes squinting at something beneath her. Her left arm is waving madly in the direction of the other searchers, her right clutching the kind of walkie-talkie you'd buy in the toy section at Walmart.

I look around—I'm the closest one by several yards. The rest are coming, running in our direction, but I'm here now. I take a step closer and she looks up at me, her eyes excited yet pleading, like she wants this item to hold some kind of significance, some kind of meaning, but at the same time, she doesn't. She desperately doesn't.

"Look," she says, waving me over. "Look right there."

I step closer again and crane my neck, an electric shock jolting through my body as my eyes focus on the object nestled in the dirt. I reach for it, without thinking—a kind of knee-jerk reflex, as if someone had smacked my shin with a mallet—and pluck it from the ground. A police officer runs up behind me, panting.

"What is it?" he asks, hovering over me. His voice has a strangled quality to it, like his breath is trying to cut through a forest of phlegm. A mouth breather. His eyes bulge as he sees the item cradled in my hand. "Jesus, don't touch it!"

"Sorry," I mutter, handing it to him. "Sorry—I, I wasn't thinking. It's an earring."

The woman looks at me as the officer kneels down, chest rattling, one arm jutting out to the side to stop the others from getting too close. He plucks the earring from my palm with his gloved hand and inspects it. It's small, silver, a cluster of three diamonds at the top forming an inverted triangle, the tip of the triangle attached to a single pearl dangling at the bottom. It looks nice, something that would have caught my eye in the window of a local jeweler. Too nice for a fifteen-year-old.

"Okay," the cop says, pushing wisps of hair across his

sweat-soaked forehead. He deflates just slightly. "Okay, this is good. We'll bag it, but remember: We're in a public place. There are thousands of graves in here, which means hundreds of visitors daily. This earring could belong to anybody."

"No," the woman shakes her head. "No, it doesn't. It belongs to Aubrey."

She reaches into her cargo pocket and pulls out a piece of paper, creased into quarters. She unfolds it: Aubrey's *MISSING* poster. I recognize the image from the one I saw this morning, plastered across my TV screen. The single image that will define her existence. She's smiling wide, that black eyeliner smeared across her lids, pink lip gloss reflecting the flash of the camera. The picture cuts off just above her chest, but I can see that she's wearing a necklace, a necklace I didn't notice before, nestled in the puddle of skin between her collarbones—three small diamonds attached to a single pearl. And there, fastened to the lobes peeking out from behind the thick, brown hair tucked behind her ears, is a pair of matching earrings.

CHAPTER TEN

Lena wasn't a nice girl, but she was nice to me. I won't make excuses for her; I won't sugarcoat the facts. She was a troublemaker, a perpetual pain in the ass who seemed to get off on making other people uncomfortable, watching them squirm. Why else would a fifteen-year-old wear a push-up bra to school, twirling her French braid around a bitten-down fingernail as she chewed on the side of her pillowy lip? She was a woman in a girl's body, or a girl in a woman's body; both seemed to make sense. Simultaneously too old and too young—a figure and mind beyond her years. But there were parts of her, somewhere, hidden beneath the depths of her slathered-on makeup and the cloud of cigarette smoke that seemed to envelope her each day after the ring of the high school bell that reminded you that she was just a girl. Just a lost, lonely girl.

Of course, I didn't see that side of her when I was twelve. She always seemed like an adult to me, despite the fact that she was the same age as my brother. Cooper never seemed like an adult with his burping and his Game Boy and his stash of dirty magazines he kept hidden under the loose floorboard beneath his bed. I'll never forget the day I found those, snooping through his room in search of a stash of cash. I had wanted to buy myself an eye shadow palette, a nice pale pink I had seen Lena wear. My mother refused to buy me makeup before high school, but I had wanted it. I wanted it badly enough to steal for it. So I crept into Cooper's room, lifted up that creaky plank, and was slapped in the face with a pair of cartoon tits that sent me reeling back so fast I whacked the back of my head on his box spring. Then I immediately told my dad.

The Crawfish Festival had been in early May that year, the prologue of summer. It was hot, but not too hot. Hot by the majority of the United States' fragile standards, but not *Louisiana hot*. That wouldn't come until August, when the damp breath of the bogs wafted through the city streets each morning like a rain cloud searching for drought.

Also in August, three of the six girls would be gone.

I joke about Breaux Bridge—*the Crawfish Capital of the World*—but the Crawfish Festival really is something to brag about. My last festival had been in 1999, but it had also been my favorite. I remember wandering by myself through the fairgrounds, the sounds and smells of Louisiana permeating my skin. Swamp pop leaking from the speakers on the main stage, the scent of crawfish being prepared in every possible way: fried, boiled, bisque, boudin. I had drifted over to the crawfish race, my head snapping to the right when I noticed Cooper's moppy brown hair peeking out from inside a crowd of other kids leaning against my father's car. He always seemed to be surrounded by people back then—we were opposites in that way. They swarmed to him, trailing him around like a cloud of gnats on a muggy day. He never seemed to mind, though. Eventually, they just became a part of him: *the crowd*. Occasionally he would swat at them, annoyed. And they would obey, scatter. Find somebody else to stick to. But they never left for long; they always found their way back.

My brother seemed to sense me looking, because before long, I saw his eyes peek above the heads of the others, zeroing in on mine. I waved, smiled meekly. I didn't mind being alone—really, I didn't—but I hated the way it made others see me. Cooper, especially. I watched him push his way through his friends, dismissing some scrawny kid with a wrist-flick when he tried to follow. Then he made his way over to me and slung his arm around my shoulder.

"Bet you a bag of popcorn on number seven?"

I smiled, grateful for the company—and for the way he never acknowledged that I spent the majority of my life alone.

"Deal."

I looked over at the race, about to begin. I remember the commissioner's scream—*Ils sont partis!*—the cheering crowds, those little red mudbugs clicking their way across the target spray-painted on a ten-foot wooden board. Within seconds, I had lost and Cooper had won, so we made our way to the concession stand so he could collect his bounty.

Standing in line, I had never been happier. Those early days of summer brought so much promise, it was like the red carpet of freedom was being rolled out beneath my feet, stretching so far into the distance it felt like it couldn't possibly end. Cooper grabbed the bag of popcorn and pushed a kernel into his mouth, sucking off the salt, as I handed over the cash. Then we turned around, and Lena was there.

"Hey, Coop." She smiled at him before fixing her gaze on me. She was holding a bottle of Sprite, twisting the cap on and off between her fingers. "Hey, Chloe."

"Hey, Lena."

My brother was a popular kid, a jock, wrestling for

Breaux Bridge High School. People knew his name and
it always confused me, watching him make friends as
naturally as I kept to myself. He didn't discriminate
when it came to company—he'd hang out with his
wrestling buddies one day, make small talk with some
stoners the next. Mostly, his attention just seemed to
make you feel important, like you were somehow wor-
thy of something valuable and rare.

Lena was popular, too, but for the wrong reasons.

"Y'all want a sip?"

I eyed her carefully, her flat stomach sticking out
from beneath a skintight henley that looked two sizes
too small, pushing her cleavage up through the buttons. I caught a glint of something sparkly on her stomach—a belly-button ring—and I immediately snapped
my head back up, trying not to stare. She smiled at me,
lifting the bottle to her lips. I watched a bead of liquid
dribble down her chin before she wiped it with her middle finger.

"Do you like it?" She pulled her shirt up, rolled the
diamond between her fingers. There was a charm dangling beneath it, some kind of bug.

"It's a firefly," she said, reading my mind. "They're
my favorite. It glows in the dark."

She cupped her hands around her stomach and motioned for me to peek through; I did, my forehead
pressed against the edges of her hands. Inside, the bug
had turned a bright, neon green.

"I like to catch them," she said, looking down at her
stomach. "Put them in a jar."

"I do, too," I said, still peeking through the hole in
her hands. It reminded me of the fireflies that emerged
in our trees at night, the way I would run through the
darkness, swatting at them like I was swimming through
stars.

"And then I take them out and squish them between

my fingers. Did you know you can write your name on the sidewalk with their glow?"

I winced; I couldn't imagine squishing a bug with my bare hands, listening to it pop. But that did seem kind of cool, getting to rub its liquid between my fingers, watching it radiate up close.

"Somebody's staring," she said, dropping her hands. I snapped my head up and looked in the direction of her gaze, directly at my father. He was across the crowd, staring at us. Staring at Lena, with her shirt pulled up to her bra. She smiled at him, waved with her free hand. He ducked his head down and kept walking.

"So," she said, pushing the Sprite bottle in Cooper's direction and wiggling it in the air. "Do you want a sip?"

He glanced over to where my dad once stood, finding a gap instead of his watchful eye, then back at the bottle, snatching it from her hand and taking a fast swig.

"I'll take some," I said, grabbing it from him. "I'm so thirsty."

"No, Chloe—"

But my brother's warning came too late; the bottle was on my lips then, the liquid pouring into my mouth and down my throat. I didn't just take a sip, I took a *gulp*. A gulp of what tasted like battery acid burning my esophagus the whole way down. I yanked the bottle from my mouth and heaved, the feeling of vomit rising up my throat. My cheeks inflated, and I started to gag, but instead of puking, I forced the liquid down so I could finally breathe.

"Ugh," I choked, wiping my mouth on the back of my hand. My throat was on fire; my tongue was on fire. For a second, I started to panic that maybe I had been poisoned. *"What was that?"*

Lena giggled, taking the bottle from my hand and finishing it off. She drank it like water; it amazed me. "It's vodka, silly. You've never had vodka before?"

Cooper looked around, his hands shoved deep in his pockets. I couldn't talk, so he talked for me.

"No, she's never had vodka before. She's twelve."

Lena shrugged, unfazed. "Gotta start somewhere."

Cooper thrust the popcorn in my direction and I shoved a handful deep into my mouth, trying to chew away that awful taste. I felt the fire traveling from my throat down to my stomach, blazing in the pit of my belly. My head was starting to spin just slightly; it was weird, but kinda funny. I smiled.

"See, she likes it," Lena said, looking at me. Smiling back. "That was an impressive swig. And not just for a twelve-year-old."

She pulled her shirt down then, covering her skin, her firefly. She tossed her braids behind her shoulders and turned on her heel, a ballerina-type twirl that sent her whole body into motion. When she started to walk away, I couldn't stop watching her, the way her hips swayed in unison with her hair, the way her legs were skinny but toned in all the right places.

"You should pick me up in that car of yours sometime," she yelled back, raising the bottle into the air.

I was drunk for the rest of the day. Cooper seemed annoyed at first, annoyed at me. At my stupidity, my naivety. At my slurring words and random giggles and running into light poles. He had left his friends for me, and now he was stuck babysitting me—*drunk* me—but how was I supposed to know that was alcohol? I didn't know alcohol came in Sprite bottles.

"You need to loosen up," I had said, tripping over myself.

I looked up at him, registered the shocked expression on his face as he stared down at me. At first I thought he was mad; I started to regret it. But then his shoulders loosened, his hard expression melted into a smile, then a laugh. He rubbed his hand through my hair and shook his head, and my chest swelled with something that felt like pride. He bought me a crawdog after that and watched in amusement as I gobbled it down in two bites.

"This was fun," I said as we walked back to the car together, hand-in-hand. I didn't feel drunk anymore; I felt droopy. It was getting darker then; our parents had left hours before, leaving us with a twenty-dollar bill for dinner, a kiss on my forehead, and instructions to be home by eight. Cooper had just gotten his driver's license and had ordered me not to talk when he saw them walking toward us, cautious of my heavy tongue and slurring words. So I didn't. Instead, I watched. I watched the way my mother chattered incessantly about *another successful year* and *goodness my feet are aching* and *C'mon, Richard, let's leave these kids to it.* I watched the way her cheeks flushed with red and the edges of her dress rippled when the wind blew. I felt my chest swelling again, but it wasn't pride that time. It was contentment, love. Love for my mother, my brother.

Then I glanced over to my dad and almost immediately, the swelling died down. He seemed . . . off. Preoccupied. Distracted, somehow, but not by anything going on around us. Distracted in his mind. I tried to get a whiff of my breath, worried that he could smell the vodka on me. I wondered if he saw Lena hand us that bottle—after all, I saw him watching. Watching her.

"I bet it was," Cooper said, smiling down at me. "But don't get in the habit of that, okay?"

"Habit of what?"

"You know what."

I furrowed my eyebrows. "But you did it."

"Yeah, I'm older. It's different."

"Lena said you gotta start somewhere."

Cooper shook his head. "Don't listen to her. You don't want to be like Lena."

But I did. I did want to be like Lena. I wanted her confidence, her radiance, her spirit. She was like that Sprite bottle; from the outside, she seemed one way, but on the inside, she was something completely different. Dangerous, like poison. But also addicting, freeing. I had had my taste and she left me wanting more. I remember getting home that night and seeing the lightning bugs in our driveway, twinkling like constellations in the sky, the way they always did. But that night, it felt different. *They* felt different. I remember catching one in my palm, feeling it flutter between my fingers as I brought it in, placing it delicately inside a water glass, covering the lip in plastic. Poking little air holes and watching it flicker in the dark for hours, trapped, as I lay beneath the sheets in my bedroom, breathing slowly, thinking of her.

I memorized everything about Lena that day—the way her hair got frizzy around the edges, leaving her with a kind of blonde halo when the air turned moist. The way she teased people with her wiggling bottle and wiggling hips and wiggling fingers as she waved in the direction of my dad. The way she wore her hair and her clothes and especially that little firefly dangling from her belly button, the way it glowed in the dark when she cupped her hands around her stomach and pulled me in.

And that's why I remembered it so vividly when I saw it again, four months later, hidden in the back of my father's closet.

CHAPTER ELEVEN

The discovery of Aubrey's earring is not a good one. The sight of it pushed into the graveyard dirt had made my blood run cold, the implications of it draping over the entire search party like a fire blanket, extinguishing the flame that had been pulsing through the cemetery minutes before. Everyone's shoulders sagged a little more after that, their heads hung a little lower.

And I was left thinking of Lena.

I drove straight to my office after I left Cypress Cemetery; I couldn't take it anymore. I couldn't take the noises—the screaming cicadas and the crunching of shoes against dead grass, the occasional snorts and spits of the search party, the buzz of a mosquito followed by a rogue slap of the skin in the distance. Khaki-cargo-pants seemed to be under the impression that we were now a team after the police officer walked away with her discovery safely sealed inside an evidence bag. She stood up from her frog-legged squat, hands on hips, and looked at me, expectantly, as if I was supposed to tell her where we should go to find the next clue. I felt like an intruder in that moment, like I shouldn't have been there. Like I was playing some kind of role in a movie, pretending to be something that I'm just not. So I turned around and walked away without uttering another word. I could feel eyes on my back until the moment I got into my car and drove away, and even then, I still felt like I was being watched.

I park outside my office building and walk frantically up the steps, inserting my key into the lock, twisting, pushing. I flip on the lights to my empty waiting room and walk into my office, my hands shaking a little bit less with each step that takes me closer to my desk. Now I settle into my chair and exhale, leaning to the side and pulling open my bottom drawer. The mountain of bottles stare back at me, each one pleading to be chosen. I eye them all, chew on the side of my cheek. I pick up one, then another, comparing them side-by-side, before settling on 1 milligram of Ativan. I study the little five-sided pill in my palm, the powdery white, the raised *A*. It's a low dose, I reason. Just enough to cloak my body in a sense of calm. I pop it into my mouth and swallow it dry before pushing the drawer closed with my foot.

I twist in my office chair, thinking, before glancing over to my phone and noticing a blinking red light—one voice mail. I turn on speakerphone and listen to the familiar voice radiate through the room.

Doctor Davis, this is Aaron Jansen with *The New York Times*. We just spoke on the phone earlier and, uh, I would really appreciate just an hour of your time to talk. We'll be running this article no matter what, and I'd like to give you the opportunity to say your part. You can call me back directly on this number.

There's silence next, but I can hear him breathing. Thinking.

I'll be reaching out to your father, too. I just thought you'd want to know.

Click.

I sink lower into my chair. I've been actively avoiding my father for the last twenty years, in every sense of the word. Speaking to him, thinking about him, talking about him. It was hard to do at first, right after his arrest. People harassed us, showed up at our house at night screaming obscenities and waving signs as if we, too, partook in the slaying of those innocent young girls. As if we somehow knew and turned a blind eye. They egged our house, slit the tires of my father's truck still parked in the yard, spray-painted *PERVERT* on the side in dripping red paint. Someone broke through my mother's bedroom window one night with a rock, shattering the glass across her body as she slept. It was all over the news, the discovery of Dick Davis as the Breaux Bridge serial killer.

And then there were those words: *serial killer.* It seemed so official. For some reason, I never thought of my father as a *serial killer* until I saw it plastered across the newspapers, labeling him as such. It seemed too harsh for my father, a gentle man with a gentle voice. He was the one who taught me how to ride a bike, jogging alongside me with his hands clutching the handlebars. The first time he let go, I had crashed into a fence, smacking straight into the wooden beam and feeling a searing pain in my cheek. I remember him running up behind me, scooping me in his arms, followed by the warmth of a damp washcloth as he pressed it against the gash beneath my eye. Drying my tears with his shirtsleeve, kissing my tangled hair. Then he fastened my helmet tighter and made me try again. My dad tucked me under the covers at night, wrote his own bedtime stories, shaved his facial hair into cartoon mustaches just to watch me laugh as he emerged from the bathroom, pretending like he didn't understand why I was wailing into the couch cushions, tears streaming from my cheeks. That man couldn't be a *serial killer*. Serial killers didn't do things like that . . . did they?

But he was, and they did. He killed those girls. He killed Lena.

I remember the way he watched her that day at the festival, his eyes tracing her fifteen-year-old body like a wolf eying a dying animal. I'll always credit that moment as the beginning of it all. Sometimes, I blame myself—she was talking to me, after all. She was holding up her shirt for me, showing off her belly-button ring for me. Had I not been there, would my father have seen her like that? Would he have *thought* of her like that? She came over a few times that summer, stopping by to give me some old hand-me-down clothes or used CDs, and every time my father walked into my bedroom and saw her there, lying belly-side down on the hardwood floor, her legs kicking freely in the air and her ass busting out of her ripped-up denim shorts, he stopped. Stared. Cleared his throat, then walked away.

His trial was televised; I know because I watched. My mother wouldn't let us at first, Cooper and me, kicking us out of the room when we wandered in to find her crouched on the floor, her nose practically touching the screen. *This isn't for children's eyes,* she would say. *Go outside and play, get some fresh air.* She was acting like it was nothing more than a rated-R movie, like our father wasn't on TV being tried for murder.

But then one day, even that changed.

The doorbell had been jarring, I remember, the way it had reverberated through our perpetually silent house, vibrating off the grandfather clock, creating a tinny buzzing that made my arm hair bristle. We had all stopped what we were doing and stared at the door. Nobody visited us anymore—and the ones who did had abandoned polite formalities like that long ago. They came by screaming, throwing things—or even worse, without making a single sound. For a while, we had been finding foreign footprints littered throughout our property, left behind by some stranger slinking across our yard at night, peeking through windows with a sick fascination. It made me feel like we were a collection of curiosities preserved behind a museum glass case, something haunted and strange. I remember the day I caught him, finally, walking up that dirt pathway and seeing the back of his head as he peered inside, thinking no one was home. I remember pushing up my sleeves, charging at him blind with nothing but adrenaline and anger forcing me forward.

"WHO ARE YOU?" I had screamed, my little fists balled up by my sides. I was so sick of our lives being put on display. Of people treating us like we weren't human, weren't real. He had swung around then, stared at me with wide eyes and hands raised, like he hadn't even considered the fact that people still lived here. Turned out, he was just a kid, too. Barely even older than me.

"Nobody," he had stammered. "I'm—I'm nobody."

We had become so used to it—to intruders and prowlers and threatening phone calls—that when we heard the bell politely ring that morning, we were almost more afraid to know who was behind that thick slab of cedar, patiently waiting for us to invite them inside.

"Mom," I had said, my eyes drifting from the door to her. She was sitting at the kitchen table, her hands woven between her thinning hair. "Are you gonna get that?"

She had looked at me, confused, as if my voice were something foreign, the words no longer intelligible. Every day, her appearance seemed to change. Wrinkles etching themselves deeper into her sagging skin, dark shadows smeared beneath her eyes, bloodshot and worn. Finally, she stood up wordlessly and peered out the small, circular window. The creak of the hinges; her soft, startled voice.

"Oh, Theo. Hi. Come in."

Theodore Gates—my father's defense attorney. I watched as he walked into our house with his slow, lumbering footsteps. I remember his shiny briefcase, the thick, gold band stretched across his wedding finger. He had smiled at me, sympathetic, but I had grimaced back. I didn't understand how he could sleep at night, defending what my father had done.

"Can I get you some coffee?"

"Sure, Mona. Yeah, that would be great."

My mother stumbled around the kitchen, clanking the ceramic mug against the tile counter. That coffee had been sitting in the pot for three straight days and I watched as she poured it, absentmindedly spinning a spoon in circles even though she hadn't poured in any creamer to mix. Then she handed it to Mr. Gates. He took a small sip, clearing his throat, before placing it back down on the table and sliding it away with his pinkie.

"Listen, Mona. I have some news. I wanted you to hear it from me first."

She was silent, staring out the small window situated above our kitchen sink, tinted green with mildew.

"I got your husband a plea deal. A good one. He's going to take it."

She had snapped her head up then, as though his words had clipped a rubber band that had been stretched tight down the back of her neck.

"Louisiana has the death penalty," he said. "We cannot risk that."

"Kids, upstairs."

She looked at Cooper and me, still sitting on the living room rug, my finger picking at the burnt hole from where my father's pipe had landed. We obeyed, standing up and skulking silently past the kitchen and up the stairs. But when we reached our bedroom doors, we closed them, loudly, before tiptoeing back toward the bannister, taking a seat on the top step. And then we listened.

"You can't possibly think they'd give him *death,*" she had said, her voice a whisper. "There's barely any evidence. No murder weapon, no bodies."

"There is evidence," he had said. "You know that. You've seen it."

She sighed, the kitchen chair screeching as she pulled it back and took a seat herself.

"But you think that's enough for . . . death? I mean, we're talking the *death penalty,* Theo. That's irreversible. They can't be sure, beyond a reasonable doubt—"

"We're talking six murdered girls, Mona. *Six.* Physical evidence found inside your home, eyewitness testimony confirming that Dick had been in contact with at least half of 'em in the days prior to their disappearance. And there are stories now, Mona. I'm sure you've heard them. About Lena not being the first one."

"Those stories are total speculation," she said. "There is no evidence to suggest that he was responsible for that other girl."

"That *other girl* has a name," he spat. "You should say it out loud. Tara King."

"*Tara King,*" I had whispered, curious as to how it would feel on my lips. I had never heard of a Tara King before. Cooper's hand shot out to the side, slapping my arm.

"*Chloe.*" My name hissed through his teeth. "*Shut up.*"

The kitchen was silent—my brother and I held our breath, waiting for my mother to appear at the base of the stairs. But instead, she kept talking. She must not have heard.

"Tara King was a runaway," she said at last. "She told her parents she was leaving. She left a note almost a year before any of this started. It doesn't fit the pattern."

"That doesn't matter, Mona. She's still missing. No-body has heard from her, and the jury is seething. They're thinking with their emotions on this one."

She was silent, refusing to respond. I couldn't see into the room, but I could picture it—her, sitting there, her arms crossed tightly. Her gaze somewhere far away, and getting farther. We were losing my mother, and we were losing her fast.

"It's tough, you know. With a case this sensational-ized," Theo said. "His face already plastered across the television. People have made up their minds, no matter what we argue."

"So you want him to give up."

"No, I want him to live. Plead guilty, and the death penalty is off the table. It's our only option."

The house was quiet—so quiet, I started to worry that they would be able to hear our breath, low and slow, as we sat just out of sight.

"Unless you have anything else I can work with," he added. "Anything at all you haven't told me."

I held my breath again, straining to hear against the deafening silence. My heart pulsing in my forehead, my eyes.

"No," she said at last, defeat in her voice. "No, I don't. You know everything."

"Right," Theo said, sighing. "That's what I thought. And Mona—"

I pictured my mother staring up at him then, tears in her eyes. All her fight gone.

"As a part of the deal, he's agreed to take the police to the bodies."

The silence returned again, but this time, we were all left speechless. Because when Theodore Gates walked out of our house that day, in an instant, everything changed. My father was no longer presumed guilty; he *was* guilty. He was admitting it, not only to the jury, but also to us. And slowly, my mother stopped trying. Stopped caring. The days went by and her eyes turned dull, like they had morphed into glass. She stopped leaving the house, then her room, then her bed, and Cooper and I were left pressing our own noses to the screen. He pled guilty, and when his sentencing finally aired, we watched the entire thing.

"Why did you do it, Mr. Davis? Why did you kill those girls?"

I watched my father look down at his lap, away from the judge. The room was silent, a collective held breath hanging heavy in the air. He seemed to be considering the question, really thinking about it, chewing it over in his mind as if it were the first time he had ever really stopped to consider the word *why*.

"I have a darkness inside of me," he said at last. "A darkness that comes out at night."

I looked at Coop, searching his face for some kind of explanation, but he just kept staring at the TV, mesmerized. I turned back.

"What kind of darkness?" the judge asked.

My father shook his head, letting a single tear erupt from his eye and drip down his cheek. The room was so quiet, I could have sworn I heard the flick as it landed on the table.

"I don't know," he said quietly. "I don't know. It's so strong, I couldn't fight it. I tried, for a long time. A long, long time. But I couldn't fight it anymore."

"And you're telling me that this *darkness* is what forced you to kill those girls?"

"Yes." He nodded. Tears were streaming down his face then, snot dripping from his nostrils. "Yes, it did. It's like a shadow. A giant shadow always hovering in

the corner of the room. Every room. I tried to stay out
of it, I tried to stay in the light, but I couldn't do it anymore. It drew me in, it swallowed me whole. Sometimes I think it might be the devil himself."

I realized in that moment that I had never seen my
father cry before. In my twelve years spent living under
his roof, never once had he shed a tear in my presence.
Watching your parents cry should be a painful experience, uncomfortable even. One time, after my aunt
had passed away, I had barged into my parents' bedroom and caught my mother crying in bed. When she
lifted her head, there was the imprint of a face on her
pillow, her tears, snot and spit marking the very spots
where her features had been, like some kind of fun-
house smiley face stained into the fabric. It was a jarring scene—otherworldly, almost, her splotchy skin
and her reddened nose and the self-conscious way she
tried to push back the wet hair stuck to the side of her
cheek and smile at me, pretending that everything was
okay. I remember standing in the doorframe, stunned,
before slowly backing up and shutting it closed without uttering a single word. But watching my father
sob on national television—watching his tears pool in
the crease above his lip before staining the notepad
positioned on the table below him—I felt nothing but
disgust.

His emotion seemed authentic, I thought, but his
explanation felt forced, scripted. Like he was reading
from a screenplay, acting out the role of the serial killer
confessing to his sins. He was looking for sympathy, I
realized. He was casting the fault in every direction but
his own. He wasn't sorry for what he had done; he was
sorry he got caught. And the fact that he was blaming this fictional thing for his actions—this devil that
lurked in the corners, forcing his hands to squeeze their
necks—sent a shot of inexplicable anger through my

body. I remember balling my hands into fists, my fingernails drawing blood from my palms.

"Fucking coward," I spit. Cooper looked at me, shocked at my language, my rage.

And that was the last time I saw my father. His face on my television screen, describing the invisible monster that made him strangle those girls and bury their bodies in the woods behind our ten-acre lot. He made good on his promise to take the police there. I remember hearing the slam of the cruiser doors, refusing to even glance out the window as he led a team of detectives into the trees. They found some remnants of the girls—hairs, clothing fibers—but no bodies. An animal must have gotten to them first, a gator or a coyote or some other hidden creature of the swamp desperate for a meal. But I knew it was the truth because I had seen him one night—a dark figure, emerging from the trees, covered in dirt. A shovel slung across his shoulder as he slumped back to our house, oblivious to me watching from behind my bedroom window. The idea of him burying a body before returning home and kissing me goodnight had made me want to crawl out of my skin and live somewhere else. Somewhere far away.

I sigh, the Ativan making my limbs tingle. The day I turned off that television screen was the day I decided that my father was dead. He isn't, of course. The plea deal made sure of that. Instead, he's serving six consecutive life sentences in Louisiana State Penitentiary without the possibility of parole. But to me, he is dead. And I like it that way. But suddenly, it's getting harder and harder to believe my lie. Harder and harder to forget. Maybe it's the wedding, the thought of him not walking me down the aisle. Maybe it's the anniversary—*twenty years*—and Aaron Jansen forcing me to acknowledge this horrible milestone I never wanted to be a part of.

Or maybe it's Aubrey Gravino. Another fifteen-year-old girl gone too soon.

I look back at my desk and my eyes land on my laptop. I open the lid, the screen glowing to life, and launch a new browser window, my fingers hovering over the keys. Then I start to type.

First, I Google *Aaron Jansen, New York Times*. Pages of articles fill the screen. I jump to one, then another. Then another. It's becoming clear now that this man makes his living writing about the murder and misfortune of others. A headless body found in the bushes of Central Park, a string of missing women across the Highway of Tears. I click over to his bio. His headshot is small, circular, black-and-white. He's one of those people whose face and voice don't match up, like it was stitched on as an afterthought, two sizes too big. His voice is deep, masculine, but his image is far from it. He looks skinny, wears brown, tortoiseshell glasses that don't actually look prescription. They look like blue-blockers—glasses made for people who wish they had glasses.

Strike one.

He's wearing a fitted, checkerboard, button-up shirt with the sleeves rolled to his elbows, a thin knit tie hanging limp against his scrawny chest.

Strike two.

I scan the article, looking for a strike three. For another reason to dismiss this Aaron Jansen as just another journalist prick looking to exploit my family. I've had these interview requests before, lots of them. I've heard the whole *I want to hear your side of the story*. And I'd believed them. I'd let them in. I'd told them my side of the story, only to read the article in horror days later as they painted my family as some kind of accomplice to my father's crimes. As they blamed my mother for the affairs that were discovered in the wake of the investigation; for cheating on my father and leaving him *emotionally vulnerable* and *angry at women*. They blamed her for allowing the girls into our home, too distracted by her suitors to notice my father eying them, sneaking out at night, and coming home with dirt on his clothes. Some of the articles even suggested she knew about it—she *knew* about the darkness in my dad and simply turned a blind eye. Maybe that's what drove her to cheat: his pedophilia, his rage. And it was the guilt that drove her mad, the guilt about her role in it all that made her recoil into herself and abandon her children when they needed her most.

And the children. Let's not even get started on the children. Cooper, the golden boy, who my father supposedly envied. He saw the way girls looked at him, with his boyish good looks and wrestler biceps and charmingly lopsided grin. Cooper kept porn in the house, like any normal teenaged boy, but my father had found it, thanks to me. Maybe that's what caused the darkness to creep in from the corners; maybe flipping through those magazines unleashed something in him he had been suppressing for years. A latent violence.

And then there was me, Chloe, the pubescent daughter who had started wearing makeup and shaving her legs and hiking up her shirt to show her belly button the way Lena had done that day at the festival. And I walked around like that, around my house. Around my dad.

It had been classic victim blaming. My father, another middle-aged white man with a meanness he couldn't explain. He offered no concrete explanations, no valid reason why. He offered only *the darkness*. And surely, that couldn't be possible—people refused to believe that otherwise average white men murder without a reason why. And so *we* became the reason: the neglect of his wife, the taunting of his son, the budding promiscuity of his daughter. It was all too much for his fragile ego, and eventually, he snapped.

I still remember those questions, those questions I had been asked years ago. My answers that were twisted and printed and archived on the internet to be summoned across computer screens for the rest of time.

"Why do you think your father did this?"

I remember tapping my pen against my nameplate, still shiny and scratchless; that interview had taken place during my first year at Baton Rouge General. It was supposed to be one of those feel-good stories they run on Sunday mornings: The daughter of Richard Davis had turned into a psychologist, channeling her childhood trauma to help other young, troubled souls.

"I don't know," I had said finally. "Sometimes these things don't have a clear answer. He obviously had a need for dominance, for control, that I didn't see when I was a child."

"Should your mother have seen it?"

I stopped, stared.

"It wasn't my mother's job to notice every red flag that my father exhibited," I said. "Oftentimes, there are no blatant warning signs until it's too late. Just look at Ted Bundy, Dennis Rader. They had girlfriends and wives, families at home completely oblivious to what they were doing at night. My mother wasn't responsible for him, for his actions. She had her own life."

"It certainly sounds like she had her own life. It came out during the sentencing that your mother had been involved in several extramarital affairs."

"Yeah," I said. "Clearly she wasn't perfect, but nobody is . . ."

"One specifically with Bert Rhodes, Lena's father."

I was silent, that mental image of Bert Rhodes's unraveling still fresh in my mind.

"Did she neglect your father, emotionally? Was she planning on leaving him?"

"No," I said, shaking my head. "No, she didn't neglect him. They were happy—or, I thought they were happy. They *seemed* happy—"

"Did she neglect you, too? After the sentencing, she tried to kill herself. With two young children still under the age of eighteen, still dependent on her."

I knew in that moment that the story had already been written; nothing I could have said would have swayed the narrative. Worse, they were using my words—my words as a psychologist, my words as his daughter—to reinforce their blind notion. To prove their point.

I click out of the *Times*'s website and open up a new window, but before I can start typing, a breaking news alert chirps across the screen.

AUBREY GRAVINO'S BODY FOUND

CHAPTER TWELVE

I don't even bother to click into the news alert. Instead, I get up from my desk and close my laptop, the Ativan fog lifting me across my office and into my car. I float weightlessly down the road, through town, through my neighborhood, through my front door, and eventually find myself on the couch, my head sinking deep into the cushions as my eyes bore into the ceiling above.

And that's where I remain for the rest of the weekend.

It's Monday morning now and the house still smells like chemically produced lemon from the cleaner I used to wipe down the wine-soaked kitchen counters on Saturday morning. My surroundings feel clean, but I do not. I haven't showered since my return from Cypress Cemetery, and I can still see the dirt from Aubrey's earring wedged beneath my fingernails. My roots are damp with grease; when I run my fingers through my hair, the strands remain stuck in one spot instead of cascading across my forehead the way they usually do. I need to shower before work, but I can't find the motivation.

What you're experiencing is akin to the symptoms of post-traumatic stress disorder, Chloe. Feelings of anxiety persisting despite the absence of any immediate danger.

Of course, it's easier to dole out advice than to actually take it. I feel like a hypocrite, an imposter, reciting the words I would say to a patient while willfully ignoring them when the recipient is myself. My phone vibrates beside me, sending it fluttering across the marble island. I glance at the display: one new text message from Daniel. I swipe at the screen and scan the paragraph before me.

> Good morning, sweetheart. I'm headed into the opening session now—will be unavailable most of the day. Make it a good one. I miss you.

My fingers touch the screen, Daniel's words lifting the heaviness from my shoulders just slightly. This effect he has on me, I can't explain it. It's as if he knows what I'm doing at this very moment; the way I'm slipping underwater, too tired to even look for a branch to cling to, and he's the hand that juts out from the trees, grabbing my shirt and yanking me back to land, back to safety, just in time.

I text him back and place my phone on the counter, turning on the coffee maker before walking into the bathroom and twisting the knob in the shower. I step into the hot water, the violent spray feeling like needles against my naked body. I let it burn me for a while, pelting my skin raw. I try not to think about Aubrey, about her body found in the cemetery. I try not to think about her skin, scratched and dirty and covered in maggots swarming eagerly around a meal. I try not to think about who might have found her—maybe it was that cop, all nasally and winded as he walked her earring back to the safety of his locked cruiser. Or maybe it was khaki-cargo-pants, leapfrogging into a ditch or a particularly dense patch of crabgrass, the scream getting caught in her throat, instead coming out like a deep, wet choke.

Instead, I think about Daniel. I think about what he's doing right now—walking into a cold auditorium in New Orleans, probably clutching a Styrofoam cup of complimentary coffee as he scans the crowd for an empty chair, a lanyard with his name dangling around his neck. He's having no problem meeting people, I imagine. Daniel can talk to anyone. After all, he managed to turn an emotionally guarded stranger he met in a hospital lobby into his fiancée within a matter of months.

I had initiated our first date, though. I'll give myself that. After all, it was his business card that was pushed into the pages of my book that day. I had his number, but he didn't have mine. I vaguely remember slipping the book back into the box that was resting on top of my car before loading it into the back seat and driving away, watching him disappear into Baton Rouge General in my rearview. I remember thinking he was nice, handsome. His card said *Pharmaceutical Sales,* which explained why he was there. It also made me wonder if that's why he was flirting with me—I could be just another client to him. Another paycheck.

I never forgot about the card; I always knew it was there, calling to me quietly from the corner. I left it there for as long as I could, leaving that box of books still untouched until, three weeks later, it was the last one left. I remember pulling stacks out by their spines, dusty and cracking, and slipping them into their spots on the bookshelf until finally, there was only one left. I peered down into the empty box, Bird Girl staring back at me with her cold, bronze eyes. *Midnight in the Garden of Good and Evil.* I bent over and picked it up, turned it to its side. I ran my fingers along the edge of the pages, fingering the gap where his business card still rested. I stuck my thumb inside and flipped it open, once again staring at his name.

Daniel Briggs.

I picked up the card and tapped it between my fingers, thinking. His number stared back at me, a silent dare. I understood my brother's aversion to dating, to getting too close to anyone. On the one hand, my father had taught me that it's entirely possible to love someone without ever really knowing them, and that thought kept me up at night. Every time I found myself getting interested in a man, I couldn't help but wonder—what are they hiding? What aren't they telling me? Which closet are their skeletons lurking in, buried in the dark? Like that box in the back of my father's, I was terrified of finding them, of learning their true essence.

But on the other hand, Lena had taught me that it's also possible to love someone and lose them for no reason at all. To find a perfectly good person and wake up one morning to learn that they're gone without a trace, either by force or by will. What if I *did* find someone, someone good, and he was taken from me, too?

Wouldn't it just be easier to go through life alone?

So that's what I had done, for years. I had been alone. I went through high school in a kind of daze. After Cooper graduated and I was on my own, I started getting jumped in the gymnasium, tough boys trying to prove their disdain for violence against women by taking a switchblade to my forearm, carving zigzags in my skin. *This is for your father,* they'd spit, the irony lost. I remember walking home, the blood dripping from my fingers like melted wax from a candlestick, a little dotted line snaking through town like a treasure map. *X* marks the spot. I remember telling myself that as long as I got into college, I could get out of Breaux Bridge. I could get away from it all.

And that's what I did.

I dated boys at LSU, but it was mostly superficial; drunken hookups in the back of a crowded bar, sneaking into a frat house bedroom, leaving the door cracked to make sure I could still hear the muffled noise of the party going on outside. The shitty music vibrating through the walls, the laughter of girls in packs echoing down the hallway, their open-faced palms slapping the door. Their whispers and their glares when we emerged from the bedroom, hair rumpled, zippers down. The slurring words of the boy I had zeroed in on hours earlier, the target of my meticulous checklist that minimized all risk of him getting too attached or killing me in the darkened corners of his bedroom. He was never too tall, never too muscular. If he got on top of me, I could easily push him off. He had friends (I couldn't risk an angry loner), but he also wasn't the life of the party (I couldn't risk an entitled blowhard, either. A guy who views the body of a female as nothing more than his own plaything). He was always just the right amount of drunk—not too drunk to get it up, but just drunk enough to be unsteady on his feet, his eyes glassed over. And *I* was just the right amount of drunk, too—tingly and confident and numb, my inhibitions lowered just enough to let him kiss my neck without pulling away, but not enough to lose my alertness, my coordination, my sense of danger. Maybe he wouldn't remember my face in the morning; certainly he wouldn't remember my name.

And that's the way I liked it: anonymity, the kind of thing I was never granted in childhood. The luxury of closeness—the beating of another heart against my chest, the trembling of fingers intertwined with mine—without the possibility of getting hurt. My only semiserious relationship didn't end well; I wasn't ready to date. I wasn't ready to fully trust another person. But again, I did it to feel normal. I did it to drown out the solitude, the physical presence of another body tricking my own into feeling less alone.

Somehow, it did the opposite.

After graduation, the hospital had given me friends, coworkers, a community I could surround myself with during the daytime hours before retreating home at night and settling into my isolated routine. And it had worked, for a while, but ever since I'd launched my own business, I had found myself *completely* alone. All day and all night. On the day I held Daniel's card again, I hadn't spoken to another human being in weeks, outside of the occasional text message from Coop or Shannon or Mom's place calling to remind me to come visit. I knew that would change once clients started trickling through the doors, but that wasn't the same. Besides, they were supposed to be talking to me for support, not the other way around.

Daniel's business card was hot in my hands. I remember walking over to my desk and taking a seat, leaning back in the chair. I picked up my phone and dialed, the ringing on the other end dragging on for so long I almost hung up. Then suddenly, a voice.

"This is Daniel."

I was quiet on the line, my breath caught in my throat. He waited a few seconds before trying again.

"Hello?"

"Daniel," I said finally. "This is Chloe Davis."

The silence on the other end made my stomach lurch.

"We met a few weeks ago," I reminded him, cringing. "In the hospital."

"Doctor Chloe Davis," he responded. I could hear the smile stretching across his lips. "I was starting to think you weren't going to call."

"I've been unpacking," I said, my heart rate slowing. "I . . . lost your card, but I just found it, at the bottom of my last box."

"So, you're all moved in?"

"Just about," I said, looking around the cluttered office.

"Well, that's cause for celebration. Do you want to grab a drink?"

I had never been one to agree to drinks with a stranger; every real date I had ever been on had been set up by mutual friends, a well-intentioned favor I knew was mostly motivated by the awkwardness that ensued when I was the only one in a group that showed up alone. I hesitated, almost made up an excuse as to why I was busy. But instead, as if my lips were moving in opposition to the brain that controlled them, I heard myself agree. Had I not been so starved for conversation that day, for any kind of human interaction, that phone call probably would have been the end of it.

But it wasn't.

An hour later, I was sitting at the bar at the River Room, swirling a glass of wine in my hand. Daniel was on the barstool next to me, his eyes studying my silhouette.

"What?" I had asked, self-consciously tucking a strand of hair behind my ear. "Do I have food in my teeth or something?"

"No," he laughed, shaking his head. "No, it's just . . . I can't believe I'm sitting here. With you."

I had eyed him then, trying to judge his comment. Was he flirting with me, or was it something more sinister? I had Googled Daniel Briggs before our date—of course I had—and this was the moment I was going to find out if he had done the same. Searching Daniel's name had yielded nothing more than a Facebook page with assorted pictures of him. Holding a whiskey at various rooftop bars. One hand clutching a golf club while the other clasped a sweating beer. Sitting cross-legged on a couch while holding a baby the caption identified as his best friend's son. I had found his

LinkedIn profile, confirming his profession in pharmaceutical sales. He was mentioned in a newspaper article from 2015 printing his finishing time for the Louisiana Marathon: four hours and nineteen minutes. It was all very average, innocent, almost boring, even. Exactly what I wanted.

But if he had Googled me, he would have found more. So much more.

"So," he said. "Doctor Chloe Davis, tell me about yourself."

"You know, you don't have to call me that all the time. *Doctor Chloe Davis*. So formal."

He smiled, took a sip from his whiskey. "What should I call you, then?"

"Chloe," I said, looking at him. "Just Chloe."

"All right, Just Chloe—" I smacked his arm with the back of my hand, laughing. He smiled back. "Really, though, tell me about yourself. I'm sitting here having drinks with a stranger; the least you could do is assure me that you're not dangerous."

I felt the goose bumps prickle across my skin, lifting the hair on my arms.

"I'm from Louisiana," I said, testing the waters. He didn't flinch. "Not Baton Rouge, a small town about an hour from here."

"Baton Rouge born and raised," he said, tilting his drink toward his chest. "What made you move here?"

"School," I said. "I got my PhD from LSU."

"Impressive."

"Thank you."

"Any possessive older brothers I should know about?"

My chest lurched again; all of these comments could be innocent flirtation, but they could also be perceived as a man trying to coax a truth out of me that he had already learned for himself. All of my other bad first dates came flooding back to me, the moment I had realized that the person I was making small talk with already knew everything there was to know. Some of them had asked me outright—*"You're Dick Davis's daughter, aren't you?"*—their eyes hungry for information, while others waited impatiently, tapping their fingers against the table while I spoke about other things, as if admitting that I shared DNA with a serial killer was something I should be eager to reveal.

"How'd you know?" I asked, trying to keep the tone light. "Is it that obvious?"

Daniel shrugged. "No," he said, turning back toward the bar. "It's just that I had a little sister once, and I know I was. I knew every guy who ever looked at her. Shit, if you were her, I'd probably be lurking in the corner of this bar right now."

He hadn't Googled me, I would learn on a later date. My paranoia about his line of questioning was just that—paranoia. He had never even heard about Breaux Bridge and Dick Davis and all those missing girls. He was only seventeen when it happened; he didn't really watch the news. I imagine his mother tried to shield it from him the same way mine had tried to shield it from me. I had told him the story one night as we lay sprawled across my living room couch; I don't know what made me choose that particular moment. I suppose I had realized that, at some point, I had to come clean. That my truth, my history, would be the make-or-break moment that determined our life together, our future—or lack thereof.

So I just started talking, watching as his forehead wrinkled deeper with every passing minute, every gruesome detail. And I told him *everything*: about Lena and the festival and the way I had watched my father get arrested in our living room, those words he had uttered before being whisked away into the night.

I had told him what I had seen through my bedroom window—my father, that shovel—and the fact that my childhood home was still sitting there, empty. Abandoned in Breaux Bridge, the memories of my youth twisted into a real-life haunted house, a ghost story, the place kids ran past with their breath held tight for fear of summoning the spirits that surely haunted its walls. I had told him about my father in prison. His plea deal and consecutive life sentences. The fact that I hadn't seen or spoken to him in almost twenty years. I had gotten completely lost in that moment, letting the memories spill from me like the rancid innards of a gutted fish. I hadn't realized how badly I needed to get them out, how they were poisoning me from the inside.

When I was done, Daniel was silent. I picked at a fraying thread on the couch, embarrassed.

"I just thought you needed to know," I had said, my head downcast. "If we're gonna be, you know, *dating* or something. And I completely understand if this is too much. If it freaks you out, trust me, I get it—"

I felt his hands on my cheeks then, gently pushing my head higher, forcing me to meet his gaze.

"Chloe," he said, softly. "It's not too much. I love you."

Daniel then went on to tell me that he understood my pain; not in the artificial way friends and family claim to *know what you're going through,* but really understood it. He had lost his sister when he was seventeen; she had gone missing, too, the same year as the Breaux Bridge girls. For one horrifying second, my father's face flashed through my mind. Had he killed outside of town? Had he traveled an hour away into Baton Rouge and murdered here, too? I thought briefly of Tara King, the other missing girl who was not like the rest. The break in the pattern. The one that didn't fit—still a mystery, decades later. And although Daniel shook his head, he provided little explanation other than her name. *Sophie.* She was thirteen.

"What happened?" I finally asked, my voice a distant whisper. I had been praying for a resolution, for concrete evidence that my father couldn't have possibly been involved. But I never got it.

"We don't really know," he had said. "That's the worst part. She was at a friend's house one night and was walking home in the dark. It was only a few blocks; she did it all the time. And nothing bad had ever happened, until that night."

I nodded, imagining Sophie walking alone down an old abandoned road. I had no idea what she looked like, so her face was blacked out. It was just a body. A girl's body. Lena's body.

My skin is scalding now, an unnatural bright red as my toes find their way to the bath mat. I wrap myself in a towel and walk into my closet, my fingers flipping between a handful of button-up blouses before selecting a hanger at random and hooking it on the doorknob. I drop my towel and start to dress, remembering Daniel's words. *I love you.* I had no idea how starved I had been for those words; how glaringly absent they had been from my life up until that moment. When Daniel had said them only a month into our courtship, for a fleeting second I had racked my brain to try to remember the last time I had heard them, the last time they had been uttered to me and me alone.

I couldn't remember.

I walk into the kitchen and pour a cup of coffee into my to-go mug, scratching my fingers through my still-damp hair, trying to dry the strands. You would think that strange coincidence between Daniel and me would have wedged distance between us—my father was a taker, and his sister had been taken—but it did the opposite. It brought us closer, gave us an unspoken bond. It made Daniel possessive of me, almost, but in a good way. A caring way. The same way Cooper is possessive, I suppose—because they both understand the inherent danger of existing as a woman. Because they both understand death, and how quickly it can take you. How unfairly it can claim possession over its next victim.

And they both understand *me*. They understand why I am the way that I am.

I walk toward the door with my coffee in one hand and purse in the other, stepping outside into the humid morning air. It's amazing what a single text message from Daniel can do to me—how thinking about him can alter my entire mood, my outlook on life. I feel invigorated, as if the shower water had washed not only the dirt from my nails but the memories that had come with it; for the first time since seeing Aubrey Gravino's picture on my TV screen, that sense of impending dread that has been hovering over me has all but evaporated.

I'm starting to feel normal. I'm starting to feel safe.

I get into my car and crank the engine; the drive to work is automatic. I keep the radio off, knowing I'll be too tempted to flip to the news and listen to the grisly details of Aubrey's recovered body. I don't need to know that. I don't want to know that. I imagine it's front-page news; avoiding it will be impossible. But for now, I want to stay clean. I pull into my office and swing open the front door, the light from inside indicating that my receptionist has already arrived. I walk into the lobby and turn toward the center of the room, expecting to see the regular venti Starbucks cup perched on top of her desk, hear her singsong voice greeting me hello.

But that's not the scene before me.

"Melissa," I say, stopping abruptly. She's standing in the middle of the office, her cheeks patchy and red. She's been crying. "Is everything okay?"

She shakes her head no, buries her face into her hands. I hear a sniffle before she starts wailing into her palms, the tears dripping to the ground from between her fingers.

"It's so awful," she says, shaking her head over and over again. "Did you see the news?"

I exhale, relax slightly. She's talking about Aubrey's body. For a second, I'm irritated. I don't want to talk about this right now. I want to move on; I want to forget. I keep walking, pushing toward my closed office door.

"I did," I say, inserting my keys into the lock. "You're right, it's awful. But at least her parents have some closure now."

She lifts her head from her hands and stares at me, her face confused.

"Her body," I clarify. "At least they found it. That's not always the case."

Melissa knows about my father, my history. She knows about the Breaux Bridge girls and how those parents weren't lucky enough to get their bodies back. If murder was judged on a sliding scale, *presumed dead* would be the furthest to the end. There's nothing worse than a lack of answers, a lack of closure. A lack of certainty despite all the evidence pointing squarely in the face of the horrible reality you know in your heart to be true—but without a body, can't possibly prove. There's always that shred of doubt, that sliver of hope. But false hope is worse than no hope at all.

Melissa sniffs again. "What—what are you talking about?"

"Aubrey Gravino," I say, my tone harsher than I intend it to be. "They found her body on Saturday in Cypress Cemetery."

"I'm not talking about Aubrey," she says slowly.

I turn toward her, my face the one twisted now. My key is still stuck in the lock, but I haven't turned it yet. Instead, my arm hangs limp in the air. She walks to the coffee table and grabs a black remote, pointing it to the television mounted on the wall. I usually keep the TV off during office hours, but now she turns it on, the black screen coming alive to reveal another bright red headline:

BREAKING: SECOND BATON ROUGE GIRL GOES MISSING

Above the marquee of scrolling information is the face of another teen girl. I take in her features—sandy blonde hair obscuring her blue eyes and white lashes; muted freckles cascading across her pale, porcelain skin. I'm mesmerized by her perfectly clear complexion—her skin looks like a doll's, untouchable—when the air exits my lungs and my arm falls to my side.

I recognize her now. I know this girl.

"I'm talking about Lacey," she says, a tear gliding down her cheek as she stares into the eyes of the girl who sat in this very lobby three days ago. "Lacey Deckler is missing."

CHAPTER THIRTEEN

Robin McGill was my father's second girl, his sequel. She was quiet, reserved, pale, and rail thin, with hair the color of a fiery sunset, something of a walking matchstick. She was not like Lena in any conceivable manner, but that didn't matter. It didn't save her. Because three weeks after Lena went missing, Robin did, too.

The fear that followed Robin's disappearance had doubled in size from the fear that followed Lena's. When a single girl goes missing, you can blame it on a lot of things. Maybe she was playing by the bog and slipped underwater, her body pulled down by the jaws of a creature lurking somewhere beneath the surface. A tragic accident—but not murder. Maybe it was a crime of passion; maybe she pissed off one too many boys. Or maybe she got pregnant and ran, a theory that had floated through town as thick and foul as marsh fog up until the day Robin's face started appearing on the TV screen—and everybody knew Robin didn't get pregnant and run. Robin was smart; she was bookish. Robin kept to herself and never wore a dress shorter than mid-calf. Until Robin's disappearance, I had actually believed those theories. A runaway teen didn't seem *that* unlikely, especially for Lena. Besides, it had happened before. It had happened with Tara. In a town like Breaux Bridge, murder seemed far more outlandish.

But when two girls go missing within the course of a month, it's not a coincidence. It's not an accident. It's not circumstance. It's calculated and cunning and far more terrifying than anything we had ever experienced before. Anything we thought possible.

Lacey Deckler's disappearance is not a coincidence. I know it in my bones. I know it the way I knew it twenty years ago when I saw Robin's face on the news; right now, standing in my office with my eyes glued to the television screen as Lacey's freckled face stares back, I might as well be twelve again, getting off the school bus from summer camp as dusk approaches, running down that old dusty road. I see my father, crouching for me on the porch; I'm running toward him when I should have been running away. Fear grips me like a squeezing hand against my throat.

Someone is out there. Again.

"Are *you* okay?" Melissa's voice shakes me from my stupor; she's looking at me, a worried expression cloaking her features. "You're looking kind of pale."

"I'm fine," I say, nodding my head. "It's just . . . memories, you know?"

She nods; she knows not to press it.

"Can you cancel my appointments today?" I ask. "Then you can head home. Get some rest."

She nods again, looking relieved, before shuffling behind her desk and picking up her headset. I turn back toward the television and raise the remote to the air, turning up the volume. The anchor's voice fills the room like a gradient, soft to loud.

For those of you just tuning in, we have gotten word that another girl from the Baton Rouge, Louisiana, area has been reported missing—the

second in just one week. Again, we have confirmed that two days after the body of fifteen-
year-old Aubrey Gravino was found in Cypress
Cemetery on Saturday, June first, another girl
has been reported missing—this time it's fifteen-
year-old Lacey Deckler, also from Baton Rouge.
Our very own Angela Baker is live now at Baton
Rouge Magnet High School. Angela?

The camera cuts away from the news desk and
Lacey's picture disappears from the green screen;
I'm now staring at a high school situated mere blocks
from my office. The reporter on camera nods along,
her finger pushed to her earpiece, before she begins
to speak.

Thank you, Dean. I'm here at Baton Rouge Magnet High School where Lacey Deckler is currently
wrapping up her freshman year. Lacey's mother,
Jeanine Deckler, told authorities that she picked
her daughter up from this school on Friday afternoon after track practice before bringing her to an
appointment just a few blocks away.

My breath catches in my throat; I glance over at
Melissa to see if she registered the comment, but
she isn't listening. She's on the phone, tapping away
on her laptop as she reschedules the day's appointments. I feel bad for canceling an entire day on her
like this, but I can't imagine seeing clients right now.
It wouldn't be fair, charging them for my time when
they wouldn't be getting it. Not really. Because my
mind would be elsewhere. It would be on Aubrey and
Lacey and Lena.
I glance back to the TV.

After her appointment, Lacey was supposed to walk to a friend's house, where she was to be spending the weekend—but she never arrived.

The camera cuts now to a woman identified as Lacey's mother; she's crying into the lens, explaining how she just thought Lacey had turned off her phone, as she sometimes does: "She's not like the other kids, glued to their Instagram; Lacey needs to disconnect sometimes. She's sensitive." She's recounting how the discovery of Aubrey's body had been the catalyst she needed to officially report her daughter as missing, and in classic female fashion, she feels the need to be defensive, to prove to the world that she's a good mother, an attentive mother. That this isn't her fault. I'm listening to her sobs—"Never in my wildest dreams would I have thought that something had *happened* to her, otherwise of course I would have reported it earlier . . ."—when the realization hits me: Lacey left her appointment on Friday afternoon, her appointment with me, and never made it to her next destination. She stepped out my front door and vanished, which means that this office, *my* office, is the last place she would have been seen alive—and I'm the last person who would have seen her.

"Doctor Davis?"

I turn around. The voice doesn't belong to Melissa, who's standing behind her desk, staring at me, clutching her headset around her neck. It's deeper; a male voice. My eyes dart to my doorframe and I register the pair of police officers standing just outside my office. I swallow.

"Yes?"

They step inside in unison and the one on the left, the smaller of the two, raises his arm to reveal a badge.

"My name is Detective Michael Thomas, and this is my colleague, Officer Colin Doyle," he says, jerking his head to the large man standing to his right. "We'd like to have a few words with you about the disappearance of Lacey Deckler."

CHAPTER FOURTEEN

The police station was warm—uncomfortably warm.
I remember the miniature fans positioned all around
the sheriff's office, the stale, recycled air blowing in
every conceivable direction, the Post-it Notes stuck
to his desk flapping in the warm breeze. Wisps of my
baby hair dancing in the crossfire, tickling my cheek. I
watched the beads of moisture drip down Sheriff Dooley's neck, soaking into his collar and leaving a dark, wet
stain. The first day of fall had come and gone, but still,
the heat was oppressive.

"Chloe, honey," my mother said, squeezing my fingers in her sweaty palm. "Why don't you show the
sheriff what you showed me this morning."

I looked down at the box in my lap, avoiding eye contact. I didn't want to show him. I didn't want him to
know what I knew. I didn't want him to see the things
that I had seen, the things in this box, because once he
did, it would all be over. Everything would change.

"Chloe."

I looked up at the sheriff, leaning toward me from
across his desk. His voice was deep, stern but somehow
sweet at the same time, probably from the unmistak-
able Southern drawl that made every word sound thick
and slow like dripping molasses. He was eying the box

in my lap; the old, wooden jewelry box my mother used to keep her diamond earrings and Grandma's old brooches in before my father had bought her a new one last Christmas. It had a ballerina inside that twirled when the lid opened, dancing to a rhythm of delicate chimes.

"It's okay, sweetheart," he said. "You're doing the right thing. Just start from the beginning. Where did you find the box?"

"I was bored this morning," I said, holding it close to my stomach, my fingernail chipping away at a splinter in the wood. "It's still so hot, I didn't wanna go outside, so I decided to play with some makeup, mess around with my hair, that kind of thing."

My cheeks reddened, and both my mother and the sheriff pretended not to notice. I had always been something of a tomboy, always preferring to roughhouse with Cooper in the yard over brushing my hair, but ever since that day with Lena, I had started to notice things about myself that I had never noticed before. Things like the way my collarbones popped when I pinned my bangs back or how my lips seemed juicier when I slathered them in vanilla gloss. I released the box then and wiped my mouth against my forearm, suddenly self-conscious that I was still wearing some.

"I understand, Chloe. Go on."

"I went into Mom and Dad's room, started digging around in the closet. I didn't mean to snoop—" I continued, looking at my mom then. "Honest, I didn't. I thought I'd grab a scarf or something to tie in my hair, but then I saw your jewelry box with all of Grandma's nice pins."

"It's okay, honey," she whispered, a tear dripping down her cheek. "I'm not mad."

"So I grabbed it," I said, looking back down at the box. "And I opened it."

"And what did you find inside?" the sheriff asked.

My lips started trembling; I hugged the box closer.

"I don't want to be a tattle," I whispered. "I don't want to get anyone in trouble."

"We just need to see what's in the box, Chloe. Nobody's getting in trouble just yet. Let's see what's in the box, and we can go from there."

I shook my head, the severity of the situation finally settling over me. I never should have showed Mom this box; I never should have said anything. I should have slammed the lid shut and pushed it back into that dusty corner and forgotten all about it. But that's not what I did.

"Chloe," he said, sitting up straighter. "This is serious now. Your mother has made a major allegation, and we need to see what's in that box."

"I changed my mind," I said, panicking. "I think I was just confused or something. I'm sure it's nothing."

"You were friends with Lena Rhodes, weren't you?"

I bit my tongue, nodded slowly. Word travels fast in a small town.

"Yes, sir," I said. "She was always nice to me."

"Well, Chloe, someone murdered that girl."

"Sheriff," my mom said, leaning forward. He held his arm out and continued to stare in my direction.

"Someone murdered that girl and dumped her somewhere so terrible, we haven't even been able to find her yet. We haven't been able to find her body and return her to her parents. What do you think about that?"

"I think it's horrible," I whispered, a tear slipping down my cheek.

"I do, too," he said. "But that's not all. When this person was done with Lena, he didn't stop there. This same person murdered five more girls. And maybe he'll murder five more before the year is over. So if you know something about who this person may be, we need to know it, Chloe. We need to know it before he does it again."

"I don't want to show you anything that could get my dad in trouble," I said, tears streaming down my cheeks. "I don't want you to take him away."

The sheriff settled back into his chair, his eyes sympathetic. He was quiet for a minute before leaning forward and opening his mouth again.

"Even if it could save a life?"

I glance up at the two men sitting before me now—Detective Thomas and Officer Doyle. They're in my office, seated in the lounge chairs usually reserved for patients, staring at me. Waiting. Waiting for me to say something, just like Sheriff Dooley had been waiting on me twenty years ago.

"I'm sorry," I say, sitting up a little straighter in my chair. "I got lost in thought for a second there. Can you repeat the question?"

The men glance at each other before Detective Thomas pushes a photograph across my desk.

"Lacey Deckler," he says, tapping the image. "Does the name or image ring a bell?"

"Yes," I say. "Yes, Lacey is a new patient. I saw her Friday afternoon. Judging by the news, I imagine that's probably why you're here."

"That would be correct," Officer Doyle says.

This is the first time I've heard the officer speak and my neck snaps in his direction. I recognize his voice. I've heard it before, that raspy, strangled sound. I heard it just this weekend in the cemetery. It's the same officer who came running over when we found Aubrey's earring. The same officer who snatched it out of my hand.

"Lacey left your office at around what time Friday afternoon?"

"She, uh, she was my last appointment," I say, peeling my eyes from Officer Doyle and directing them back to the detective. "So I imagine she left around six thirty."

"Did you see her leave?"

"Yes," I say. "Well, no. I saw her leave my office, but I didn't see her leave the building."

The officer looks at me quizzically, as if he recognizes me, too.

"So, for all you know, she never left the building?"

"I think it's safe to assume she left the building," I say, swallowing my annoyance. "Once you leave the lobby, there isn't really anywhere left to go but out. There's a janitor's closet that's always locked from the outside and a small bathroom by the front door. That's it."

The men nod, seemingly satisfied.

"What did you talk about during your appointment?" the detective asks.

"I can't tell you that," I say, shifting in my chair. "The relationship between psychologist and patient is strictly confidential; I don't share anything my clients tell me within these walls."

"Even if it could save a life?"

I feel a punch in my chest, like the wind has been knocked straight from my lungs. The missing girls, the police asking questions. It's too much, too similar. I blink hard, trying to shake the bright light that's surging through my peripheral vision. For a second, I think I might faint.

"I'm—I'm sorry," I stutter. "What did you just say?"

"If Lacey told you anything during your session on Friday that could potentially save her life, would you tell us?"

"Yes," I say, my voice shaking. I glance down at my

desk drawer, at my sanctuary of pills just barely out of reach. I need one. I need one now. "Yes, of course I would. If she had told me anything that raised even the slightest suspicion that she was in danger, I would tell you."

"So why did she come into a therapist's office, then? If there wasn't anything wrong?"

"I'm a psychologist," I say, my fingers quivering. "It was our first appointment together; it was very introductory. Just getting to know each other. She has some . . . family issues that she needs help dealing with."

"Family issues," Officer Doyle repeats. He's still looking at me suspiciously, or at least, I think he is.

"Yes," I say. "And I'm sorry, but that's really all I can tell you."

I stand up, a nonverbal cue that it's time for them to leave. I was at the crime scene where Aubrey's body was found—this very officer walked up on me *holding* a piece of evidence, for Christ's sake—and now I'm the last person Lacey saw before her disappearance. These two coincidences, paired with my last name, would put me squarely in the center of this investigation— somewhere I desperately don't want to be. I glance around my office, looking for any clues that could give away my identity, my past. I keep no personal mementoes here, no pictures of family, no allusions to Breaux Bridge. They have my name and only my name, but if they wanted to know more, that would be enough.

They look at each other again and stand in unison, the screech of their chairs making my arm hair bristle.

"Well, Doctor Davis, we appreciate your time," Detective Thomas says, nodding his head. "And if you think of anything that may be pertinent to our investigation, anything at all that you think we should know—"

"I'll tell you," I say, smiling politely. They walk

toward the door, opening it wide before peering out into the now-empty lobby. Officer Doyle turns around, hesitates.

"I'm sorry, Doctor Davis, one more thing," he says. "You look so familiar, and I can't seem to place it. Have we met before?"

"No," I say, crossing my arms. "No, I don't believe so."

"Are you sure?"

"I'm pretty sure," I say. "Now, if you'll excuse me, I have a day full of appointments. My nine o'clock should be here any minute."

CHAPTER FIFTEEN

I step into my lobby, the quiet stillness amplifying the sound of my own breath. Detective Thomas and Officer Doyle have left. Melissa's purse is gone, her computer black. The TV is still blaring, Lacey's face haunting the room with her invisible presence.

I lied to Officer Doyle. We have met before—in Cypress Cemetery, as he lifted the earring of a dead girl out of my palm. I also lied about having appointments today. Melissa cleared them—I explicitly asked her to—and now it's nine fifteen on a Monday morning, and I have nothing to do but sit in an empty office and let the darkness of my own thoughts devour me whole before regurgitating my bones.

But I know I can't do that. Not again.

I hold my phone in my palm, thinking about who I can talk to, who I can call. Cooper is out of the question—he would worry too much. Ask me questions that I don't want to answer, jump to conclusions that I'm actively trying to avoid. He would look at me with concern, his eyes flickering to my desk drawer and back up again, silently wondering what kind of remedies I have in there, hidden in the dark. What kind of twisted thoughts they're creating, swirling in my mind.

No, I need calm, rational. Reassuring. My next thought is Daniel, but he's at a conference. I can't bother him with this. It's not that he would be too busy to listen to me—that's the opposite of the problem. It's that he would drop everything and rush to my aid, and I can't let him do that. I can't drag him into this. Besides, what is *this,* anyway? It's nothing more than my own memories, my own unresolved demons, bubbling to the surface. There's nothing he could do to fix the problem, nothing he could say to me that hasn't been said before. That's not what I need right now. I just need someone to listen.

My head jerks up. Suddenly, I know where I need to go.

I grab my purse and keys, locking my office door before jumping back in my car and heading south. Within minutes, I'm pulling past a sign that reads *Riverside Assisted Living,* a familiar collection of pollen-colored buildings looming in the distance. I always assumed the color choice was meant to mirror sunshine, happiness, feel-good things like that. At one point, I actually believed it, convincing myself that a paint color could artificially lift the mood of the residents trapped inside. But the once-bright yellow is faded now, the siding perpetually discolored with the merciless effects of weather and age, missing blinds turning the windows into gap-toothed grins, weeds peeking through the sidewalk cracks like they, too, are struggling to escape. I approach the buildings now and I no longer see sunshine gleaming back in my direction, the color of warmth and energy and cheer. Instead, I see neglect, like a stained bedsheet or the yellowing of forgotten teeth.

If I were a patient, I already know what I'd say to myself.

You're projecting, Chloe. Is it possible that you sense neglect in these buildings because you feel as if you've neglected someone inside?

Yes, yes. I know the answer is yes, but that doesn't make it any easier. I swerve into a parking spot near the entrance and slam my door a little too hard before walking through the automatic entryway and arriving in the lobby.

"Well, hello there, Chloe!"

I turn toward the front desk and smile at the woman waving in my direction. She's big, busty, her hair pulled back into a tight bun, her patterned scrubs faded and soft. I wave back before leaning my arms against the counter.

"Hey, Martha. How are you today?"

"Oh, not bad, not bad. You here to see your mama?"

"Yes, ma'am." I smile.

"It's been a while," she says as she pulls out the guest book and pushes it in my direction. There's judgment in her tone, but I try to ignore it; instead, I look down at the book. The page is fresh and I write my name in the top spot, noticing the date in the upper right-hand corner—Monday, June 3. I swallow hard, trying to ignore the pinch in my chest.

"I know," I say at last. "I've been busy, but that's no excuse. I should have come sooner."

"The wedding's comin' up now, isn't it?"

"Next month," I say. "Can you believe it?"

"Good for you, honey. Good for you. I know your mama's happy for you."

I smile again, grateful for the lie. I'd like to think my mom is happy for me, but the truth is, it's impossible to tell.

"Go ahead," she says, pulling the book back into her lap. "You know the way. A nurse should be in there with her."

"Thanks, Martha."

I turn around and face the interior of the lobby; there are three hallways, all jutting out in different directions. The hallway to my left leads to the cafeteria and kitchen, where residents are served from vats of various mass-produced meals at the same time every day—woks full of watery scrambled eggs, spaghetti with meat sauce, poppy-seed chicken casseroles served with wilted lettuce drowning in salty salad dressing. The one in the middle leads to the living room, a wide-open area with televisions and board games and surprisingly comfortable lounge chairs that I have fallen asleep in more than once. I take the hallway to the right—the hallway littered with bedrooms, hallway number three—and walk down the endless stretch of marbled linoleum until I reach room 424.

"Knock, knock," I say, tapping on the partially cracked-open door. "Mom?"

"Come in, come in! We're just getting cleaned up in here."

I peek into the bedroom and catch a glimpse of my mother for the first time in a month. As always, she looks the same, but different. The same as she has looked for the last twenty years, but different from the way my mind still chooses to remember her—young, beautiful, full of life. Colorful sundresses that grazed her tanned knees, her long, wavy hair clipped back at the sides, her cheeks flushed from the summer heat. Now I see her pale, frail legs peeking out from behind the opening of a robe as she perches in her wheelchair, expressionless. The nurse is brushing her hair, now cut to her shoulders, as she stares out a window overlooking the parking lot.

"Hey, Mom," I say, moving closer. I sit on the side of the bed and smile. "Good morning."

"Good morning, honey," the nurse says. This one is

new—I don't recognize her. She seems to sense that and continues talking. "My name's Sheryl. Your mama and I have been getting close over these last few weeks, haven't we, Mona?"

She taps my mother's shoulder and smiles, brushes a few more times before placing the comb on her bedside table and wheeling her around to face me. My mother's face still comes as a shock, even after all these years. She isn't disfigured or anything; she isn't maimed beyond recognition. But she is different. The little things that made her *her* have changed—her once perfectly manicured eyebrows are overgrown, giving her face a more masculine appearance. Her skin is waxy and devoid of all makeup, her hair washed with cheap store-brand shampoo that leaves the ends wiry and wild.

And her neck. That long, thick scar that still rests across her neck.

"I'll leave y'all to it," Sheryl says, walking toward the door. "If you need anything, just holler."

"Thank you."

I'm alone with my mother now, her eyes boring into mine, and those feelings of neglect come raging back. Mom was placed in a home in Breaux Bridge after her suicide attempt. We were still too young to care for her ourselves—at twelve and fifteen, we were sent to live with an aunt on the outskirts of town—but the plan was to take her out when we could. Care for her when we could. Then Cooper turned eighteen, and it was clear that she couldn't go with him; he couldn't stay put for long enough. Couldn't sit still. She needed routine. Clean, simple routine. So we decided to move her to Baton Rouge when I got into LSU, and I would take over after I finished college . . . but then we came up with excuses for that, too. How would I get my PhD caring for a dependent and disabled mother? How would I ever meet someone, date someone, get married—although

I had been doing a pretty good job of sabotaging my chances of that without her help, anyway. So we kept her here, in Riverside, still telling ourselves it was temporary. After graduation. After we had enough savings. After I opened my own practice. The years stretched on, and we quieted our guilt by visiting every weekend. Then we started taking turns, Cooper and I, going every other week, rushing through each visit, checking our phones because we crammed it between other obligations. Now we mostly visit when the nurses call and ask us to. They're good people, but I'm sure they talk about us when we're not around. Judge us for abandoning our mother, leaving her fate in the hands of strangers.

But what they don't understand is that she abandoned us, too.

"Sorry I haven't come to visit in a while," I say, my eyes searching her face for any sign of movement, any sign of life. "The wedding's in July, so we've got a lot of last-minute planning to do."

The silence between us stretches out, lazy, though I'm used to it by now. Talking to myself. I know she won't respond.

"I promise I'll bring Daniel by to meet you soon," I say. "You'd like him. He's a really good guy."

She blinks a few times, taps her finger against her armrest. My eyes dart over to her hand. Staring, I ask again.

"Would you like to meet him?"

She taps her finger again, gently, and I smile.

I found our mother sprawled across the floor of her bedroom closet shortly after Dad was sentenced—the closet where I found that box. That box that sealed his fate. The poetic symbolism was not lost on me, even at twelve. She had tried to hang herself using one of his leather belts until the wooden beam snapped, sending her crashing to the ground. By the time I had found her,

her face was purple, her eyes bulging, her legs twitching. I remember screaming for Cooper, screaming for him to say something, to do something. I remember him standing in the hallway, stunned, motionless. *DO SOMETHING!* I screamed again, and I had watched him blink, shake his head, then run into the closet and attempt to perform CPR. At some point, it dawned on me to call 9-1-1, so I did. And we were able to save some of her, just not all of her.

She was in a coma for a month; Cooper and I weren't old enough to make any medical decisions, so that decision rested on our father, from prison. He didn't want to pull the plug. He wasn't able to come visit her, but her condition was made clear—she would never be able to walk again, talk again, do anything on her own again. But still, he refused to give up on her. That poetic symbolism wasn't lost on me, either—that he spent his days outside of a cell taking lives, but once he was incarcerated, he was apparently determined to save them. We watched for weeks on end as our mother lay motionless in a hospital bed, her chest rising and falling with the help of a machine, until one morning, she made a movement on her own—her eyes fluttered open.

She never regained movement. She never regained speech. She had suffered from anoxia—a severe lack of oxygen to the brain—which left her in what the doctors called a *minimally conscious state.* They used words like *extensive* and *irreversible.* She's not all there, but she's not gone, either. The depths of her understanding are still murky; some days, when I find myself rambling on about my life or Cooper's, about all the things we've seen and done in the years since she decided we were no longer important enough to stay alive for, I can see a flicker in her eyes that tells me that she hears me. She understands what I'm saying. She's sorry.

Then other times, when I look into her inky black pupils, nothing stares back but my own reflection.

Today is a good day. She hears me. She understands. She can't communicate verbally, but she can move her fingers. I've learned through the years that a tap means something—her version of a head nod, I think, a subtle indication that she's following along.

Or maybe that's just my own wishful thinking. Maybe it means nothing at all.

I look at my mother, a living, breathing embodiment of the pain my father has caused. If I'm being honest with myself, that's the real reason I've left her here for all these years. It's a big responsibility, yes, caring for a person with a disability as severe as hers—but I could do it if I really wanted to. I have the money to hire help, maybe even get a live-in nurse. The truth is, I don't want to. I can't imagine looking into her eyes every day and being forced to relive the moment we found her over and over and over again. I can't imagine allowing the memories to come flooding into my home, the one place I've tried so hard to maintain some semblance of normalcy. I abandoned my mother because it's easier this way. Just like I abandoned our childhood home, refusing to dig through our belongings and relive the horrors that took place there, instead just letting it sit and rot, as if refusing to acknowledge its existence would somehow make it less real.

"I'll bring him by before the wedding," I say, actually meaning it this time. I want Daniel to meet my mother, and I want my mother to meet him. I rest my hand on her leg; it's so frail I almost recoil, twenty years of immobility deteriorating the muscles and leaving nothing but skin and bone. But I force myself to hold it there, squeezing her gently. "But actually, Mom, that's not what I wanted to talk about. That's not why I'm here."

I look down at my lap, knowing full well that once the words escape my lips, I can't reel them back in, swallow them back down. They'll be trapped inside the mind of my mother—a locked box with a missing key. And once they're in there, she won't be able to get them out. She won't be able to talk about it, verbalize it, get it off her chest the way that I can—the way that I *am,* right here, right now. Suddenly, it feels incredibly self-ish. But I can't help myself. I say it anyway.

"There are more missing girls. Dead girls. Here in Baton Rouge."

I think I see her eyes widen, but then again, I could be wishing.

"They found the body of a fifteen-year-old in Cypress Cemetery on Saturday. I was there, with the search party. They found her earring. Then this morning, another one was reported missing. Another fifteen-year-old. And this time, I *know* her. She's a patient of mine."

Silence settles over the room, and for the first time since I was twelve, I yearn for my mother's voice. I desperately need her practical yet protective words to drape over my shoulders like a blanket in winter, keep-ing me safe. Keeping me warm.

This is serious, honey, but just be careful. Be vigilant.

"It feels familiar," I say, gazing out the window. "Something about it all just feels . . . I don't know. The same. It's like I'm having déjà vu. The police came to speak with me, at my office, and it reminded me of . . ."

I stop, look at my mother, wonder if she, too, can still remember our conversation in Sheriff Dooley's office. The humid air, the Post-it Notes flicking in the breeze, the wooden box resting on my lap.

"Entire conversations are bubbling back to the sur-face," I say. "Like I'm having the exact same ones all over again. But then I think about the last time I felt this way . . ."

I stop again, remembering that *this* memory is one my mother certainly doesn't share. She doesn't know about the last time, the time in college when the memories came flooding back again, memories so realistic that I couldn't separate the past from the present, the *then* from the *now*. The real from the imagined.

"With the anniversary coming up, I know I'm probably just being paranoid," I say. "You know, more than usual, I mean."

I laugh, lifting my arm from her leg to stifle the noise. My hand brushes up against my cheek and I feel wetness, a tear, running down my face. I hadn't realized I was crying.

"Anyway, I just needed to say it out loud, I guess. Say it to someone to help me hear how stupid it sounds." I wipe the tear from my cheek and rub my hand against my pants. "God, I'm glad I came to you before I said it to anyone else. I don't know what I'm so worried about. Dad's in prison. It's not like he can be involved or anything."

My mother stares at me, her eyes filled with questions I know she wants to ask. I glance down at her hand, at the imperceptible twitch of her fingers.

"I'm back!"

My body jumps as I twist around to face the voice behind me. It's Sheryl, standing in the doorframe. I lift my hand to my chest and exhale.

"Didn't mean to scare you, baby," she laughs. "Y'all havin' a good time?"

"Yes," I say, nodding. I glance back at my mother. "Yes, it's nice catching up."

"You're just getting all kinds of visitors this week, aren'tcha, Mona?"

I smile, relieved to hear that Cooper made good on his promise to visit.

"When did my brother swing by?"

"No, not your brother," Sheryl says. She walks behind my mother and puts her hands on the back of her wheelchair, her foot releasing the brake on her wheels. "It was another man. A family friend, he said he was."

I look at her, my eyebrows furrowed.

"What other man?"

"Kind of trendy looking, not from around here. Said he was visiting from the city?"

Something in my chest squeezes.

"Brown hair?" I ask. "Tortoiseshell glasses?"

Sheryl snaps before pointing her finger at me. "That's the one!"

I stand up, grabbing my purse from the bed.

"I have to go," I say, walking briskly over to my mom and hugging her around the neck. "I'm sorry, Mom. For . . . everything."

I run out her open door and down the long hallway, the anger in my chest building with every strike of the heel. How dare he? How *dare* he? I reach the front desk and slam into the counter, panting. I have an idea who this mystery visitor may be, but I need to know for sure.

"Martha, I need to see the guest book."

"You already signed it, sweetie. Remember, when you came in?"

"No, I need to see past visitors. From this weekend."

"I'm not sure I can let you do that, honey—"

"Someone in this building let a man in to see my mother who is not authorized. He said he's a family friend, but he is not a friend. He's dangerous, and I need to know if he was here."

"Dangerous? Sweetheart, we don't let people in who aren't—"

"Please," I say. "Please, just let me look."

She stares at me for a second before leaning over and grabbing the book from her desk. She slides it across the counter and I whisper a *thank you* before flipping through old pages filled with signatures. I come across yesterday's section—the day I spent wasting away on my living room couch—and skim down the list of names, my heart stopping when I glimpse the one I was desperately hoping not to see.

There, in messy script, is the proof I have been looking for.

Aaron Jansen was here.

CHAPTER SIXTEEN

The phone rings twice before that familiar voice greets me.

"Aaron Jansen."

"You *asshole*," I say, not bothering with an introduction. I'm storming through the parking lot in the direction of my car. I had called into my office voice mail the second I handed over the guest book and replayed Aaron's last message to me from Friday night.

You can call me back directly on this number.

"Chloe Davis," he responds, the hint of a smile in his voice. "I thought I might hear from you today."

"You visited my *mother*? You had no right."

"I told you I'd be reaching out to your family in my voice mail. I gave you fair warning."

"No," I say, shaking my head. "No, you said my father. I don't give a fuck about my father, but my mother is off-limits."

"Let's meet. Obviously, I'm in town. I'll explain everything."

"Fuck you," I spit. "I am not meeting with you. What you did was unethical."

"You really want to talk to me about ethics?"

I stop, inches from my parked car.

"What's that supposed to mean?"

"Just meet me today. I'll make it quick."

"I'm busy," I lie, unlocking my car and easing inside. "I have appointments."

"I'll come to your office, then. I'll wait in the lobby until you have an opening."

"No—" I exhale, closing my eyes. I lean my forehead against the steering wheel. This back-and-forth is pointless, I realize. He's not going to give up. He flew to Baton Rouge from New York City to meet with me, and if I want this man to stop digging around in my life, I'm going to have to speak with him. Face-to-face. "No, please don't do that. I'll meet you, okay? I'll meet you right now. Where do you want to go?"

"It's still early," he says. "How about coffee. My treat."

"There's a place on the river," I say, pinching the skin between my eyes. "BrewHouse. Meet me there in twenty minutes."

I hang up on him before slamming my car into reverse and driving in the direction of the Mississippi. I'm only ten minutes from the café, but I want to make it there before him. I want to be sitting at a table of my choosing the moment he walks through the doors. I want to be in the driver's seat for this conversation, not riding along as a powerless passenger. Not on the defensive, caught off guard the way I was just now.

I pull into a nearby spot and duck into the little café, a hidden gem on River Road partially cloaked by live oaks dripping in gray-green foliage. It's dim inside, and I order a latte, my eyes landing on a bulletin board of flyers by the cream-and-sugar stand. Wedged between violin lessons being advertised with those little paper flaps and an upcoming concert poster is Lacey Deckler's face, *MISSING* scrawled across the top in Sharpie. It's stapled on top of another piece of the paper, the corners peeking out. I reach over and push the picture aside with my finger, revealing Aubrey's poster behind it—already, she's been replaced, taped over like a broken vending machine.

I slide into a table in the corner, choosing the seat that faces the front door. My fingers tap anxiously against the rim of my mug, and I force myself to hold them still, despite the nervous energy radiating from my every pore. Then I wait.

Fifteen minutes later, my latte is cold. I consider getting up to ask them to reheat it, but before I can move, I see Aaron walk in. I recognize him immediately from his picture online—he's wearing another checkered, button-up shirt, the same stupid blue-blocker glasses— though he's not as skinny as he was in his headshot. He fills out his clothes more than I had expected him to, his leather computer bag hanging heavy over one shoulder, pulling the fabric tight against a bicep I was not expecting to see. I wonder how long ago that picture was taken; immediately after college, I suppose. When he was still just a boy. I continue to stare, watching him amble through the café, browsing the pastry cooler and squinting at the menu bolted behind the coffee bar. He orders a cappuccino and pays with cash, lazily licking his fingers before counting out the bills and dropping his change in the tip jar. Then he eyes the artwork on the wall while he waits for his espresso to brew, the scream of the steamer making my skin crawl.

For some reason, his calmness is bothering me. I was expecting him to run inside, eager to beat me the way I was eager to beat him. I wanted him panting, sweaty, playing catch-up. Thrown off guard by my waiting. But instead, he shows up late. He's acting like he has all the time in the world. He's acting like *he's* the one calling the shots—and that's when I realize.

He knows I'm here. He knows I'm watching.

This calm demeanor, this careless attitude. It's a show

put on just for me. He's trying to unnerve me, to get under my skin. The thought pisses me off more than it should.

"Aaron," I yell, waving my hand too animatedly. He jerks his head up and looks in my direction. "I'm over here."

"Chloe, hi," he says, smiling. He walks over to the table and puts his bag on the chair. "Thank you for meeting me."

"It's Doctor Davis," I say. "And you didn't give me much of a choice."

He grins.

"I'm just waiting on my cappuccino," he says. "Can I buy you anything?"

"No," I say, motioning to the mug in my hands. "I'm good, thanks."

"You been here long?" he asks. "Your drink looks cold."

I eye him, wondering how he could possibly know that. I must look confused, because I see him smirk just slightly before motioning to the condensation beading along the inner rim of my glass.

"No steam."

"Just a couple minutes," I say.

"Huh," he says, eying my drink. "Well, if you want me to have that warmed up for you—"

"No. Let's just get started."

He smiles, nods. Then turns back toward the bar to grab his drink.

Well, it's confirmed, I think, bringing my latte to my lips and wincing at the room-temperature liquid, forcing myself to drink. *He's an asshole.* Aaron slides into the chair opposite me and pulls a notebook from his bag as I set my mug down. I steal a glance at his press card, clipped neatly to the lip of his shirt, the *New York Times* logo printed large at the top.

"Before you start taking any notes, I need to be clear," I say. "This is not an interview. This is a very frank conversation of me telling you to stop harassing my family."

"I hardly think calling you twice would be considered harassing."

"You visited my mother's assisted-living home."

"Yeah, about that," he says, pushing his sleeves to his elbows. "I was in her room for two, three minutes tops."

"I'm sure you got some really great information," I say, glaring at him. "She's a real talker, isn't she?"

He's silent for a while, staring at me from across the table.

"Honestly, I didn't realize her . . . disability . . . was as severe as it is. I'm sorry."

I nod, satisfied with this tiny win.

"But talking to her isn't why I went," he says. "Not really. I thought I could maybe get a little bit of information, but mostly I went because I knew it would get your attention. I knew it would force you to meet with me."

"And why is it that you're so desperate to meet with me? I already told you. I don't speak with my father. We don't have a relationship. I can't give you anything of value. Honestly, you're wasting your time—"

"The story has changed," he says. "That's not the angle anymore."

"Okay," I say, unsure of where this conversation is now headed. "What's the angle, then?"

"Aubrey Gravino," he says. "And now Lacey Deckler."

I feel my heartbeat start to rise in my chest. My eyes dart around the room, though the café is practically empty. I lower my voice to a whisper.

"Why would you think I have anything to say about those girls?"

"Because their deaths . . . I don't think it's a coincidence. I think they have something to do with your father. And I think you can help me figure out what that is."

I shake my head, squeezing my hands tightly around my mug to keep them from shaking.

"Look, you're reaching here. I know you think this makes for a good story, but as I'm sure you know—given your beat, and everything—this kind of thing happens all the time."

Aaron smiles, impressed.

"You've researched me," he says.

"Well, you know everything about me."

"That's fair," he says. "But look, Chloe. There are similarities. Similarities you can't deny."

I think back to the conversation with my mother just this morning. The creeping déjà vu I had just admitted to, the unsettling familiarity of it all. But this isn't the first time I've felt this way, the first time I've re-created my father's crimes in my mind. This has happened once before, and last time, I was wrong. Very, very wrong.

"You're right, there are similarities," I say. "A teenage girl got murdered by some creep roaming the streets. It's unfortunate, but like I said, it happens all the time."

"The twenty-year anniversary is coming up, Chloe. Abductions happen all the time, but serial killers do not. There's a reason this is happening right here, right now. You know there is."

"Whoa, who said anything about a serial killer? You are jumping so far into that conclusion. We have one body. *One*. For all we know, Lacey ran away."

Aaron looks at me, a flicker of disappointment in his eyes. Now he's the one who lowers his voice.

"You and I both know that Lacey didn't run away."

I sigh, glance over Aaron's shoulder and through the

window outside. The breeze is picking up, the Spanish moss swaying in the wind. I notice the sky is quickly morphing from robin's-egg blue to a bloated storm gray; even inside, I can feel the heaviness of impending rain. Lacey is staring at me from her *MISSING* poster; her eyes followed me here, to this very table. I can't bring myself to meet them.

"So what is it that you think is going on, exactly?" I ask, still staring outside at the trees in the distance. "My father is in prison. He's a monster, I'm not denying that, but he's not the boogeyman. He can't hurt anyone anymore."

"I know that," he says. "I know it's not him, obviously. But I think it's someone trying to *be* him."

I glance back at Aaron, gnaw at the inside of my lip.

"I think we're dealing with a copycat here. And I'm willing to bet that before the week is over, someone else will be dead."

CHAPTER SEVENTEEN

Every serial killer has their signature. Like a name scrawled in the corner of a painting or an Easter egg planted in the scenes of a film, artists want their work to be recognized, immortalized. Remembered beyond their years.

It's not always as grisly as they portray in the movies—encrypted monikers scratched across the skin, detached body parts showing up around town. Sometimes it's as simple as the cleanliness of the crime scene or the way in which the bodies are placed on the floor. Stalking patterns strung together by unsuspecting witnesses or ritualistic procedures that occur over and over and over again until eventually, a pattern emerges. A pattern that isn't too dissimilar to the way ordinary people go through their routines in a methodical rhythm each morning, as if there were no other way to make a bed, to clean a dish. Human beings are habitual creatures, I've learned, and the act of taking a life can reveal a lot about a person. Each kill is unique, like a fingerprint. But my father left behind no bodies upon which he could leave his mark, no crime scenes to preserve his autograph, no fingerprints to lift or analyze. Which left the town wondering: How do you leave a signature without a canvas?

The answer is, you can't.

The Breaux Bridge Police Department spent the summer of '99 scouring Louisiana for a single clue to his identity. They listened for whispers of evidence that pointed in the direction of one viable suspect, a hidden signature at a crime scene that seemed not to exist. But of course, they found nothing. Six girls dead and not a single witness could pinpoint a man lurking near the county pool or a car inching down the street at night, stalking its prey. In the end, I was the one who'd found the answer. A twelve-year-old girl playing dress-up with her mother's makeup, rummaging through the back of a closet in search of scarves to tie in her hair. And it was then, holding that little wooden box, when I saw it—the thing nobody else had been able to see.

Instead of leaving evidence, my father was taking it.

"Even if it could save a life, Chloe?"

I watched the sweat drip down Sheriff Dooley's neck. He was staring at me with an intensity I had never seen before. He was staring at me, and he was staring at the box clutched in my hands.

"If you hand over that box, you could save a life. Think about that. What if someone could have saved Lena's life, but chose not to because they were afraid of stirring up trouble?"

I looked down at my lap, nodded slightly. Then I thrust my arms forward before I had time to change my mind.

The sheriff wrapped his gloved hands around mine, the rubber slippery but warm, before pulling the box gently from my grip. He looked down at the lid before placing his fingers on the lip and opening it wide, the sound of chimes filling the room. I avoided his expression, instead choosing to stare at the ballerina, twirling in slow, perfect circles.

"It's jewelry," I said, my eyes still on the dancing girl. It was mesmerizing, watching her spin in that faded pink tutu, her arms raised high. She reminded me of Lena, the way she twirled at the festival.

"I see that. Do you know who it belongs to?"

I nodded. I knew he was looking for more of an answer, but I couldn't bring myself to say it. Not voluntarily, at least.

"Who does the jewelry belong to, Chloe?"

I heard a sob erupt from my mother beside me, and I glanced in her direction. Her hand was clamped over her mouth, her head shaking violently. She had already seen the contents of this box; I had shown it to her, back home. I had wanted her to give me an explanation other than the one that was forming in my own mind. The only explanation that made sense. But she couldn't.

"Chloe?"

I looked back at the sheriff.

"The belly-button ring is Lena's," I said. "Right there, in the middle."

The sheriff reached into the jewelry box and plucked out the small, silver firefly. It looked dead, having spent weeks in the dark. No sunshine to fuel its glow.

"How do you know that?"

"I saw Lena wearing it at the Crawfish Festival. She showed it to me."

He nodded, lowering it back into the box.

"And the others?"

"I know that pearl necklace," my mother said, her voice wet. The sheriff glanced at her before reaching into the box again and lifting up a string of pearls. They were large, pink, and tied together in the back with a ribbon. "That belongs to Robin McGill. I . . . I saw her wearing it. At church one Sunday. I commented on how much I liked it, how unique it was. Richard was with me. He saw it, too."

The sheriff exhaled, nodding again before placing it back inside. Over the next hour, the rest of the jewelry would come to be identified—Margaret Walker's diamond earrings, Carrie Hollis's sterling silver bracelet, Jill Stevenson's sapphire ring, Susan Hardy's white gold hoops. There was no DNA found on anything—they had been meticulously cleaned, the box wiped down—but their parents confirmed our suspicions. They had been presents for eighth-grade graduations, confirmations, birthdays. Tokens meant to celebrate the milestones of their girls growing up, instead forever memorialized by their untimely deaths.

"This is helpful, Chloe. Thank you."

I nodded, the rhythm from the chimes soothing me into a kind of stupor. Sheriff Dooley slapped the lid closed, and I jerked my head up, the trance broken. He was staring at me again, his hand placed on top of the closed box.

"Did you ever witness your father interacting with Lena Rhodes or any of the other missing girls?"

"Yes," I said, my mind flashing back to the festival. The way he was staring at her and her long, smooth stomach. The way he ducked his head when he realized he was caught. "I saw him watching her once at the Crawfish Festival. When she was showing me her belly-button ring."

"What was he doing?"

"Just . . . staring," I said. "She had her shirt pulled up. She caught him looking, and she waved."

My mother scoffed beside me, shook her head.

"Thank you, Chloe," the sheriff said. "I know this wasn't easy for you, but you did the right thing."

I nodded.

"Before we let you go, is there anything else you'd like to tell us about your father? Anything that might be important for us to know?"

I exhaled, held myself tightly in my own arms. It was hot in there, but suddenly, I felt myself shiver.

"I saw him with a shovel once," I said, avoiding my mother's stare. This was news to her. "He was walking across our yard, coming from the swamp behind our house. It was dark, but . . . he was there."

Everyone was silent, this new revelation settling over the room like a heavy morning fog.

"Where were you when you saw him?"

"In my room. I couldn't sleep, and I have this bench, right below my window, where I like to read . . . I'm sorry I didn't say anything sooner," I said. "I . . . I didn't know . . ."

"Of course you didn't, sweetheart," Sheriff Dooley said. "Of course you didn't. You've done more than enough."

A roll of thunder shudders through my house now, making the wineglasses hanging upside down from our liquor cabinet rattle like chattering teeth. Another summer storm is rolling through. I can feel the electric charge in the air, taste the impending rain.

"Chlo, did you hear me?"

I glance up from my wineglass, half full of cabernet. The memory of Sheriff Dooley's office starts melting away slowly; instead, I see Daniel, standing at our kitchen counter, sleeves rolled up to his elbows and a butcher knife in one hand. He got back from his conference earlier this afternoon; when I arrived home from the office, I found him dancing to Louis Armstrong through the kitchen in my gingham apron, the ingredients for tonight's dinner spread across the island. The image makes me smile.

"Sorry, no," I say. "What was that?"

"I said you've done more than enough."

I squeeze my glass a little more tightly, the delicate

stem threatening to snap from the pressure between my fingers. I rack my brain, trying to remember what we were just talking about. I've been so lost in thought these last few days, so consumed in memories. Especially with Daniel being gone and the house being empty, it's almost felt as if I've been living in the past again. When the words escape Daniel's lips, I can't tell if they actually came from him or if I imagined them, conjured them up from the recesses of my mind and placed them into his mouth to regurgitate back to me. I open my lips to speak, but he cuts me off.

"Those cops had no right to show up at your office like that," he continues, his eyes focused on the cutting board beneath him. He chops some carrots, moving the blade in quick, fluid motions before scraping them to the side of the board and moving on to the tomatoes. "Thank God you didn't have any clients in there yet. That could have really hurt your reputation, you know?"

"Oh, yeah," I say. I remember now. We had been talking about Lacey Deckler, about Detective Thomas and Officer Doyle questioning me at work. It felt like something I should tell him, in case her last known location ever became public knowledge. "Well, I was the last person to see her alive, I guess."

"She might still be alive," he says. "They haven't found her body yet. It's been a week now."

"That's true."

"And the other girl . . . she was missing for, what, three days before they found her?"

"Yeah," I say, swirling the wine in my glass. "Yeah, three days. So it sounds like you've been following all of this, then?"

"Yeah, you know. It's been on the news. Kind of hard to avoid."

"Even in New Orleans?"

Daniel keeps chopping, the tomato juice running across the cutting board and pooling onto the counter. Another roll of thunder vibrates the house. He doesn't reply.

"Does it sound like it could have been the same person to you?" I ask, trying to keep my tone light. "Do you think they're, you know . . . related?"

Daniel shrugs.

"I don't know," he says, wiping the tomato juice off the blade with his finger before popping it into his mouth. "Too early to tell, I think. So what kinds of questions did those guys ask you?"

"Not much, really. They were trying to get me to tell them what we talked about in our session. Obviously, I wouldn't, which kind of bothered them."

"Good for you."

"They asked if I saw her leaving the building."

Daniel glances at me, his brows furrowed.

"Did you?"

"No," I say. "I saw her leave my office, but I didn't see her leave the building. I mean, I assume she did. There really isn't anywhere else to go. Unless she was grabbed from inside, but . . ."

I stop, look down at the ruby-red liquid coloring the sides of my glass.

"That seems kind of unlikely."

He nods and looks back down at the cutting board before scooping up the chopped vegetables and placing them in a searing pan. The scent of garlic fills the room.

"Other than that, it was pretty pointless," I say. "Seems to me like they don't even know where to start."

A steady sheet of rain erupts outside, and the house is filled with the sound of millions of fingers tapping on the roof, eager to get in. Daniel glances out the window before walking over and cracking it open, the earthy aroma of a summer storm gushing into the kitchen, mixing with the scent of a home-cooked meal. I stare at him for a while, the way he glides around the kitchen so naturally, cracking pepper into the skillet of sautéing vegetables, rubbing Moroccan spices across a slab of pink salmon. He flings a dish towel over one husky shoulder, and my heart surges with warmth at the perfection of it all. The perfection of him. I'll never understand why he chose me: *damaged Chloe*. He acts as though he's loved me since the moment he met me, the moment he knew my name. But there's still so much about me that he doesn't know. So much that he doesn't understand. I think about the small pharmacy hidden in my office—my lifeline—that collection of faked prescriptions that I used his name to obtain. I think about my childhood, my past. The things I've seen. The things I've done.

He doesn't know you, Chloe.

I try to shake Cooper's words out of my mind, but I know he's right. Excluding my family, Daniel knows me more than anyone else in the world, but that isn't saying much. It's still surface level. It's still staged. Because I know if I were to show him all of me—if I were to show him *damaged Chloe,* expose my rancid, pulsing core—he would take one whiff and recoil. He couldn't possibly like what he'd see.

"Enough about all of that," he says, leaning over the counter as he fills up my diminishing glass. "How was the rest of your week, then? Did you get any wedding planning done?"

I think back to Saturday morning, the morning Daniel left for New Orleans. I had intended on getting some wedding planning done—I had opened my laptop and responded to some emails before the news of Aubrey Gravino filled my living room, the memories trapping me inside my own mind like a car submerged in

water. I remember leaving the house and driving mindlessly through town, coming across the search party in
Cypress Cemetery, finding Aubrey's earring, leaving
minutes before her body was discovered. I think about
Aaron Jansen, visiting my mother, the theory he shared
with me that I've been actively trying to deny all week.
It's Friday now; Aaron predicted another body would
turn up by Monday. So far, it hasn't, and every day that
goes by, a small weight is lifted from my shoulders. A
moment of relief that he might be wrong.

I think, for a second, about what I should tell Daniel,
and I decide that I'm not ready for him to know me
yet—not this side of me, at least. The side that self-
medicates to calm my nerves. The side that joins a cemetery search party in an attempt to find the answers to
questions I've been asking myself for the last twenty
years. Because Daniel doesn't let me hide; he doesn't let
me be afraid. He throws me surprise parties and plans
a wedding in July, spitting in the face of all my irrational fears. If he knew what I had spent my week doing
while he was away—drugging myself into a stupor, en-
tertaining a reporter's fictional scenario, dragging my
mother into it all despite her inability to protest, to talk
back—he would be ashamed. *I'm* ashamed.

"It was fine," I say at last, taking a sip from my glass.
"I decided on caramel cake."

"Progress!" Daniel shouts, before leaning farther over
the counter and kissing me on the lips. I return the kiss
before pulling back slightly, taking in his features. He
analyzes my face, his eyes searching every surface of
my skin.

"What is it?" he asks, dipping his hand into my hair.
He cradles my skull, and I lean into his outstretched
palm. "Chloe, what's wrong?"

"Nothing's wrong," I say, smiling. A band of thunder rolls gently through the room, and I feel my skin

prickle; I can't tell if it's reacting to the bolt of lightning that flashes outside or the way Daniel's fingers are caressing my neck, making slow circles in the spot of delicate skin just beneath my ear. I close my eyes. "I'm just happy you're home."

CHAPTER EIGHTEEN

It's still raining when I wake up, the kind of slow, lazy rain that threatens to pull you back to sleep. I lie in the dark, feeling the warmth of Daniel beside me, his bare skin pressed against mine. His breath rhythmic and slow. I listen to the drizzle outside, to the low rumbles of thunder. I close my eyes and imagine Lacey, her body half buried in the mud somewhere, the rain washing away any traces of evidence that might have been left behind.

It's Saturday morning. One week from the discovery of Aubrey's body. Five days since the news of Lacey's disappearance and my face-to-face meeting with Aaron Jansen.

"What makes you think this is the work of a copycat?" I had asked, hunched over my cold coffee. "We hardly know anything about these cases at this point."

"The location, the timing. Two fifteen-year-old girls who fit the profile of your father's victims show up missing and dead weeks before the twentieth anniversary of Lena Rhodes's disappearance. Not only that, but they happen in Baton Rouge—the city where Dick Davis's family now lives."

"Okay, but there are differences, too. They never found the bodies of my dad's victims."

"Right," Aaron said. "But I think this copycat *wants* the bodies to be discovered. He wants credit for his work. He dumped Aubrey in a cemetery, in her last known location. It was just a matter of time before she was found."

"Yeah, but that's what I'm saying. That doesn't sound like he's copying my dad. It sounds like he selected Aubrey at random, killed her on the spot, and left her body there in a hurry. This wasn't a calculated crime."

"Or the spot where he dumped her has some sort of significance. It holds special meaning. Maybe there are clues on her body that he wanted to be found."

"Cypress Cemetery does not hold any special meaning to my dad," I said, getting agitated. "The timing of her murder, it's just a coincidence—"

"So, it's also just a coincidence that Lacey was snatched next, minutes after walking out of *your* office?"

I hesitated.

"I wouldn't be surprised if you've seen this guy around before, Chloe. Copycats—they copy for a reason. Maybe they revere the guy they're trying to emulate or maybe they revile him, but either way, they copy their style. Their victims. They try to *become* the killer that came before them, maybe even beat them at their own game."

I raised my eyebrows, took another sip of my coffee.

"Copycats murder because they're obsessed with another murderer," Aaron continued, placing his arms on the table and leaning in. "They know everything about them—which means that this person could very well know you. He could be watching you. He could have seen Lacey walking out of your office. I'm just asking you to trust your gut here. Pay attention to what's going on, and listen to your instincts."

I thought back to Cypress Cemetery, to the feeling

of eyes on my back as I walked to my car and drove to my office. I shifted in my chair, growing more uncomfortable by the minute. Talk of my dad always left me feeling guilt-ridden, but I could never tell where the guilt was supposed to be aimed. Did I feel guilty for betraying him, for being the sole finger pointed in his direction and locking him in a cage for the rest of his days? Or did I feel guilty for sharing his blood, his DNA, his last name? So many times, when talk of my father came up, I felt the overwhelming need to apologize. I wanted to apologize to Aaron, to Lena's parents, to the town of Breaux Bridge. I wanted to apologize to everyone for simply existing. There would be so much less pain in the world if Richard Davis had never been born.

But he was, and because of that, so was I.

I feel a movement next to me and glance over toward Daniel, lying awake and staring in my direction. He's watching me, watching my eyes flicker across the ceiling as I replay that conversation with Aaron in my mind.

"Good morning." He sighs, his voice thick with sleep, as he wraps his arms around me and pulls me closer. His skin is warm, safe. "What are you thinking about?"

"Nothing," I say, moving deeper into his arms. I brush against his hips and smile, the bulge in his boxers rubbing against my leg. I twist around so I'm facing him before gripping my legs tightly around his hips, and soon we begin to make love in mutual, somnolent silence. Our bodies are pressed together, slightly damp with early morning sweat, and he kisses me hard, his tongue down my throat, his teeth on my lip. His hands start to snake across my body, up my legs and across my stomach, before passing my chest and working their way toward my throat.

I continue kissing him, trying to ignore the feeling

of his hands around my neck. Waiting for him to move them somewhere else, anywhere else. But he doesn't. He keeps going, his hands still resting there as he pumps harder and harder, faster and faster. He starts to squeeze, and I let out a scream before shooting backward, moving as far away from him as I can.

"What?" he asks, sitting up. He's staring at me with a startled look. "Did I hurt you?"

"No," I say, my heart pounding in my chest. "No, you didn't. It's just that—"

I look at him, at the confused look on his face. At the concern in his eyes over causing me pain, the hurt he must feel at the prospect of me physically recoiling from his touch, his fingers like matches, leaving burn marks on my skin. But then I think about the way he kissed me last night, in the kitchen. The way he felt the pulse beneath my jaw with his fingers, the way he grabbed my neck gently yet firmly.

I lean my head back onto my pillow and sigh.

"I'm sorry," I say, pinching my eyes shut. I need to get out of my head. "I'm just wound kind of tight right now. I'm jumpy, for some reason."

"It's okay," he says, folding his arm around my waist. I know I've ruined the moment—his arousal is gone, and mine is, too—but he holds me anyway. "There's a lot going on right now."

I know he knows I'm thinking about Aubrey and Lacey, but neither of us mentions it. We lie in silence for a while, listening to the rain. Just as I think he might have fallen back asleep, his voice breaks into a whisper.

"Chloe?" he asks.

"Mmm?"

"Is there anything you want to tell me?"

I'm quiet, my outstretched silence telling him all he needs to know.

"You can talk to me," he says. "About anything. I'm your fiancé. That's what I'm here for."

"I know," I say. And I believe him. After all, I've told Daniel all about my father, my past. But it's one thing to recount memories with detachment, relaying them as simple facts that happened and nothing more. It's another thing completely to relive them in his presence. To see the face of my dad in every darkened corner, to hear the words of my mother echoed in the voices of others. And it's even worse because this *has* happened before—this feeling of déjà vu. I'll never forget the look on Cooper's face as he stared at me that day, years ago, as I tried to explain myself, explain my reasoning. The look of concern intermixed with genuine fear.

"I'm fine," I say. "Really, I am. It's just a lot all at once. Those girls disappearing, my dad's anniversary coming up—"

My phone vibrates violently across my bedside table, the light from the screen partially illuminating our still-dark bedroom. I lean on my elbow and squint at the unknown number trying to reach me.

"Who's that?"

"I'm not sure," I say. "It shouldn't be for work, this early on a Saturday morning."

"Go ahead and answer it," he says, rolling over. "You never know."

I pick up my phone and let it vibrate in my hand before swiping the screen and lifting it to my ear. I clear my throat before answering.

"This is Doctor Davis."

"Hi, Doctor Davis, this is Detective Michael Thomas. We met at your office on Monday regarding the disappearance of Lacey Deckler."

"Yes," I say, glancing in Daniel's direction. He's on his phone now, scrolling through emails. "I remember. How can I help you?"

"Lacey's body was found early this morning in the alleyway behind your office. I'm sorry to have to tell you this over the phone."

I gasp, my hand instinctively moving to my mouth. Daniel looks at me, lowers his phone. I shake my head silently as tears begin to well in my eyes.

"We need you to come down to the morgue this morning. Take a look at the body."

"I, um . . ." I hesitate, unsure if I heard him correctly. "I'm sorry, Detective, I've only met Lacey once. Surely you'll want her mother to come identify her instead? I barely know her—"

"She's been identified," he says. "But since she was found right outside your office, and the last place her mother saw her was dropping her off there, it's safe to assume at this point that you were the last person to see her alive. We'd like you to take a look at her and tell us if anything seems different than it did when you saw her for your appointment. If anything looks out of place."

I exhale, moving my hand from my mouth to my forehead. The room seems to be getting hotter, the rain outside louder.

"I really don't know how much help I can be. We were together for one hour. I barely remember what she was wearing."

"Everything helps," he says. "Maybe the sight of her will jog your memory. The earlier you can get here, the better."

I nod, agreeing, before hanging up the phone and sinking back into bed.

"Lacey's dead," I say, not as much to Daniel as admitting it to myself. "They found her outside my office. She was *killed* right outside my office. I was probably still upstairs."

"I already know where you're going with this," he says, leaning against the headboard. His hand finds mine in the sheets, and our fingers intertwine. "There's nothing you could have done, Chloe. Nothing. You would have had no way of knowing."

I think back to my father, that shovel slouched over one arm. An inky outline making his way through our backyard, slowly. Like he had all the time in the world. Me, upstairs, curled up on my bench with that little reading light, peering through a window. Present for the entire thing, yet completely unaware of what I was witnessing.

I'm sorry I didn't say anything sooner. I . . . I didn't know . . .

Had Lacey told me something that could have saved her life? Had I seen someone that day that looked suspicious, someone lingering around the office, but failed to notice? Just like before?

Aaron's words echo through my mind.

This person could very well know you. He could be watching you.

"I should go," I say, releasing Daniel's hand before swinging my legs out of bed. I feel exposed sliding out of the sheets, my nakedness no longer the powerful, intimate thing it was just minutes before. Now it reeks of vulnerability, of shame. I feel Daniel's eyes watching me as I walk across the bedroom and into the bathroom, moving quickly in the dark before closing the door behind me.

CHAPTER NINETEEN

"Cause of death was strangulation."

I'm hovering over Lacey's body, the pallor of her face an icy blue. The coroner stands to my left, clutching a clipboard; to my right, Detective Thomas hovers too close. I don't know what to say, so I say nothing, my eyes flickering over the girl that I had just barely known. The girl who had wandered into my office one week ago and told me about her problems. Her problems that she had trusted me to solve.

"You can tell by the bruising, just there," the coroner continues, pointing to her neck with a pen. "You can see the finger marks. Same size and spacing as the ones found on Aubrey. Same ligature marks on the wrists and ankles, too."

I glance at the coroner and swallow.

"So, you're thinking they're related, then? It's the same guy?"

"That's a conversation for another time," Detective Thomas interrupts. "Right now, we're focusing on Lacey. Like I said, she was found in the alley behind your office. You ever go back there?"

"No," I say, staring down at the body before me. Her blonde hair is wet from the rain, sticking to her face like a web of spider veins. Her pale skin is even paler now, somehow, making her collection of scars even more visible, those thin, red slits checkered across her arms and chest and legs. "No, I rarely go back there. It's really just for the garbage trucks to empty the dumpster. Everyone parks out front."

He nods, exhaling loudly. We stand in silence for a minute as he allows me to take it all in, to process the grisly sight before me. I realize, in this moment, that although I've been surrounded by death my entire life, this is the first time I've ever actually seen a dead body. The first time I've actually looked one in the eye. I imagine I'm supposed to be remembering right now— remembering Lacey's face, the way it looked in my office that afternoon, the way it looked before this—but my mind is a blank slate. I can't conjure up any images of Lacey with pink skin and twitchy fingers and tears welling in her eyes as she sits in my leather recliner, talking about her dad. All I can see is this Lacey. Dead Lacey. Lacey on a medical table being poked at by strangers.

"Does anything look different to you?" he asks finally, nudging me along. "Missing any clothes?"

"I really can't say," I respond, scanning her body. She's wearing a black T-shirt and faded jean shorts, dirty Converse sneakers with doodles on the sides. I try to imagine her drawing on her shoes in school, bored, passing the time with a ballpoint pen. But I can't. "Like I said, I wasn't really paying attention to what she was wearing."

"Okay," he says. "It's okay. Just keep trying. Take your time."

I nod, wondering if this is what Lena looked like a week after her life was taken. As she lay in a field or in a shallow grave somewhere. Before her skin peeled off and her clothes disintegrated, I wonder if she looked like this. Like Lacey. Pale and bloated from the hot, humid air.

"She talk to you about that?"

Detective Thomas nudges his head toward her arms, toward the tiny cuts in her skin. I nod.

"A little bit."

"How about that?"

He glances at the larger scar on her wrist, that thick, fleshy purple lightning bolt I had spotted days before.

"No," I say, shaking my head. "No, we didn't get to that."

"Fucking shame," he says quietly. "She was too young to feel pain like that."

"Yeah," I nod. "Yeah, she was."

The room is quiet for a minute, all three of us taking a moment of silence to mourn not only the violence of this girl's death, but of her life, too.

"Didn't you check the alley before?" I ask. "I mean, back when she was first reported missing?"

Detective Thomas looks at me, and I see anger flash across his face. The fact that the body of this girl was found mere feet from the place she was last seen and it took almost a week to find her doesn't look good, and he knows it.

"Yeah," he says at last, sighing loudly. "Yeah, we did. Either she was somehow missed, or she was placed there later. Killed in another location and moved."

"It's a pretty small area," I say. "Narrow. The dumpster takes up most of the space. If you checked back there, I can't imagine you would have missed her. There aren't many places to hide—"

"How do you know all this if you rarely go back there?"

"I can see it from my lobby." I say. "My window points in that direction."

He stares at me for a second, and I can tell he's trying to make an assessment, determine if he's just caught me in a lie.

"I obviously don't have the best view," I add, trying to smile.

He nods, either satisfied with my answer or filing it away to revisit at another time.

"That's who found her," he says at last. "The garbage-men. She was wedged behind the dumpster. When they lifted it up to empty it, they saw her body fall out."

"Then she was definitely moved," the coroner interrupts, tapping the backs of her arms. "That right there is livor mortis. The pooling indicates that she died on her back, not in a seated position. Or *wedged* any-where."

A wave of nausea rolls through my stomach, and I try to stop my eyes from scanning her body again, evaluating her wounds, but I can't. She's bruised, mostly, her pale skin looking marbled in places where I now know gravity forced the blood to settle. The coroner had mentioned ligature marks, and my eyes trace the length of her limbs, from her shoulders down to her fingertips.

"What else do you know?" I ask.

"She was drugged," the coroner says. "We found heavy traces of Diazepam in her hair."

"Diazepam. That's Valium, right?" Detective Thomas asks. I nod. "Was Lacey on medication for anxiety? Depression?"

"No." I shake my head. "No, I had prescribed her some. But she wasn't taking anything yet."

"The growth level suggests the drugs were ingested about one week ago," the coroner adds. "So, at the time of her murder."

Detective Thomas glances at the coroner after this new revelation, and I feel a sudden impatience reverberate through the room.

"How soon can you have the full autopsy?"

The man looks at the detective, then at me.

"The sooner I can get started, the sooner I can have it for you."

I feel both men glance over at me, a nonverbal cue that I've been less than helpful. But my eyes are still glued to Lacey's arm. To the tiny cuts littering her skin, to the ligature marks on her wrist and the jagged purple scar stretching across her veins.

"Well, no offense, Doctor Davis, but I really didn't bring you here for small talk," Detective Thomas says. "If there's nothing else that you can remember, you're free to go."

I shake my head, my eyes boring into her wrist.

"No, I remembered something," I say, tracing the path her razor must have taken to make such a crooked mark. It must have been messy. "Something about Lacey that day. Something that's different."

"Okay," he says, shifting his weight. He eyes me carefully. "Let's hear it."

"Her scar," I say. "I noticed her scar on Friday. I noticed she was trying to cover it up with a bracelet. Wooden beads with a little silver cross on it."

The detective looks down at her arm now, her wrist bare. I remember that rosary dangling there, in front of her veins, maybe a reminder for the next time she felt the urge to cut into her skin. It was definitely there, on her wrist, when she was sitting in my office that afternoon, fidgeting in my leather recliner. And it was there when she got up and left, when she was grabbed outside my front door. When she was drugged, when she was killed.

But now it's not.

"Someone took it."

CHAPTER TWENTY

My breath is ragged when I finally reach my car, parked outside the morgue. I'm inhaling massive, unsteady gulps of air, trying to wrap my mind around the implications of what I just saw.

Lacey's bracelet is gone.

I try to tell myself that it could have fallen off; just like Aubrey's earring was found mashed into the dirt in Cypress Cemetery, Lacey's bracelet could have been flung from her wrist in a struggle, snagged on the side of the dumpster when the police dragged her body out from behind it. It could be buried in the trash somewhere, lost forever. But I'm sure Aaron would disagree.

I'm just asking you to trust your gut here. Listen to your instincts.

I exhale, try to stop the shaking in my fingers. What are my instincts telling me?

The coroner's statement about the bruises on Lacey's neck and ligature marks on her arms make it impossible to disagree with one fact: The same person is responsible for the deaths of both Aubrey Gravino and Lacey Deckler. Same method of killing, same finger marks on the neck. As much as I was trying to deny it before, convincing myself Lacey could have run away, maybe

taken her own life—after all, she had tried to before—
some part of me known this all along. Abductions
happen. Especially abductions involving young, attractive girls. But two abductions over the course of one
week? Two abductions within miles of each other?

It was too coincidental.

Still, proof that Aubrey and Lacey had lost their lives
to the same person doesn't necessarily mean this person is a copycat. It doesn't mean these murders have
anything to do with my father, with me.

*He dumped Aubrey in a cemetery, in her last known
location.*

I think about Lacey, dropped behind a dumpster in
the alley behind my office—her last known location.
Hidden in plain sight. Not only that, but now I know that
she was *moved* there. She wasn't grabbed at random and
killed on the spot, the way I had assumed Aubrey had
been. She was taken from my office, drugged, killed in
another location, and then brought back.

For a split second, my heart forgets to beat as a
thought materializes in my mind, a thought too terrifying to entertain. I try to push it out, try to discount the
idea as paranoia or déjà vu or purely raw and unfiltered
fear. Another irrational coping mechanism my mind
simply generated to try to make sense out of something
so senseless.

I try, but I can't.

What if the killer wanted the bodies to be found . . .
but not by the police? What if he wanted them to be
found by *me*?

Aubrey's body turned up minutes after I had left
the search party. I was there. Did this person somehow
know I would be there?

Even more terrifying—was he there, too?

I move on to Lacey, to the mental image of her body
dumped feet from my office door. I was telling Detec-

tive Thomas the truth—I rarely go into that alleyway—but I can see it from a window in my office, very clearly. I can see the dumpster, and it's entirely likely that had I not been in such a distracted daze this week, I could have noticed Lacey slumped behind it from the viewpoint of my lobby.

Did this person somehow know that, too?

Maybe there are clues on her body that he also wanted found.

My mind is racing faster than I can keep up. Clues on the body, clues on the body. Maybe the missing bracelet is the clue. Maybe the killer took it on purpose. Maybe he knew that if I found the body, and if I noticed the missing bracelet, I would put the pieces together. I would understand.

My car is hot at a stifling 85 degrees, but somehow, I still have goose bumps. I crank the engine, letting the air-conditioning blow through my hair. I glance over to my glove compartment and remember the bottle of Xanax I picked up last week. I imagine myself pushing the pill onto my tongue, that bitter pinch in the jaw before it dissolves into my bloodstream and loosens my muscles, cloaks my mind. I open the door and the bottle rattles to the front. I pick it up, turn it over in my hands. Twist off the cap and dump a pill into my palm.

My phone vibrates beside me, and I turn toward the illuminated screen, Daniel's name and picture staring back at me. I look down at the pill in my palm, then back to the phone. I exhale, reaching for the phone and swiping to answer.

"Hey," I say, still holding the Xanax, inspecting it between my fingers.

"Hey," he says, hesitant. "So, are you done?"

"Yeah, I'm done."

"How was it?"

"It was awful, Daniel. She looks . . ."

My mind wanders back to Lacey's body on the table, her skin the color of frostbite, her eyes made of wax. I think about the little cuts across her skin like wild cherry Tic Tacs. The giant cut across her wrist.

"She looks awful," I finish. I can't think of any other word to describe it.

"I'm sorry you had to do that," he says.

"Yeah, me, too."

"Did you find anything helpful?"

I think back to the missing bracelet and start to open my mouth before realizing that, without context, this revelation means nothing. To explain the significance of the missing bracelet, I would have to explain my trip to Cypress Cemetery and finding Aubrey's earring minutes before her body was discovered. I would have to explain my meeting with Aaron Jansen and his theory about a copycat. I would have to revisit all the dark places my mind has been wandering to this past week, revisit them in front of Daniel. *With* Daniel.

I close my eyes, rub my fingers against my eyelids until I'm seeing stars.

"No," I say finally. "Nothing. Like I said to the detective, I was only with her for an hour."

Daniel exhales; I can visualize him running his hands through his hair as he sits up in bed, his bare back leaning against the headboard. I can see him resting the phone against his shoulder, rubbing his eyes with his fingers.

"Come home," he says at last. "Come home and get back into bed. Let's relax today, okay?"

"Okay." I nod. "Okay, that sounds good."

I fidget in my seat, pushing the pill and its bottle back into the glove compartment. I get ready to shift into Drive when Aaron's voice echoes around me again. I hesitate, wonder if I should go back inside, tell Detective Thomas everything. Tell him Aaron's theory. If

I keep this to myself, how many other girls could go missing?

But I can't do that. Not yet. I'm not ready to be thrust back into the middle of something like this; to explain his theory, I would need to explain who I am, my family. My past. I don't want to open that door again, because once I do, it would never be closed.

"I have to run a quick errand first," I say instead. "It shouldn't take longer than an hour."

"Chloe—"

"It'll be fine. I'm fine. I'll be home before lunch."

I hang up before Daniel can convince me to change my mind; then I dial another number, my fingers tapping impatiently against my steering wheel until that familiar voice picks up on the other end of the line.

"This is Aaron."

"Hi, Aaron. It's Chloe."

"Doctor Davis," he says, his voice light. "This is certainly a more pleasant greeting than the last time you called."

I glance out the window and crack a small smile for the first time since Detective Thomas's number appeared on my phone this morning.

"Listen, are you still in town? I want to talk."

CHAPTER TWENTY-ONE

After my conversation with Sheriff Dooley, he had given us two options: Stay in the station until they obtained a warrant to arrest my father, or go home, tell no one, and wait.

"How long will it take to obtain the warrant?" my mother had asked.

"Can't say for certain. Could be hours, could be days. But with this evidence, my guess is we'll have him before the night is up."

My mother looked at me as if waiting for an answer. As if I were the one who should be making the decision. Me, age twelve. The smart thing to do, the *safe* thing to do, would be to stay in the station. She knew it, I knew it, Sheriff Dooley knew it.

"We'll go home," she said instead. "My son is at home. I can't leave Cooper alone with him."

Sheriff Dooley shifted in his chair.

"We can always go get the boy, bring him here."

"No." My mother shook her head. "No, that would look suspicious. If Richard starts to suspect something before you obtain the warrant . . ."

"We'll have officers patrolling the neighborhood, undercover. We won't let him run."

"He won't hurt us," my mother said. "He won't. He won't hurt his family."

"With all due respect, ma'am, but this is a serial murderer we're talking about. A man suspected of killing six people."

"If anything happens that makes me think we're in danger, we'll leave immediately. I'll call the police and have one of the officers come to the house."

And so her decision had been made. We were going home.

I could tell from the look on Sheriff Dooley's face that he was wondering why—why was she so adamant about going back to my father? We had just presented him evidence that all but proved that her husband was a *serial killer,* and still, she wanted to go home. But I wasn't wondering; I knew. I knew she would go back because she had always gone back. Even after she brought those men into our home, into her room, she still went back to Dad at the end of every night, cooking him dinner and carrying it over to his chair before ducking silently into her bedroom and closing the door behind her. I glanced over to my mother, to the stubborn expression on her face. Maybe she was having doubts, I thought. Maybe she wanted to see him, one last time. Maybe she wanted to say goodbye in her own subtle way.

Or maybe it was simpler than that. Maybe she just didn't know how to leave.

Sheriff Dooley sighed in obvious disapproval before getting up from his desk and opening his office door, allowing my mother and me to walk out of the police station in numb, mutual silence. We rode for fifteen minutes without speaking a word, me strapped into the front seat of her used red Corolla, sputtering toward home. There was a hole in the cushion, and I stuck my finger in it, ripping it wider. They made me leave the box at the police station, the box with my father's trophies. I liked that box, with the chimes and the ballerina twirling to the music. I wondered if we'd ever get it back.

"You did the right thing, sweetie," my mother said at last. Her voice was comforting, but somehow the words felt hollow. "But we need to act normal now, Chloe. As normal as possible. I know that's going to be hard, but it won't be for long."

"Okay."

"Maybe you can go into your room when we get home, close the door. I'll tell Dad you're not feeling well."

"Okay."

"He's not going to hurt us," she said again, and I didn't answer. I got the feeling she was speaking to herself that time.

We pulled into the long driveway toward home, that gravel road that I used to run down, my shoes kicking up dust, the shadows from the forest moving in the trees. I wouldn't have to run anymore, I realized. I wouldn't have to be scared. But as our house inched closer through the bug-splattered windshield, I had the overwhelming urge to open the door and fling myself out, scramble into the woods, and hide. It felt safer in there than out here. My breath started to quicken.

"I don't know if I can do this," I said. I started to suck in quick, hollow breaths, and soon I was hyperventilating, my surroundings growing spotty and bright. For a second, I thought I might die right there in the car. "Can I at least tell Cooper?"

"No," my mother said. She looked at me, the way my chest was rising and falling at an alarming speed. She released the wheel with one hand and turned my face toward hers, rubbing my cheek with her fingers.

"Chloe, breathe. Can you breathe for me? Breathe in through your nose."

I closed my lips and inhaled deep through my nostrils, letting my chest fill with air.

"Now out through your mouth."

I pursed my lips and pushed it out slowly, feeling my heartbeat slow just slightly.

"Now do it again."

I did it again. In through the nose, out through the mouth. With each successful breath, my vision started to return, until finally, once our car pulled up to our porch and my mother killed the engine, I found myself breathing normally as I stared at our home looming before us.

"Chloe, we tell no one," my mother said again. "Not until the police are here. Do you understand?"

I nodded, a tear dripping down my cheek. I turned toward my mother and saw the way she was staring, too. Staring at our house as if it were haunted. And it was then, looking at her hardened features, the feigned confidence masking the terror I could see in the depths of her eyes, that I realized her true intentions. I understood why we were here, why we had come back. It wasn't because she felt like she had to; we didn't come back because she was weak. We came back because she wanted to prove to herself that she could stand up to him. She wanted to prove that she could be the strong one, the fearless one, instead of running from her problems the way she had always done. Hiding from them, hiding from him, pretending they didn't exist.

But now she was afraid. She was just as afraid as I was.

"Let's go," she said, opening her door. I did the same, slamming it shut before walking toward the front of the car and staring at our wraparound porch, at the rocking chairs creaking in the breeze, at my favorite magnolia tree casting shade across the hammock my dad had tied to its trunk years ago. We walked inside, the door groaning as we pushed it open. My mother nudged me toward the staircase, and I started toward my bedroom before a voice stopped me mid-step.

"Where have you two been?"

I froze in place, turning my neck to see my father sitting on the living room couch, staring in our direction. He was holding a beer, his fingers ripping at the damp label, a little pile of paper scraps collecting on the television tray. Sunflower seeds scattered across the wood. He was clean, showered, his hair combed back and his face freshly shaven. He seemed put together, dressed in khakis and a button-down, shirt tucked in. But he also seemed tired. Exhausted, even. His skin seemed saggy and his eyes sunken in, like he hadn't slept in days.

"We got lunch," my mother said. "Girls' trip."

"That sounds nice."

"But Chloe isn't feeling well," she said, looking at me. "I think she might be coming down with something."

"Sorry to hear that, honey. Come here."

I glanced at my mom and she nodded slightly. I walked back down the steps and into the living room, my heart hammering in my chest as I approached my father. He looked at me, curiosity in his eyes as I stood before him. Suddenly, I wondered if he had realized his box was missing. I wondered if he was going to ask me about it. He reached his hand toward my forehead and pressed.

"You're hot," he said. "Sweetheart, you're sweating. You're *shaking*."

"Yeah," I said, my eyes to the floor. "I think I just need to lie down."

"Here." He grabbed his beer and pushed it against my neck, and I flinched, the cold glass numbing my skin, its sweat dripping down my chest and dampening my shirt. I felt my pulse, hard against the bottle, a cool beating. "Does that help?"

I nodded, forcing myself to smile.

"I think you're right," he said. "You should lie down. Take a nap."

"Where's Coop?" I asked, suddenly aware of his absence.

"He's in his room."

I nodded. His room was on the left side of the stairs; mine, the right. I wondered if I could sneak in there without my parents noticing, curl into his bed, and pull the covers over my eyes. I didn't want to be alone.

"Go ahead," he said. "Go lie down. I'll come get you in a few hours, take your temperature."

I turned on my heel and started walking back toward the stairs, the bottle still pressed to my neck. My mother followed me, her closeness comforting, until we hit the hallway.

"Mona," my dad called out. "Hang on a second."

I felt her turn around, face his direction. She was silent, so my father spoke again.

"Is there something you need to tell me?"

Aaron's eyes are drilling into my skull as I gaze out toward the river. I turn to him, unsure if I heard him correctly, or if my memories are flooding my subconscious again, clouding my judgment, confusing my brain.

"Well?" he asks again. "Is there?"

"Yeah," I say, slowly. "That's why I called you here. This morning, I got a call from Detective Thomas—"

"No, before we get to that. Something else. You lied to me."

I look back toward the river and lift a coffee to my lips; we're sitting on a bench by the water, the bridge in the distance looking even more industrial and bleak with the settling fog.

"About what?"

"About this."

He holds his phone in front of me, and I grab it with my free hand; I'm looking at a picture of myself, wandering amidst a crowd of people. Immediately, I know where this was taken. My gray T-shirt and topknotted hair, the mangled trees dripping in Spanish moss, the yellow police tape blurry in the distance. This picture was taken one week ago in Cypress Cemetery.

"Where did you find this?"

"There's an article online," he says. "I was looking in the local paper, trying to identify some people to talk to, when I came across images from the search party. Imagine my surprise when I saw that you were there."

I sigh, silently berating myself for not paying closer attention to those journalists I had seen walking around with cameras slung from their necks. I hope Daniel doesn't see this article—or worse, Officer Doyle.

"I never told you I *wasn't* there."

"No, but you told me Cypress Cemetery held no special meaning to your family. That there would be no reason to think dumping Aubrey's body there would be suspicious."

"It doesn't," I say. "There's not. I just stumbled across the search party, okay? I was driving around, trying to clear my head. I saw it in the distance and decided to look around."

He stares at me, his eyes narrowing.

"In my line of work, trust is everything. Honesty is everything. If you lie to me, I can't work with you."

"I'm not lying," I say, holding up my hands. "I swear."

"Why did you decide to look around?"

"I don't really know," I say, taking another sip of my

coffee. "Curiosity, I guess. I was thinking about Aubrey. And Lena."

Aaron is quiet, his eyes trained on me.

"What was she like?" he asks at last, curiosity creeping into his voice. He can't help it; I know he can't. Nobody ever can. "Were you friends with her?"

"Something like that. I thought we were, when I was little. But now I see it for what it really was."

"And what is that?"

"She was an older cool kid looking out for a younger nerd," I say. "She was nice to me. She gave me hand-me-downs, taught me how to put on makeup."

"That's a friend," Aaron says. "The best kind, if you ask me."

"Yeah," I say, nodding. "Yeah, I guess you're right. There was something about her that was just . . . I don't know. Magnetic, you know?"

I glance at Aaron, and he nods knowingly. I wonder if he had a Lena, too. I imagine everyone has a Lena in their life at some point. A person who comes blazing in like a shooting star and fizzles out just as fast.

"She used me a little bit, and I knew it, but I didn't even care," I continue, tapping my fingers against my coffee cup. "She didn't have the best home life, so our house was something of an escape for her. Besides, I think she had a crush on my brother."

Aaron raises his eyebrows.

"Everyone had a crush on my brother," I say, my lips twitching into a gentle smile, reminiscing. "He didn't like her like that, but I think that's the reason why she came around so much. I remember, there was this one time—"

I stop, catching myself before I go too far.

"Sorry," I say. "You probably don't care about that."

"No, I do," he says. "Go on."

I exhale, push my fingers into my hair.

"There was this one time, that summer. Back before everything happened. Lena was at our house—she was always making excuses about why she needed to come to our house—and she convinced me to break into Cooper's room. I didn't really do stuff like that . . . you know, break the rules. But Lena had a way about her. She made you want to push the boundaries. Live your life without fear."

I remember that afternoon so vividly—the warmth of the afternoon sun stinging my cheeks, the blades of grass pushing deep into my back, itching my neck. Lena and I lying in the backyard, making shapes out of the clouds.

"You know what would make this even better?" she had asked, her voice raspy. "Some weed."

I rolled my head on its side so I was facing her direction. She was still staring into the clouds, her eyes focused, her teeth digging into the side of her lip. She held a lighter in one hand, absentmindedly flicking it on and off between her bitten-down fingernails, the other held above the flame, moving closer and closer until a little black circle appeared on her palm.

"I'm *positive* your brother has some."

I watched an ant crawl slowly up her cheek, toward her eyebrow. I got the feeling that she knew it was there; that she could feel it, crawling closer. That she was testing it, testing herself. Waiting to see how long she could take it—just like that fire, searing her skin—how close it could get before she was forced to reach her hand up and brush it away.

"Coop?" I asked, tilting my head back. "No way. He doesn't do drugs."

Lena snorted, pushing herself up onto her elbow.

"Oh, Chloe. I love how naive you are. That's the beauty of being a kid."

"I'm not a kid," I said, sitting up, too. "Besides, his room is locked."

"Do you have a credit card?"

"No," I said, embarrassed again. Did Lena have a credit card? I didn't know any fifteen-year-olds with credit cards—Cooper definitely didn't have one—but then again, Lena was different. "I have a library card."

"Of course you do," she said, pushing herself up from the grass. She held her hand out, her palms rippled with the indents from the blades, specks of soil stuck to the skin. I took it, damp with sweat, and stood up, too, watching as she picked the weeds from the backs of her thighs. "Let's go. Honestly, I have to teach you everything."

We walked inside, stopping by my room to grab the small purse that held my library card before crossing the hall to Cooper's.

"See," I said, jiggling the handle. "Locked."

"Does he always lock his bedroom?"

"Ever since I found these gross magazines under his bed."

"Cooper!" she said, raising her eyebrows. She looked more impressed than disgusted. "Naughty boy. Here, give me the card."

I handed it over, watching as she stuck it through the crack.

"First, check the hinges," she said, jostling the card. "If you can't see them, it's the right kind of lock. You need the slant of the latch to be facing towards you."

"Okay," I said, trying to fight down the panic that was rising in my throat.

"Next, insert the card at an angle. Once the corner is in, straighten it up. Like this."

I watched, mesmerized as she pushed the card deeper and deeper into the opening, applying pressure to the door. The card started to bend, and I said a prayer that it wouldn't break.

"How do you know how to do this?" I finally asked.

"Oh, you know," she said, wiggling the card. "You get grounded so many times and you learn to let yourself out."

"Your parents lock you inside your room?"

She ignored me, giving the card a few more good yanks until, finally, the door pushed open.

"Ta-da!"

She twirled around, a look of satisfaction on her face until I saw her expression slowly change. Mouth open, eyes wide. Then, a smile.

"Oh," she said, placing her hand on a popped hip. "Hey, Coop."

Aaron laughs now, polishing off his latte before placing the to-go cup on the ground by his feet.

"So he caught you?" he asks. "Before you even got inside?"

"Oh, yeah," I say. "He was standing right behind me, watching the whole thing from the stairwell. I think he was just waiting to see if we could get in."

"No weed for you, then."

"No," I say, smiling. "That would have to wait a few years. But I don't think that's what Lena was really after, anyway. I think she wanted to get caught. To get his attention."

"Did it work?"

"No," I say. "That kind of thing never worked on Cooper. It kind of had the opposite effect, actually. He sat me down that night and talked to me about not doing drugs, the importance of good role models, blah, blah, blah."

The sun is peeking out now, and almost instantly, the temperature seems to rise a few degrees, the humidity getting thick like churning milk. I feel my cheeks start to burn—I can't tell if it's from the sun on my face or from sharing this intimate memory with a stranger. I don't really know what drove me to tell it.

"So, why did you want to meet me?" Aaron asks, sensing my desire to change the subject. "Why the change of heart?"

"I saw Lacey's body this morning," I say. "And the last time we met, you were telling me to trust my instincts."

"Wait, back up," he interrupts. "You saw Lacey's body? How?"

"She was found in the alleyway behind my office. Stashed behind a dumpster."

"Jesus."

"They asked me to look at her, try to identify if anything looked different from the last time I saw her. If anything was missing."

Aaron is quiet, waiting for me to continue. I exhale, turn toward him.

"She was missing a bracelet," I say. "And back when I was at the cemetery, I came across an earring. An earring that belonged to Aubrey. At first I thought it probably just fell out of her ear when her body was being dragged or something, but then I realized that it was a part of a set. She had a matching necklace, too. I never saw Aubrey's body, but if she was found without that necklace—"

"You think the killer is taking their jewelry," Aaron interrupts. "As a kind of prize."

"That was my dad's thing," I say, the admission, even after all these years, still making me nauseated. "They caught him because I found a box of his victims' jewelry hidden in the back of his closet."

Aaron's eyes widen before he looks down at his lap, processing the information I just gave him. I wait a minute before continuing again.

"I know it's a stretch, but I think it's at least worth looking into."

"No, you're right." Aaron nods. "It's a coincidence we can't ignore. Who would have known about that?"

"Well, my family, obviously. The police. The victims' parents."

"Is that it?"

"My dad took a plea deal," I say. "Not all of the evidence was presented publicly. So yeah, I think so. Unless somehow the word got out."

"Can you think of anybody on that list that would have a reason to do something like this? Any police officers who got too obsessed with the case, maybe?"

"No." I shake my head. "No, the cops were all—"

I stop, a realization settling over me. My family. The police.

The victims' parents.

"There was one man," I start, slowly. "One of the victims' parents. Lena's dad. Bert Rhodes."

Aaron looks at me, nods for me to continue.

"He . . . didn't handle things well."

"His daughter was murdered. I don't think most people would."

"No, this wasn't normal grief," I say. "This was something different. This was rage. And even before the murders, there was something about him that was just . . . off."

I think back to Lena, jimmying my brother's locked door. Her involuntary admission, that slip of the tongue. Pretending not to hear when I pressed her for more.

Your parents lock you inside your room?

Aaron nods, blows a steady stream of air through his pursed lips.

"What did you say the other day about copycats?" I ask. "They can either *revere* or *revile*?"

"Yeah," Aaron says. "There are two different

categories of copycats, generally speaking. There are people who admire a murderer and want to mimic their crimes as a form of respect, and then there are people who disagree with a murderer in some way—maybe they have an opposing political belief or just think they're overhyped and want to do it better—so they mirror their crimes as a way to draw attention away from their predecessor and toward themselves. But either way, it's a game."

"Well, Bert Rhodes *reviled* my father. For good reason, but still. It seemed unhealthy. Like an obsession."

"Okay," Aaron says at last. "Okay. Thanks for telling me this. Are you going to bring it to the police?"

"No," I say, probably too quickly. "Not yet, at least."

"Why, is there more?"

I shake my head, deciding not to mention the other part of my theory—that the person taking these girls is talking to me, specifically. Taunting me. Testing me. Wanting me to put the pieces together. I don't want Aaron to start to doubt my sanity here, to discount everything I just said if I take it a step too far. I want to do some research of my own first.

"No. I'm just not ready for that yet. It's too soon."

I stand up, pushing a wisp of hair from my forehead that the wind has loosened from my bun. I exhale, turning toward Aaron to say goodbye, when I notice him looking at me in a way I've never seen from him before. There's concern in his eyes.

"Chloe," he says. "Hang on a second."

"Yeah?"

He hesitates, as if trying to decide if he should continue. He makes up his mind and leans toward me, his voice low and steady.

"Just promise me you'll take care of yourself, okay?"

CHAPTER TWENTY-TWO

I remember seeing Lena's parents once, Bert and Annabelle Rhodes, sitting in the audience of Breaux Bridge High School's annual end-of-year play. That year, the year of the killings, they were putting on *Grease,* and Lena was Sandy, her tight-as-skin pleather pants shimmering every time the fabric caught the glare of the auditorium lights at just the right angle. Her usual French braids were replaced with a perm, a fake cigarette peeking out from behind one ear (although I very much doubted it was fake; she probably smoked it in the parking lot after the curtain had dropped). Cooper was in it, too, which was why we were there. He was good at sports—but acting, not so much. The pamphlet identified him as some tertiary role like *Student #3.*

But not Lena. Lena was the star.

I was with my parents, sliding through the rows of seats looking for three empty chairs together, apologizing as we knocked into the knees of the other already-seated parents.

"Mona," my dad called, waving his hand. "This way."

He motioned toward three chairs in the center of the room, situated right next to the Rhodes'. I watched my mother's eyes bulge for a fraction of a second before she plastered a smile on her face and put her hand on my back, pushing me forward with too much force.

"Hey, Bert," my father said, smiling. "Annabelle. These seats taken?"

Bert Rhodes smiled at my father and gestured to the open seats, ignoring my mother completely. In the moment, it struck me as rude. He had met my mother; I had seen him at our house, just weeks before. He installed security systems for a living; I remember his tanned, leathery arms as he knelt outside in the dirt of our backyard before she tapped him on the shoulder and invited him inside. I watched through my window as he looked up at her, his arm wiping the moisture from his forehead, the unnatural loudness of her laugh as she pulled him in. They went into the kitchen, where I heard them talking in hushed voices; from the bannister on the stairs, I saw her lean over the counter, her chest pushed together as she cradled a glass of sweet iced tea.

We took our seats just before the lights dimmed, and Lena pranced across the stage, her twirling hips making her white hoop skirt fly around her waist. My father shifted in his chair, crossed his legs. Bert Rhodes cleared his throat.

I remember looking over at him then, at the stiffness in his posture. At my mother's eyes, glued to the stage. And at my father in between them, oblivious to it all. Bert Rhodes wasn't rude, I realized. He was uncomfortable. He was hiding something. And my mother was, too.

The news of their affair came as a shock to me after my father's arrest; I suppose all children think of their parents as perfectly happy people, some kind of subhuman life form devoid of feelings and opinions and problems and needs. At age twelve, I didn't understand the complexities of life, of marriage, of relationships. My father was at work all day while my mother was home alone. Cooper and I were at school or wrestling practice or camp most of the time, and I never really stopped to wonder what she did all day. Our languid nighttime routine of dinner served atop TV trays, followed by my father nodding off in his La-Z-Boy while my mother cleaned the kitchen and retreated to their bedroom with a book in her hand seemed like just that to me: routine. I never thought about how lonely it must have been, how stale. Their lack of intimacy seemed normal—I never once saw them kiss, hold hands—because I had never witnessed anything else. I had never *known* anything else. So when she started inviting a steady stream of men into our house over the course of that summer—the gardener and the electrician and the man who installed our security system, the man whose daughter would later vanish—I didn't think of it as anything more than friendly Southern hospitality. Helping them beat the heat with a glass of homemade sweet tea.

Some people speculated that my father killed Lena as payback, as a sick way of evening the scales after he found out about Bert and my mother. Maybe Lena, his first kill, was the onset of his darkness. Maybe it crept in from the corners after that, became bigger and messier, harder to control. Bert Rhodes certainly believed that.

I thought back to him standing next to Lena's mother during that first televised press conference, before Lena's status shifted from *missing* to *presumed dead*. He was a man undone, barely forty-eight hours into his daughter's disappearance and already unable to string words together to form a coherent sentence. But when my father was identified as the man who killed her, he snapped completely.

I remember Cooper pulling me into the house one

morning because Bert Rhodes was outside, pacing like a rabid animal in our front yard. This wasn't like our other visitors, throwing things from a distance or scampering away when we chased them out. This time, it was different. Bert Rhodes was a full-grown man. He was angry, frantic. My mother had already left us, at that point—mentally, at least—and Cooper and I didn't know what to do, so we huddled in my bedroom and watched through my window. We watched as he kicked at the dirt and shouted curse words at our home. We watched as he screamed in our direction and ripped at his clothes, his hair. Eventually, Cooper went outside. I had begged him not to, pulling on his shirtsleeve, tears streaming down my cheeks. Then I had watched helplessly as he walked down our front steps, emerging into the yard. I watched as he shouted back, pushing his outstretched finger into Bert's beefy chest. Eventually, Bert left, with promises of retaliation.

This ain't over! I heard him scream, his gruff voice echoing through the vast nothingness that was our home.

We later learned that the rock that came hurtling through my mother's bedroom window that night had come from his callused hands, the slits in my father's truck tires the work of his blade. In his mind, it was his fault. He had slept with a married woman, after all, and within that same stretch of summer, her husband had murdered his daughter. Karma had been served, and the guilt was too much to bear. He was angry to his core. If Bert Rhodes had been able to get his hands on my father after he confessed to Lena's murder, I'm positive he would have killed him, and not quickly. Not mercifully. He would have killed him slowly, painfully. And he would have enjoyed it.

But of course, he couldn't. He couldn't get his hands

on my father. He was in police custody, safely locked
behind bars.

But his family wasn't, so he set his sights on us.

I unlock the front door now and peek my head into the
house, searching for Daniel. I'm home before lunch, as
promised, and I can smell fresh coffee brewing in the
kitchen. I eye my laptop in the living room, and I want
to grab it, open it, start typing furiously.

I want to learn more about Bert Rhodes.

He knew about Lena's belly-button ring. He knew
about the way my father looked at his daughter at the
fair and at the school play and as she laid flat on my bedroom floor, those long legs in the air. All of the other
girls—Robin, Margaret, Carrie, Susan, Jill—they were
victims, too. But they were random. They were taken
out of necessity or convenience or some mixture of the
two. They were at the wrong place at the wrong time,
the exact time the darkness crept in and my father
could no longer fight it off—when he found the first
young, innocent, defenseless girl he could get his hands
on and he squeezed, hard, until it retreated back into
the corner like a beetle scuttling away from the light.
But Lena seemed to be more than that, she always had.
With Lena, it was personal. She was his first. She was
taken because of who she was, because of the way she
made my father feel. The way she teased him with her
waving fingers before she disappeared into a crowd; the
way Bert teased him by sleeping with his wife before
turning around and smiling at him in public, pretending to be friends.

I walk across the hall to the living room and sit on
the couch, pulling my computer into my lap and powering it on. Bert Rhodes was violent, angry, unforgiv-
ing. Bert Rhodes had a grudge. Was he still stewing
over this, twenty years later? He hadn't forgotten my fa-

ther's crimes—and maybe he didn't want us to forget them, either. I can't shrug off the feeling that I'm onto something, so I tap my fingers across the keys, typing his name into the search engine and hitting *Enter*. A series of articles come up, almost all of them related to the Breaux Bridge killings. I scroll through the pages, skimming the headlines. They're all outdated, and I've read them all before. I decide to refine my search to *Bert Rhodes Baton Rouge* and try again.

This time, a new result pops up. It's the website for Alarm Security Systems, a Baton Rouge–based security company. I click on the link and watch as the website loads, reading the homepage.

Alarm Security Systems is a locally owned and operated on-demand security company. Our trained installation experts will personally install and monitor your home, 24/7, to keep you and your family protected.

I click on a tab titled *Meet The Team* and watch as Bert Rhodes's face loads onto the screen. My eyes drink in his picture, his once-sharp jawline now padded with excess fat and saggy skin, stretched like pizza dough and left to hang. He looks older, fatter, balder. He looks terrible, to be honest. But it's him. It's definitely him.

Then, the realization hits me.

He lives here. Bert Rhodes lives *here,* in Baton Rouge. I'm engrossed in his image, in the way he stares at the camera, the way his face completely lacks an expression. He's neither happy nor sad nor angry nor irritated—he just *is,* a shell of a human. Empty inside. His lips droop into a gentle frown, his eyes emotionless and black. They seem to suck the light from the camera flash deep into their center instead of reflecting it back, the way the other pictures do. I lean closer to the monitor, so absorbed in the image on my screen, in this face from my past, that I don't notice the sound of footsteps walking toward me.

"Chloe?"

I jump, my hand shooting to my chest. I look up to see Daniel hovering above me, and instinctively, I shut my computer. He glances at it.

"What are you looking at?"

"Sorry," I say, my eyes darting from my computer and back to him. He's fully dressed and holding a giant mug in his hands, staring at me. He pushes it in my direction, and I take it, reluctantly, even though I just downed a venti with Aaron thirty minutes before, and the caffeine—or at least, I think it's the caffeine—is already making me jittery. I don't answer, so he tries again.

"Where were you?"

"Just running an errand," I say, pushing my laptop to the side. "I was already in town, so I figured I might as well knock it out—"

"Chloe," he interrupts. "What were you really doing?"

"Nothing," I snap. "Daniel, I'm fine. Really. I just needed to drive around for a little bit, okay?"

"Okay," he says, holding up his hands. "Okay, I get it."

He turns around, and a wave of guilt washes over me. I think of every other relationship I've had, all over before they even began because of my inability to let people in. To trust them. Because of my paranoia and my fear silencing every other emotion in my body screaming to be acknowledged.

"Wait, I'm sorry," I say, reaching my arm toward him. I wiggle my fingers, and he turns around and walks back toward me, sitting next to me on the couch. I drape my arm over his back and lean my head against his shoulder. "I know I'm not handling this very well."

"What can I do to help?"

"Let's do something today," I say, sitting up straighter. My fingers are still itching to get back to my laptop, to dive back into Bert Rhodes, but right now, I need to be with Daniel. I can't keep blowing him off like this. "I know you said we could spend the day in bed, but I don't think that's what I need right now. I think we need to go *do* something. Get out of the house."

He sighs, running his fingers through my hair. He looks at me with a mixture of affection and sadness, and I can already tell that I'm not going to like what he's about to say next.

"Chloe, I'm sorry. I need to drive to Lafayette today. You know that one hospital I've been struggling to meet with? They called me, while you were . . . running your errand. They're giving me an hour this afternoon, and I might even be able to take a few of the doctors to dinner. I have to go."

"Oh, okay." I nod. For the first time since I walked in, his appearance really registers. He isn't just dressed; he's dressed well. He's dressed for work. "Okay, that's . . . of course that's fine. Do what you need to do."

"But *you* should get out of the house," he says, poking me in the chest. "You should go do something. Get some fresh air. I'm sorry I can't be there with you, but I should be home first thing tomorrow morning."

"It's fine," I say. "I have some wedding stuff I should be catching up on anyways. Emails to answer. I'll settle in here and knock it out, maybe grab a drink with Shannon later."

"Atta girl," he says, pulling me in and kissing me on the forehead. He pauses for a minute, and I can feel his eyes drilling into the laptop behind me, still closed shut. He keeps me tight against his chest with one arm as his free hand snakes across the couch and reaches for the computer, pulling it closer. I try to reach for it, too, but he grabs my wrist first, holding it tight, while he slides the computer onto his lap, opening it wordlessly.

"Daniel," I say, but he ignores me, his grip on my wrist getting tighter. "Daniel, come on—"

I swallow hard as the screen illuminates his face, wait while his eyes scan the page I know is still pulled up—Alarm Security Systems, and the picture of Bert Rhodes. He's quiet for a while, and I'm sure he recognizes the name. He knows what I'm up to. After all, he knows about Lena. I open my mouth, getting ready to explain, before he cuts me off.

"Is this what you've been so worked up about?"

"Look, I can explain," I say, still trying to wriggle my wrist free. "After Aubrey's body showed up, I started to get worried . . ."

"You want a security system installed?" he asks. "You're worried whoever is doing this to those girls might come for you next?"

I'm quiet, trying to decide if I should let him go down this path or explain the truth. Again, I open my mouth, but he keeps going.

"Chloe, why didn't you say something to me? God, you must be so scared." He lets go of my wrist, and I feel the blood rush back into my hand, an icy tingle pulsing through my fingers. I hadn't realized how tightly he had been squeezing. Then he pulls me into his chest again, his fingers trailing against my neck and down my spine. "The memories this must be bringing back for you . . . I mean, I knew you were thinking about it, about your dad, but I didn't realize it had gotten to *this*."

"I'm sorry," I say, my lips pressed into his shoulder. "It just . . . it felt a little ridiculous, you know? Being afraid."

It's not the truth, exactly. But it isn't a lie, either.

"You'll be fine, Chloe. You don't have anything to worry about."

My mind flashes to that one morning with my mom, with Cooper, twenty years ago. Crouched in the hallway with our backpacks on. Me, crying. My mom, comforting.

She does have something to worry about, Cooper. This is serious.

"This guy, whoever he is, he likes teenagers, remember?"

I swallow, nod, and my mind formulates the words I already know he's going to say before he has the chance to say them. As if I'm standing in that hallway again, letting my mother wipe away my tears.

"Don't get into a car with strangers, don't walk down dark alleys alone."

Daniel pulls back and smiles at me, and I force a smile back.

"But if getting a security system installed will make you feel better, I think you should do it," he adds. "Call this guy and get him over here. At the very least, it'll give you peace of mind."

"Okay." I nod. "I'll look into it. These things, though, they're expensive."

Daniel shakes his head.

"Your peace of mind is more valuable," he says. "Can't put a price on that."

I smile, a genuine one this time, and wrap my arms around him one last time. I can't blame him for being angry with me, for being curious. I've been secretive these last few days and he knows it. He still has no idea I'm not actually shopping for security systems, that I'm investigating the man on the screen and not the piece of equipment he installs, but still. I can tell that the emotion in his voice is authentic. He means it.

"Thank you," I say. "You're amazing."

"As are you," he says, kissing my forehead before standing up. "Now I've got to go. Get some work done, and I'll text you when I get there."

CHAPTER TWENTY-THREE

As soon as I see Daniel's car pull out of the driveway, I run back to my computer and grab my phone, starting a new text to Aaron.

Bert Rhodes lives here. In Baton Rouge.

I don't know what to do with this information. It's a lead, definitely. It has to be more than coincidence. But still, it's not enough to approach the police with. For all I know, they haven't made the connection with the missing jewelry on their own, and I still don't want to be the one to bring that up. Seconds later, my phone vibrates with Aaron's response.

Looking into it. Give me ten minutes.

I put the phone down and glance back at my computer, at Bert's image still glowing on my screen, his own face proof of the trauma he has experienced. When people get hurt physically, you can see it in the bruises and the scars, but when they're hurt emotionally, mentally, it runs deeper than that. You can see every sleepless night in the reflection of their eyes; you can see every tear stained into their cheeks, every bout of anger etched into the creases in their foreheads. The thirst for blood cracking the skin on their lips. I hesitate for a minute as my eyes drink in the face of this broken person. I start to empathize, and I start to wonder—how could a man who lost his daughter in such a tragic way turn around and take a life in the exact same manner? How could he subject another innocent family to the exact same pain? But then I remember my clients, the other tortured souls I see day in and day out. I remember myself. I remember that statistic I learned in school, the one that made my blood run cold—forty percent of people who are abused as children will go on to become abusers themselves. It doesn't happen to everyone, but it happens. It's cyclical. It's about power, control—or rather, the lack of control. It's about taking it back and claiming it as your own.

I, of all people, should understand that.

My phone starts to vibrate and I see Aaron's name on the screen. I pick it up after the first ring.

"What did you find?" I ask, my eyes still glued to my computer.

"Assault resulting in a bodily injury, public drunkenness, DUI," he says. "He's been in and out of jail over the last fifteen years, and it looks like his wife filed for divorce a while ago after a domestic violence dispute. There's a restraining order."

"What did he do?"

Aaron is silent for a second, and I can't tell if he's reading his notes or if he just doesn't want to answer the question.

"Aaron?"

"He strangled her."

I let the words settle over my body, and instantly the room feels twenty degrees colder.

He strangled her.

"It could be a coincidence," Aaron says.

"Or it couldn't."

"There's a big difference between an angry drunk and a serial killer."

"He could be escalating," I say. "Fifteen years of violent misdemeanors seems to be a pretty good indication that he's capable of something more. He attacked his wife in the same way his daughter was attacked, Aaron. In the same way Aubrey and Lacey were murdered—"

"Okay," Aaron says. "Okay. We'll keep an eye on him. But if this is really concerning you, I think you should go to the police. Tell them the theory, you know. About the copycat."

"No." I shake my head. "No, not yet. We need more."

"Why?" Aaron asks, sounding agitated. "Chloe, you said that last time. This *is* more. Why are you so afraid of the police?"

His question stuns me. I think about the way I've been lying to Detective Thomas and Officer Doyle, hiding evidence from the investigation. I've never thought of myself as being *afraid* of the police, but then I think back to college, to the last time I got involved in something like this, and how badly it had ended. How wrong I had been.

"I'm not afraid of the police," I say. Aaron is silent, and I feel like I should continue, explain more. I feel like I should say *I'm afraid of myself.* But instead, I sigh.

"I don't want to talk to them for the same reason I didn't want to talk to you," I say, my tone harsher than I intend it to be. "I didn't ask to be involved in this. In any of it."

"Well, you are," Aaron snaps back. He sounds hurt, and in this moment, even more than the moment on the dock as he listened to me recount that memory with Lena, our relationship starts to feel like something more than journalist and subject. It starts to feel personal. "Whether you like it or not, you're involved."

I glance toward the window just in time to see the

outline of a car through the blinds, pulling into my driveway. I'm not expecting anyone, so I glance at the clock—Daniel has been gone for about thirty minutes. I look around the house, wondering if he forgot something and had to turn around and drive back.

"Look, Aaron, I'm sorry," I say, pinching my nose between my fingers. "I didn't mean it like that. I know you're trying to help. You're right, I'm involved in this, whether or not I want to be. My dad made sure of that."

He's silent, but I can feel the tension evaporating on the other side of the line.

"All I'm saying is I'm not ready for the police to start digging around in my life just yet," I continue. "If I bring this to them, if I tell them who I am, I can't turn back from that. I'll be picked apart and scrutinized all over again. This is my home, Aaron. My life. I'm normal here . . . or as normal as I can get, anyway. I like it like that."

"Okay," he says at last. "Okay, I understand. I'm sorry for pushing it."

"It's fine. If we find any more proof, I'll tell them everything. I swear."

I hear the slam of a car door outside and turn to see the silhouette of a man walking up my driveway, approaching my home.

"But hey, I need to go. I think Daniel's home. I'll call you later."

I hang up and toss my phone on the couch before walking toward the front door. I can hear the sound of footsteps on the stairs, and before Daniel can come inside, I swing open the door and place a hand on my hip.

"You just couldn't stay away, could you?"

My eyes register the man before me, and my smile fades, my playful expression replaced with one of horror. This man isn't Daniel. My hand drops to my side as I look him up and down, his husky frame and dirty clothes, his wrinkled skin and dark, dead eyes. They're even darker than they were in his picture, still pulled up on my laptop screen. My heart starts to accelerate, and for one terrifying second, I grasp the doorframe to stop myself from passing out.

Bert Rhodes is standing on my doorstep.

CHAPTER TWENTY-FOUR

We stare at each other for what seems like forever, each one silently daring the other to speak first. Even if I had something to say, I wouldn't be able to say it. My lips are frozen in place, the sheer terror of Bert Rhodes in the flesh rendering me immobile. I can't move, I can't speak. All I can do is stare. My gaze travels down from his eyes to his hands, callused and dirty. They're large. I imagine them gripping my neck easily, squeezing gently at first before increasing the pressure with every gag. My nails clawing at his grasp, my eyes bulging as they stare into his, searching for a hint of life in the darkness. His cracked lips snaking into a smile. The finger-shaped bruises Detective Thomas would find on my skin.

He clears his throat.

"Is this the residence of Daniel Briggs?"

I stare at him for another second, blinking a few times, as if my mind is trying to shake itself from a stupor. I don't know if I heard him correctly—he's looking for Daniel? When I don't answer, he speaks again.

"We got a call from Daniel Briggs 'bout thirty minutes ago asking to install a security system at this address." He looks down at his clipboard before glancing at the street sign behind him, as if checking to make sure he's at the right place. "Said it was urgent."

I glance behind him at the car parked in my driveway, the *Alarm Security Systems* logo printed across the side. Daniel must have called the company himself as soon as he got in the car—it was a sweet gesture, well intentioned, but one that also lured Bert Rhodes directly to me. Daniel has no idea of the danger he's just put me in. I look back at this man from my past, lingering on my doorstep, waiting politely to be invited inside. The realization dawns on me slowly.

He doesn't recognize me. He doesn't know who I am.

I hadn't noticed it before, but I'm breathing rapidly, my chest rising and falling violently with each desperate inhale. Bert seems to notice at the same moment I do; he's eying me suspiciously, rightfully curious as to why his presence is making a stranger hyperventilate. I know I need to calm myself down.

Chloe, breathe. Can you breathe for me? Breathe in through your nose.

I imagine my mother and close my lips, inhaling deep through my nostrils and letting my chest fill with air.

Now out through your mouth.

I purse my lips and push out the stale air slowly, feeling my heartbeat slow. I clench my hands to stop them from shaking.

"Yes," I say, stepping to the side and gesturing for him to come in. I watch as his foot crosses the threshold of my home, my sanctuary. My safe haven and my escape, carefully crafted to exude normalcy and control, an illusion that instantly shatters the moment this presence from my past steps inside. There's an atmospheric shift in the air, a buzzing of particles that makes my arm hair bristle. Standing closer to me now, inches from my face, he seems even larger than I remembered, despite the fact that the last time I was in a room with this man, I was twelve years old. But he doesn't seem to know that. He doesn't seem to have any idea that I am the twelve-year-old girl who shares blood with the man who murdered his daughter; I am the girl who screamed when the rock he threw came crashing through my mother's window. I am the girl who hid beneath my bed when he showed up on our doorstep stinking of whiskey and sweat and tears.

He doesn't seem to have any idea of the history we share. And now, with him standing in my home, I wonder if I can use this to my advantage.

He steps farther into the house and looks around, his eyes scanning the hallway, the attached living room, the kitchen, and the staircase that leads to the second floor. He takes a few steps and peeks into each room, nodding to himself.

Suddenly, a terrifying thought washes over me. What if he *does* recognize me? What if he's just checking to see if I'm alone?

"My husband is upstairs," I say, my eyes darting to the staircase. Daniel keeps a gun stashed in our bedroom closet, in case of intruders. I rack my brain, trying to remember where the box is, exactly. I wonder if I can make an excuse to run upstairs and grab it, just in case. "He's on a conference call, but if you need anything, I can just go ask him."

He squints at me before licking his lips and smiling, shaking his head gently, and I get the distinct feeling that he's laughing at me, mocking me. That he knows I'm lying about Daniel, and that I am here completely alone. He walks back in my direction, and I notice him rubbing his hands against his pants, as if wiping the sweat from his palms. I start to panic and consider bolting outside before he twists around and points to the door, tapping it twice with his index finger.

"No need, I'm just assessin' your entry points. Two

main doors, front and back. You got lots of windows in here, so I would suggest we install some glass-break sensors. You want me to take a look upstairs?"

"No," I say. "No, downstairs is fine. That all—that all sounds fine. Thank you."

"You want cameras?"

"What?"

"Cameras," he repeats. "They're tiny little things we can place throughout the property, then you can access the video from your phone—"

"Oh, yeah," I say, quickly, absentmindedly. "Yeah, sure. That'll be good."

"All right," he says, nodding. He scribbles some notes on his clipboard before thrusting it in my direction. "If you could just sign here, I'll get my tools."

I take the clipboard and look down at the order form as he steps outside and walks toward his car. I can't sign my name, obviously. My *real* name. Surely, he would recognize that. So instead, I sign *Elizabeth Briggs*—my middle name paired with Daniel's last—and hand him the clipboard as he walks back inside. I watch as he scans my signature before making my way back to the couch.

"I appreciate you showing up on such short notice," I say, shutting my laptop and stuffing my phone into my back pocket. "That was extremely quick."

"On-demand, 24/7," he says, reciting the slogan from the website. He's walking around the house now, sticking sensors on each window. The thought of this man knowing exactly which areas to avoid to bypass the alarm is suddenly concerning; for all I know, he could be skipping a spot, keeping a mental note of which window to crawl through when he comes back later. I wonder if this is how he chooses his victims—maybe he first saw Aubrey and Lacey when installing systems in *their* homes. Maybe he stood inside their bedrooms, took a peek inside their panty drawers. Learned their routines.

I'm quiet as he stalks through my house, poking his head into various corners, his fingers into every crack. He grabs a footstool and grunts as he climbs, sticking a small, circular camera in the corner of the living room. I stare into it, a microscopic eye staring right back.

"Are you the owner?" I ask at last.

"No," he says. I expect him to elaborate further, but he doesn't. I decide to keep pressing.

"How long have you been doing this?"

He climbs off the ladder and looks at me, his mouth opening as if he wants to say something. Instead, he reconsiders and closes it again before walking toward the front door, pulling out a drill from his tool bag and fastening the security panel to the wall. I watch the back of his head as the sound of the drill fills my hallway, and try again.

"Are you local to Baton Rouge?"

The drilling stops, and I see his shoulders tense. He doesn't turn around, but now the sound of his voice is what fills the empty room.

"Do you really think I don't know who you are, Chloe?"

I freeze, his response stunning me into silence. I keep watching the back of his head until, slowly, he turns around.

"I recognized you the second you answered the door."

"I'm sorry." I swallow. "I don't know what you're talking about."

"Yes, you do," he says, taking a step closer. Still clutching the drill. "You're Chloe Davis. Your fiancé gave me your name when he called. He's on his way to Lafayette, and he said you'd let me in."

My eyes grow wide as I register what he just admitted—he knows who I am. He has this whole time. And he knows I'm here alone.

He takes another step closer.

"And the fact that you lied about your name on the order form tells me that you know who I am, too, so I really don't know what you're playin' at, askin' me these questions."

My phone is hot in my back pocket. I could pull it out, call 9-1-1. But he's right in front of me now, and I'm terrified that any movement on my part will send him hurtling in my direction.

"You wanna know what brought me to Baton Rouge?" he asks. He's getting angry now; I can see his skin reddening, his eyes getting darker. Little bubbles of spit multiplying on his tongue. "I've been here for a while, Chloe. After Annabelle and I got divorced, I needed a change of scenery. A fresh start. I was in a dark place for a while there, so I picked up and moved, got the fuck out of that town and all the memories that come with it. And I was doin' okay, all things considered, until a few years ago, I opened the Sunday paper, and guess who I saw starin' right back at me."

He waits for a second, his lip curling into a smile.

"It was a picture of you," he says, pointing the drill in my direction. "A picture of you beneath some cheeky little headline about you *channeling your childhood trauma* or some bullshit like that right here in Baton Rouge."

I remember that article—that interview I had granted the paper when I started working at Baton Rouge General. I thought that article would be a redemption piece, of sorts. A chance to redefine myself, to write my own narrative. But of course, it wasn't. It was just another exploration of my father, another gaudy glorification of violence masquerading under the façade of journalism.

"I read that article," he continues. "Every fuckin' word. And you know what? It just pissed me off all over again. You makin' excuses about your dad, capitalizin' on what he did, for the good of your own career. And then I read about your *mom,* tryin' to take the cowardly way out after the role she played in all of this. So she didn't have to live with herself no more."

I'm silent as his words settle over me, as I take in the way he's staring at me with pure hatred in his eyes. The way his hands are clutching the drill so hard I can see the whites of his knuckles, threatening to tear straight through his skin.

"Your entire family makes me sick," he says. "And no matter what I do, I can't seem to escape you."

"I never made excuses for my father," I say. "I never tried to *capitalize* on anything. What he did . . . it's, it's inexcusable. It makes *me* sick."

"Oh, is that right? It makes you sick?" he asks, tilting his head. "Tell me, does owning your own practice make you sick, too? That nice little office you got downtown? Does your six-figure paycheck make you sick? Your fuckin' Garden District, two-story home and picture-perfect fiancé? Do they make you sick?"

I swallow hard. I underestimated Bert Rhodes. Inviting him inside was a mistake. Trying to play detective and interrogate him was a mistake. Not only does he know me—he knows everything *about* me. He's been researching me the same way I've been researching him—but for much, much longer. He knows about my practice, my office. Maybe that means he knows that Lacey was a patient—and he was there, waiting, the day she stepped outside and disappeared.

"Now, tell me," he growls. "Why is it fair that Dick Davis's daughter gets to grow up and live a perfect life while mine is rotting in the ground wherever that fucker dumped her body?"

"I am not living a perfect life," I say. Suddenly, I'm angry, too. "You have no idea what I've been through, how fucked up I am after what my father did."

"What *you've* been through?" he yells, pointing the drill at me again. "You want to talk about what *you've* been through? How fucked up *you* are? What about my daughter? What about what *she* went through?"

"Lena was my friend. Mr. Rhodes, she was my *friend*. You are not the only one who lost someone that summer."

His expression shifts slightly—a softening of the eyes, a loosening of the forehead—and suddenly, he's looking at me like I'm twelve again. Maybe it was the way I said his name, *Mr. Rhodes,* the same way I said it when my mother introduced us in our kitchen one evening after I burst in from camp, sweating and dirty and confused as to who this man was, standing so close to my mother. Or maybe it was the mention of *her* name—Lena. I wonder how long it's been since he's heard it spoken out loud, a name so sweet it tastes like sap dripping down a piece of bark on the tongue. I try to take advantage of this momentary shift and keep talking.

"I am so sorry about what happened to your daughter," I say, taking a step back, putting some distance between us. "Truly, I am. I think about her every day."

He sighs, lowering the drill to his legs. He turns to the side, gazing at something outside through the blinds, a faraway look in his eyes.

"You ever think about what it feels like?" he finally asks. "I used to keep myself up at night, wondering. Imagining. Obsessing over it."

"All the time. I can't imagine what she went through."

"No," he says, shaking his head. "I'm not talking

about her. Not Lena. I never wondered what it was like to lose my life. Honestly, if I did, I wouldn't care."

He turns toward me now. His eyes have morphed back into two inky black voids, any trace of softness now gone completely. He's wearing that expression again, that same expression of flat, emotionless indifference. He almost looks inhuman, like an empty mask hanging against a pitch-black wall.

"I'm talking about your father," he says. "I'm talking about taking one."

CHAPTER TWENTY-FIVE

I don't move until I hear the roar of the engine and the *thud* of his truck reversing over the curb and peeling out of my driveway. I stand completely still, listening to the sound of his retreating vehicle growing fainter in the distance, until finally, I'm met with silence.

You really think I don't know who you are, Chloe?

His words had trapped me, rendered me immobile the second he turned around and looked me in the eye. I was paralyzed the same way I was paralyzed as I watched my father slink through the backyard at night, shovel in hand. I knew I was witnessing something wrong, something terrible. Something dangerous. I knew I should run, screaming. I knew I should sprint out the open door, flailing my arms. But just as my father's slow, lumbering steps had held me captive, Bert Rhodes's eyes had entranced me, bolted my feet to the floor. His voice had coiled around my body like a snake, refusing to let go. It was dense like salt water; trying to run from it, from him, felt like trying to run through the swamp, the mud heavy and thick and sticking to your ankles. The harder you try to push through, the more exhausted you feel, the weaker you become. The deeper you sink.

I wait another minute, until I'm sure he's gone, and

take a slow step forward, the weight of my heel forcing the wood beneath my feet to creak.

I'm not talking about her. Not Lena. I never wondered what it was like to lose my life.

I take another step—slow, cautionary, as if he's lurking behind the still-open front door, waiting to strike.

I'm talking about your father. I'm talking about taking one.

I take one last step to the front door and slam it shut, locking the dead bolt before pushing my back hard against the wood. I'm shaking violently as the room starts to get brighter; I'm fighting back that unearthly feeling that sweeps over your body after a shot of unexpected adrenaline wears off—twitchy fingers, spotty vision, ragged breathing. I slide down the wall and sit on the floor, pushing my hands through my hair, trying not to cry.

Eventually, I look up at the security panel installed on the wall above me, glowing bright. I stand up and set the code on the keypad before pushing *Enable,* watching the little lock icon turn from red to green. I exhale, although I can't help but feel that it's pointless. For all I know, he didn't install it correctly. He skipped a few windows, set an override code. Daniel wanted to get a security system installed to help me feel safer, but right now, I've never felt more afraid.

I need to go to the police with this. I can't put it off any longer. Bert Rhodes not only knows who I am, but he knows where I live. He knows I'm here alone. Maybe he knows that I'm onto him. As much as I don't want to thrust myself into another missing girls investigation, that encounter was the extra evidence I had been looking for; Bert Rhodes's rambling—his anger over my life and how I turned out, his wondering what it felt like to take a life—was practically an admission of guilt and a threat of future violence all at once. I reach a shaky hand into my back pocket and yank out my phone, pulling up my previous calls and tapping on the number that appeared on my screen just this morning, the number that confirmed my biggest fear: that Lacey Deckler was dead. I listen to the ringing on the other end, bracing myself for the conversation I know we're about to have. The conversation I had been desperately hoping to avoid.

It stops abruptly as a voice greets me on the other end.

"Detective Thomas."

"Hi, Detective. This is Chloe Davis."

"Doctor Davis," he says, sounding surprised. "What can I do for you? Did you remember something else?"

"Yes," I say. "Yes, I did. Could we meet? As soon as possible?"

"Of course." I hear shuffling on the other end, like he's moving around papers. "Can you come to the station?"

"Yes," I say again. "Yes, I can do that. I'll be there soon."

I hang up, my mind swirling as I grab my keys and walk outside, double-checking that the door is locked behind me. I get in the car and crank the engine. He didn't have to give me directions; I already know where I'm going. I've been to the Baton Rouge Police Department before, although I hope that part of my past isn't dragged up, too, when I reveal to him who I am. It shouldn't be, but it could. And even if it is, there's nothing I can do about that but try to explain.

I pull into visitors' parking and kill the engine as I stare at the entrance looming before me. This building looks the same as it did ten years ago, only older. Less maintained. The tan bricks are still tan, but the paint is cracking at the seams, large chips peeling off and landing in piles on the concrete. The landscaping is patchy and brown, the chain-link fence separating the station from the neighboring strip mall wobbly and bent. I step out of the car and slam the door behind me, pushing myself inside before I can change my mind.

I walk to the front counter and stand behind the clear plastic divider, watching as the woman behind the desk taps her acrylic nails against a keyboard.

"Hi," I interrupt. "I have an appointment with Detective Michael Thomas?"

She glances at me from behind the plastic and chews on the side of her cheek, as if she's trying to decide if she believes me. My statement came out more like a question, undoubtedly because the certainty I felt back home about coming clean to the police all but evaporated the second I stepped inside.

"I can text him," I say, holding up my phone, trying to convince both her and myself that letting me in is a good idea. "Tell him I'm here."

She looks at me for another few seconds before picking up her phone and dialing an extension, propping it between her shoulder and chin while she continues typing. I hear the line ring before Detective Thomas's voice picks up.

"There's someone here to see you," she says. She looks at me, eyebrows raised.

"Chloe Davis."

"A *Chloe Davis*," she repeats. "Says she has an appointment."

She hangs the phone up quickly and gestures to the door on my right, guarded by a metal detector and security personnel who looks agitated and tired.

"He said you can go in. Place all metal and electronics in the bin. Second door on the right."

Inside the station, Detective Thomas's office door is cracked open. I peek my head through, knocking gently on the wood.

"Come in," he says, looking at me from above a desk

cluttered with various papers, manila folders, and an open box of Saltine crackers, half a sleeve sticking out and a trail of crumbs littered across the wood. He follows my gaze and ducks his head, shoving the sleeve back into the box and closing the flap. "Sorry for the mess."

"It's fine," I say, walking inside and pushing the door shut behind me. I linger for a second before he points to the chair opposite him. I take a seat, my mind flashing back to earlier this week when the roles were reversed. When I was seated behind *my* desk, in *my* office, gesturing for *him* to sit where I commanded. I exhale.

"So," he says, folding his hands on the table. "What is it that you remembered?"

"First, I have a question," I say. "Aubrey Gravino. Was she found wearing any jewelry?"

"I don't really see how that's relevant."

"It is. I mean, depending on what the answer is, it could be."

"Why don't you tell me what you remember first, and then we can look into that."

"No." I shake my head. "No, before I share this, I need to know for certain. I promise, it matters."

He looks at me for another few seconds, weighing his options. He sighs loudly, trying to convey his annoyance, before shuffling through the folders on his desk. Then he grabs one, opens it, and flips through a few pages.

"No, she wasn't found with any jewelry," he says. "One earring was found near the body in the cemetery—sterling silver with a pearl and three diamonds."

He looks up at me, his eyebrows raised, as if to question: *Are you happy now?*

"So, no necklace?"

His eyes linger on mine for another few seconds before looking back down.

"No. No necklace. Just the earring."

I exhale, pushing my hands into my hair. He's looking at me carefully again, waiting for me to say something, to do something. I lean back into my chair and spit it out.

"That earring was a part of a set," I say. "There's a matching necklace she would have been wearing at the time of her abduction. She wears them together in all of her pictures. On the *MISSING* poster, her yearbook photos, tagged pictures on Facebook. If she was wearing the earrings, she was also wearing the necklace."

He lowers the folder to his desk.

"How do you know this?"

"I checked," I say. "Before I came to you with this, I wanted to be sure."

"Okay. And why do you think this matters?"

"Because Lacey was wearing a piece of jewelry, too. Remember?"

"That's right," he says. "You mentioned a bracelet."

"A beaded bracelet with a metal cross. I saw it on her wrist in my office. She wore it to cover her scar. But when I looked at her body this morning . . . it wasn't there."

The room is uncomfortably quiet. Detective Thomas continues to stare, and I can't tell if he's actually considering what I'm telling him, or if he's concerned about my well-being. I talk faster.

"I think the killer is taking his victim's jewelry, as mementos," I say. "And I think he's doing that because my father used to do that. Richard Davis, you know. From Breaux Bridge."

I watch his reaction as the pieces fall into place. It's always the same, every time someone realizes who I am: a visible loosening of the face before the jaw gets tight, like they have to physically restrain themselves from lunging at me from across the table. Our last names, our similar features. I've always been told that I have my father's nose, oversized and slightly crooked, by far my least favorite thing on my face—not because of vanity, but because of the constant reminder of our shared DNA every time I look in the mirror.

"You're Chloe Davis," he says. "Dick Davis's daughter."

"Unfortunately, yes."

"You know, I think I read an article about you." He's pointing at me now, waving his finger as he allows the memory to take over. "I just . . . I didn't put it together."

"Yeah, that ran a few years ago. I'm relieved to hear you forgot."

"And you think these murders are somehow related to the ones your father committed?"

He's still staring at me with that look of disbelief, as if I'm an apparition hovering above the carpet, unsure if I'm real.

"At first, I didn't," I say. "But the twenty-year anniversary is coming up next month, and I recently discovered that the father of one of my father's victims lives here in Baton Rouge. Bert Rhodes. And he's . . . angry. He has a record. He tried to strangle his wife—"

"You think this is a copycat?" he interrupts. "That the *victim's father* has turned into a copycat?"

"He has a record," I repeat. "And . . . my family. He *hates* my family. I mean, understandably so, but he showed up to my house today, and he was very angry, and I felt very unsafe—"

"He came to your house unannounced?" he sits up straighter and reaches for a pen. "Did he threaten you in any way?"

"No, it wasn't really unannounced. He installs security systems, and my fiancé, he called them to have one installed—"

"So you invited him to your house?" he leans back again, putting the pen down.

"Will you stop interrupting me?"

The sentence comes out louder than I intend it to, and Detective Thomas looks at me, stunned, with a mixture of shock and unease as an uncomfortable silence settles across the room. I bite my lip. I hate that look. I've seen that look before. I've seen that look from Cooper. I've seen that look from police officers and detectives, right here, in this very building. That look that shows the very first hint of concern—not for my safety, but for my mind. That look that makes me feel like my words are not to be trusted, that my slow unravel is getting faster and faster, spiraling out of control, until pretty soon, I'll be nothing.

"I'm sorry," I say, exhaling. Forcing myself to calm down. "I'm sorry, it's just that I feel like you're not really listening to me. You asked me to look at Lacey's body today and tell you if I remembered anything that could be important. This is me telling you what I believe may be important."

"Okay," he says, holding his hands in the air. "Okay, you're right. I'm sorry. Please continue."

"Thank you," I say, feeling my shoulders relax a little. "Anyway. Bert Rhodes is one of the few people, possibly the *only* person, who would know that detail, lives in the area where these current murders are taking place, and has a motive for murdering these girls in the same way my father murdered his daughter twenty years ago. It's a coincidence that can't be ignored."

"And what do you believe his motive is, exactly? Does he know these girls?"

"No—I mean, I don't know. I don't think so. But isn't that your job to figure out?"

Detective Thomas raises his eyebrow.

"I'm sorry," I say again. "Just . . . look. It could be a

lot of things, okay? Maybe it's revenge, targeting girls I know to harass me or make me feel the same pain he felt when his daughter was taken. An eye for an eye. Or maybe it's grief, a need for control, the same fucked-up reason victims of abuse will go on to become abusers themselves. Maybe he's trying to make a point. Or maybe he's just sick, Detective. Twenty years ago, he wasn't exactly the best father either, okay? Even as a girl, I just had a *feeling* about him. That something wasn't right."

"Okay, but a *feeling* isn't a motive."

"All right, well how's this for motive?" I spit. "Today, he told me that after Lena's death, he found himself obsessing over what it would feel like to take somebody's life. Who *says* that? Who imagines what it's like to take a life after your own daughter has just been murdered? Shouldn't it be the other way around? He's empathizing with the wrong person here."

Detective Thomas is silent for a minute before sighing again, this time in what sounds like resignation.

"Okay," he says. "Okay, we'll look into him. I agree—it's a coincidence that deserves to be checked out."

"Thank you."

I get ready to stand from the chair before the detective looks at me again, a question forming on his lips.

"Real quick, Doctor Davis. You said that maybe this man, this—"

He looks down at the paper below him, devoid of any notes. I feel irritation gurgling up my throat like bile.

"Bert Rhodes. You should write it down."

"Right, Bert Rhodes," he says, scribbling the name in the corner, circling it twice. "You said he might be targeting girls you know specifically."

"Yeah, maybe. He admitted to knowing where my office was, so maybe that's why he took Lacey. Maybe he was watching me and he saw her walking out. Maybe he dumped her in the alley behind my office because he knew I might find her there, notice the missing jewelry, make the connection. That I'd be forced to acknowledge the fact that all these girls are still dying because of . . ."

I stop, swallow. Force myself to say the words.

"Because of my dad."

"Okay," he says, tracing his pen along the edge of his paper. "Okay, that's a possibility. But then what exactly is your connection to Aubrey Gravino? How do you know her?"

I stare at him, my cheeks growing hot. It's a valid question—one I somehow hadn't thought to ask myself before. I was there just before Aubrey's body had been found, which seemed coincidental, then Lacey going missing the day she left my office took it to a whole new level. But in terms of an actual shared connection between Aubrey and me . . . I can't think of one. I remember seeing her image on the news for that first time, the vague familiarity of her features, like I had seen her somewhere before, maybe in a dream. I had just chalked it up to all the adolescent girls who streamed through my office on a weekly basis, the way they all seem to look somewhat the same.

But now I start to wonder if maybe it was something more.

"I don't know Aubrey," I admit. "I can't think of any connection right now. I'll keep thinking on it."

"Okay." He nods, still eying me carefully. "Okay, Doctor Davis, I appreciate you coming in. I'll be sure to follow up on this lead and let you know as soon as I learn more."

I push myself up from the chair and turn to leave; his office feels claustrophobic now, the closed door and the closed windows and the clutter piling high on every surface making my palms sweat and my heartbeat pound loudly in my chest. I walk quickly to the door and grasp the knob, feeling his eyes still drilling into my back, watching. It's clear that Detective Thomas is wary of my story; with something this shocking, I had suspected that might be the case. But in coming here and revealing my theory, I had hoped to at least point the spotlight on Bert Rhodes, to get the police to start watching him closely, making it harder for him to lurk in the dark.

But instead, I feel like it's pointed directly at me.

CHAPTER TWENTY-SIX

It's late afternoon by the time I make it back home. When I enter the hallway, our new alarm system beeps twice, sending a jolt of panic through my chest at the sound. I immediately reengage it once I close the door behind me, increasing the sound to the highest setting. Then I look around my house, quiet and still. Despite my best efforts, Bert Rhodes's presence is everywhere I look. The sound of his voice seems to echo across the empty halls, his dark eyes peering at me from behind every unturned corner. I can even smell him, that musky scent of sweat mixed with a hint of alcohol that trailed him around as he wandered through my home, touching my walls, inspecting my windows, injecting himself into my life once again.

I walk into the kitchen and take a seat at the island, placing my purse on the counter and fishing out the Xanax bottle I retrieved from my glove compartment. I twist it in my hands, shaking the bottle slightly and listening to the rattle of the pills as they tumble around inside. I've been craving a Xanax since the second I left the morgue this morning; that was only a matter of hours ago—sitting in my car, the mental image of Lacey's blue body making my fingers shake as I held the pill in my palm—but given all that's happened since, it feels like a lifetime ago. I twist open the cap and dump one in my hand, tossing it back and swallowing it dry before another phone call can interrupt me. Then I glance at the refrigerator, realizing that I've barely eaten all day.

I jump up from the island and walk over to the fridge, opening the door and leaning against the cool stainless steel. Already, I'm starting to feel better. I told the police about Bert Rhodes. Detective Thomas didn't seem very convinced, but I did what I could. He'll be looking into him now. Surely, he'll be watching him, watching his movements, his patterns. He'll be noting which houses he visits, and if another girl goes missing from one of those houses, then he'll know. He'll know I was right, and he'll stop looking at me as if *I'm* the crazy one. As if *I'm* the one with something to hide.

My eyes land on the leftover salmon from last night, and I pull the Pyrex container out, removing the lid before placing it in the microwave, the kitchen quickly filling with the smell of spices mixing in the air. It's too late for lunch, so I'll call it an early dinner, which means it's entirely within my rights to enjoy a glass of that cabernet that paired so well with it last night. I walk over to the wine cabinet and retrieve a glass, pouring the ruby red liquid to the brim and taking a long drink before dumping the rest of the bottle into the glass and then tossing it into the recycling bin.

Before I can pull out my barstool, there's a knock at the door—a loud, closed-fist pounding that sends my hand to my chest—followed by a familiar voice.

"Chlo, it's me. I'm comin' in."

I hear the sound of a key in the lock, a quiet clicking as the latch slips out of place. I watch the doorknob begin to turn when I remember the alarm.

"No, wait!" I yell, jogging to the door. "Coop, don't come in. Hang on a second."

I reach the keypad and punch in the code just before the door swings open; when it does, I turn to face the porch, my brother's surprised eyes staring in my direction.

"You got an alarm?" he asks, his feet planted on the *Welcome!* mat, a bottle of wine clutched in his hand. "If you wanted your key back, you could have just asked."

"Very funny." I smile. "You're going to have to start giving me a heads-up when you're coming over. This thing will call the cops on you."

I tap the keypad and gesture for him to come inside, walking back to the island and leaning against the cool marble.

"And if you try to break in, I'll see you on my phone."

I lift up my cell phone and wiggle it in the air before pointing at the camera in the corner.

"Is that actually recording?" he asks.

"Sure is."

I open up the security app on my phone and turn it around so Cooper can see; he's standing in the center of my cell phone screen.

"Huh," he says, turning back around and waving into the camera. He looks back at me and grins.

"Besides," I say. "As much as I love your visits, I'm not the only one who lives here now."

"Yeah, yeah," Cooper says, taking a seat on the edge of a stool. "Speaking of which, where is your fiancé?"

"Traveling," I say. "For work."

"Over the weekend?"

"He works a lot."

"Hm," Cooper says, twirling his bottle of merlot on the table. The liquid glistens under the kitchen lights, casting bloodred shadows across the wall.

"Cooper, don't," I say. "Not now."

"I didn't."

"But you were about to."

"Doesn't it bother you?" he asks, the words pressed and urgent, like if he didn't speak them now, they would come ripping out on their own. "How often he's gone? I mean, I don't know, Chlo. I always pictured you with someone who was around to keep you feeling safe. After everything you've been through, you deserve that. Someone present."

"Daniel is present," I say, reaching for my wineglass and taking a deep drink. "He keeps me feeling safe."

"So, what's the alarm for?"

I think about how to respond to that, my fingernails tapping against the grooved glass.

"It was his idea," I say at last. "See? Keeping me safe, even when he's not here."

"All right, whatever," Cooper says, standing from the barstool with a sigh. He walks over to the cabinet and grabs a corkscrew, twisting the cork from his own bottle. Even though I know it's coming, the *pop* makes me jump. "Anyway, I was going to suggest we drink, but it looks like you've already gotten started."

"Why are you here, Cooper? Are you here to argue with me again?"

"No, I'm here because you're my sister," he says. "I'm here because I'm worried about you. I wanted to make sure you're doing okay."

"Well, I'm fine," I say, raising my arms in a shrug. "I don't really know what to tell you."

"How are you dealing with all this?"

"With what, Cooper?"

"Come on," he says. "You know."

I sigh, my eyes flickering over to the empty living room, to the couch that suddenly seems so comfortable, so inviting. I let my shoulders slouch a little; they're so tight. I'm tight.

"It's bringing back memories," I say, taking another drink. "Obviously."

"Yeah. For me, too."

"Sometimes it's hard for me to determine what's real and what's not."

The words escape before I have a chance to reel them back in; I can still taste them on my tongue, that admission I had been trying so hard to just swallow down. Forget was ever there. I look down at my wine-glass, suddenly half empty, then back up at Cooper.

"It's just so familiar, I mean. There are so many sim-ilarities. Doesn't it seem a little coincidental to you?"

Cooper eyes me, his lips parting gently.

"What kind of similarities, Chloe?"

"Forget it," I say. "It's nothing."

"Chloe," Cooper says, leaning toward me. "What are those?"

I follow his stare toward the bottle of Xanax still on the counter, that tiny orange bottle holding a mountain of pills inside. I look back down at my wineglass again, at the finger of liquid remaining.

"Have you been taking those?"

"What? No," I say. "No, those aren't mine—"

"Did Daniel give you those?"

"No, Daniel didn't give me those. Why would you say that?"

"His name is on the bottle."

"Because they're *his*."

"Then why are they open on the counter when he's out of town?"

Silence settles between us. I glance out the window, at the sun beginning to set outside. The noises of the night are starting to emerge—the scream of the cicadas and chirping of crickets and all of the other animals that begin to come alive in the dark. Louisiana at night is a noisy place, but I prefer it to silence. Because when it's silent, you can hear everything. Muffled breaths in the distance, footsteps digging deep into drying leaves. A shovel being dragged through the dirt.

"I've been worried about this." Cooper exhales, pushing his hands through his hair. "It's not safe for him to be bringing all those drugs into the house with your history."

"What do you mean *all those drugs*?"

"He's a pharmaceutical sales rep, Chloe. His briefcase is full of that shit."

"So? I have access to drugs, too. I can prescribe them."

"Not to yourself."

I feel a wave of tears pricking at my eyes. I hate that Daniel is taking the blame for this, but I can't think of another explanation. Another way out without telling Cooper that I've been calling pills in for myself under Daniel's name. So instead, I'm quiet. I let Cooper believe it. I let his distrust for my fiancé sink deeper, simmer louder.

"I'm not here to fight," he says, standing up from the stool and walking toward me. He wraps my body in a deep hug, his arms thick and warm and familiar. "I love you, Chloe. And I know why you do it. I just wish you would stop. Get some help."

I feel a tear escape, gliding down my cheek and leaving a trail of salt in its wake. It lands on Cooper's leg, leaving a small, dark stain. I bite my lip, hard, trying to stop the rest from falling.

"I don't need help," I say, pushing down on my eyes with my palms. "I can help myself."

"I'm sorry I upset you," he says. "It's just—this relationship you're in. It doesn't seem healthy."

"It's fine," I say, lifting my head from his shoulder, wiping the back of my hand across my cheek. "But I think you should go."

Cooper tilts his head. This is the second time in one week I've threatened to choose Daniel over my brother. I think back to the engagement party, standing on my back porch. That ultimatum I'd given him.

I want you in this wedding. But it's happening, with or without you.

But I can see now, from the hurt in his eyes, that he hadn't believed me.

"I can see that you're trying," I say. "And I get it, Cooper. I really do. You're protective, you care. But no matter what I say, Daniel is never going to be good enough for you. He's my *fiancé*. I'm marrying him next month. So if he's not good enough for you, I guess I'm not, either."

Cooper takes a step back, his fingers curling into his open palm.

"I am just trying to help you," he says. "To look after you. That's my job. I'm your *brother*."

"It's not your job," I say. "Not anymore. And you need to leave."

He stares at me for a second longer, his eyes darting back and forth from me to the pills on the counter. He extends his arm, and I think he's going to grab them, take them, but instead, he hands me the key ring that holds my spare. The memory of me giving it to him flashes through my mind—years ago, when I had first moved in, I had wanted him to have it. *You're always welcome here,* I had said as we sat cross-legged on the mattress in my bedroom, foreheads damp with sweat from assembling my headboard, Chinese takeout cartons spilling onto the floor. The oily noodles leaving greasy smears on the hardwood. *Besides, I'm going to need someone to water my plants when I'm gone.* I stare at the key now, dangling from his pointer finger. I can't bring myself to take it back—because once I do, I know that it's final. That it can't be returned. So instead, he places it gently on the counter, turns around, and walks out the door.

I stare at the key, fighting the urge to pick it up, walk outside, and push it back into his hands. Instead, I grab it and the Xanax and toss them into my purse before walking over to the door and setting the alarm. Then I grab Cooper's wine bottle, still mostly full, and pour myself another glass before picking it up along with the salmon, now cold, and walking back into the living room, settling in on the couch, and turning on the TV.

I think about everything that has happened today and immediately, I'm exhausted. Seeing Lacey, my meeting with Aaron. The scuffle with Daniel and the interaction with Bert Rhodes and going to Detective Thomas, telling him everything. The argument with my brother, the concern in his eyes when he saw those pills. When he saw me, alone, drinking at the kitchen island.

Suddenly, more than exhausted, I feel lonely.

I pick up my phone, tap the screen until the background illuminates in my hand. I think about calling Daniel, but then I picture him at dinner, ordering another bottle at some five-star Italian restaurant, the roars of laughter as he insists on just one more. He's probably the life of the party—cracking jokes, grabbing shoulders. The thought makes me feel even lonelier, so I swipe up at the screen and open up my Contacts.

And there, at the very top, I'm greeted with another name: Aaron Jansen.

I could call Aaron, I think. I could fill him in on everything that has happened since the last time we spoke. He probably isn't doing anything, alone in an unfamiliar town. He's probably doing the same thing as me, as a matter of fact—sitting on the couch, half drunk, leftovers perched between his outstretched legs. My finger hovers over his name, but before I can tap it, the screen goes dark. I sit for a minute, wondering. My

mind is feeling a little foggy now, like it's been wrapped
in a thick, wool blanket. I put the phone down, deciding
against it. Instead, I close my eyes. I imagine how he
might react when I tell him about Bert Rhodes showing
up on my doorstep. I imagine him yelling at me through
the phone after I admit to letting him in. I smirk a little bit, knowing that he'd be worried. Worried about
me. But then I would tell him how I got him out of the
house, called Detective Thomas, went to the police. I
would relay our conversation, word by word, and smile
again, knowing that he'd be proud.

I open my eyes and take another bite of salmon, the
drone of the TV sounding more distant as my mind
starts to focus instead on the sound of my chewing. The
clank of the fork against the Pyrex. My heavy breathing. The image on the television is starting to grow fuzzy
on the screen, and I realize that my eyelids are feeling
heavier with every subsequent sip of wine. Pretty soon,
my limbs are tingling.

I deserve this, I think, sinking deeper into the couch.
I deserve to sleep. To rest. I'm just exhausted. So, so
exhausted. It's been a long day. I turn my phone off—no
disruptions—and place it on my stomach before pushing my dinner onto the coffee table. I take another sip
of wine and feel a little bit dribble down my chin. Then
I let myself close my eyes, just for a second, and feel
myself drift into sleep.

It's dark outside when I wake up. I'm disoriented,
my eyes fluttering open as I lie on the couch, the half-
empty wineglass still propped between my arm and
stomach. Miraculously, it didn't spill. I sit up and tap
my phone, looking for the time, until I remember that
I turned it off. I squint at the television—the time on
the newscast says it's just past ten. My pitch-black living room is partially illuminated in an eerie blue glow,
so I reach for the remote and turn off the TV before

pulling myself off the couch. I look at the wineglass in my hand and down the rest of the liquid before placing it on the coffee table, walking upstairs, and collapsing into bed.

I sink into the mattress immediately, and pretty soon, I'm in a dream—or maybe it's a memory. It feels a little bit like both, somehow strange yet familiar at the exact same time. I'm twelve years old, sitting in my reading nook, my bedroom pitch-black, with the glow of my tiny reading light illuminating my face just slightly. My eyes are skimming the book in my lap, engrossed in the words on the page, when a noise from outside breaks my concentration. I look out the window and see a figure in the distance, moving silently across our yard in the dark. It's coming from the trees just beyond our property, the trees that line the entrance to a swamp spanning miles in either direction.

I squint at the figure, and pretty soon, I can tell it's a body. A fully grown adult body dragging something behind it. The sound begins to drift across the backyard and leaks through my cracked-open window, and soon, I recognize it as the scraping of metal against dirt.

It's a shovel.

The body walks closer to my window and I press my face against the glass, dog-earing my book and putting it down. It's still dark, and I'm still struggling to make out a face or features. As the body inches even closer, almost directly below my window now, a floodlight turns on and I find myself squinting at the sudden brightness, my hand shielding my face as my eyes try to adjust to the light. I remove my hand and confusion washes over me as the person below my window is finally illuminated enough to see. It isn't the body of a man, as I had originally assumed. It isn't my father, the way the memory should have actually played out.

This time, it's a woman.

She turns her head to the sky and looks at me, as if she knew I was there all along. We make eye contact, and I don't recognize her at first. She looks vaguely familiar, but I don't know how or why. I look at her individual features—eyes, mouth, nose—and that's when it finally clicks. I feel the blood drain from my face.

The woman below my window is *me*.

Panic starts to surge through my chest as twelve-year-old me stares into the eyes of myself, twenty years older. They're completely black, like the eyes of Bert Rhodes. I blink a few times and look down at the shovel in her hand, covered in a red liquid I somehow know in my gut to be blood. Slowly, a smile forms on her lips, and I break out into a scream.

My body shoots upright, and I'm covered in sweat, my screaming still ringing throughout the house. But then I realize—I'm not screaming. My mouth is open, panting, but there's no sound coming out. The sound I'm hearing is coming from somewhere else; it's a loud, screeching sound, almost like a siren.

It's an alarm. It's *my* alarm. My alarm is going off.

Suddenly, I remember Bert Rhodes. I remember him in my home, sticking sensors on my windows, pointing his drill in my direction. I remember his warning.

I never wondered what it was like to lose my life. I'm talking about taking one.

I fling myself from bed, hearing the frantic sound of footsteps downstairs. He's probably trying to disable it, stop the ringing before coming upstairs and strangling the life from my lungs the same way he strangled those girls. I run toward the closet and fling open the door, my hands searching blindly across the floor for the box that holds Daniel's gun. I've never used a gun. I have no idea how to use a gun. But it's here, and it's loaded, and as long as I can have it in my hands when Bert walks into my bedroom, I'll feel like I have a fighting chance.

I'm flinging dirty clothes across the floor when I hear the sound of footsteps coming up the stairs. *Come on,* I whisper. *Come on, where is it?* I grab a couple of shoe-boxes, opening them up before tossing them to the side when I see nothing but boots nestled inside. The foot-steps are closer now, louder. The alarm is still blaring through the house. The neighbors are surely awake, I think. He can't get away with this. He can't kill me with the alarm going off like this. Still, I keep search-ing until my hands find another box pushed into the corner. I grab it, yank it closer, inspect it in my grip. It looks like a jewelry box—why would Daniel have a jewelry box? But it's long, slender, about the right size for a gun, so I open the lid quickly, feeling the presence of a person just outside my closed door.

My breath catches in my throat as I look down at the box now opened in my lap. Inside, there is no gun, but something far more terrifying.

It's a necklace with a long silver chain, a single pearl on the end, and three small diamonds clustered at the top.

CHAPTER TWENTY-SEVEN

Chloeeee.

I hear a voice outside my bedroom door, barely audible above the shrieking of the alarm. It's calling my name, but my eyes are still glued to the box in my hands. The box I found pushed to the back of the closet. The box that holds Aubrey Gravino's necklace draped gently inside. All of a sudden, the sounds swirling around me evaporate away and I'm twelve again, sitting in my parents' bedroom, watching that tiny ballerina twirl. I can almost hear the chimes, that rhythmic lullaby lulling me into a trance as I stare at the pile of jewelry ripped from dead skin.

CHLOE!

My eyes glance up just as my bedroom door starts to creak open. Instinctively, I shut the box and slide it back into the closet, throwing a pile of clothes on top of it. I look around, looking for something, *anything,* to arm myself with when I see a man's leg step into the bedroom, followed by a body. I'm so sure I'm about to see Bert Rhodes's dead eyes and outstretched arms come barreling toward me that I barely even register Daniel's face as he turns the corner and stares at me, huddled on the floor.

"Chloe, my God," he says. "What are you doing?"

"Daniel?" I push myself up from the floor and start to run toward him until I stop in my tracks, remembering the necklace. Wondering how the hell that could have found its way into our closet unless someone put it there . . . and I know *I* didn't put it there. I hesitate. "What are you doing here?"

"I called you," he yells. "How do you turn this fucking thing off?"

I blink a few times before pushing past him and running down the stairs, pounding a string of numbers into the system and shutting off the alarm. The deafening siren has now been replaced with deafening silence, and I can feel Daniel behind me, staring at me from the stairs.

"Chloe," he says. "What were you doing in the closet?"

"I was looking for the gun," I whisper, too afraid to turn around. "I didn't know you were coming home tonight. You said tomorrow."

"I called you," he says again. "Your phone was off. I left a message."

I hear him walk down the stairs and make his way over to me. I know I should turn around; I know I should face him. But right now, I can't look at him. I can't bring myself to look at his expression because I'm too terrified of what it might reveal.

"I didn't want to stay away all night," he says. "I wanted to get home to you."

I feel his arms snake around my waist, and I bite my lip as he pushes his nose into my shoulder, inhaling slowly before kissing the side of my neck. He smells . . . different. Like sweat mixed with honey and vanilla perfume.

"I'm sorry if I scared you," he says. "I missed you."

I swallow, my body tense against his. The medicated calm I felt earlier tonight has evaporated completely, and

I can feel my heart crashing against my chest with startling force. Daniel seems to feel it, too, and squeezes me
tighter.

"I missed you, too," I whisper, because I don't know
what else to say.

"Let's get back into bed," he says, running his hands
up my shirt and across my stomach. "I'm sorry I woke
you."

"It's fine," I say, trying to pull away. But before I can,
he flips me around so I'm facing him, and his arms hug
me tighter, his lips pressing hard against my ear. I feel
his breath hot on my cheek.

"Hey, you don't have to be afraid," he whispers, his
fingers combing my hair. "I've got you."

My jaw clenches as I remember those exact words ex-
iting the mouth of my father. Me, running down that
gravel roadway and up our steps, slamming into his
outstretched arms. Him, hugging me tight. His body a
vessel of warmth and safety and protection, whispering
into my ear.

I've got you. I've got you.

That's what Daniel has always been to me: warmth.
Safety. Protection not only from the outside world, but
also from myself. But in this moment, locked in his
arms, the heat of his breath sending goose bumps up
my neck, a dead girl's necklace hidden in the depths of
our closet, I start to wonder if there is more to this man
than what I've always thought. I think back to all those
times I've gotten involved with someone and wondered:
What are they hiding? What aren't they telling me?

I think about my brother's words, all of his warnings.

*How can you really know someone that well in a
year?*

Daniel releases me from his grip and holds me by my
shoulders, smiling in my direction. He looks tired, his
skin uncharacteristically baggy and his hair ruffled out

of place. I wonder what he's been up to tonight, why he looks like this. He seems to notice me scanning his features because he runs his hand over his face, pulling his eyelids down with it.

"Long day," he says, sighing. "Lots of driving. I'm going to shower, then let's get to sleep."

I nod, watching as he turns around and walks up the stairs. I refuse to move until I hear the hiss of the showerhead come alive, and only then do I exhale, unclench my fists, and follow behind him, cocooning myself as tightly as I can in the covers of our shared bed. When Daniel emerges from the shower, I pretend to be asleep, trying hard not to flinch when his bare skin slides against mine, when his hands start to massage the nape of my neck, or when he emerges from the covers minutes later, tiptoes across the bedroom, and slides the closet door shut.

CHAPTER TWENTY-EIGHT

I wake up to the smell of popping bacon grease and the sound of Etta James's earthy vocals traveling down the hall. I don't remember falling asleep. I had been actively trying not to, the weight of Daniel's arms draped across my torso constricting me like a body bag. But I suppose it was inevitable; I couldn't fight it forever, especially after the tranquilizer cocktail I had downed just before he came home. I sit up in bed, trying to ignore the gentle pounding in my skull, the puffiness of my eyes constricting my vision to two crescent-shaped slits. I glance around the room—he's not here. He's downstairs, making me breakfast, the way he always does.

I slip out of the covers and creep down the stairs, listening for the sound of his humming. I hear it, confirming that he is, in fact, downstairs, probably hopping around in that gingham apron as he flips chocolate-chip pancakes with little drawings etched inside. A cat with whiskers drawn on with a toothpick, a smiling face, a bulging heart. I slink back up the stairs, back into the bedroom, and slide open our closet door.

The necklace I found last night belongs to Aubrey Gravino. I have no doubt in my mind. Not only did I see it in her *MISSING* picture, but I saw the matching

earring. I held it in my hand, inspected the trinity of diamonds and the pearl apex. I start to push the laundry
aside, my mind less hazy now that the wine and Xanax
are fully out of my system. I think back to the list of
people I recounted to Aaron. The people who would
know about the jewelry my father took and stashed in
the back of his closet.

My family. The police. The victims' parents.

And Daniel. I had told Daniel. I had told him *everything*.

I didn't even think to include Daniel . . . because why
would I? Why would I have reason to suspect my own
fiancé? I still don't know the answer to that question, but
it's one I need to find out.

I lift up the LSU sweatshirt I remember tossing over
the box and reach my hand out to grab it . . . but it's not
there. The box isn't there. I push aside more laundry,
grabbing heaps of clothes and throwing them to the
side. I sweep my arms across the floor, hoping to feel
it hiding beneath a pair of jeans or a tangled-up belt or
a rogue shoe.

But I don't feel it. I don't see it. It's not there.

I lean back onto my legs, a sinking feeling settling in
my stomach. I know I saw it. I remember grabbing the
box, holding it in my hands, opening the lid and seeing the necklace nestled inside . . . but I also remember hearing Daniel get up last night to close the closet
door. Maybe he grabbed the box then, too. Hid it somewhere else. Or maybe he woke up early this morning
and moved it when I was sleeping.

I exhale slowly, trying to formulate a plan. I need
to find that necklace. I need to know what it's doing in
my house. The thought of bringing this evidence to the
police—the thought of bringing *Daniel* to the police—
makes my stomach lurch. It's almost laughable, how
ridiculous it seems. But I can't just ignore it. I can't

pretend that I didn't see it. That I didn't smell that perfume on Daniel last night, that I didn't notice the way his collar was damp with sweat. Suddenly, another memory rises to the surface. My brother, last night, his weary eyes resting on that bottle of pills.

His briefcase is full of that shit.

I think back to Lacey's autopsy, to the coroner poking at her rigid limbs.

We found heavy traces of Diazepam in her hair.

Daniel would have the drugs. Daniel would have the opportunity. He disappears for days on end, alone. I think back to all the times he has taken off on a business trip I didn't know about or remember, and instead of questioning him, I had blamed myself for forgetting. I went to Detective Thomas yesterday with a tip about Bert Rhodes based on far less than this. It was a theory formed out of circumstance and suspicion and a hint of hysteria, if I'm being honest with myself. But this . . . this isn't suspicion. This isn't hysteria. This seems like proof. Solid, concrete proof that my fiancé is somehow involved in something he shouldn't be. Something terrible.

I stand up, sliding the closet door shut and sitting on the edge of my bed. I hear the clatter of a skillet being lowered into the sink, the *hiss* of steam as the faucet sprays water onto the hot surface. I need to know what's going on. If not for myself, then for those girls. For Aubrey. For Lacey. For Lena. If I can't find the necklace, I need to find something. Something that will lead me to answers.

I walk down the stairs again, ready to face Daniel. I turn the corner to find him standing in the kitchen, placing two plates of pancakes and bacon on our small breakfast-nook table. There are two mugs of coffee steaming on the kitchen island, a pitcher of orange juice with sweat dripping down the sides.

It was just one week ago when I thought that this was karma. The perfect fiancé in exchange for the worst possible father. Now I'm not so sure.

"Good morning," I say, standing in the doorway. He looks up and flashes a smile. It seems genuine.

"Good morning," he says, grabbing a mug. He walks over and hands it to me, kissing the top of my head. "Interesting night last night, huh?"

"Yeah, sorry about that," I say, scratching at the spot his lips just left. "I think I was kind of in shock, you know. Waking up to the alarm like that and not knowing it was you downstairs."

"I know, I feel horrible," he says, leaning against the island. "I must have scared you to death."

"Yeah," I say. "A little bit."

"At least we know the alarm works."

I try to crack a smile. "Yeah."

This isn't the first time I've struggled to find the words to say to Daniel, but usually it's because nothing ever seems good enough to say. Nothing ever seems to convey how deep my feelings are, how absolutely I had fallen for him in such a short amount of time. But now, the reasons are so vastly different, it's hard to wrap my mind around. It's hard to believe that this is actually happening. For a split second, my eyes glance over at my purse on the counter, at the bottle of Xanax I know is tucked inside. I think about the pill I took before chasing it with two glasses of wine, the way I had sunken into the couch as if I had been falling through clouds, the memory-like dream I was experiencing just before the alarm screeched to life. I think about college, the last time something like this happened. The last time I was mixing drugs with alcohol in such a reckless manner. I think about the way the police had stared at me then the same way Detective Thomas was staring at me in his office yesterday afternoon—the same way

Cooper was staring—silently questioning the validity of my mind, my memories. Me.

I wonder, for a second, if maybe I imagined the necklace. If maybe it wasn't there at all. If maybe I was just confused, conflating the past with the present, the way I have so many times before.

"You're mad at me," Daniel says, walking over to the table and taking a seat. He gestures to the chair across from him, and I follow, dropping my phone on the counter before sitting down and staring at the food below me. It looks good, but I'm not hungry. "And I don't blame you. I've been gone . . . a lot. I've been leaving you here all by yourself in the middle of all of this."

"In the middle of all what?" I ask, my eyes drilling into the chocolate chips poking out of the browned batter. I pick up my fork and stab one with a single prong, scraping it off with my teeth.

"The wedding," he says. "Planning everything. And, you know, what's been on the news."

"It's okay. I know you've been busy."

"But not today," he says, cutting into his breakfast and taking a bite. "Today, I'm not busy. Today, I'm yours. And we've got plans."

"And what exactly are those plans?"

"It's a surprise. Dress comfortably, we're going to be outside. Can you be ready in twenty minutes?"

I hesitate for a second, wondering if it's a good idea. I open my mouth, start to come up with an excuse, when I hear my phone vibrate on the kitchen counter.

"One second," I say, pushing my chair back, grateful for the excuse to step away, to stop talking. I walk over to the counter and see Cooper's name on the screen and suddenly our argument last night feels so trivial. Maybe Cooper was right. All this time, maybe he had seen something in Daniel that I couldn't see. Maybe he's been trying to warn me.

This relationship you're in. It doesn't seem healthy.

I swipe my finger across the screen, ducking into the living room.

"Hey, Coop," I say, my voice low. "I'm glad you called."

"Yeah, me, too. Look, Chloe. I'm sorry about last night—"

"It's fine," I say. "Really, I'm over it. I overreacted."

The line is quiet and I can hear his breath. It sounds shaky, like he's walking fast, his pounding feet on the pavement sending a vibration up his spine.

"Is everything okay?"

"No," he says. "No, not really."

"What is it?"

"It's Mom," he says at last. "Riverside called me this morning, they said it was urgent."

"What was urgent?"

"Apparently she's been refusing to eat," he says. "Chloe, they think she's dying."

CHAPTER TWENTY-NINE

I'm out the front door in less than five minutes; my shoes are barely on, the fabric on the back of my sneakers digging blisters into my heels as I run across the driveway.

"Chloe," Daniel calls after me, his open hand slapping the door, pushing it back open. "Where are you going?"

"I have to go," I yell back. "It's my mom."

"What about your mom?"

He's rushing out of the house now, too, tugging a white T-shirt over his head. I'm fumbling through my purse, trying to find the keys to unlock my car.

"She isn't eating," I say. "She hasn't eaten in days. I have to go, I have to—"

I stop, drop my head in my hands. All these years, I've been ignoring my mother. I've been treating her like an itch that I refused to scratch. I guess I thought that if I focused on it, on her, it would be overbearing, impossible to focus on anything else. But if I ignored it, eventually the pain would just subside on its own. It would never be *gone*—I knew it would still be there, it would always be there, ready to begin prickling across my skin as soon as I would let it—but it would be less noticeable, like background noise. Static. Just like my father, the reality of what she is—what she

did to herself, to us—had been too much to handle. I
had wanted her gone. But never, not once, did I stop
to think about how I would feel if she actually *were*
gone. If she passed away, by herself in that musty room
in Riverside, unable to express her final words, her
dying thoughts. The realization I have always known
settles over me; it's thick and suffocating, like trying to
breathe through a damp towel.

I have abandoned her. I have left my mother to die
alone.

"Chloe, hang on a second," Daniel says. "Talk to me."

"No," I say, shaking my head, digging my hands
back into my purse again. "Not now, Daniel. I don't
have time."

"Chloe—"

I hear the jangling of metal behind me, and I freeze
in place, turning around slowly. Daniel is behind
me, holding my keys in the air. I grab for them, and
he yanks them back, out of my reach.

"I'm coming with you," he says. "You need me for
this."

"Daniel, no. Just give me my keys—"

"Yes," he says. "Goddamn it, Chloe. It's nonnegotia-
ble. Now get in the car."

I look at him, shocked at this sudden flare of anger.
At his flushed-red skin and bulging eyes. Then, almost
as suddenly, his expression shifts back.

"I'm sorry," he says, exhaling and reaching out toward
me. He puts his hands on mine, and I flinch. "Chloe, I'm
sorry. But you have to stop pushing me away. Let me
help you."

I look at him again, at the way his face has completely
changed in seconds. At the concern bunching his eyebrows now, the folds in his forehead, shiny and deep. I
drop my hands in surrender; I don't want Daniel there.
I don't want him in the same room as my mother—my

dying, vulnerable mother—but I don't have the energy to fight. I don't have the *time* to fight.

"Fine," I say. "Drive fast."

I recognize Cooper's car as soon as we pull into the lot; I jump out before Daniel can even put ours in Park, running through the automatic doors. I can hear Daniel behind me, his sneakers squeaking on the tile, trying to catch up, but I don't wait. I take a right down my mother's hallway, run past the collection of cracked doors, the quiet murmurs of televisions and radios and residents mumbling to themselves. When I turn in to her room, I see my brother first, sitting on her bedside.

"Coop." I run toward him, collapsing onto my mother's bed as I let Cooper pull me into a hug. "How is she?"

I look over at my mother, her eyes closed. Her already thin frame looks even thinner, as if she's lost ten pounds in a week. Her wrists look as if they could snap, her cheeks two hollowed out caves draped in tissue paper skin.

"You must be Chloe."

I jump at the voice coming from the corner of the room; I hadn't noticed the doctor there, standing in a white coat with a clipboard pushed against his hip.

"My name is Doctor Glenn," he says. "I'm one of the on-call doctors at Riverside. I spoke to Cooper this morning, over the phone, but I don't believe we've met."

"No, we haven't," I say, not bothering to stand. I look back down at my mother, at the gentle rise and fall of her chest. "When did this happen?"

"It's been a little under a week."

"A *week*? Why are we just now learning about this?"

A noise erupts from the hallway that diverts our collective attention; it's Daniel, his body slamming into the doorframe. I see a bead of sweat trickle down his forehead, and he wipes it with the back of his hand.

"What is he doing here?" Cooper starts to stand, but I put my hand on his leg.

"It's fine," I say. "Not now."

"We are typically equipped to handle these types of situations; as you can imagine, it's fairly common in older patients," the doctor continues, his eyes darting between Daniel and us. "But if it continues on for any longer, we're going to need to transfer her to Baton Rouge General."

"Do we know what the underlying cause is?"

"Physically, she's in fine health. There is no illness we can identify that could be causing an aversion to food. So, in short, we don't know—and in all the years that she's been in our care, we've never once had this issue with her."

I look back down at her, at the sagging skin on her neck, her collarbones popping out like two drumsticks.

"It's almost as if she just woke up one morning and decided it was time."

I glance at Cooper, looking for answers. My entire life, I have always found what I've been searching for somewhere in his expression. In the imperceptible twitch of his lip as he tried to stifle a smile, the way his cheek dimpled slightly when he chewed on the inside of his mouth in thought. There has only been one time I can remember when my gaze was met with nothing but a blank stare; just one time when I had turned to Cooper and realized, with sinking dread, that even he couldn't help—that nobody could help. It was in our living room, our legs pretzeled on the floor. Our eyes illuminated from the glow of the TV screen, listening to our father talk about his darkness, ankle chains rattling, the drip of a rogue tear staining his legal pad.

But now I see it again. Cooper's eyes, not meeting mine, but staring straight ahead. Boring into Daniel's, both their bodies stiff as boards.

"Your mother is uncommunicative, of course," Doctor Glenn continues, oblivious to the tension in the room. "But we were hoping, maybe by coming here, you could try to get through."

"Yes, of course," I say, peeling my eyes from Cooper and looking back down to my mom. I grab her hand, hold it in mine. She's still, at first, until I feel a gentle tapping, her fingers moving slowly against the thin skin of my wrist. I look down at the tiny flicker of movement. Her eyes are still closed, but her fingers—they're moving.

I look back at Cooper, at Daniel, at Doctor Glenn. None of them seem to notice.

"Can I have a moment alone with her?" I ask, my heartbeat rising into my neck. My palms start to feel slick with sweat, but I refuse to let go of her hand. "Please?"

Doctor Glenn nods, walking silently past her bed and out the door.

"You, too," I say, looking first at Daniel and then at Cooper. "Both of you."

"Chloe," Cooper starts, but I shake my head.

"Please. Just a couple minutes. I'd like to, you know . . . just in case."

"Sure." He nods gently, placing his hand on top of mine and squeezing. "Whatever you need."

Then he stands up, pushes past Daniel, and walks into the hallway without another word.

I'm alone with my mother now, and memories of our last meeting start rushing through my mind. The way I had told her about the missing girls, the similarities of it all. The déjà vu. And if Doctor Glenn's time line is correct, that would have been around the time she had stopped eating.

I don't know what I'm so worried about, I had said. *Dad's in prison. It's not like he can be involved or anything.*

The tapping of her fingers, frantic, before I had rushed out of the room, our visit cut short. I've never told Cooper or Daniel or anyone else about the way I believe my mother can communicate—the gentle movement of her fingers, a tap means *Yes, I hear you*—because, quite honestly, I wasn't even sure if I believed it myself. But now, I wonder.

"Mom," I whisper, somehow feeling both ridiculous and terrified. "Can you hear me?"

Tap.

I look down at her fingers. They moved again—I know they did.

"Does this have something to do with what we talked about the last time I was here?"

Tap, tap.

I exhale, my eyes darting from her palm to the hallway, the door still open.

"Do you know something about these murdered girls?"

Tap, tap, tap. Tap, tap.

I pull my eyes away from the hallway and back toward my hand, at my mother's fingers twitching frantically across my palm. This cannot be a coincidence; it has to mean something. Then I pull my gaze higher, toward my mother's face, and immediately, my body flies backward, a jolt of adrenaline and fear that causes me to rip my hand away from her palm and cover my mouth in disbelief.

Her eyes are open, and she is staring straight at me.

CHAPTER THIRTY

Daniel and I are in the car again, silent other than the gentle pounding of the wind as it rips through our open windows, giving me a much-needed breath of fresh air. I can't stop thinking about my mother, about the conversation that just took place in her room.

"Do you think you could spell it?" I had stuttered, staring into her wide, watery eyes. Tears were stuck to her eyelashes like beads of dew on grass, quivering. I looked down at her fingers, convulsing against mine. "Give me one second."

I walked back into the hallway, poking my head into the waiting room. Daniel and Cooper were sitting with a few chairs between them, silent and stiff, their backs facing my direction. Then I shuffled across the hall, toward the living area, riffling through the table filled with old books that smelled like mothballs, pages stained brown. I grabbed a random assortment of DVDs, the donated rejects that nobody wanted to watch, and pushed them aside until I reached the board games. Then I hurried back to my mother's room, pulling a small, velvet bag from my pocket. Scrabble tiles.

"Okay," I said, feeling self-conscious as I dumped them onto her comforter and started flipping them over, one by one, until we had a full alphabet, each letter facing up. I couldn't imagine this possibly working, but I had to try. "I'm going to point to a letter. We'll start simple: *Y* means yes, *N* means no. Tap when I hit the one you want."

I looked down at the rows of letters on her bed, the prospect of having an actual conversation with my mother for the first time in twenty years both exhilarating and mind-numbing. I took a deep breath, and then I started to talk.

"Do you understand how this is going to work?"

I pointed to the *N*—nothing. Then I pointed to the *Y*. *Tap.*

I exhaled, my heart beating faster. All these years, my mother knew. She understood. She was hearing me talk. I just never took the time to let her talk back.

"Do you know something about these murdered girls?"

N—nothing. *Y*—*tap.*

"Are these murders somehow related to Breaux Bridge?"

N—nothing. *Y*—*tap.*

I stopped, thinking hard about my next question. I knew we didn't have a lot of time; soon, Cooper or Daniel or Doctor Glenn would walk back in, and I didn't want them to catch me like this. I looked back down at the tiles, then I asked my final question.

"How do I prove it?"

I had started with the *A*, my finger pointing to the tile in the top left corner—nothing. I moved on to *B*, then *C*. Finally, when I pointed at *D*, her fingers moved.

"*D*?"

Tap.

"Okay, first letter, *D*."

Then I started back at the beginning—*A*.

Tap.

My heart lurched in my chest.

"*D-A?*"

Tap.

She was spelling Daniel. I blew the air through my pursed lips, slowly, trying to stay calm. I lifted my fingers and pointed to the *N,* my eyes drilling into her fingers . . . until a noise from the hallway jolted me into action.

"Chloe?" I could hear Cooper getting closer, feet from the open door. "Chloe, you doing okay?"

I swept my arm across the bedspread and collected the tiles, grabbing them all into my palm and turning around just as Cooper appeared in the doorway.

"I just wanted to check on you," he said, his eyes moving from me to my mother. A gentle smile cracked across his lips as he moved toward us, sitting on the edge of the bed. "You got her eyes to open."

"Yeah," I said, the sweat from my palm making the tiles greasy, slipping against each other in my grip. "Yeah, I did."

Daniel flips on his blinker now, and we pull into a gravel driveway, the sound of kicked-up pebbles flicking off the windshield forcing him to close the windows. I lift my head slowly, shaking myself from my memory, and realize that I no longer recognize our surroundings.

"Where are we?" I ask. We're winding down dusty side roads now; I don't know how long we've been driving, but I do know this is not the route back home.

"We're almost there," Daniel says, smiling at me.

"Where is *there*?"

"You'll see."

Suddenly, it feels claustrophobic in here. I reach for the air-conditioning and push the knob all the way to the right, leaning into the blast of cold air.

"Daniel, I need to go home."

"No," he says. "No, Chloe, I am not letting you

wallow in self-pity at home right now. I told you I had
plans for us today, and we're going to do them."

I inhale deeply, turning to face my window, watching the trees fly past as we inch deeper into the woods. I
think about my mother, spelling out Daniel's name. How
could she possibly know? How could she know who he
is if they've never met? The uneasiness I felt this morning is quickly returning. I look down at my phone, at
the single bar of service, appearing and disappearing
as it struggles to find a signal. Here I am—miles from
home, trapped in a car with a man in possession of a
dead girl's necklace, no way to call for help. Maybe
he saw me holding it last night; maybe I didn't stash it
back into the closet as quickly as I thought I did. My
feet graze my purse and I think about my pepper spray,
dutifully tucked into the bottom. At least I have that.

*Don't be ridiculous, Chloe. He won't hurt you. He
won't.*

A shock wave jolts through my body, and I realize
that I sound just like my mother. I *am* my mother. I am
my mother sitting in Sheriff Dooley's office, making
rationalizations about my father despite the growing
mountain of evidence stacking up against him. My eyes
sting as a pool of tears wells up inside, threatening
to break free. I lift my hand and wipe at them quickly,
careful not to let Daniel see.

I think of my mother, bed-bound back in Riverside,
her life confined to the ever-shrinking walls of her own
troubled mind. And I understand now. I understand why
she did it. I always thought she went back to my father because she was weak; because she didn't want
to be alone. Because she didn't know how to leave
him—she didn't *want* to leave him. But now, in this
moment, I understand my mother more than I ever have
before. I understand that she went back to him because

she was desperately searching for any trace of evidence that would point in the opposite direction, a scrap of something she could cling to that proved she wasn't in love with a monster. And when she couldn't find it, she was forced to take a good hard look at herself. She was forced to ask herself the very questions that are now swirling in my own mind, constricting in the same way hers must have been.

She was forced to acknowledge the fact that she *was* in love with a monster. And if she was in love with a monster . . . what did that make her?

I feel the car start to roll to a stop. I glance out the window again and see that we're deep in the woods, the only break in the trees a small, swampy stream, presumably the entrance to a larger body of water.

"We're here," he says, turning off the car and stuffing the keys in his pocket. "Now get out."

"Where is *here*?" I ask again, trying to keep my voice light.

"You'll see."

"Daniel," I say, but he's already out of the car, walking over to the passenger side and opening my door for me. What used to feel like a chivalrous act now feels more ominous, like he's forcing me out against my will. I reluctantly take his hand and step out of the car, wincing as he slams the door shut behind me, my purse, phone, and pepper spray still inside.

"Close your eyes."

"Daniel—"

"Close them."

I close my eyes, taking in the absolute silence around us. I wonder if this is where he took them, Aubrey and Lacey. I wonder if this is where he did it. It's the perfect spot—isolated, hidden. *He won't hurt you.* I hear the buzzing of mosquitos around us, the scamper of some animal rustling the leaves in the distance. *He won't.* I hear footsteps, Daniel's, walking back toward my car, unlocking the trunk, pulling something out. *He won't hurt you, Chloe.* I hear a thud as whatever it is is yanked from inside and lands on the ground. He's walking back toward me now, carrying something. I hear it scraping against the ground. The scraping of metal against dirt.

A shovel.

I swing around, ready to sprint into the woods and hide. Ready to scream at the top of my lungs, hoping against all odds that there is someone else out here. Someone to hear me. Someone to help. When I face Daniel, his eyes are wide. He wasn't expecting me to turn around. He wasn't expecting me to fight. I look down at his hands, at the long, slender thing he's clutching in his palms. I raise my arms to block him from striking me with it when I get a good, hard look at it and realize . . . it's not a shovel. Daniel isn't holding a shovel.

It's an oar.

"I thought we'd go kayaking," he says, his eyes darting over to the water. I turn, looking at the small opening where the trees part and the swamp water peeks through. Next to it, partially hidden behind the foliage, is a wooden rack with four kayaks perched inside, covered in leaves and dirt and spiderwebs. I exhale.

"This place is pretty hidden, but it's been here forever," he says, holding the oar sheepishly in his hands. He steps closer and holds it out for me to take. I grab it, feeling the heaviness of it in my arms. "The kayaks are free to use, you just need to bring your own paddle. It wouldn't fit in my car, so I took your keys and loaded it into your trunk this morning."

I look at him, studying him closely. If he were planning on using this thing as a weapon, he wouldn't have handed it to me. I look down at the paddle and then back to the kayaks, the stillness of the water, the cloudless sky. I glance over at the car—my only way out of here, I know. The keys are in his pocket; I have no other way home. So I decide in this moment—if he can act, so can I.

"Daniel," I say, dropping my head. "Daniel, I'm sorry. I don't know what's wrong with me."

"You're tense. And that's completely understandable, Chloe. That's why we're here. So I can help you relax."

I look at him, still unsure if I can trust him. I can't ignore the flood of evidence over the last few hours. The necklace and the perfume, the way Cooper had glared at him at Riverside, as if he could sense something in him that I couldn't—something evil, something dark. My mother's warning. The way he had grabbed my wrist yesterday, pinning me to the couch; the way he had snapped at me this morning, dangling my keys just out of reach.

But then there are the other things, too. He had a security system installed. He took me to Riverside to see my mother and threw a surprise party and planned a day for just us two. It's exactly the type of romantic gesture that he has always done from the moment we first met, lifting that box out of my arms and hoisting it onto his shoulder. The type of gesture I was looking forward to enjoying for the rest of our lives. I can't help but smile as I take in his self-conscious grin—habit, I suppose—and that's when I make up my mind: Daniel may hurt people, but I don't yet believe that he would hurt me.

"Okay," I say, nodding. "Okay, let's go."

Daniel's smile grows wider, forging ahead to the kayak stand and lifting one down from the wooden pegs. He drags it across the forest floor and brushes off the debris, clearing out the cobwebs that have collected in the center before pushing it into the water.

"Ladies first," he says, holding out his arm. I let him

grab my hand and take a shaky first step into the boat before instinctively clutching his shoulder as he helps lower me down. He waits until I'm situated before he jumps into the seat behind me and pushes us off from the dirt, and I feel us floating away.

Once we pass the clearing, I can't help but gasp at the beauty of this place. The bayou is wide and lazy, peppered with cypress trees emerging from the murky water, their knees breaking the surface like fingers reaching for something to grab. There are curtains of Spanish moss cascading the sunlight into millions of twinkling pinpricks, a chorus of frogs croaking in unison with their wet, guttural sounds. Algae floats sluggishly along the surface, and out of the corner of my eye, I see the slow creep of an alligator, his beady eyes watching an egret before it lifts gracefully from its skinny legs and flaps into the safety of the trees.

"It's beautiful, isn't it?"

Daniel is paddling quietly behind me, the sound of the sloshing water pushing past the kayak lulling me into a daze. My eyes stay on the alligator, on the way it lurks so silently, hidden in plain sight.

"Gorgeous," I say. "It reminds me of . . ."

I stop, my unfinished thought hanging heavy in the air.

"It reminds me of home. But . . . in a good way. Cooper and I, we used to go to Lake Martin sometimes. Watch the alligators."

"I'm sure your mother loved that."

I smile, remembering. Remembering the way we would scream through the trees: *See ya later, alligator!* The way we would catch turtles with our bare hands, counting the rings on their shells to learn their age. The way we would slather our faces with mud like war paint, chasing each other through the brush before slamming through the front door of our home, getting

scolded by our mother, snickering all the way to the
bathroom before she scrubbed our skin until it was
fleshy and raw. Pushing our nails into our mosquito
bites, little Xs peppering our legs like human tic-tac-
toe boards. Somehow, only Daniel could draw these
memories from me. Only Daniel could coax them out
of their hiding place, out of the hidden recesses of my
mind, out of the secret room I had banished them to
the moment I saw my father's face on the television
screen, crying not for the six lives he had taken, but because he had gotten caught. Only Daniel could force me
to remember that it wasn't all bad. I lean back into the
kayak and close my eyes.

"This is my favorite part," he says, pushing our boat
around a corner. I open my eyes, and there, in the distance, is Cypress Stables. "Only six more weeks."

The property is even more breathtaking from the
water, that large, white farmhouse looming over acres
of perfectly manicured grass. The rounded columns
holding up its triple wraparound porches, the rocking chairs still dancing in the breeze. I watch them
sway, back and forth, back and forth. I imagine myself
walking down those magnificent wooden steps, walking toward the water, toward Daniel.

Then suddenly, out of nowhere, Detective Thomas's
words start to echo across the water, disturbing my perfect reverie.

What exactly is your connection to Aubrey Gravino?

I don't have one. I don't know Aubrey Gravino. I try
to silence the sound, but for some reason, I can't get it
out of my head. I can't get *her* out of my head. Her liner-
smudged eyes and ashy brown hair. Her long, skinny
arms. Her youthfully tan skin.

"From the moment I saw it, I wanted it," Daniel says
from behind me. But I barely register his words. I'm too
focused on those rocking chairs, swaying back and forth

in the wind. They're empty now, but they weren't always empty. There was a girl before. A tan, skinny girl rocking lazily against the column in her leather riding boots, sun-bleached and worn.

That's my granddaughter. This land has been in our family for generations.

I remember Daniel waving. The uncrossing of the legs and the pulling down of the dress. The self-conscious way she dipped her head before waving back. The sudden emptiness of the porch. The rocking chair slowing to a halt.

She likes to come here sometimes after school. Do her homework on the porch.

Until two weeks ago, when she didn't make it.

CHAPTER THIRTY-ONE

I'm staring at a picture of Aubrey on my laptop, a picture I've never seen before. It's a small image, slightly pixelated from me zooming in on her face, but clear enough to know for sure. It's her.

She's seated on the ground with her legs tucked under a white dress, those same leather riding boots hiked up to her knees, her hands resting on a perfectly manicured lawn of pristine green grass. It's a family portrait, and she's surrounded by her parents. Her grandparents. Her aunts and her uncles and her cousins. The image is framed with the same moss-draped oak trees I had envisioned framing the aisle of my wedding; in the background, those same white stairs I had imagined myself walking down, with my veil trailing behind me, are ascending to that giant wraparound porch. To those chairs that never seem to stop moving.

I lift a cardboard cup of coffee to my lips, my eyes still scanning the image. I'm on the official Cypress Stables website, reading about its owners. It really has been in the Gravino family for centuries—what started as a sugarcane farm built in 1787 had gradually transitioned into a horse farm, then eventually, an event venue. Seven generations of Gravinos had lived there, producing some of Louisiana's best cane syrup. Once they realized they were sitting on such a desirable piece of land, they renovated the farmhouse and decorated the barn, the immaculately ornamented inside and meticulously pruned outside providing the perfect Louisiana backdrop for weddings, corporate events, and other celebrations.

I remember the vague familiarity of seeing Aubrey's *MISSING* picture. That nagging feeling that I knew her, somehow. And now I know why. She was there the day we visited the Stables. She was there when we had toured the grounds, when we had booked the venue for our wedding. I had seen her. *Daniel* had seen her.

And now, she's dead.

My eyes move from Aubrey's face to the face of her parents. The parents I had seen on the news almost two weeks ago. Her father had been crying into his hands. Her mother had been pleading into the camera: *We want our baby back.* Next, I look at her grandmother. That same sweet woman struggling with that iPad, trying to calm my fabricated fears with promises of air-conditioners and bug spray. I imagine the fact that Aubrey Gravino came from a locally famous family was mentioned in the news at some point, but I hadn't known that. After the discovery of her body, I had been deliberately avoiding the news. I had been driving around town with the radio turned off. And once her headshot was replaced by Lacey's, that detail no longer mattered. The media had moved on. The world had moved on. Aubrey was just another vaguely familiar face lost in a sea of other faces. Of other missing girls just like her.

"Doctor Davis?"

I hear a knock and look up from my laptop, at Melissa peering at me from behind the cracked door. She's in running shorts and a tank top, her hair pulled back into a bun, and a gym bag flung over one shoulder. It's six thirty a.m., the sky outside my office just barely starting to morph from black to blue. There's something inherently lonely about a morning spent awake when nobody else seems to be—being the one to turn on the coffee, the only car on an abandoned highway, arriving to an empty office building and flipping on the lights. I had been so engrossed in Aubrey's image, so deafened by the absolute silence surrounding me, I hadn't even heard her come in.

"Good morning." I smile, waving her inside. "You're here early."

"I could say the same for you." She steps inside and closes the door behind her before wiping a bead of sweat trickling down her forehead. "Do you have an early appointment today?"

I sense a panic in her expression, a fear that she had overlooked something on my calendar and now, here she was, showing up to work in gym clothes. I shake my head.

"No, I'm just trying to catch up on some work. Last week was . . . well, you know how it was. I was distracted."

"Yeah, we both were."

The truth is, I couldn't stand to be in the same house as Daniel for a minute longer than necessary. Sitting in that kayak, the water bobbing us gently as I stared at Cypress Stables in the distance, I had finally allowed myself to be scared. Not just suspicious . . . scared. Scared of the man who was sitting right behind me, my neck within grabbing distance of his hands. Scared of sharing a roof with a monster—a monster that hid in plain sight, like that alligator gliding across the surface of the water. Like my father twenty years ago. Not only did I have the necklace nagging at my conscience, Cooper's distrust, and my mother's warning, but now I had this. I had another dead girl linked to me—linked to

Daniel. And just like I had been keeping secrets from Daniel, in that moment, I was positive that he had been keeping them from me, too. Cooper was right—we don't know each other. We're engaged to be married. We're living under the same roof, sleeping together in the same bed. But we're strangers, this man and I. I don't know him. I don't know what he's capable of.

"I'm getting a bit of a headache," I had said to him then, not exactly lying. A wave of nausea was rolling through my stomach as I stared at that house in the distance, at those empty rocking chairs being pushed by phantom legs. I wondered if Aubrey had been wearing the necklace at that very moment, the necklace that was now tucked away somewhere in my home. "Can we turn back?"

Daniel was quiet behind me; I wondered what he was thinking. Why did he take me there? Was he gauging my reaction? Was this part of the fun for him—dangling the truth in front of me, just barely out of reach? Was he warning me? Does he *know* I know? I thought back to my conversation with Aaron, about Cypress Cemetery holding some kind of special meaning. I should have put it together sooner. I first saw Aubrey at Cypress Stables, and her body was found in Cypress Cemetery. I didn't think anything of it before—that name is so common—but now, like Lacey's body showing up behind my office, it seems too coincidental. Too perfect to have been left to chance. Did Daniel want me to recognize Aubrey when her body was found? Or was he genuinely confident enough to show me another piece of the puzzle and expect me not to see the bigger picture that was starting to form?

"Daniel?"

"Sure." His voice was offended, quiet. "Sure, yeah, we can turn back. Everything okay, Chlo?"

I nodded my head, forced myself to peel my eyes from

the farmhouse and focus on something else. Anything else. We paddled back to the landing and rode home in silence, Daniel with his eyes on the road and his lips pursed shut, and me resting my head against the window, massaging my temple with my fingers. When we pulled into the driveway, I muttered something about a nap before retreating to our bedroom, locking the door, and crawling into bed.

"Hey, Mel," I ask now, looking up at my assistant. "Can I ask you a question? It's about the engagement party."

"Sure." She smiles, taking a seat opposite my desk.

"What time did Daniel get there?"

She chews on the inside of her cheek, thinking.

"Not much earlier than you, honestly. Cooper, Shannon, and I were there first. Daniel was running late from work, so we let everyone else in until he showed up, maybe twenty minutes before you did."

I feel that familiar pang in my chest again. Cooper, trying to push his feelings aside. He had been trying to be there for me, despite it all—or maybe because of it all. I imagine him standing at the back of my living room, his face hidden in the crowd. Watching me scream, my arm shooting into my purse, searching frantically. Daniel pulling me in, hands on my hips, working the crowd. It would have been too much for him to handle, I'm sure. Watching Daniel flash that iridescent smile, manipulating me into submission. So he had turned around before I could see him, ducking into the backyard, alone with his pack of cigarettes. Waiting for me there. I don't know how I didn't see it before— stubbornness, I suppose. Selfishness. But now, it was obvious: It had been the same way Cooper had always been there for me—quietly, in the background, the same way his head had bobbed over the sea of other faces at the Crawfish Festival, breaking apart from the crowd. Finding me, comforting me, when I had been alone.

"Okay." I nod, trying to focus. Trying to think back to that day. Lacey had left my office at six thirty; I had left closer to eight, spending some time saving her notes, packing up my office, and taking that call from Aaron. Then I had made a stop at the CVS before pulling into my driveway, probably around eight thirty. That would have given Daniel two hours to grab Lacey from outside my office building, take her to wherever he was keeping her before he stashed her behind the dumpster, and get to the house before I made it home.

Was it possible?

"What did he do when he got there?"

Melissa shifts in her chair, hooking one foot behind the other. She's tenser than she was when she walked in; she knows there's something about these questions that's personal.

"He went upstairs to freshen up; I think he took a shower and changed clothes. He said he'd been driving all day. Then he came back down just as we saw your headlights pull into the driveway. He poured a few glasses of wine and then . . . you walked in."

I nod, smiling again to let her know I appreciate the information, even though inside, I feel like screaming. I remember that moment so perfectly. That moment I saw the sea of people part and Daniel emerge from the crowd. That moment he started walking toward me, wineglasses in hand, and the wave of relief that washed over my panic-stricken body the instant he snaked his arm around my waist and pulled me in. I remember the smell of his spiced body wash, his bleached white grin. I remember feeling so lucky, so goddamn lucky, in that exact moment with him by my side. But now . . . I can't help but wonder what he had been doing immediately *before* that moment. If his soap smelled so strong because he had intentionally lathered it up to wash away the scent of something else. If the clothes he had been wearing before he changed were even in our house anymore, or if he had dumped them somewhere on the side of the road or burned them with matches, incinerating any evidence that could link him to his crimes. Were there traces of her somewhere on his skin as our naked bodies lay intertwined in bed that night—a strand of her hair, a drop of her blood, a ripped out fingernail embedded somewhere that had yet to be found? I wonder about Aubrey, about the night she went missing, and about what we might have done together after he got home. Did Daniel jump into the shower the same way he always did after returning home from a long, lonely drive? Did I decide to join him that night, peeling away his clothes for him as the bathroom fogged up with steam? Did I help him wash her away?

I pinch my nose, closing my eyes. The thought of it makes me sick.

"Chloe?" I hear Melissa's voice, a soft, concerned whisper. "Are you okay?"

"Yeah," I say, lifting my head, smiling weakly. The heaviness of the situation settles over my shoulders. My inexplicit involvement reminds me of twenty years ago—of seeing and not realizing. Of unknowingly leading girls to a predator, or rather, leading a predator to them. I can't help but wonder—if it weren't for me, would they still be alive? All of them?

Suddenly, I feel tired. So, so tired. I barely slept at all last night, Daniel's skin radiating like a furnace, warning me not to get too close. I glance down at my desk drawer, at the collection of pills waiting to be beckoned from the dark. I could tell Melissa to leave. I could close the curtains, escape it all. It's not even seven a.m.

yet—plenty of time to cancel the day's appointments. But I can't do that. I know I can't.

"What does my calendar look like?"

Melissa reaches into her purse and pulls out her phone, navigating to her calendar app and skimming the day's appointments.

"You're pretty full," she says. "Lots of reschedules from the other week."

"Okay, what about tomorrow?"

"Tomorrow, you're booked until four."

I sigh, massaging my temples with my thumbs. I know what I need to do, I just don't have the time to do it. I can't keep canceling on my clients, or else pretty soon, there won't be any left.

But still, I picture my mother's fingers dancing madly across my palm.

How do I prove it?

Daniel. The answer is Daniel.

"You're pretty open on Thursday," Melissa offers, using her forefinger to swipe at her screen. "Appointments in the morning, then nothing after noon."

"Okay," I say, sitting up straighter. "Block the rest of that day off for me, please. Friday, too. I need to take a trip."

CHAPTER THIRTY-TWO

"I'm proud of you, babe."

I glance up from our bedroom floor at Daniel leaning against the doorframe, smiling at me. He's fresh out of the shower, a crisp white towel knotted around his waist and his arms crossed against his bare torso. He walks across the bedroom and starts flipping through a line of pressed white button-ups hanging in the closet. I stare at him for a second, at his perfectly tanned body. His toned arms, his dewy skin. I squint, noticing a scratch across his side, trailing from his stomach to his back. It looks fresh, and I try not to wonder how it got there. Where it came from. Instead, I look back down at my suitcase, at the pile of clothes heaped inside. It's mostly jeans and T-shirts, practical things, and I realize I should probably toss in a dress and some stilettos for appearance's sake—after all, that's the kind of thing you wear on a bachelorette party.

"Who's going to be there, again?"

"It's small," I say, nestling some heels into the corner of the bag. Heels I know I won't be wearing. "Shannon, Melissa, some old work friends. I don't want to make it a big thing."

"Well, I think it's great," he says, picking a shirt from the hanger and hoisting it over his back. He walks toward me, the buttons still gaping open. Normally, I would have stood up, wound my arms around his bare skin, pressed my fingers into the muscles in his back. Normally, I would have kissed him, maybe led him back to bed before we both left for the day, no longer smelling like body wash but instead like each other.

But not today. I can't today. So instead, I smile at him from the floor, then look back down at the clothes in my lap, focusing intently on the shirt I was folding.

"It was your idea," I say, trying to avoid his eyes. I can feel them burrowing into my temple, trying to wade through the coils. "At the engagement party, remember?"

"I remember. I'm glad you listened."

"And when you went to New Orleans, I thought that could be fun," I say, glancing up at him. "An easy drive, not too expensive."

I see his lips twitch, an invisible flicker I never would have noticed had I not already known the truth—that he was never in New Orleans. That the conference he had told me about in such detail—networking on Saturday followed by golfing on Sunday and sessions for the rest of the week—had never actually taken place. Actually, that's a lie. It *had* taken place. Pharmaceutical sales reps had flocked to the city from all across the country, but not Daniel. He wasn't there. I know because I had found the conference website, called the hotel, and asked them to send over a copy of his invoice, claiming to be his assistant filing an expense report. And he wasn't there. No Daniel Briggs had checked in or out of the hotel, let alone registered for the conference. I had no way to confirm his recent trip to Lafayette, but I had a hunch that was a lie, too. That all of these trips he took, all of these long weekends and overnight drives that brought him home deliriously tired yet somehow more alive than ever were just a cover-up for something else. Something dark. And there was only one way to find out for sure.

There are so many things I don't know about my fiancé, but living together has made one thing clear: He is a creature of habit. Every day, when he gets home, he tucks his briefcase neatly into the corner of the dining room, locked and ready for his next trip. And every morning, he goes for a run—four, five, six miles around the neighborhood, followed by a long, hot shower. And so, every day this week, after he kissed my forehead and stepped out of our house, I had crept into the dining room, my fingers pushing the digits back and forth on the combination lock, trying to crack the code. It had been easier than I had expected—he's predictable, in a way. I had tried to think about all the numbers in Daniel's life that could hold some type of meaning—his birthday, my birthday. The address of our home. After all, if Aaron had taught me anything, it's that copycats are sentimental; their lives revolve around hidden messages, secret codes. After days of no luck, I sat down on the dining room floor, thinking, my eyes darting back and forth between his briefcase and our dining room window, just waiting for him to appear.

But then I stood back up, a thought creeping into my mind.

I glanced out the window again before trying one more combination: 72619. I remember lining the numbers up against the little tick marks etched into the lock's side; I remember pushing the slider, hearing that click as the latch unlocked. The creak of the hinges as the satchel fell open, its contents organized neatly inside.

It had worked. The code had worked. 72619.

July 26, 2019.

Our wedding day.

"I'm going to text Shannon and make sure she sends

me pictures," Daniel says now, turning toward the dresser and opening his underwear drawer. He steps into his boxers, a pair of red and green flannel ones I bought him for Christmas, and laughs. "I want photo evidence of you straddling those bartenders on Bourbon Street, you know the ones with the little test-tube shots—"

"No," I say, probably too fast. I turn toward him, watch as his eyes narrow a fraction, then scramble to come up with an excuse believable enough to convince him not to text Shannon, or Melissa, or anyone for that matter, because none of them are going to my bachelorette party. *I'm* not even going to my bachelorette party. Because it doesn't exist.

"Please don't," I say, lowering my eyes. "I mean, it's my bachelorette party, Daniel. I don't want to be self-conscious the entire time, worried about making a fool out of myself and having it wind up on your phone."

"Oh, come on now," he says, putting his hands on his hips. "Since when are you insecure about having a few too many drinks?"

"We're not supposed to be communicating!" I say, trying to make it playful. "It's just one weekend. Besides, I doubt they'll even respond. I've already been read the rules—no calls, no texts. We're being cut off. Girls' weekend."

"Fine," he says, holding his hands up in surrender. "What happens in New Orleans stays in New Orleans."

"Thank you."

"You'll be home Sunday, then?"

I nod, the prospect of four full, uninterrupted days enough to make me melt into the carpet. It's a relief, really. Getting away. Getting to stop the pretending, the constant acting that's required of me every time I step foot in my own home. And hopefully, after this trip, I won't need to act anymore. I won't need to pretend. I won't need to sleep with my body pressed against his, concealing the cringe that shudders down my back every time his lips graze against my neck. After this trip, I will have the evidence I need to go to the police, finally. To make them believe me, finally.

But that doesn't make what I'm about to do any easier.

"I'll miss you," he says, sitting on the edge of the bed. I've been distant since the night of the alarm and he knows it. He can sense it, sense me pulling away. I tuck a strand of hair behind my ear and force myself to stand, to walk over toward him and take a seat by his side.

"I'll miss you, too," I say, holding my breath as he pulls me in for a kiss. He holds my head in his hands, cradling my skull in that familiar way. "But hey, I have to go."

I pull back, standing up and walking to my suitcase, closing the flap and zipping it shut.

"I have a few appointments this morning, then I'm leaving straight from the office. Melissa and I are riding together, and we'll pick up Shannon on the way."

"Have fun." He smiles. For a brief second, watching him sit on the edge of the bed by himself, his fingers laced together as his palms rest heavy in his lap, I sense a sadness that I've never seen in him before. The kind of desperate longing that I had once recognized in myself, before Daniel, when I felt the loneliest in the company of others. Just weeks ago, I would have felt guilty, that familiar pang in the chest when you lie to someone you love. I am sneaking around behind his back, digging into his past the way I have always chastised others for doing to me. But this is different, I know. This is serious. Because Daniel isn't me—I know he's not me. But I'm becoming increasingly certain that he may be just like my father.

I arrive at my office thirty minutes before my first appointment, duffel bag slung over one shoulder. I walk quickly past Melissa's desk, waving at her as she takes a sip of her latte, trying to avoid lengthy conversation about my upcoming trip. I told her it was for wedding planning, but beyond that very vague description, I'm lacking any legitimate details. My primary concern had been providing a believable alibi to Daniel, and so far, I think I've done pretty well.

"Doctor Davis," she says, placing her cup on the desk. I'm halfway through my office door before turning toward the sound of her voice. "Sorry, but you have a visitor. I told him you have an appointment, but . . . he's been waiting."

I turn toward my waiting room, glancing at the cluster of couches in the corner that I had completely ignored on my way in, and there, sitting on the far edge of one of them, is Detective Thomas. He's holding a magazine open in his lap and smiles in my direction before flipping it closed and tossing it back on the coffee table.

"Good morning," he says, standing up to greet me. "Going somewhere?"

I look down at my duffel bag, then back up to the detective, who has already halved the distance between us.

"Just a little trip."

"Where to?"

I chew on the side of my cheek, very aware of Melissa's presence behind me.

"New Orleans," I say. "I'm running some last-minute wedding errands. They have some boutiques there, different vendors I wanted to check out."

When I find myself caught up in a lie, I've found it's always best to simplify it. To stick to the same version as often as possible. If Daniel thinks I'm in New

Orleans, then Melissa and Detective Thomas might as well think the same thing. I catch Detective Thomas's eyes glancing down at the ring on my finger before looking back up, nodding gently.

"This will just take a few minutes."

I extend my arm to my office, turning around and smiling at Melissa as I lead him across the waiting room, attempting to convey a sense of calm and control despite the panic rising in my chest. The detective follows me inside and shuts the door.

"So, what can I do for you, Detective?"

I walk behind my desk and set my bag on the ground, pulling out my chair and taking a seat. I hope he'll follow my lead and do the same, but he remains standing.

"I wanted to let you know that I spent the week following up on your lead. Bert Rhodes."

I raise my eyebrows; I forgot about Bert Rhodes. So many things have happened over the past week that have shifted my focus—the necklace in our closet and the revelation about Aubrey Gravino, the perfume on Daniel's shirt and the lying about the conference and the scratch across his side. The visit with my mother, the things I had found in Daniel's briefcase, now tucked into my own duffel bag. The evidence I had been looking for, and the evidence I'm traveling this weekend to find. The memory of Bert Rhodes in my home, holding that drill, his eyes boring into mine, feels so distant to me now. But I still remember that feeling of paralysis, of fear. Of my feet firmly planted on the ground despite the mounting sense of danger. But now danger has taken on a whole new meaning. At least I wasn't living under the same roof as Bert Rhodes; at least he didn't have a key to access the doors that I had locked behind me. I'm feeling almost nostalgic for last week, yearning for that moment—standing in my hallway, back against the door—when the line between *good* and *bad* was so clearly defined.

Detective Thomas shifts on his feet and suddenly, I feel guilt, too. Guilt for sending him down this rabbit hole. Yes, Bert Rhodes is a bad man. Yes, I felt unsafe in his presence. But the evidence I've uncovered in the past week doesn't point in his direction—and I feel like I should say so. But still, I'm curious.

"Oh, really. What did you find?"

"Well, for starters, he wants to take out a restraining order. Against you."

"What?" The shock of his statement sends me shooting up from my desk, the screech of my chair against the hardwood floor like jagged nails on a chalkboard. "What do you mean, a restraining order?"

"Please take a seat, Doctor Davis. He told me he felt threatened during his little visit to your house."

"He felt threatened?" I'm raising my voice now; I'm sure Melissa can hear, but at this point, I don't care. "How in the world did he feel threatened? *I* felt threatened. I was unarmed."

"Doctor Davis, take a seat."

I stare at him for a moment, blinking back my disbelief, before slowly lowering myself into my chair again.

"He claims that you lured him into your home under false pretenses," he continues, taking a step closer to my desk. "That he arrived under the impression that he was completing a job, but once he stepped inside, he realized you had other intentions. That you were interrogating him, pushing his buttons. Trying to get him to admit to something incriminating."

"That's ridiculous. I didn't call him to my house, my fiancé did."

I feel a lurch in my chest at that word—*fiancé*—but force myself to push it down.

"And how did your fiancé get his number?"

"I imagine from the website."

"And why were you looking at the website? It seems like a pretty big coincidence, considering your history."

"Look," I say, pushing my hands through my hair. I can already see where this is going. "I had his website pulled up, okay? I had just realized that Bert Rhodes lives in town and I was thinking about how coincidental it is, to your point. I was thinking about those girls and how desperately I wanted to figure out what was happening to them. My fiancé saw it pulled up on my laptop and called him without me knowing. It was just a stupid misunderstanding."

Detective Thomas nods in my direction. He doesn't believe me, I can tell.

"Is that all?" I ask, irritation dripping from my tongue.

"No, that's not all," he says. "We also discovered that this isn't the first time this has happened with you. It sounds eerily familiar, actually. The stalking, the conspiracy theories. Even the restraining order. Does the name *Ethan Walker* ring a bell?"

CHAPTER THIRTY-THREE

I first saw him at a house party, dipping a plastic cup into a cooler of neon-red liquid. He had a certain quality about him that I couldn't quite define—ethereal, almost, like everyone else in the room had dimmed, and he stood there glowing, drawing all the light to his center.

I took a drink out of my own cup and winced; frat party liquor was never of the highest quality, but that wasn't really the point. I was drinking just enough to feel a little tingly, a little numb. The Valium coursing through my veins had already helped to quiet my nerves, to cloak my mind in a sense of chemically induced calm. I looked down into my cup, at the last remaining finger of liquid, and knocked it back.

"His name's Ethan."

I looked over to my left; my roommate, Sarah, was standing next to me, nodding in the direction of the boy I had been staring at. *Ethan.*

"He's cute," she said. "You should go talk to him."

"Maybe."

"You've been staring at him all night."

I shot a look in her direction as heat rose to my cheeks.

"No, I haven't."

She smirked, twirled the liquid in her own cup before taking a sip herself.

"Well, fine," she said. "If you won't talk to him, I will."

I watched Sarah saunter over in his direction, pushing through the haze of drunken body heat and noise with a certain determination, a woman on a mission. I stayed firmly planted in my usual spot against the wall—a spot that allowed me to survey the room, always aware of my surroundings, never in a position to be approached from behind, surprised in any way. This was so typical of Sarah. Our entire college friendship had been dominated by her taking the things I so clearly wanted—the bottom bunk in our dorm followed by the bedroom with the walk-in closet in our current apartment, the last open spot in an Abnormal Psych lecture, the only size medium beige top left hanging in the boutique window. A top she was currently wearing.

And now, Ethan.

I watched her approach him, tap him on the shoulder. He glanced over at her, smiling wide before wrapping her in a friendly hug. *It's fine,* I thought. *He doesn't fit the checklist, anyway.* And it was true. He was a little too big for my liking, the muscles in his arms bulging as he squeezed Sarah against his chest. He could have held her there if he had wanted to; he could have kept squeezing, like a boa constrictor, until she snapped. He seemed too popular, too. Too used to getting what he wanted. I never got involved with a guy who seemed entitled, who would get angry if I suddenly changed my mind.

I looked over at the front door, a portal away from this stuffy house and back into the cool, crisp air of LSU in fall. I always made it a point never to walk home alone, but now it seemed like Sarah was going to be here for a while, and I didn't have much of a choice. I had a pepper spray key chain dangling from my apartment key, and it was only a couple of blocks, after all. I hesitated in my spot, wondering if I should walk over to her and tell her goodbye, or if I should just turn around and leave. I doubted anyone would notice, anyway.

I had made my decision, turning back from the door to the party to take one last look around before I made my exit, when I noticed them looking at me. Both Ethan and Sarah, staring in my direction. Sarah was whispering into his ear, a dainty hand cupped over her lips, and Ethan, smiling, nodding along gently. I felt my heartbeat rise into my throat; I looked down into my empty cup, desperately wishing there was something there for me to sip on, if only to give my hands something to do instead of hanging limply by my side. Before I could move from my spot, Ethan started to walk toward me, zeroing in on my eyes as if there were nobody else in the room. Something about him made me nervous, and not in the way men usually made me nervous—guarded, on edge. He made me nervous in a good way, an excited way. I gripped the cup in my hands so hard I heard the plastic crack. When he approached me, finally, he brushed his thick arms against mine so I could feel the soft cotton of his henley shirt against my skin.

"Hi," he said, smiling wide. His teeth were so white, so straight. He smelled like that cool blast of fragrance that hits you when you walk past a store in a shopping mall. Clover and sandalwood. I didn't know it then, but I would come to know that smell so well over the next couple of months; the way it would linger on my pillow for weeks on end, long after the warmth of his body had left. The way I would recognize it anywhere—in the places that he had been, in the places that he shouldn't have been.

"So, you're Sarah's roommate?" he asked, nudging me along. "We know each other from class."

"Yeah," I said, glancing over at my friend, who had now partially vanished into the crowd. I shot her a silent apology in my mind for automatically assuming the worst. "I'm Chloe."

"Ethan," he said, thrusting a drink in my direction as opposed to a handshake. I took it, slipping the heavy cup into my empty one and drinking from the double-stacked lip. "Sarah mentioned that you're pre-med?"

"Psychology," I said.

"Wow," he said. "That's amazing. Hey, it's kind of loud in here—do you want to find somewhere quiet to talk?"

I remember the distinct drop of my chest in that moment; the realization that he was just like the rest. I felt like I couldn't judge him, though. I had done it, too. Used people. Used their bodies to feel less alone. But this time, it felt different. I was on the receiving end.

"I was actually just about to leave—"

"That came out weird," he interrupted, holding up his hand. "I know guys probably say that a lot. *Somewhere quiet,* like my bedroom, right? That's not what I meant."

He smiled sheepishly as I chewed on the side of my lip, trying to decipher what it was that he *did* mean. He didn't fit my checklist, that tried-and-true system I had used to keep myself safe for so long, physically and emotionally. He was hard to pin down, with his picture-perfect smile and tousled blonde surfer's hair. Chiseled forearms that seemed effortless, like he had never actually stepped foot inside of a gym. Talking to him somehow seemed both safe and dangerous, like strapping into a roller coaster and feeling your chest lurch back as the clicking of the chains starts to move your body forward, too late to turn back.

"How about in there?"

He gestured over to the kitchen, dirty with old, sticky

cups and empty cases of Natural Light beer stacked on the counters, the door removed clean from the hinges. It was empty, though. Quiet enough to talk, but visible enough to feel safe. I nodded, and let him trail me down the crowded hallway and into the fluorescently lit room. He grabbed a towel and wiped down a counter, patting it twice with a grin. I walked over and leaned against it, placing my hands on the surface and hoisting myself up until I was sitting on the edge, my feet dangling in the air. He sat down next to me and tipped his old plastic cup against mine. We each took a sip, staring at each other from above the plastic.

And that's where we sat for the next four hours.

CHAPTER THIRTY-FOUR

"Doctor Davis, can you answer the question, please?"

I look up at Detective Thomas and attempt to blink away the memory. I can still feel the stickiness on my hands from the spilt drinks on the counter, the tingling in my legs from sitting there, motionless, for so many hours. So deep in conversation. Oblivious to the world outside of that dilapidated old kitchen. The buzz of the party around us evaporating until suddenly, we were the last ones left. The quiet walk home in the dark, Ethan's finger hooked gently around mine as the fall wind trickled through the trees on campus. The way he led me up the sidewalk to my apartment, waited on the street corner until I unlocked my front door and waved him good night.

"Yes," I say quietly, the knot in my throat tightening. "Yes, I know Ethan Walker. But it sounds like you know that already."

"What can you tell me about him?"

"He was my boyfriend in college. We dated for eight months."

"And why did you split up?"

"We were in college," I repeat. "It wasn't that serious. It just didn't work out."

"That's not what I heard."

I'm glaring at him now, a hatred boiling in my chest that momentarily startles me. Clearly, he knows the answer already. He just wants to hear me say it.

"Why don't you tell me the whole story, in your words," Detective Thomas says. "Start from the top."

I sigh, glancing at the clock hanging above my office door. Fifteen minutes before my first appointment is supposed to arrive. I've told my version of this story a hundred times before—I know he can just look at the department records, probably listen to a recording of me recounting the exact same thing—but I desperately want this man out of my office by the time my appointment arrives.

"Ethan and I dated for eight months, like I said. He was my first real boyfriend, and we got close fast. Too fast for a couple of kids. He was over at our apartment all the time, almost every night. But at the start of that summer, right after classes ended, he started to distance himself. It was also right around that time that my roommate, Sarah, went missing."

"Was it reported as a Missing Persons case?"

"No," I say. "Sarah was spontaneous; a free spirit. She was known to take off on weekend trips and things of that nature, but something about it didn't feel right to me. I hadn't heard from her in three days, so I started to get concerned."

"That seems normal," Detective Thomas says. "Did you go to the police?"

"No," I say again, knowing how it sounds. "You have to remember, this was in 2009. People weren't attached to their cell phones like they are today. I tried to tell myself that maybe she just took a last-minute trip and left her phone behind, but then I noticed that Ethan was starting to act strange."

"Strange how, exactly?"

"Every time I mentioned her name, he got flustered.

Kind of rambled a little bit and changed the subject. He didn't even seem concerned that she was gone—he just offered up vague ideas about where she could be. He would say something like, *'It's summer break, maybe she went home to visit her parents,'* but when I said I wanted to call them and make sure she was there, he told me I was overreacting and needed to stop inserting myself into other people's business. I started to think that the way he was acting, it was like he didn't want her to be found."

Detective Thomas nods in my direction; I wonder if he really has heard this all before, from the recording at the police station, but his expression gives away nothing.

"I went into her room one day and started poking around, trying to see if I could find a clue or something as to where she had gone. Like a note or something, I don't know."

The memory is so vivid, pushing her bedroom door open with one finger, listening to it creak. Stepping inside, quiet, like I was breaking some kind of unspoken rule. Like she could come barreling in at any moment, catch me digging through her laundry or reading her diary.

"I ripped her comforter off her bed and I noticed that there was a bloodstain on her mattress," I continue. "A big one."

I can still see it, so clearly. The blood. Sarah's blood. The spot taking up almost the entire bottom half of her bed, no longer bright but a burnt, rusty red. I remember pushing my hand into it, feeling the moisture seep up from somewhere deep inside. Smears of scarlet on my finger pads, still wet. Still fresh.

"And I know this sounds strange, but I could *smell* Ethan on her bed," I say. "He had a very . . . distinct smell."

"Okay," he says. "Surely, at that point, you went to the police."

"No. No, I didn't. I know I should have, but—" I stop, compose myself. I need to make sure I word this correctly. "I wanted to be absolutely certain that there was some kind of foul play involved before going to the police. I had just moved to Baton Rouge to escape my name, my past. I didn't want the police dragging that back to the surface again. I didn't want to lose the normalcy that I was finally starting to find."

He nods, judgment in his eyes.

"But just like I had invited Lena into my house and introduced her to my father, I was starting to feel the same way about Sarah and Ethan," I continue. "I had given him a key to our apartment. And now she was missing, and it was starting to feel like maybe she was in trouble, and if Ethan had something to do with it, I felt obligated to do everything I could to figure that out. I was starting to feel responsible."

"Okay," he says. "What happened next?"

"Ethan broke up with me that week. It came out of nowhere. I was blindsided, but the fact that this was happening right around the time of Sarah's disappearance felt like proof to me. Proof that he was hiding something. He told me he was getting out of town for a few days, heading home to his parents' house to *work through everything.* So I decided to break into his place."

Detective Thomas raises his eyebrows, and I force myself to keep talking, to push on, before he can interrupt me again.

"I thought I could get some evidence to take to the police," I say, my mind on the jewelry box in my father's closet, the physical embodiment of undeniable proof. "I knew from my father's murders that evidence was critical—without it, there's just suspicion. Not enough to make an arrest or to even take an accusation seriously. I don't know what I was expecting to find, exactly. Just something I could put my hands on. Something to make me feel like I wasn't going crazy."

I flinch slightly at my own choice of words—*crazy*—and continue.

"So I broke in through a window I knew he kept unlocked and started looking around. But pretty soon, I heard a noise coming from his bedroom, and I realized that he was home."

"And what did you find when you went into his bedroom?"

"He was there," I say, my cheeks flushing at the memory. "And so was Sarah."

In that moment—standing in Ethan's bedroom doorway, staring at him and Sarah tangled between his ratty sheets—I remembered their hug at that party, the night we met. I remembered the way she cupped her hand over her lips and leaned in close, whispering into his ear. Ethan and Sarah had known each other from class—that much was true. But I would later find out that wasn't the extent of their relationship. They had hooked up the previous year, and after a few months of us dating, they started it back up again, behind my back. Turns out I had been right about Sarah. Always taking what I wanted. Introducing us had been a game to her, a way to dangle herself in front of Ethan and then swoop in and reclaim him, once again proving that she was better than me.

"And how did he react to you barging in like that? Breaking into his apartment?"

"Not well, obviously," I say. "He started screaming at me, saying he had been trying to break up with me for months but I was being clingy. Refused to listen. He painted me as the crazy ex-girlfriend breaking into his apartment . . . and he took out a restraining order."

"And the blood stain on Sarah's mattress?"

"Apparently she had accidentally gotten pregnant," I say in a matter-of-fact numbness. "But she had a miscarriage. She was pretty upset about it, but she wanted to keep it a secret. For starters, she didn't want anyone to know she had gotten pregnant, but she especially didn't want them to know it had been with her roommate's boyfriend. She had been holing up at Ethan's apartment for the week, trying to work through it. That's why Ethan didn't want me to freak out about it and call her parents—or, God forbid, report her missing."

Detective Thomas sighs, and I can't help but feel stupid, like a teenager being scolded for trying to get drunk off mouthwash. *I'm not mad, I'm disappointed.* I wait for him to say something, anything, but instead, he just continues to stare in my direction, scrutinizing me with those questioning eyes.

"Why are you making me tell you this story?" I ask finally, my irritation from before creeping back in. "You obviously know it already. How is it relevant to this case at all?"

"Because I was hoping that recounting this memory would help you see what I see," he says, taking a step closer to me. "You have been hurt in your life by people you loved. People you trusted. You have an inherent distrust in men, that much is clear—and who can blame you, after what your father did? But just because you don't know where your boyfriend is every second of the day doesn't mean that he's a murderer. You learned that the hard way."

I feel my throat constrict and I immediately think of Daniel—of my other boyfriend (no, *fiancé*) who I am now investigating on my own accord. Of the suspicions that have been piling up in my mind, of the plans I have for this weekend. Plans that are no different from breaking through Ethan's apartment window, really.

It's an invasion of privacy. A proverbial snoop through the diary. My eyes flicker to the duffel bag at my feet, zipped and ready.

"And just because you have a distrust of Bert Rhodes doesn't mean that he is capable of murder, either," he continues. "This seems to be a pattern with you—injecting yourself into conflicts that don't concern you, trying to solve the mystery and be the hero. I understand why you're doing it—you were the hero who put your father behind bars. You feel like it's your duty. But I'm here to tell you that it needs to stop."

This is the second time I've heard those words in a week; the last was with Cooper, back in my kitchen, his eyes on my pills.

I know why you do it. I just wish you would stop.

"I'm not *injecting myself* into anything," I say, my fingers digging deep into my palms. "I'm not trying to *be the hero,* whatever that means. I'm trying to be helpful. I'm trying to give you a lead."

"False leads are worse than no leads at all," Detective Thomas says. "We spent close to a week on this guy. A week we could have spent on someone else. Now, I don't necessarily believe that you have malicious intentions here—I *do* believe that you were trying to do what you think is best—but if you ask my opinion, I think that you need to consider getting some help."

Cooper's voice, pleading.

Get some help.

"I'm a psychologist," I say, my eyes trained on his, regurgitating the same words I had spit back at Cooper; the same words I have been reciting in my own mind my entire adult life. "I know how to help myself."

A silence settles over the room, and I can almost hear Melissa's breathing outside, her ear pushed against the closed door. Surely, she heard our entire conversation. As did my next patient, probably sitting outside in the waiting room now. I imagine her eyes widening as she overhears a detective telling her psychologist that *she needs help*.

"Ethan Walker's restraining order, the one he filed after you broke into his apartment. He mentioned that you had some substance abuse problems in college. You were reckless with prescription Diazepam, mixing it with alcohol."

"I don't do that anymore," I say, my pill drawer radiating against my leg.

We found heavy traces of Diazepam in her hair.

"I'm sure you know that those drugs can have some pretty serious side effects. Paranoia, confusion. It can be tough to separate reality from fantasy."

Sometimes it's hard for me to determine what's real and what's not.

"I don't have a prescription for any drugs," I say, not exactly a lie. "I'm not paranoid, I'm not confused. I'm just trying to help."

"Okay." Detective Thomas nods. I can tell he feels bad for me; he's pitying me, which means he's never again going to take me seriously. I didn't think it was possible to feel more alone than I did before, but right now, I do. I feel completely alone. "Okay, well. I think that means we're done here."

"Yes, I think so."

"Thank you for your time," he says, walking toward the door. He reaches for the handle and hesitates, turning around again. "Oh, one more thing."

I raise my eyebrows, a silent cue for him to continue.

"If we see you at any more crime scenes, we will take the appropriate disciplinary actions. Tampering with evidence is a criminal offense."

"What?" I ask, genuinely stunned. "What do you mean tampering with—?"

I stop, mid-sentence, realizing what he's talking

about. Cypress Cemetery. Aubrey's earring. The officer plucking it out of my palm.

You look so familiar, and I can't seem to place it. Have we met before?

"Officer Doyle recognized you from Aubrey Gravino's crime scene the minute we stepped into your office. We were waiting to see if you would say anything to us. Mention that you were there. It's a pretty big coincidence."

I swallow, too stunned to move.

"But you never did. So when you came to the station because you had *remembered something,* that's what I thought you were going to tell me," he continues, shifting. "But instead, you had a theory about a copycat. Stolen jewelry. Bert Rhodes. Only, you told me that seeing Lacey's body had been the catalyst of that theory. But I had a hard time wrapping my mind around that, because that was *after* Officer Doyle saw you holding that earring. It didn't make sense."

I think back to that afternoon in Detective Thomas's office, to the way he had been looking at me, uneasy. Unbelieving.

"How would I have gotten Aubrey's earring?" I ask. "If you genuinely think that I *planted* it there, that must mean you think that I . . ."

I stop, unable to speak the words. He can't possibly think that I have something to do with all of this . . . can he?

"There are different theories floating around." He digs a pinky nail into his teeth, inspects it. "But I can tell you that her DNA wasn't on it. Anywhere. Only yours."

"What are you trying to say?"

"I'm saying we can't prove how or why that earring got there. But the common thread binding all this together seems to be you. So don't make yourself look any more suspicious than you already do."

I realize now, even if I do find Aubrey's necklace hidden somewhere in my home, that the police will never believe me. They clearly think that I'm planting evidence to point them in a certain direction, a desperate attempt to prove another one of my baseless ideas, placing the blame on yet another untrustworthy man in my life. Or worse, they think *I* had something to do with it. Me, the last person to see Lacey alive. Me, the first person to find Aubrey's earring. Me, the living, breathing DNA of Dick Davis. The spawn of a monster.

"Okay," I say. There's no point in fighting him on this one. No point in trying to explain. I watch Detective Thomas nod again, satisfied with my response, before turning around and disappearing behind my office door.

CHAPTER THIRTY-FIVE

The rest of the morning goes by in a daze. I have three appointments, back-to-back, none of which I remember very clearly. For the first time, I'm thankful for the little icons on my desktop—I can go back and listen to my recordings later when I'm less distracted, more engaged. I cringe, imagining the emotionless mumbling I'm sure to hear coming from my side of the conversation; the distant *mhmms* I had administered instead of asking genuine questions. The long, drawn-out silences before my eyes refocused and I remembered where I was, what I was doing. My first appointment was in the waiting room when Detective Thomas walked out. I saw the look on her face when I finally pulled myself from my chair and walked into the lobby, the way her eyes darted from me to the door as if she were trying to decide whether or not she wanted to come into my office or just get up and leave.

I rise from my desk at 12:02—I don't want to seem too eager—and snatch my duffel bag, powering down my computer before opening up my desk drawer and tapping my fingers across the sea of pills. I look at the Diazepam nestled in the corner and turn away, deciding instead on a bottle of Xanax, just in case, before securing the drawer and rushing past Melissa with hurried instructions to lock the door on her way out.

"You'll be back Monday, right?" she says, standing up.

"Yes, Monday," I say, turning around and trying to flash a smile. "I'm just doing some wedding shopping. Knocking out the last-minute errands."

"Right," she says, eying me carefully. "In New Orleans. You said that."

"Right." I try to think of something else to say, something normal, but the silence stretches between us, awkward and uncomfortable. "Well, if that'll be all—"

"Chloe," she says, picking at her cuticle. Melissa hardly ever uses my first name in the office; she always keeps distinct boundaries between personal and professional. Clearly, what she's about to say to me now is personal. "Is everything okay? What's been going on with you?"

"Nothing," I say, smiling again. "Nothing's going on, Melissa. I mean, other than my patient being murdered and my wedding coming up in a month."

I try to laugh at my pathetic attempt at a joke, but it comes out strangled. Instead, I cough. Melissa doesn't smile.

"I've just had a lot of stress lately," I say. It feels like the first honest thing I've said to her in a while. "I need a break. A mental health break."

"Okay," she says, hesitating. "And that detective?"

"He was just asking some follow-up questions about Lacey, that's all. I was the last one to see her alive. If I'm their strongest witness, they obviously don't have much to go on at the moment."

"Okay," she says again, this time more confidently. "Okay, well, enjoy your break. I hope you can come back refreshed."

I walk out to my car, tossing my duffel bag onto the passenger seat like junk mail before getting into the driver's seat and cranking the engine. Then I pull out my phone, navigate to my Contacts, and start typing a message.

On my way.

The drive to the motel is quick, only forty-five minutes from my office. I reserved the room on Monday, immediately after I told Melissa to block my calendar. I had found the first cheap all-nighter I could find on Google with a rating over three stars—I wanted to pay in cash, and I knew I wouldn't be spending much time in the room, anyway. I pull into the parking lot and walk into the lobby, avoiding small talk with the clerk while retrieving my key.

"Room twelve," he says, dangling it in front of me. I grab it, shoot him a weak smile, almost like I'm apologizing for something. "You're right next to the ice machine, lucky you."

I feel my phone vibrate in my pocket as I'm unlocking the door. I dig it out, read the message—*I'm here*—and shoot off a text with the room number before tossing my bag onto the single queen bed. Then I glance around the room.

It's bleak in that fluorescently lit way only highway motels can be. The efforts at décor almost make the place sadder, with its mass-produced beach scene hung crookedly over the bed, the chocolate placed delicately on my pillow, warm and slightly squishy between my fingers. I look at the bedside table, open the drawer. There's a Bible inside with the cover ripped off. I walk into the bathroom and splash water on my face before twisting my hair into a topknot. There's a knock at the door, and I exhale slowly, stealing one final glance at myself in the mirror, trying to ignore the bags under my eyes that seem amplified in the harsh light. I force myself to flip the switch and walk back toward the door, a silhouette looming outside the closed curtains. I grasp the knob firmly and swing the door open.

Aaron is standing on the sidewalk, his hands shoved deep into his pockets. He looks uncomfortable, and I don't blame him. I try to smile in an attempt to lighten the mood, to draw attention away from the fact that we're meeting each other in a nondescript motel room on the outskirts of Baton Rouge. I haven't told him why he's here, what we're really doing. I haven't told him why I can't sleep in my own home tonight when we're within an hour's drive of my neighborhood. All I said when I called him on Monday was that I had a lead he wouldn't want to ignore—a lead I needed his help to follow.

"Hey," I say, leaning against the door. It groans under my body weight, so I straighten back up, crossing my arms instead. "Thanks for coming. Let me just grab my purse."

I motion for him to come inside, and he does, stepping self-consciously across the threshold of the door. He looks around, unimpressed with my new digs. We've barely spoken since I asked him to look into Bert Rhodes last weekend, and that seems like a lifetime ago. He has no idea about the confrontation I had with Bert, my trip to the police station, and the subsequent threat from Detective Thomas to stay out of the investigation—the exact opposite of what I am doing right now. He also has no idea that my suspicions have shifted from Bert Rhodes to my own fiancé, and that I am enlisting his help to prove my theory right.

"How's the story coming?" I ask, genuinely curious if he's been able to uncover anything more than me.

"My editor is giving me until the end of next week

to dig something up," he says, sitting on the edge of the mattress with a creak. "Otherwise it's time to pack it up and head home."

"Empty-handed?"

"That's right."

"But you came all this way. What about your theory? The copycat?"

Aaron shrugs.

"I still believe it," he says, his fingernail picking at the seam of the comforter. "But honestly, I'm getting nowhere."

"Well, I may be able to help."

I walk over to the bed and sit down next to him, the slouch of the mattress bringing our bodies closer together.

"And how is that? Does it have to do with this mysterious lead of yours?"

I look down at my hands. I need to word my response carefully, giving away only the information that Aaron needs to know.

"We're going to speak with a woman named Dianne," I say. "Her daughter went missing around the time of my father's murders—another young, attractive teenager—and just like his victims, her body was never found."

"Okay, but your dad never confessed to her murder, right? Only the six?"

"No, he didn't," I say. "And there was no jewelry of hers, either. She doesn't really fit the pattern . . . but since her abductor was never found, I think it's worth looking into. I was thinking that maybe *he* could be the copycat, you know? Whoever he is. That maybe he started mimicking my father's crimes way earlier than we thought—maybe even while they were still happening. He went dark for a while, and maybe now, for the twentieth anniversary, he's popping back up again."

Aaron looks at me, and I half expect him to stand up and walk back outside, insulted that I brought him all the way out here for such a half-assed clue. But instead, he slaps his hands on his legs, exhaling loudly before standing up from the sunken bed.

"Well, okay," he says, offering his hand to help me up. I can't tell if he's actually sold on my story, if he's desperate enough for a lead that he's willing to follow me blindly, or if he's just going along with it to make me happy. Either way, I'm grateful. "Let's go talk to Dianne."

CHAPTER THIRTY-SIX

Aaron drives as I navigate the directions on my phone, taking us deeper into a part of town that slowly morphs from middle-class modular homes into a dilapidated corner of Baton Rouge, barely recognizable. It happens so gradually I hardly realize it; one minute, I'm looking out the window at a toddler splashing in an inflatable pool—his mother soaking her feet, distracted on her phone with a lemonade in hand—and the next, I'm staring at a skeleton of a woman pushing a shopping cart full of trash bags and beer. The houses are falling apart now—bars on windows, paint peeling—and we turn in to a long, gravel roadway. Finally, I see a two-story with the number 375 bolted to the vinyl siding and motion for him to pull over.

"We're here," I say, unbuckling my seat belt. I steal another look at myself in the rearview mirror, the thick reading glasses I had put on before we left the motel partially obscuring my face. It feels cartoonish, putting on a pair of glasses as a disguise. Something out of a bad movie. I don't think Dianne has ever seen a picture of me, but I can't know for certain. For that reason, I want to make myself look different—and I want Aaron to do most of the talking.

"Okay, so what's the plan, again?"

"We knock on the door, tell her that we're investigating the deaths of Aubrey Gravino and Lacey Deckler," I say. "Maybe flash her your credentials. Make it seem official."

"Okay."

"Tell her that we know her daughter was kidnapped twenty years ago and that her abductor was never caught. We're curious if she can tell us anything about her daughter's case."

Aaron nods, not asking questions, and grabs his computer bag from the back seat before placing it on his lap. He seems nervous, but I can tell he doesn't want it to show.

"And you are?"

"Your colleague," I say, before getting out of the car and slamming the door behind me.

I walk toward the home, the scent of cigarette smoke lingering heavy in the air. It doesn't smell freshly smoldered, like someone was just out here, sitting on the stoop, sneaking a smoke before dinner. It smells like it's engrained in the place, coming out in little puffs from a timed air freshener, a permanent aroma that seeps into your clothes and never really leaves. I hear Aaron slam his door, hurrying behind me as I climb the steps toward the front porch. I turn around to face him, raising my eyebrows as if to ask: *Are you ready?* Aaron nods, a subtle tilt of the head, before raising his fist and knocking twice on the door.

"*Who is it?*"

I hear the voice of a woman erupt from inside, high-pitched and screechy. Aaron looks at me, and I lift my fist this time, knocking on the door again. My arm is still raised in the air when the door swings open, an older-looking woman glaring at us from behind a dirty screen. I notice a dead fly trapped in the mesh.

"What?" she asks. "Who are you? What do you want?"

"Um, my name is Aaron Jansen. I'm a reporter for *The New York Times*." Aaron looks down at his shirt, points to the press badge clipped to his collar. "I was wondering if I could ask you a few questions."

"A reporter for what?" the woman asks, her eyes darting from Aaron to myself. She stares at me for a second, her forehead crumpled, a dark blue shadow to the right of her nose. Her eyes are gelatinous and yellow, the consistency of Goo Gone, like even her tear ducts can't be saved from the nicotine in the air. "You said you work for a newspaper?"

For a moment, I'm terrified that she recognizes me. That she knows who I am. But almost as quickly as her eyes settle on mine, they dart back over to Aaron, squinting at the ID on his shirt.

"Yes, ma'am," he says. "I'm writing a story about the deaths of Aubrey Gravino and Lacey Deckler, and it came to my attention that you also lost a daughter, twenty years ago. A daughter who went missing and was never found."

My eyes scan the woman, the weariness in her features, like she doesn't trust a person in the world. I look her up and down, take in the ratty, oversized clothes she's wearing, the sleeves covered in microscopic moth holes. Her arthritic thumbs thick and crooked like baby carrots, the red and purple shiners marbling her arms. I can almost make out little finger marks, and in this moment, I realize that the shadow beneath her eye isn't a shadow at all. It's a bruise. I clear my throat, deflecting the attention from Aaron to myself.

"We would love to ask you a few questions," I say. "About your daughter. Finding out what happened to her is just as important as finding out what happened to

Aubrey and Lacey, even after all these years. And we were hoping—I was hoping—that you might be able to help us."

The woman looks at me again before glancing behind her shoulder, sighing in what seems like defeat.

"Okay," she says, pushing the screen door open and motioning for us to come inside. "But you'll need to make it fast. I need you gone by the time my husband gets home."

We walk inside, and the dirtiness of the place over-powers all my senses; there's trash everywhere, heaped in the corners of every room. Paper plates with caked-on food forming leaning towers on the floor, flies buzzing around fast-food bags stained with ketchup smears and grease. There's a mangy cat resting on the edge of the sofa, its fur patchy and wet, and she swats at it, sending it scampering across the floor with a squawk.

"Sit," she says, motioning to the couch. Aaron and I look at each other briefly, then back down at the sofa, trying to find enough fabric peeking out from behind the magazines and dirty clothes. I decide to just sit on top of it, the crunch of paper beneath my weight unnaturally loud. She sits in the seat opposite the coffee table and grabs a carton of cigarettes from the surface—there seem to be cartons everywhere, littered across the room like reading glasses—peeling one from the pack with her thin, wet lips. She grabs a lighter and raises the cigarette to the flame, inhaling deeply before blow-ing smoke in our direction. "So, what do you want to know?"

Aaron grabs a notebook from his briefcase and flips it to a clean page, clicking his pen repeatedly against his leg.

"Well, Dianne, if you could just start by telling me

your full name, for the record," he says. "Then we can get into the disappearance of your daughter."

"Okay." She sighs, sucking in another cloud of smoke. When she exhales, I watch her eyes grow distant as she stares out the window. "My name is Dianne Briggs. And my daughter, Sophie, went missing twenty years ago."

CHAPTER THIRTY-SEVEN

"What can you tell us about Sophie?"

Dianne glances in my direction, as if she had forgotten about my existence entirely. It feels wrong that this is the way I'm meeting my would-be future mother-in-law. She clearly has no idea who I am, and as long as I can avoid giving her my name, it should stay that way. I no longer have Facebook, so I never post pictures of myself online—and even if I did, Daniel doesn't speak to his parents anymore. They aren't invited to the wedding. I wonder if she even knows he's engaged.

She seems to consider the question for a second, as if she's forgotten, lifting her hand to scratch at the leathery skin on her arm.

"What can I tell you about Sophie," she echoes, sucking down the last of her cigarette before putting it out on the wooden table. "She was a wonderful girl. Smart, beautiful. Just beautiful. That's her, just there."

Dianne points to a single, framed picture on the wall, a school portrait that features a smiling girl with pale skin and frizzy blonde hair, a turquoise backdrop that looks like pool water. It strikes me as odd to see her class picture displayed—that, and nothing else. It seems staged and unnatural, like a sad sort of shrine. I wonder if the Briggs family wasn't big on cameras, or if there just weren't any moments worth remembering. I look around for pictures of Daniel, but I don't see any.

"I had big dreams for her," she continues. "Before she went missing."

"What kind of dreams?"

"Oh, you know, just getting out of here," she says, gesturing to the room around us. "She was better than this. Better than us."

"Who is *us*?" Aaron asks, resting the tip of his pen against his cheek. "You and your husband?"

"Me, my husband, my son. I just always thought she would be the one to get out of here, you know. To make something of herself."

My chest lurches at the mention of Daniel; I try to imagine him growing up here, getting buried alive in the clouds of cigarette smoke and mountains of trash. I've been wrong about him, I realize. His perfect teeth, his smooth skin, his expensive education and high-paying job. I had always assumed those things were a product of his upbringing, of his privilege. That he is inherently better than me, than *damaged Chloe*. But it isn't; he isn't. He's damaged, too.

He doesn't know you, Chloe. And you don't know him.

It's no wonder he's so meticulously clean now, so immaculately put together. He's been trying so hard to become the exact opposite of *this*.

Or maybe he's been trying to hide who he really is.

"What can you tell us about your husband and son?"

"My husband, Earl. He's got a temper, as I'm sure you've noticed." She looks at me, smirks a little, as if we share some kind of unspoken bond over men. The things they do. *Boys will be boys.* I divert my gaze from the bruise beneath her eye, but this woman isn't stupid. She must have caught me looking. "And my son, well.

I don't know much about him anymore. But I've always worried that the apple doesn't fall too far from the tree."

Aaron and I glance at each other, and I nod at him to go on.

"What do you mean by that?"

"I mean that he's got a temper, too."

I think of Daniel's hand on my wrist, squeezing.

"He used to try to fight off his daddy, protect me when he came home after a night of drinking," she continues. "But as he got older, I don't know. He stopped trying, just let it happen. I think he got desensitized. I guess I can blame myself for that."

"Okay." Aaron nods, scribbling notes in his notebook. "And how did your son—I'm sorry, what did you say his name was?"

"Daniel," she says. "Daniel Briggs."

I feel a squeeze in my stomach as I rack my brain to remember if I've ever mentioned Daniel's full name to Aaron. I don't think I have. I glance over at him, at the concentration warping his forehead as he scrawls the name on his notepad. It doesn't seem to register.

"Okay, and how did Daniel react to Sophie's disappearance?"

"Honestly, he didn't seem to care," she says, reaching for the pack of cigarettes and lighting another. "I know it's not very *maternal* of me to say things like that, but it's true. A little part of me always wondered . . ."

She stops, stares into the distance, then shakes her head gently.

"Wondered what?" I ask. She looks at me now, her daze broken. There's a certain intensity in her eyes, and for a second, I'm convinced that she knows who I am. That she's speaking to *me*, Chloe Davis, the woman engaged to her son. That she's trying to warn me.

"Wondered if he had somethin' to do with it."

"What makes you say that?" Aaron asks, his voice growing more urgent with each question. He's writing faster now, trying to remember every detail. "That's quite the accusation."

"I don't know, just a feeling," she says. "I guess you could call it a mother's instinct. When she first went missing, I would ask Daniel if he knew where she was, and I could always tell he was lying. He was hiding something. And sometimes, when we were watchin' the news, listening to them report on her disappearance, I would catch him smiling—no, like *smirking*, like he was laughing at some secret that the rest of the world didn't know."

I can feel Aaron looking at me, but I ignore him, keeping my focus on Dianne.

"And where is Daniel now?"

"I ain't got a fuckin' clue," Dianne says, leaning back into the sofa. "He moved out the day after he graduated high school, and I haven't heard from him since."

"Do you mind if we look around?" I ask, suddenly eager to cut this conversation short before Aaron uncovers too much. "Maybe poke around in Daniel's room, see if we can find anything that may point us in the right direction?"

She holds her arm out, gesturing to the staircase.

"Be my guest," she says. "I already told this to the police twenty years ago, didn't amount to nothin'. In their opinion, no teenaged boy could have gotten away with it."

I stand up, take exaggerated steps over the obstacles in the living room and toward the stairs, the beige carpet dirty and stained.

"First one on the right," Dianne yells as I take them one at a time. "Haven't touched that room in years."

I make my way upstairs and look at the closed door. My hand finds the knob, and I twist it open, unveiling the bedroom of a teenaged boy, all the lights off, a stream of sunshine through the window revealing specks of dust floating in the air.

"Sophie's, either," she continues, her voice distant. I hear Aaron stand up from the couch, make his way upstairs behind me. "No reason for me to go up there anymore. Truthfully, I didn't really know what to do with them."

I step inside, holding the air in my cheeks like a child stepping over a sidewalk crack, a weird superstition. Like bad things will happen if I breathe. This is Daniel's bedroom. There are posters on the wall, '90s rock bands like Nirvana and the Red Hot Chili Peppers fraying at the edges. A blue-and-green plaid comforter rumpled messily across a mattress on the floor, like he had just woken up and walked outside. I imagine Daniel lying in bed, listening to his father come home, drunk and disorderly. Angry. Loud. I imagine the screaming, the clatter of pots and pans, the sound of a body slamming against the wall. I imagine him motionless, listening to it all. Smiling. *Desensitized.*

"We should probably go," Aaron whispers, creeping up behind me. "I think we got what we came for."

But I don't listen. I can't listen. I keep walking, drinking in this place from Daniel's past. I trail my fingers along the wall, leading to a bookshelf, where there are rows of dusty books with yellowing pages, a couple decks of cards, an old baseball resting in a mitt. My eyes skim the titles—Stephen King, Lois Lowry, Michael Crichton. It all seems so adolescent, so normal.

"Chloe," Aaron says, but suddenly, I feel like there's cotton in my ears. I can barely hear him over the sound of my own rushing blood. I reach out my arm and grab a book, pulling it from its home. I hear Daniel's voice in my mind on that first day we met. The day he had grabbed this same book out of my box and trailed his fingers along the cover, that glisten in his eye as he held my copy of *Midnight in the Garden of Good and Evil.*

No judgment, he had said, flipping through its pages. *I love this book.*

I blow the dust from the cover so I'm staring at that famous statue of a young, innocent girl, her neck tilted as if asking me: *Why?* I run my fingers against the glossy cover the same way he had. Then I turn it to the side and see a gap in the pages, the same way his business card had left a gap in mine after he had wedged it deep inside.

Got a thing for murder?

"Chloe," Aaron says again, but I ignore him. Instead, I take a deep breath and stick my nail into the crack, flipping the pages open. I look down and feel that same twist in my chest as my eyes scan a name. Only this time, it's not Daniel's name. And it's not a business card. It's a collection of old newspaper clippings, pushed flat from two decades of being wedged between these pages. My hands are shaking, but I force myself to pick them up. To read the first headline that stretches across the top in boldfaced print.

RICHARD DAVIS NAMED AS BREAUX BRIDGE
SERIAL KILLER, BODIES STILL UNFOUND

And there, staring back at me, is a picture of my father.

CHAPTER THIRTY-EIGHT

"Chloe, what is that?"

Aaron's voice sounds distant, like he's calling to me from the other end of a tunnel. I can't stop looking into my father's eyes. Eyes I haven't seen since I was a little girl, twelve years old, crouched on my living room floor, gazing into them through the static of a television screen. In this moment, I think back to the night I told Daniel about my father, the concern etched into his features as he listened to me detail his crimes in such gruesome specificity. The way he shook his head, claimed he had never heard, he had no idea.

But that was a lie. All of it, a lie. He already knew about my father. He knew about his crimes. He kept an article describing every detail tucked away in his childhood bedroom, hidden between the pages of a novel like a bookmark. He knew how he was able to take those girls and hide their bodies somewhere secret, somewhere never to be found.

Had Daniel done something similar to his sister, something terrible? Had my father been his inspiration? Is he still?

"Chloe?"

I look up at Aaron, my eyes wet with tears. Suddenly, I realize that if Daniel had known about my father, that means he had known about me, too. I think about the way we ran into each other at the hospital—a fateful coincidence, or the result of meticulous planning, being at the right place at the right time? It was common knowledge that I worked at that hospital; that article in the newspaper was proof of that. I think about the way he had looked at me, as if he had known me already. His eyes scanning my face, as though it were familiar. The way he had poked his head into the box of my belongings; the smile that snaked across his face when I told him my name. The way he seemed to fall for me instantly after that, gliding seamlessly into my life the way he's somehow able to glide seamlessly into everything and everyone.

I just can't believe I'm sitting here. With you.

I wonder if this was all a part of his plan. If I was a part of his plan. *Damaged Chloe,* another one of his unsuspecting victims.

"We need to go," I whisper, my shaking hands folding the clipping and tucking it into my back pocket. "I . . . I need to go."

I walk quickly past Aaron, charge down the steps and back toward Daniel's mother, still sitting on the living room couch, a distracted look in her eyes. When she sees us walking toward her, she looks up at us, smiles weakly.

"Find anything useful?"

I shake my head, feeling Aaron's eyes glued to the side of my face, watching suspiciously. She nods gently, as though she were expecting as much.

"Didn't think you would."

Even after all these years, the disappointment in her voice is palpable. I understand what it's like: always wondering, never being able to really let it go. But also, never wanting to admit it—that you still hold out hope that one day, you'll know the truth. That you'll understand. And that maybe, in the end, somehow, it will be worth the wait. Suddenly, I find myself drawn to this woman I barely even know. We're connected, I realize. We're connected in the same way my mother and I are connected. We love the same man, the same monster. I walk toward the couch, taking a seat on the edge of the cushion. Then I place my hand on hers.

"Thank you for talking to us," I say, squeezing gently. "I'm sure that wasn't easy."

She nods, glances down at my hand clutching hers. Slowly, I see her head tilt gently to the side, as if she's inspecting something. She flips her hand around and grabs mine, squeezing it tighter.

"Where did you get this?"

I look down and notice my engagement ring, Daniel's family heirloom, glistening on my finger. Panic rises in my chest as she lifts my hand higher, inspecting it more closely.

"Where did you get this ring?" she asks again, her eyes now fastened on mine. "This is Sophie's ring."

"Wh—what?" I stutter, trying to pull my hand back. But she's holding it too tightly; she won't let go. "I'm sorry, what do you mean, *Sophie's ring*?"

"This is my daughter's ring," she says again, louder, her eyes drilling into the ring once more, the oval cut diamond and halo of stones. The cloudy 14-karat band that sits slightly too large on my thin, bony finger. "This ring has been in my family for generations. It was my engagement ring, and when Sophie turned thirteen, I gave it to her. She always wore this ring. *Always*. She was wearing it the day she . . ."

She looks at me now, her eyes wide, terrified.

"The day she disappeared."

I stand up, ripping my hand from her grip.

"I'm sorry, we have to go," I say, walking past Aaron and throwing open the screen door. "Aaron, come on."

"Who are you?" the woman yells after us, shock bolting her to the couch. *"Who are you?"*

I run out the door and down the front steps. I feel dizzy, drunk. How could I have forgotten to take off the ring? How could I have *forgotten* that? I reach the car and pull on the handle, but the door doesn't budge. It's locked.

"Aaron?" I yell. My voice sounds strangled, like there are hands around my neck, squeezing it closed. "Aaron, can you unlock the door?"

"WHO ARE YOU?" the woman yells behind me. I can hear her getting up, running through the house. The screen door opens and slaps shut, and before I can turn around, I hear the car unlock. I grab the handle again, ripping the door open and flinging myself inside. Aaron is right behind me, running into the driver's seat and cranking the engine.

"WHERE IS MY DAUGHTER?"

The car lurches forward, flips around, and peels back down the road. I look in the rearview mirror, at the cloud of dust we've kicked up, at Daniel's mother running after us, growing more distant with each passing second.

"WHERE IS MY DAUGHTER? PLEASE!"

She's flailing her hands, running wildly, until suddenly she collapses to her knees, drops her head into her hands, and cries.

The car is silent as we drive through town, making our way back to the highway. My hands are shaking in my lap, the image of that poor woman chasing us down the street making my stomach squeeze. The ring on my finger suddenly feels suffocating, and I grab it with my other hand, pulling it off frantically and flinging it to the ground. I stare at it on the floor, imagining Daniel gently removing it from the cold, dead hand of his sister.

"Chloe," Aaron whispers, his eyes still trained on the road. "What was that?"

"I'm sorry," I say. "I'm sorry, Aaron. I'm so sorry."

"Chloe," he says again, louder this time. Angrier. "What the fuck was that?"

"I'm sorry," I repeat again, my voice shaking. "I didn't know."

"Who is that?" he asks again, his hands gripping the steering wheel. "How did you find that woman?"

I'm silent next to him, unable to answer the question. His face turns toward mine, his mouth gaping open.

"Isn't your fiancé named Daniel?"

I don't respond.

"Chloe, *answer me*. Isn't your fiancé named Daniel?"

I nod, tears streaming down my cheek.

"Yes," I say. "Yes, but Aaron, I didn't know."

"What the fuck," he says, shaking his head. "Chloe, what the *fuck*. I told that woman my name. She knows where I work. Jesus Christ, I'm going to lose my job over this."

"I'm sorry," I say again. "Aaron, please. You were the one that helped me to see it—talking about my father's jewelry, who would have known. *Daniel*. Daniel knew. Daniel knew everything."

"And was this just a hunch, or . . . ?"

"I found a necklace in our closet. A necklace that looks a lot like the one Aubrey would have been wearing the day she disappeared."

"Jesus Christ," he says again.

"Then I just started noticing things. Noticing how he smelled different when he came home from his trips. Smelled like perfume. Like other women. He claimed he was out of town when Aubrey and Lacey were taken, but he wasn't where he told me he would be. I had no idea where he would go for days on end. I had no idea what he would do—until I looked through his briefcase and found his receipts."

Aaron looks at me, finally, like I am the bane of his existence. Like he would rather be anywhere in the world than here, with me.

"What kind of receipts?"

"I'll show you back at the motel," I say. "Aaron, please. I need you to help me with this."

He hesitates, his fingers drumming against the steering wheel.

"I've told you before," he says, quieter than ever. "In my line of work, trust is everything. Honesty is everything."

"I know," I say. "And I promise, right now, I will tell you everything."

We pull into the parking lot, the motel bleak before us. Aaron turns off the ignition, sitting silently beside me.

"Please come in," I say, moving my hand to his leg. He flinches at the touch, but I can see his resolve melt. Silently, he unbuckles his seat belt and pushes the door open, stepping outside without a word.

The door to my room creaks as I open it, and we both step inside, closing it behind us. It's cold, dark. The curtains are pulled tightly, my bag still resting on the bed. I walk over to the bedside table and click on the light, the fluorescent glow casting shadows across Aaron's face as he stands by the doorway.

"This is what I found," I say, zipping open my duffel bag. I reach inside, and my hand grazes the bottle of Xanax resting gently on top, but I push it aside. Instead, I reach for a white envelope. My fingers shake as I grab it, the same way they had been shaking as I leafed through Daniel's briefcase, unsnapped on the dining room floor, digging through the papers organized in manila folders and three-ring binders. There had been packets of drug samples organized in clear dividers, memorialized like baseball cards. I had recognized the names from my own desk drawer: Alprazolam, Chlordiazepoxide, Diazepam. I remember feeling a choke lodge itself in my throat as I read that last one, imagining a single hair floating to the floor like a feather. Then I had forced myself to keep flipping until I had found what I was looking for.

Receipts. I needed to see receipts. Because I knew that Daniel kept everything, from hotels and meals to gas stops and car repairs. All of it could be expensed.

I open the flap of the envelope now and dump its contents onto the bed, a pile of receipts fluttering onto the comforter. I start flipping through each one, my eyes scanning the various addresses at the bottom.

"There are receipts from Baton Rouge, of course," I say. "Restaurants in Jackson, hotels in Alexandria. All of these receipts paint a picture of where he goes all day—and the dates at the bottom can tell us when he was there."

Aaron walks over and sits next to me, his leg pressed against mine. He grabs the receipt on the top and stares at it, his eyes trained on the bottom.

"Angola," he says. "Is that in his territory?"

"No," I say, shaking my head. "But he goes there—a lot. And that's the one that caught my attention."

"Why?"

I pluck it from him, holding it at a distance between the tips of my thumb and forefinger, like it's poisonous. Like it could bite.

"Angola is the home of the largest maximum-security prison in America," I say. "Louisiana State Penitentiary."

Aaron lifts his head. He turns to face me, his eyebrows lifted.

"The home of my father."

"Holy shit."

"Maybe they know each other," I continue, looking back at the receipt. A bottle of water, twenty dollars' worth of gas. A sleeve of sunflower seeds. I remember the way my father used to tip the whole bag into his mouth and crunch like he was chewing on a handful of fingernails. The way the shells would turn up around the house, stuck to everything. Wedged between the cracks of the kitchen table, trapped beneath my shoe. Clumping together at the bottom of a water glass, drowning in spit.

I think of my mother, spelling *Daniel* with her fingers.

"That must be why he's doing this," I say. "Why he found me. They're connected."

"Chloe, you need to go to the police."

"The police aren't going to believe me, Aaron. I've already tried."

"What do you mean, you've already tried?"

"I have a history. A past that's working against me. They think I'm crazy—"

"You are not crazy."

His words cut me short. I'm almost stunned to hear them, like he had opened his mouth and started to speak French. Because for the first time in weeks, someone believes me. Someone is on my side. And it feels so good to be believed; to have someone look at me with genuine caring instead of suspicion or worry or rage. I think about all my little moments with Aaron, moments I had been trying to push out, trying to pretend didn't mean anything. Sitting together by the bridge, talking about memories. The way I had wanted to call him that night on the couch when I was drunk and alone. I can tell he wants to keep talking, so I lean forward and kiss him once before he can say anything else. Before this feeling is gone.

"Chloe." Our faces are close, foreheads pressed together. He looks at me like he wants to pull away, like he should pull away, but instead, his hand finds its way to my leg, then up my arm and into my hair. Before long, he's kissing me back, his lips pushed hard onto mine, his fingers grabbing at anything they can find. I snake my own hands through his hair before working my way down the buttons on his shirt, his pants. I'm in college again, throwing myself at another beating heart to make my own feel less alone. He lays me down gently, his body pressed against mine, his thick arms raising my hands above my head, pinning my wrists into place. His lips work their way down my neck, my chest, and for a couple minutes, feeling Aaron slide inside of me, I let myself forget.

It's dark outside when we're finished, the only light coming from the dim glow of the bedside table. Aaron is lying beside me, his fingers playing with my hair. We haven't spoken a word.

"I believe you," he says at last. "About Daniel. You know that, right?"

"Yeah." I nod. "Yeah, I do."

"So you'll go to the police tomorrow?"

"Aaron, they won't believe me. I'm telling you. I've been starting to think—" I hesitate, turn to the side, so I'm facing him. He's still staring at the ceiling, a silhouette in the dark. "I've been starting to wonder if maybe I need to go see him. My father."

He sits up, leans his bare back against the headboard. His head swivels to face mine.

"I'm just starting to think that maybe he's the only one with answers," I continue. "Maybe he's the only one that can help me understand—"

"That's dangerous, Chloe."

"How is it dangerous? He's in prison, Aaron. He can't hurt me."

"Yes, he can. He can still hurt you from behind bars. Maybe not physically, but . . ."

He stops, runs his hands over his face.

"Sleep on it," he says. "Promise me you'll sleep on it? We can decide tomorrow. And if you want me to go with you, I will. I'll talk to him with you."

"Okay," I say at last. "Okay, I will."

"Good."

He flings his legs out of bed, leaning over to grab his jeans from the floor. I watch as he shimmies them on and walks into the bathroom, flipping on the light. I shut my eyes, hearing the squeak of the faucet, the rush of running water. When I open them, he's walking back into the bedroom again, a glass of water in his hand.

"I have to go for a while," he says, pushing it in my direction. I grab it and take a sip. "My editor hasn't heard from me all day. Are you going to be okay?"

"I'll be fine," I say, rolling back onto my pillow. I watch as Aaron looks down, his eyes landing on something on the floor. He leans over and picks up my Xanax bottle, still resting at the top of my bag.

"Do you want one of these? To help you fall asleep?"

I stare at the bottle, the collection of pills inside. Aaron shakes them gently, his eyebrows lifting, and I nod, extend my hand.

"Would you judge me if I took two?"

"No." He smiles, opening the cap and dumping two in my palm. "You've had a hell of a day."

I inspect the pills in my palm and toss them back, swallowing them down with the water, feeling each one tear down my esophagus like jagged nails trying to claw their way back up.

"I can't help but feel responsible," I say, leaning my head against the headboard. I'm thinking of Lena. Of Aubrey. Of Lacey. Of all the girls whose deaths are on my conscience. Of all the girls I have inadvertently lured into the hands of a monster—first, my father. And now, Daniel.

"You're not responsible," Aaron says, sitting on the edge of the bed. He lifts his hand and brushes it through my hair. The room starts to spin gently, my eyelids begin to droop. When I close my eyes, an image from my dream flashes into my mind—me, standing beneath my childhood window, holding a shovel covered in blood.

"It's my fault," I say, my words slurred. I can still feel Aaron's hands, warm on my forehead. "All of it, my fault."

"Get some sleep," I hear him say, almost like an echo. He leans down to kiss my forehead, his lips sticking to my skin. "I'll lock the door behind me."

I nod once before feeling myself drift away.

CHAPTER THIRTY-NINE

I wake up to the sound of my phone vibrating on the bedside table, shaking violently across the wood until it tips over the side and clatters to the floor. I open my eyes, groggy, and squint at the alarm clock.

It's ten p.m.

I try to open my eyes wider but my vision is bleary, my head pounding. I think back to my trip to Daniel's home—his mother in that dilapidated old shack, the newspaper clipping stuck between the pages of that book. Suddenly, I feel nauseated, and I drag myself from the bed and run into the bathroom, throwing open the toilet seat before heaving into the bowl. Nothing comes up but bile, acid yellow and burning my tongue. A skinny string of spit dangles from the back of my throat, making me gag. I wipe my mouth with the back of my hand and walk into the bedroom, perching on the edge of the bed. I reach for the glass of water on the table, but I see that it's on its side, the water dripping from the rim and onto the carpet. My phone must have knocked it over. Instead, I reach down and grab my phone, pressing the side to illuminate the screen.

There are a few missed calls from Aaron, some messages checking in. In an instant, I remember the feeling of his body on top of mine. His hands on my wrists, his lips on my neck. That was a mistake, what we did, but I'll have to deal with that later. I have to scroll to get through the rest of the missed calls and text messages—mostly, they're from Shannon, with a few from Daniel thrown in. *How do I have this many missed calls?* I wonder. It's only ten o'clock—I've been asleep for four hours, tops. Then I notice the date on the screen.

It's ten p.m. on *Friday*.

I've been asleep for an entire day.

I unlock my phone and look at my text messages, alarm starting to creep in as I skim each one.

Chloe, call me please. This is important.

Chloe, where are you?

Chloe, call me NOW.

Shit, I think, rubbing my temples. They're still throbbing, still screaming at me in protest. Taking two Xanax on an empty stomach was clearly a mistake, but I knew that as I was doing it. All I wanted was to sleep. To forget. After all, I've barely slept in a week with Daniel pushed up against me. Clearly, it caught up with me.

I scroll to Shannon's name and hit *Call,* holding the phone to my ear as it rings. They've obviously discovered my lie. Daniel must have texted her like he said he would, even though I asked him not to. Then, once they realized that I was lying to them both, that I was missing without a valid explanation as to where I had gone and who I was with, panic must have set in. But right now, I don't really care. I'm not going home to Daniel. I'm still not convinced that I can go to the police, either—Detective Thomas made it clear that I am to stay out of the investigation. But between the newspaper article and the engagement ring, the Angola receipts and my conversation with Daniel's mother, maybe I can get their attention this time. Maybe I can get them to listen.

Then it hits me: the engagement ring. I had pulled it off my finger in Aaron's car, thrown it to the floor. I don't think I ever picked it back up. I look down at my empty hand before twisting around and moving my fingers through the rumpled comforter on the bed. My palm hits something hard and I flip the blanket back— but it's not the ring. It's Aaron's press badge, hidden in the sheets. In a flash, I see myself unbuttoning his shirt, shrugging it off his shoulders. I pick it up, bring it close. I stare at his picture and I let myself wonder, for a minute, if maybe last night wasn't a mistake. If maybe, in some strange twist of fate, this was how we were meant to find each other.

The phone stops ringing, and when Shannon answers, I can immediately tell that something is wrong. She sniffles.

"Chloe, where the hell are you?"

Her voice is croaky, like she's been gargling nails.

"Shannon," I say, sitting up straighter. I stick Aaron's badge in my pocket. "Is everything okay?"

"No, everything is not okay," she snaps. A little sob erupts from her throat. "Where are you?"

"I'm . . . in town. I just needed to clear my head for a little bit. What's going on?"

Another sob bursts through the speaker—this time, louder—and the noise makes me physically recoil, like it slapped me through the phone. I hold my arm out, listening to the wails on the other side of the line as she tries to string enough words together to form a complete thought.

"It's . . . Riley . . ." she says, and immediately, I feel like I'm going to be sick again. I already know what she's going to say before she has the chance to say it. "She's . . . she's *gone*."

"What do you mean, 'she's gone'?" I ask, although I know what she means. I know it in my gut. I picture Riley at our engagement party, slouched down in our living room, her skinny legs crossed. Her sneaker feet kicking against the leg of the chair. Her phone in one hand, her hair twirling in the other.

I think about Daniel, the way he was staring at her. The words he said to Shannon, words I once thought were reassuring, their meaning now much more sinister.

One day, they'll just be distant memories.

"I mean, she's *gone*." She takes three little breaths in quick succession. "We woke up this morning, and she wasn't in her room. She snuck out again, through the window, but she hasn't come home. It's been an entire day."

"Did you call Daniel?" I ask, hoping the tension in my voice doesn't give anything away. "I mean, when you couldn't reach me?"

"Yes," she says, her voice tense now. "He was under the impression that we were together. At your bachelorette party."

I close my eyes, lower my head.

"There's obviously something going on with you two. You've been lying to us about something. But you know what, Chloe? I don't have time for it. I just want to know where my daughter is."

I'm quiet, unsure of where to even begin. Her daughter is in trouble, Riley is in trouble, and I'm pretty sure I know why. But how do I break that news to her? How do I tell her that Daniel probably has her? That he was probably there, waiting, when she tossed her sheet out her bedroom window and climbed down into the dark? That he knew she would be there because Shannon had told him herself, that night in our home? That he chose last night because *I* was gone, giving him the freedom to roam around as he pleased?

How do I tell her that her daughter is probably dead because of me?

"I'm going to come over," I say. "I'm going to come over now and explain everything."

"I'm not home now," she says. "I'm in the car, driving around. I'm looking for my daughter. But we could use your help."

"Of course," I say. "Just tell me where to be."

I hang up with instructions to drive down every side street within a ten-mile radius of their home. I stand up from the bed and look down, my duffel bag resting by my feet, Daniel's receipts piled on top of that white envelope. I reach down and push everything back into my bag and grab the handle, flinging it over my shoulder. Then I look back down at my phone, at the texts from Daniel.

Chloe, can you call me, please?
Chloe, where are you?

I have a voice mail, and for a second, I consider deleting it. I can't hear his voice right now. I can't hear his excuses. But what if he has Riley? What if I can still save her? I press the recording and lift the phone to my ear. His voice seeps into my brain, slippery like oil, filling every corner, every gap. Coating everything.

Hi, Chloe. Listen . . . I don't really know what's going on with you right now. You're not at your bachelorette party. I just talked to Shannon. I don't know where you are, but obviously, something is wrong.

The line is quiet for too long. I look down at my phone, to see if the voice mail is over, but the timer is still ticking forward. Finally, he speaks again.

I'm going to be gone by the time you get home. God knows where you are right now. I'll be gone by tomorrow morning. This is your house. Whatever it is that you're trying to work through, you shouldn't feel like you can't do it from here.

My chest constricts. He's leaving. He's *running*.

I love you, he says. It comes out more like a sigh. *More than you know.*

The recording ends abruptly, and I'm left standing in the middle of the motel room, Daniel's voice still echoing around me. *I'll be gone by tomorrow morning.* I glance at the alarm clock again—it's ten thirty now. Maybe he's still there. Maybe he's still home. Maybe I can get there before he leaves, figure out where he's running to, and notify the police.

I walk quickly toward the door, stepping into the parking lot. The sun has already descended below the trees, the glow of the streetlights turning their branches into gnarled shadows. I stop in my tracks, instinctively uneasy of the darkness. The cloak of night. But then I think of Riley. Of Aubrey and Lacey. I think of Lena. I think of the girls, of all the missing girls out there, and I force myself to keep walking toward the truth.

CHAPTER FORTY

I turn my headlights off as soon as I pull onto our street, though I quickly realize it's pointless. Daniel won't see me coming, because Daniel is already gone. I can tell the minute my car creeps past our empty driveway. The lights, both inside and out, are off. My house, once again, looks dead.

I lean my head against the steering wheel. I'm too late. He could be anywhere by now—anywhere with Riley. I rack my brain, trying to imagine his final movements. Trying to visualize where he would go.

Then I lift my head. I have an idea.

I remember the camera, that pinprick in the corner of my living room that Bert Rhodes installed. I pull out my phone and tap on the security app, holding my breath as the image on my screen begins to load. It's my living room—dark, empty. I half expect to see Daniel hiding in the shadows, waiting for me to walk inside. I press the slider at the bottom of the screen, moving it back in time, watching as my house illuminates and Daniel finally appears.

Thirty minutes ago, he was here. He was walking around the house, busying himself with maddeningly normal tasks like wiping down a countertop, stacking the mail two, three times before positioning it in a slightly different spot. As I watch him, I'm left thinking of those words again: *serial killer.* The taste is funny in my mouth, the same way it was twenty years ago as I watched my father hand-wash the dishes and dry each one with meticulous care, mindful not to chip the edges. *Serial killer.* Why would he care about something like that? Why would a serial killer care about preserving my grandmother's china when he didn't even care about preserving a life?

Daniel walks over to the couch and sits on the edge, rubbing his fingers absentmindedly across his jaw. I've watched him so many times before this, observed the little things he does when he thinks nobody else is looking. I've watched him make dinner in the kitchen, noticing the way he tops off my glass with the last dribbles of a bottle of wine before swiping his finger across the lip and licking it clean. I've watched him get out of the shower, tousling the strands of damp hair that cascade across his forehead before grabbing his comb and pushing them neatly to one side. And every time I've watched him, every time I've witnessed one of those little private moments, I've always been met with a sense of awe, as if he couldn't possibly be real.

And now I know why.

He isn't real. Not really. The Daniel I know, the Daniel I fell in love with, is a caricature of a man, a mask the real one donned to hide his true face. He lured me in, in the same way he lured in those girls; he showed me everything I wanted to see, told me everything I wanted to hear. He made me feel safe, he made me feel loved.

But now I think about all those *other* moments—the moments when he showed me pieces of his real self. When he let his mask slip for just a minute. I should have seen it before.

After all, it comes back to Aaron's description of

the two different kinds of copycats: those who revere and those who revile. Clearly, Daniel reveres my father. He's been following him for twenty years, mirroring his crimes since he was seventeen. He visits him in prison, but at a certain point, that wasn't enough. It wasn't enough to kill anymore. It wasn't enough to take a life and dump it somewhere; he needed to take a life and keep it. He needed to take *my* life, hijack it the way my father had. He needed to trick me every single day, the way my father had. I watch him now, those hands that pushed his sister's ring on my finger, marking his territory. Those hands that gripped my throat as he kissed me, squeezing just a little too tight. Teasing me, testing me. I am no different from a piece of jewelry tucked away safely in a darkened closet corner—his trophy, a living, breathing reminder of his accomplishments. I watch him now and feel the anger surge in my chest like a rising tide, getting higher and higher, taking me down, drowning me alive.

I watch as Daniel stands, reaching into his back pocket. He pulls something out, stares at it for a while. I squint, trying to make it out, but it's too small. I pinch my cell phone screen with two fingers, zooming in on his hand, and that's when I recognize it: the thin silver chain puddled in his palm, spilling over the edge of his wrist. A tiny cluster of diamonds glinting in the light.

I think back to him getting out of bed, creeping across the bedroom, and pushing the closet door shut. I feel the heat building from my chest and into my throat, up my cheeks, radiating through my eyes.

I was right. He did take it.

I think of all the times now that Daniel has made me doubt myself, my sanity, if only for a moment. *I'm going to New Orleans, don't you remember?* Second-guessing the things that I had seen; the things I knew in my heart to be true. He continues to stare into his palm until he finally exhales, pushing it back into his pocket. He walks toward the front door, and that's when I notice a suitcase resting in the hallway, his laptop bag leaned gently against the wall. He picks them both up, turns around. Surveys the room one final time. Then he lifts his finger to the light switch, and like a pair of pursed lips channeling breath into a flame, everything goes black.

I place my phone in my cup holder, trying to decipher what I just watched. It isn't much—but it's something. Half an hour ago, Daniel was here. He isn't too far ahead of me. I just need to figure out where he would go. The possibilities are endless, really. He could go anywhere. He has a suitcase. He could be driving across the country, prepared to hole up in a hotel room somewhere. Maybe even go south into Mexico—the border is less than ten hours away. He could be there by morning.

But then, I think of that necklace, his finger stroking the silver as it rests in his palm. I think of Riley, still missing. Her body not yet discovered. And I realize: He isn't running, because he isn't done yet. He still has work to do.

The coroner had determined that the victims' bodies had been moved after death. That they had died somewhere else before being dropped back in the same place they had vanished. So, if that's the case, *where is Riley?* Where could he possibly be keeping her? Where did he keep all of them?

And then it hits me. I know. Somehow, deep down, on a cellular level. I know.

Before I can talk myself out of it, I start my car, flip on my headlights, and drive. I try to distract myself by thinking of anything and anywhere other than where I'm about to be—but as the minutes tick by, I can feel my heartbeat accelerating. With every passing mile, it gets harder and harder to breath. Thirty minutes go by, then forty. I know I'm almost there. I glance at the clock in my car—it's just before midnight—and when I peel my eyes from the dashboard and back to the road, that's when I see it, approaching slowly in the distance. That old, familiar sign, rusted on the edges and dirty from years of mud and grime caking to the metal. I feel my palms go slick with sweat, the panic setting in as it inches closer and closer into view. A flickering light illuminating it with a sick glow.

WELCOME TO BREAUX BRIDGE:
CRAWFISH CAPITAL OF THE WORLD

I'm going home.

CHAPTER FORTY-ONE

I turn on my blinker and take the next exit. Breaux Bridge. A place I haven't seen since I left for college more than a decade ago; a place I never expected to see again.

I wind through town, through the rows of old brick buildings with moss-green awnings. In my mind, this place seems to be separated by a crisp, clean line: *before* and *after.* On one side of the line, the memories are bright, happy. A small-town childhood filled with gas station snow cones and consignment store Rollerblades; the bakery I used to duck inside every day at three p.m., picking up a complimentary slice of sourdough, still warm from the oven. Melted butter dripping down my chin as I walked home from school, jumping over the cracks on the sidewalk, picking a bouquet of flowering weeds that I would present to my mother in a cloudy juice glass.

On the other side, a bloated cloud hovers over everything.

I pass the empty fairgrounds where the festival takes place each year. I see the very spot where I stood with Lena, my forehead pressed against her warm stomach, the dampness of her sweat sticking to my skin. A metallic firefly glowing in my hands. I look across the field, at the spot where my father stood in the distance, staring at us. At her. I drive past my old school, past the dumpster where a senior boy had slammed my head against the metal, threatening to do to me what my father had done to his sister.

Daniel has been driving this same route for weeks, I realize, disappearing into the night before coming home again tired and sweaty and full of life. I approach my street and pull over onto the side of the road, just before my old driveway. I eye that long path I used to run down, kicking up dust before vanishing into the trees. Running up the porch steps, slamming into my father's outstretched arms. It's the perfect place to take a missing girl: an old abandoned house situated on ten acres of discarded land. A house that nobody visits, nobody touches. A house that's considered haunted, the very place where Dick Davis buried his six victims before ducking into my bedroom and kissing me good night.

I think back to that conversation with Daniel, both of us stretched out across my living room couch. The conversation when I had told him everything for the first time—and how he had listened, so intently. Lena and her belly-button ring, a single firefly glowing in the dark. My father, a shadow in the trees. The box in the closet holding his secrets.

And my house. I had told him about my house. The epicenter of it all.

After my father went to prison and my mother was no longer able to care for the property, the responsibility had landed on us—on Cooper and me. But just like we had abandoned my mother to Riverside, we chose to abandon this place, too. We didn't want to deal with it, didn't want to face the memories that still lived inside. So instead, we just left it here, sitting empty for years, our furniture still arranged in the exact same way, a thick layer of cobwebs probably coating everything inside. That wooden beam in my mother's closet still snapped from the pressure of her neck, the ash from my father's pipe still staining the living room carpet. All of it—a snapshot of my past, frozen in time, dust particles suspended in the air as if somebody had simply pressed *Pause*. Then turned around, closed the door, and left.

And Daniel knew. Daniel knew it was here. He knew it was empty—ready and waiting for him.

My hands clench the steering wheel, my heart pounding in my chest. I sit in silence for a few seconds, wondering what to do. I think about calling Detective Thomas, asking him to meet me here. But what would he do, exactly? What proof do I have? Then I think about my father, making his way through these very woods at night, a shovel slouched over one shoulder. I think about myself, twelve years old, watching through my open window.

Watching, waiting, but not doing anything.

Riley could be in there. She could be in trouble. I grab my purse, a shaky hand opening the lip to reveal the gun nestled inside—the gun I had grabbed from the closet before leaving on my trip, the gun I had been looking for that night of the alarm. Then I take a breath before easing myself out of the car, closing the door with a silent *click*.

The air is warm and damp like a boiled-egg burp, the sulfur from the swamp oppressive in the summer heat. I tiptoe toward the driveway and stand there for a while, peering down that road toward home. The woods on either side are pitch-black, but I force myself to take a step forward. And then another. Another. Soon, I'm approaching the house. I had forgotten how absolute the darkness is out here, with no lights from the street or neighboring houses—but with that perfect,

inky contrast, the moonlight always shines so bright. I
look up at the full moon above me, totally unobscured.
It beams on the house like a spotlight, making it glow. I
can see it now, perfectly—the chipped white paint, the
wood siding peeling under years of heat and humidity,
the grass growing wild beneath my feet. Vines crawl
up the side of the house like veins, giving it an otherworldly appearance, pulsing with devilish life. I start
to creep up the stairs, avoiding the spots that are prone
to creaking, but I notice that the blinds are open—and
with the moon this bright, if Daniel is inside, I know I
could be seen. So instead, I turn and walk around back.
I eye the junk cluttering the backyard the way it always
has—there are piles of old plywood stacked against the
back of the house along with a shovel and a wheelbar-
row with other gardening tools loaded inside. I imagine
my mother on her hands and knees, soil pushed into her
skin, a streak of dirt swiped across her forehead. I try
to peer through the windows, but back here, the blinds
are all closed, the lack of light on this side of the house
making it impossible to see anything through the gaps.
I try twisting the doorknob, jiggling it slightly, but it
doesn't open. It's locked.

I exhale, resting my hands on my hips.

Then I have an idea.

I look at the door, summoning that day with Lena to
the forefront of my mind—library card in hand, breaking into my brother's bedroom.

*First, check the hinges. If you can't see them, it's the
right kind of lock.*

I dig into my pocket and pull out Aaron's badge, still
wedged in my jeans after I had found it buried beneath
the motel room sheets. I bend it in my hands—it's
sturdy enough—and insert it into the gap at an angle,
just like Lena taught me.

Once the corner is in, straighten it up.

I start to wiggle the card, applying gentle pressure, moving it back and forth, back and forth. I push it in deeper, my free hand twisting the knob—until finally, I hear a click.

CHAPTER FORTY-TWO

The back door pushes open, and I yank hard to free the card, wrapping it in my hand as I step inside. I feel my way through the hallway, trailing my fingers along the familiar walls to keep myself straight. The darkness is disorienting; I hear creaking in every direction, but I don't know if it's simply the noises of an old house or if it's Daniel, creeping up behind me, arms extended, ready to strike.

I feel the hallway open up to our living room, and as I step inside, the room illuminates with the glow of the moon through the blinds, making it bright enough to see. I glance at my surroundings. The shadows of the room look exactly the way I remember them: my father's old La-Z-Boy recliner in the corner, the leather faded and cracking. The TV on the floor with smudges on the screen from where my fingers pressed into the glass. This is where Daniel has been going: this house. This awful, terrible house is where he vanishes each week. It's where he takes his victims, doing God-knows-what with them before returning to the spot where they disappeared and dumping their bodies. I look to my right, and that's when I notice an unusual shape on the floor, long and lean like a stack of wooden boards.

A shape like a body. The body of a young girl.

"Riley?" I whisper, running across the living room and toward the shadow. Before I reach it, I can see that it's her: eyes closed, mouth shut, hair loose around her cheeks and cascading across her chest. Even in the dark, or perhaps because of the dark, the paleness of her face is startling—she looks like a ghost, lips blue, all the blood drained from her skin, giving her a translucent glow.

"Riley," I say again, my fingers shaking her arm. She doesn't move; she doesn't speak. I look at her wrists, at the line of red starting to form across her veins. I look at her neck, preparing myself to see those faint, finger-shaped bruises beginning to marble across the skin—but they're not there. Not yet.

"Riley," I repeat, shaking her gently. "Riley, come on."

I bring my fingers beneath her ear and hold my breath, hoping to feel something, anything. And it's there—just barely, but it's there. A gentle pounding, her heartbeat, slow and labored. She's still alive.

"Come on," I whisper, trying to lift her up. Her body is deadweight heavy, but when I grab her arms, I see her eyes flicker, a rapid side-to-side movement, and she emits a gentle groan. It's the Diazepam, I realize. She's heavily drugged. "I'm going to get you out of here. I promise I'm going to—"

"Chloe?"

Immediately, my heart stops—there's someone behind me. I recognize his voice, the way my name rolls around in his mouth like a lozenge before melting on his tongue. I would recognize it anywhere.

But it doesn't belong to Daniel.

I stand up slowly, turning around to face the figure behind me. The room is just bright enough for me to make out his features.

"Aaron." I try to think of an explanation, a reason for

why he's standing here, in this house—*my* house—but my mind goes blank. "What are you doing here?"

The moon dips behind a cloud, and suddenly, the room goes dark. My eyes widen, trying to see, and when the light streams through the blinds again, Aaron seems closer—by a foot, maybe two.

"I could ask you the same question."

I turn my head to the side, looking at Riley, and I realize how this must look. Me, kneeling over an unconscious girl in the dark. I think back to Detective Thomas hovering in my office, the way he had glared at me, suspicious. My fingerprints on Aubrey's earring. His words, accusatory.

The common thread binding all this together seems to be you.

I motion to Riley and open my mouth, trying to speak, but I feel a choke lodge itself in my throat. I stop, clear it.

"She's alive, thank God," Aaron interrupts, taking a step closer. "I just found her myself. I tried to get her to wake up but I couldn't. I called the police. They're on their way."

I look at him, still unable to speak. He senses my hesitation and keeps talking.

"I remembered you had mentioned this house. How it just sits here, empty. I thought maybe she might be here. I called you a few times." He lifts his arms, as if to gesture to the room, before dropping them back to his sides. "I guess we had the same idea."

I exhale, nodding. I think back to last night, to Aaron in my motel room. His eager hands as they snaked through my hair; the way we lay there afterward, quietly. His voice in my ear: *I believe you.*

"We have to help her," I say, finding my voice. I swing back around to Riley and crouch down next to her, checking her pulse again. "We have to make her throw up or something—"

"The police are coming," Aaron says again. "Chloe, it's going to be okay. She'll be fine."

"Daniel has to be close," I say, rubbing my fingers against her cheek. It feels cold. "When I woke up, I had all these missed calls. He left me a voice mail, and I thought maybe—"

Then I stop, remembering the sequence of that night again. Of me drifting into sleep, of Aaron's chapped lips sticking to my forehead as he kissed me goodnight. I stand up slowly, turning around. Suddenly, I don't want my back to be facing him.

"Wait a second." My thoughts are moving slowly, like they're trudging through mud. "How did you know Riley was missing?"

I remember waking up, a full day later, after Aaron had left. Calling Shannon, those slow, wet sobs.

Riley's gone.

"It's on the news," he says. But there's something about the way he says it—cold and rehearsed—that I don't quite believe.

I take a small step backward, trying to put more distance between us. Trying to stand firm between Aaron and Riley. I watch his expression change as I step away—the slight hardening of his lips into a thin, tight line; his jaw muscles tensing, his fingers curling into his palms.

"Chloe, come on," he says, trying to smile. "There's a search party and everything. The whole town is out looking for her. Everyone knows."

He reaches his arms out, like he wants to grab my hands, but instead of moving toward him, I put my own hands up, motioning for him to stop moving.

"It's me," he says. "It's Aaron. Chloe, you *know* me."

The moon streams through the blinds again, and that's when I see it, lying on the ground between us. I must have dropped it when I ran to Riley, my hands frantically searching her body for a pulse: Aaron's press badge. The card I had used to jimmy the back door. But now, something about it looks . . . different.

I lean down slowly, refusing to peel my eyes from Aaron, and pick it up. I bring it to my face, looking closer, and that's when I notice that it's cracking, the force from the door causing it to break. The edges are fraying. I flick at the tattered paper, pulling it gently, and the entire face begins to peel. I feel a shiver run down my spine.

It's not a real press badge. It's fake.

I look up at Aaron, standing there, watching. Then I think back to the first time I saw this card, in that café, conveniently clipped to his shirt. Easy to read, that *New York Times* logo big and bold, printed at the top. That was the moment I had first met Aaron—but that wasn't the first time I had seen him. I had known it was him because I had seen his picture, in my office, the Ativan making my limbs tingle as I drank in his headshot online—small and grainy, black-and-white. That checkered button-up and tortoiseshell glasses. The exact same outfit he had been wearing when he stepped into that coffee shop, rolling his sleeves to his elbows. And now, I realize with a sense of sinking dread: That had been on purpose. All of it, on purpose. The outfit, something he knew I would recognize. The press badge with the name *Aaron Jansen* printed somewhere easy to see. I remember thinking that he had looked different from his picture, different from what I was expecting . . . bigger, huskier. His arms too thick, his voice two octaves too low. But I had just assumed this man was Aaron Jansen before he had even introduced himself, before he had ever uttered the name. And the way he had sauntered into that café—slowly, confidently—as if he knew I was there, where I was sitting. As if he was putting on a show, like he knew I was watching him.

It's because he had been watching me, too.

"Who are you?" I ask now, his face, in the dark, suddenly unrecognizable.

He stands in place, quiet. There's a hollowness to him that I've never noticed before, as if all the yolk has been drained from him, his body a cracked shell. He seems to consider the question for a moment, trying to determine how best to respond.

"I'm nobody," he says at last.

"Did you do this?"

I watch as he opens his mouth and closes it again, as though he's searching for the words. He doesn't respond, and I find myself thinking back to every conversation we've ever had. His words are loud now, echoing around me like the blood I can hear pulsing in my ears.

Copycats murder because they're obsessed with another murderer.

I look at this man, this stranger, who injected himself into my life at the start of all this. The man who had first shared the theory about a copycat, nudging me along until, finally, I believed it, too. Those questions he had asked, always probing, leaning in close: *There's a reason this is happening, right here, right now.* When I had talked about Lena, the childlike giddiness that had crept into his voice, almost as if he couldn't help himself, he had to know: *What was she like?*

"Answer me," I say, trying to keep my voice from shaking. "Did you?"

"Look, Chloe. It's not what you think."

I think of him in my bed, his hands on my wrists, his lips on my neck. I think of him standing up, pulling on his jeans. Bringing me that cup of water before running his fingers through my hair, lulling me to sleep before stepping back into the dark. That was the night Riley went missing. That was the night she was taken—by *him,* as I slept, my forehead dotted with sweat, my limbs still throbbing from his touch. I feel disgust bubble up from the pit of my stomach. But that's what he had told me, after all—that day on the river, cardboard cups of coffee between our feet, gazing out at the bridge in the distance, emerging gently from beneath a blanket of fog.

It's a game.

Only I didn't realize that the game was his.

"I'm calling the police," I say, knowing now that he never called them himself. That they're not coming. I push my hand into my purse, fumbling for my phone. My fingers are shaking, brushing up against everything inside—and then it hits me: My phone is in the car, still lodged inside my cup holder. It's still where I had placed it after I had watched Daniel on my camera before driving mindlessly to Breaux Bridge, parking the car, breaking inside. How could I have forgotten it? How could I have forgotten my phone?

"Chloe, come on," he says, moving closer. He's only a few feet away from me now, close enough to touch. "Let me explain."

"Why did you do it?" I ask, my hand still shoved deep into my purse, my lip quivering. "Why did you kill those girls?"

The minute the words escape my lips, I feel it again: the déjà vu, washing over me like a wave. The memory of me, sitting in this very room, twenty years ago. My fingers pressed against the television, listening as the judge asked my father the exact same question. The silence of the courtroom as everyone waited, as I waited, desperate for the truth.

"It wasn't my fault," he says at last, a dampness in his eyes. "It wasn't."

"It wasn't your fault," I repeat. "You killed two girls, and it wasn't your fault."

"No, I mean . . . It was. Yes, it was. But also, it wasn't—"

I look at this man, and I see my father. I see him on my television screen, arms chained behind him, as I sat on the floor, drinking in his every word. I see the devil that lives somewhere deep inside of him—a wet, pulsing fetus curled up in his belly, growing slowly, until one day, it burst. My father and his darkness; that shadow in the corner, drawing him in, swallowing him whole. The silence of the courtroom as he confessed, tears in his eyes. The voice of the judge, disbelieving. Full of disgust.

And you're telling me that this darkness is what forced you to kill those girls?

"You're exactly like him," I say. "Trying to blame something else for what you did."

"No. No, it's not like that."

I can practically feel my fingernails digging into my palms, drawing blood. The anger and rage that had surged through my chest as I watched him that day; my indifference at seeing him cry. I remember how I had hated him in that moment. Hated him with every cell in my body.

I remember how I had killed him. In my mind, I had killed him.

"Chloe, just listen to me," he says, taking a few steps closer. I look at his arms, reaching out toward me, soft hands outstretched. The same hands that had touched my skin, intertwined with my fingers. I had run into his arms the same way I had run into my father's, looking for safety in all the wrong places. "He made me do it—"

I hear it before I actually see it, before I can even register what I've done. It's as if I'm watching it happen to someone else: my arm, emerging from my purse, the gun in my hand. One single gunshot, exploding loud like a firecracker, jerking my arm back. A flash of bright light as his legs stagger back across the hardwood, glancing down at the pool of red expanding across his stomach before he looks back at me, surprised. The moonlight as it stretches across his eyes, glassy and confused. His lips, red and wet, parting slowly as if he's trying to speak.

Then I watch as his body slumps to the floor.

CHAPTER FORTY-THREE

I'm sitting in the Breaux Bridge Police Department, the cheap bulbs fastened to the ceiling of the interrogation room making my skin glow a radioactive algae green. The blanket they had draped over my shoulders is scratchy like Velcro, but I'm too cold to take it off.

"All right, Chloe. Why don't you take us through what happened one more time?"

I look up at Detective Thomas. He's sitting on the other side of the table alongside Officer Doyle and a Breaux Bridge cop whose name I've already forgotten.

"I already told her," I say, looking at the unnamed officer. "She has it on tape."

"Just one more time for me," he says. "And then we can take you home."

I exhale, my hand reaching for the paper cup of coffee sitting on the table in front of me. It's my third cup of the night, and as I bring it to my lips, I notice microscopic specs of blood dried to my skin. I put the cup down, pick at one spot with my fingernail, and watch as it flakes off like paint.

"I met the man I knew to be Aaron Jansen a few weeks ago," I say. "He told me he was writing a story about my father. That he was a reporter for *The New York Times*. Eventually, he claimed that his story had changed due to the disappearances of Aubrey Gravino and Lacey Deckler. That he believed it was the work of a copycat, and he wanted my help to solve it."

Detective Thomas nods, urging me to continue.

"Throughout our conversations, I started to believe him. There were so many similarities: the victims, the missing jewelry. The anniversary coming up. Initially, I believed it could have been Bert Rhodes—I told you that—but later that night, I found something in my closet. A necklace that matched Aubrey's earrings."

"And why didn't you bring this evidence to us when you found it?"

"I tried," I say. "But the next morning, it was gone. My fiancé took it—I have a video of him holding it, on my phone—and that's when I started to believe that he may have had something to do with it. But even if I did have it, during our last conversation, you made it pretty clear that you didn't believe anything I said. You practically told me to fuck off."

He stares at me from across the room, shifting uncomfortably. I stare back.

"Anyway, there's more than that. He's been visiting my father in prison. I found Diazepam in his briefcase. His own sister went missing, twenty years ago, and when I visited his mother, she told me that she actually thought he might have had something to do with it—"

"Okay," the detective interrupts, holding up a hand, fingers outstretched. "One thing at a time. What brought you to Breaux Bridge tonight? How did you know Riley Tack would be here?"

The image of Riley, ghostly pale, is still etched into my mind. Of the ambulance as it came flying down my driveway—of me, standing in the front yard, the phone I had retrieved from my car clutched in my hand as I waited, my body rigid and eyes unfocused. Unable to go back into that house, unable to face the dead body on the floor. The paramedics loading her into the back, tied to a stretcher, bags of fluids rushing into her veins.

"Daniel left me a voice mail, telling me he was leaving," I say. "I was trying to figure out where he might have been going, where he could have been bringing the girls. I just had a feeling that he was bringing them here. I don't know."

"Okay." Detective Thomas nods. "And where is Daniel now?"

I look up at him, my eyes stinging from the harsh lights, the bitter coffee, the lack of sleep. Everything.

"I don't know," I say again. "He's gone."

The room is quiet except for the buzzing of the lights overhead, like a single fly trapped inside of a tin can. Aaron killed those girls. He tried to kill Riley. Finally, I have my answers—but there is still so much that I don't understand. So much that doesn't make sense.

"I know you don't believe me," I say, looking up. "I know this sounds crazy, but I'm telling you the truth. I had no idea—"

"I believe you, Chloe," Detective Thomas interrupts. "I do."

I nod, trying not to show the relief that I feel flowing over me. I don't know what I was expecting him to say, but it wasn't this. I was expecting an argument, a demand for proof that I can't produce. And then I realize: He must know something that I don't.

"You know who he is," I say, understanding dawning on me slowly. "Aaron, I mean. You know who he really is."

The detective looks back at me, his expression unreadable.

"You have to tell me. I deserve to know."

"His name was Tyler Price," he says at last, leaning over as he pulls his briefcase onto the table. He opens it up, pulls out a mug shot, and places it between us. I stare at Aaron's face—no, *Tyler's* face. He looks like a Tyler, different without the glasses magnifying his eyes, the snugly fit button-ups, his hair buzzed short. He has one of those generic faces that seems recognizable to everybody—bland features, no easily identifiable marks—but there is a vague resemblance to that headshot I had seen online, to the real Aaron Jansen. He could pass as a second cousin, maybe. An older brother. The kind who buys liquor for high-schoolers then shows up to the party, slinking off to the corner. Sipping a beer in silence, observing.

I swallow, my eyes drilling into the table. Tyler Price. I scold myself for falling for it, for so easily seeing what he had wanted me to see—but at the same time, maybe I had seen what *I* had wanted to see. I had needed an ally, after all. Someone on my side. But it had only been a game to him. All of it, a game. And Aaron Jansen had been nothing more than a character.

"We were able to ID him almost immediately," Detective Thomas continues. "He's from Breaux Bridge."

My head snaps up, eyes wide.

"What?"

"He was already in their system for some smaller stuff a while back. Possession of marijuana, trespassing. Dropped out of school just before the ninth grade."

I look back down at his picture, trying to conjure up a memory. Any memory of Tyler Price. Breaux Bridge is a small town, after all—then again, I never had many friends.

"What else do you know about him?"

"He was seen at Cypress Cemetery," he says, pulling another picture from his briefcase. This time, it's of the search party—with Tyler in the distance, glasses off, baseball cap pulled down low over his forehead. "Murderers can be known to revisit their crime scenes, especially repeat offenders. It seems Tyler took it a step further with you. Not only revisiting the scenes, but getting involved in the case itself. At a distance, of course. It's not unheard of."

Tyler had been there, been everywhere. I think back to the cemetery, those eyes that I could feel on my back, always. Watching as I pushed through the headstones, crouched in the dirt. I imagine him holding Aubrey's earring in one gloved hand, crouching down to tie his shoe, and leaving it there, waiting for me to find it. That picture of me he had shown me on his phone. He didn't find it online, I realize. He took it himself.

And then it hits me.

I think back to my childhood, after my father's arrest. Those footprints we had found around our property. That nameless kid I had caught, staring through our windows. Propelled by a sick curiosity, a fascination with death.

Who are you? I had screamed, charging forward. His answer was the same then as it was last night, twenty years later.

I'm nobody.

"We're processing his car now," Detective Thomas continues, but I can barely hear him. "We found Diazepam in his pocket. A gold ring that we assume at this point belongs to Riley. A bracelet. Wooden beads with a metal cross."

I pinch my nose with my fingers. It's all too much.

"Hey," he says, dipping his head so he can see my eyes. I glance up, weary. "This isn't your fault."

"But it is, though," I say. "It is my fault. He found them because of me. They *died* because of me. I should have recognized him—"

He holds out his palm, gives his head a little shake.

"Don't even go there," he says. "It was twenty years ago. You were just a kid."

He's right, I know. I was just a kid, only twelve years old. But still.

"You know who else is just a kid?" he asks.

I look at him, my eyebrows raised.

"Who?"

"Riley," he says. "And because of you, she made it out alive."

CHAPTER FORTY-FOUR

Detective Thomas rests his hands on his hips as we walk out of the station, as if he's standing on a mountain peak somewhere, not in a parking lot, surveying our surroundings. It's six a.m. The air is somehow both muggy and cool, an early-morning anomaly, and I'm keenly aware of the chirping birds in the distance, the cotton-candy skies, the first few motorists on their commutes to work. I squint my eyes, feeling foggy and confused. There is no sense of time inside of a police station—no windows, no clocks. The world creeps by around you as you're being force-fed caffeine at four in the morning, smelling some off-duty cop's slightly sour leftovers heat up in the break-room kitchen. I can feel my brain struggling to understand how it's sunrise, the start of a new day, when my mind is still stuck on last night.

A bead of sweat drips down my neck, and I reach my hand back, feeling the salt water run between my fingers like blood. That's all I can seem to think about—blood, the way it pools, snaking its way across the path of least resistance. Ever since I looked down and saw Tyler's stomach, that dark puddle expanding slowly across his shirt. The way it had trickled across the floor, creeping slowly toward me. Enveloping my shoes, staining the soles. It just kept coming, like someone had taken a pair of scissors to a rubber hose, letting the liquid gush.

"Listen, what you said earlier." Detective Thomas breaks the silence. "About your fiancé."

I'm still looking at my shoes, at the line of red at the bottom. If I didn't know better, I could have stepped in spilt paint.

"Are you sure?" he asks. "There could be an explanation—"

"I'm sure," I interrupt.

"That video on your phone. You can't really get a good look at what's in his hand. It could be anything."

"I'm sure."

I can feel him looking at the side of my face before he straightens up, nods to himself.

"Okay," he says. "We'll find him. Ask him some questions."

I think of Tyler's final words to me, echoing through my house, my mind.

He made me do it.

"Thank you."

"But until then, go home. Get some rest. I'll have an undercover patrolling your neighborhood, just in case."

"Yeah," I say. "Yeah, okay."

"You need a ride?"

Detective Thomas drops me back off at my car, still parked on the road outside my childhood home. I don't let myself look up, instead shuffling straight from his cruiser into my driver's seat, eyes on the gravel, cranking the engine and driving away. I don't think about much on the ride back to Baton Rouge, my eyes focusing on the yellow line in the highway until I feel cross-eyed. I pass a sign inviting me to Angola—fifty-three miles northeast—and grip the wheel a little bit harder. It all comes back to him, after all: my father. Daniel's receipts, the way Tyler had tried to stop me from going to see him that night at the motel. *Chloe, it's danger-ous.* My father knows something. He is the key to all of this. He is the common thread between Tyler and Daniel and those dead girls and me, binding us all to-gether like flies caught in the same web. He holds the answers—him, and nobody else. I've known that, of course. I've been toying with the idea of visiting him, spinning it around in my mind like fingers working at a ball of clay, hoping for a shape to form. An answer to be revealed.

But nothing ever was.

I step through my front door and expect to hear chimes, now a familiar comfort of my alarm, but noth-ing happens. I look at the keypad, notice that it hasn't been set. Then I remember watching Daniel on my cell phone, flicking the lights off, the last one to leave. I punch the code into the keypad and walk upstairs, straight into my bathroom, dropping my purse onto the toilet seat. I run a bath, twisting the faucet as far left as it can possibly go, hoping the scalding water will burn straight through my flesh, washing Tyler from my skin.

I dip my toe into the tub and slide inside, my body turning an angry pink. The water rises to my chest, my collarbones. I sink so deep that everything is submerged but my face; I hear my heartbeat in my ears. I glance over at my purse, at the bottle of pills tucked inside. I imagine taking them all, falling asleep. The little bub-bles that would escape from my lips as I sank deeper, until finally, the last one burst. It would be peaceful, at least. Surrounded by warmth. I wonder how long it would take for them to find me. Days, probably. Maybe weeks. My skin would start to detach, little flaps rising to the surface like lily pads.

I look down at the water, notice that it's turned a pale pink. I grab a washcloth and start scrubbing at my skin, at the remnants of Tyler's blood still caked to my arms.

Even after it's gone, I keep scrubbing, pushing hard. Making it hurt. Then I lean forward, pull the stopper from the drain, and stay seated until every last drop is gone.

I put on sweatpants and a sweatshirt before walking back downstairs, entering the kitchen, and filling a glass of water. I down the entire thing, sighing when I've reached the bottom, hanging my head low. And then I look up, listening. I feel a wave of goose bumps erupt across my skin and I place the glass down gently, taking a slow step toward the living room. I can hear something. Something muffled. A subtle movement, the kind of thing I wouldn't have noticed if I wasn't so acutely aware of being alone.

I walk into my living room and feel my body stiffen as my eyes land on Daniel.

"Hey, Chloe."

I stare at him silently, standing there, picturing myself upstairs in the bathtub, eyes closed. I imagine opening them, seeing Daniel hovering above me. His hands reaching out, holding me down. Open-mouthed screams and rushing water, sputtering to death like an old car.

"I didn't want to scare you."

I glance at the keypad, the alarm that had been left unlocked. And that's when I realize: He never left. I picture him standing by the front door, exhaling before flipping that switch. The camera going dark.

But I never saw him open the door. I never saw him leave.

"I knew you wouldn't come home unless you thought I was gone," Daniel says, reading my mind. "I was just planning on waiting for you so we could talk. I even saw you outside last night, parked by the house. But then you left. And you didn't come back."

"There's an undercover cop outside," I lie. I didn't see

one when I pulled in, but there could be. There might be. "They're looking for you."

"Just let me explain."

"I met your mother."

He looks taken aback; he wasn't expecting that. I don't have a plan here, but seeing Daniel here in my home, standing smug, I'm suddenly angry.

"She told me all about you," I say. "Your father, his violence. The way you tried to intervene for a while, but eventually just stopped. Let it happen."

Daniel curls his fingers into his palms, a loose fist.

"Is that what happened to her?" I ask. "To Sophie? Was she your punching bag?"

I imagine Sophie Briggs getting home from her friend's house, pink sneakers pounding up the steps, screen door slapping. Stepping inside to see Daniel, hunched over on the couch, dead eyes and a sick grin. I imagine her running past him, tripping over trash as she ran up those carpeted stairs toward her bedroom. Daniel behind her, getting closer, grabbing her cork-screw ponytail and tugging hard. Yanking her neck back, a twig snap cracking. A strangled scream that nobody heard.

"Maybe you didn't mean to. Maybe it just went too far."

Her body at the base of the stairs, limbs flopped like wet noodles. Daniel shaking her shoulder before leaning forward, lifting her hand and letting the deadweight drop. Pulling her ring gently from her finger and pushing it into his pocket. Sometimes that's the way bad habits start: an accident, like a broken pinky leading to a drug addiction. Without the pain, you would have never even known you liked it.

"You think I killed my sister?" he asks. "Is that what this is about?"

"I know you killed your sister."

"Chloe—"

He stops mid-sentence, scrutinizing me. The way he looks at me now, it's not confusion or anger or longing in his eyes. It's that same look I've seen before, many, many times. That look I've seen in the eyes of my own brother, the police. In Ethan and Sarah and Detective Thomas. In the mirror as I gaze into my own reflection, trying to decipher the real from the imagined; the *then* from the *now*. It's the look I had been dreading to see in the eyes of my fiancé; all these months, the look I was desperately trying to avoid. But now, here it is.

That very first hint of concern—not for my safety, but for my mind.

It's pity, it's fear.

"I didn't kill my sister," he says slowly. "I saved her."

CHAPTER FORTY-FIVE

Earl Briggs drank Jim Beam Kentucky Straight. Always slightly warm from sitting open on the living room table, light beams from the windows reflecting off the bottle like fossilized amber. Always in a highball glass, liquid filled to the brim. It coated his lips in a perpetual slickness like a puddle of gasoline, giving his breath a medicinal smell. Sickly sweet like butterscotch left out in the sun.

"I always knew what kind of day it would be based on how full the bottle was," Daniel says, slumping down to the couch and staring at the floor. Normally, I would have walked to him, wrapped my arm around his back. Trailed my fingernail along the little stretch of skin between his shoulder blades. Normally. Instead, I stay standing. "I started to think of it like an hourglass, you know? It started out full, then we'd watch it slowly disappear. When it was empty, we knew to stay away."

My father had his demons, obviously, but drinking wasn't one of them. I have vague recollections of him cracking open a Bud Light after an afternoon in the yard, a sweaty neck warranting a sweaty bottle. He rarely broke into the liquor, only on special occasions. I would almost prefer it if he drank. Everybody has their vices: some people smoke cigarettes when they're

drunk; Dick Davis kills. But no, it wasn't like that. He
didn't need any kind of chemical substance to switch on
the violence. This particular demon I can't understand.

"He went after my mom for years," Daniel says.
"About everything. Every little thing would set him off."

I think about that bruise underneath Dianne's eye, her
arms red like tenderized meat. *My husband, Earl. He's
got a temper.*

"I couldn't understand why she didn't just leave," he
says. "Just take us and go. But she never did. So we
learned to navigate it, I guess. Sophie and I. We just
kept our distance, tiptoed around it. But then one day, I
came home from school—"

He looks like he's in physical pain, like he's trying
to swallow a rock. He squeezes his eyes tight, looks up
at me.

"He beat the shit out of her, Chloe. His own daughter. And that's not even the worst of it. My mom didn't
stop him."

I let myself imagine it: a young Daniel, seventeen years old, listening to those familiar wails float
through the front door as he makes his way home,
backpack slung over his shoulder. Walking inside,
living room filled with smoke. But instead of the usual
scene, he sees his mother hovered over the kitchen
sink, attempting to let the sound of the running water
drown out the noise.

"God, I tried to get her to do something. To stand up
to him. But she just let it happen. Better Sophie than
her, I guess. I honestly think she was relieved."

I picture him running down that hallway, barreling through piles of trash and the mangy cat and the
cigarette butts discarded on the carpet. Pounding on a
locked door, his screams falling on deaf ears. Running
into the kitchen, shaking his mother's arm. *DO SOME-*

THING. I imagine the same sense of panic I had felt when I stumbled into my parents' bedroom, my mother's almost-lifeless body crumpled into a heap in the closet, as if she were nothing more than dirty clothes that had spilled over the side of the hamper. Cooper, staring. Doing nothing. The realization that we were on our own.

"And that's when I knew she had to go. If I didn't get her out of there, she would never leave. She would turn into my mother, or worse. She would turn up dead."

I let myself take a step in his direction—a single step. He doesn't seem to notice; he's lost in the memory now, letting it spill freely. Roles reversed.

"I heard about your father down in Breaux Bridge, and that's where I got the idea. The inspiration. To make her disappear."

That article pushed into his bookshelf, my father's mug shot.

RICHARD DAVIS NAMED AS BREAUX BRIDGE SERIAL KILLER, BODIES STILL UNFOUND.

"She went to a friend's house after school and never came home. My parents didn't even realize she was gone until the following night. Twenty-four hours missing . . . nothing." He waves his hand, makes a *poof* motion. "I kept waiting for them to say something. I just kept sitting there, waiting for them to notice. To call the police, *something*. But they never did. She was only thirteen." He shakes his head in disbelief. "Her friend's mom called the next day, the friend whose house she had been at—I guess she left her textbook there, she knew she wouldn't need it anymore—and that's when they realized it. Someone else's parent noticed before they did.

By then, everyone just assumed the same thing happened to her as all those other girls. That she was taken."

I imagine Sophie on that dingy television, the kitchen counter kind they had plopped on top of a portable table in the living room. That same school picture, her *only* picture, flashing onto the screen. Dianne watching as Daniel smiled quietly in the corner, knowing the truth.

"Then where is she?" I ask. "If she's still alive—"

"Hattiesburg, Mississippi." He says it with an exaggerated twang, like a misplaced commuter reading it off a map. "Little brick house, green shutters. I stop by and see her when I can, when I'm driving."

I close my eyes. I recognize that town from one of his receipts. Hattiesburg, Mississippi. A diner called Ricky's. Chicken Caesar salad and a cheeseburger, medium well. Two glasses of wine. Twenty percent tip.

"She's fine, Chloe. She's alive. She's safe. That's all I ever wanted."

It's starting to make sense now, but not in the way I had expected it to. I'm still not sure if I can believe him, fully. Because there's still so much that has yet to be explained.

"Why didn't you tell me?"

"I wanted to." I try to ignore the begging in his voice, the little quiver that makes it sound like he might cry. "You have no idea how many times I almost just came out and said it."

"Then why didn't you? I told you about my family."

"That's exactly why," he says, tugging at the ends of his hair. He sounds frustrated now, like we're arguing over the dishes. "I always knew who you were, Chloe. I knew the second I saw you in that lobby. And then that day at the bar, you weren't bringing it up, and I didn't want to bring it up for you. That's not the kind of thing you should be forced into saying."

Those little nudges, the way he couldn't seem to stop staring. I think about that night on the couch, and my face flushes with blood.

"You let me tell you everything and you acted like you didn't already know."

I can't help but feel angry as the magnitude of his lies settles over me. At the things he had made me believe, the way he had made me feel.

"What was I supposed to say? Stop you mid-sentence? *Oh yeah, Dick Davis. He gave me the idea to fake my sister's murder.*" He snorts a little self-deprecating laugh, then almost as suddenly, his face goes serious again. "I didn't want you to think that everything up until that moment had been a lie."

I remember that night so vividly, the way I had felt lighter after that, after telling him everything. My insides raw but clean, a verbal purging to get the sickness out. His finger on my chin, tilting it up. Those words for the first time. *I love you.*

"Wasn't it, though?"

Daniel sighs, rests his hands on his thighs. "I don't blame you. For being mad. You have every right. But I'm not a murderer, Chloe. I can't even believe you'd think that."

"Then what are you doing with my father?"

He stares at me. His eyes look tired, like they've been drilling straight into the sun.

"If all of this has an innocent explanation, if you have nothing to hide, then why have you been visiting him?" I continue. "How do you know him?"

I watch him deflate a little, like he's sprung a leak somewhere. An old balloon hovering self-consciously in the corner, shriveling into nothing. Then he reaches his hand into his pocket, pulls out a long, silver necklace. I watch his thumb polish the pearl in the center, making tiny little circles, over and over. It feels tender, like

rubbing a rabbit's foot charm or the cheek of a new-
born, soft and juicy like an overripe peach. I have a
flash of Lacey rubbing her rosary in my office, back
and forth, up and down.

Finally, he speaks.

CHAPTER FORTY-SIX

I'm sitting at my kitchen island, an open bottle of red aerating between two full glasses. I'm twisting one in my hand, rubbing the delicate stem back and forth between my fingers. To my left, an orange bottle, the cap unscrewed.

I glance at the clock on the wall, the hour hand pointing at seven. The overgrown branches from the magnolia tree outside are scratching at my window, nails against glass. I can almost feel the knock on my door before I hear it, that moment of anticipatory silence hanging heavy in the air like the seconds after a lightning strike as you wait for the thunder to roll though. Then that quick, closed-fisted pounding—always the same, unique like a fingerprint—followed by a familiar voice.

"Chlo, it's me. Let me in."

"It's open," I yell back, my eyes staring straight ahead. I hear the creak of the door, the double chimes from my alarm. My brother's heavy footsteps as he steps inside, closing it behind him. He walks over to the island, kisses my temple before I feel his posture stiffen.

"Don't worry about it," I say, sensing his eyes on the pills. "I'm fine."

He exhales, pulls out the barstool next to mine and

takes a seat. We're quiet for a while, a game of dare. Each of us waiting for the other to go first.

"Look, I know these last couple weeks have been hard on you." He gives in, placing his hands on the counter. "They've been hard on me, too."

I don't respond.

"How are you holding up?"

I lift my wine, my lips grazing the edge of the glass. I hold them there and watch as my breath comes out in little puffs before disappearing again.

"I killed someone," I say at last. "How do you think I'm holding up?"

"I can't imagine what that must have been like."

I nod, take a sip, put my glass down on the counter. Then I turn toward Cooper. "Are you really going to make me drink alone?"

He stares at me, his eyes searching my face like he's looking for something. Something familiar. When he can't find it, he reaches for the second glass and takes a sip himself. He exhales, stretches his neck.

"I'm sorry about Daniel. I know you loved him. I just always knew there was something about him . . ." He stops, hesitates. "Whatever, it's over now. I'm just glad you're safe."

I wait silently as Cooper takes another few sips, the alcohol starting to course through his veins, loosen his muscles, until I look at him again, my eyes square on his.

"Tell me about Tyler Price."

I watch a shock wave ripple across his expression, only for a second. A tremor like a miniature earthquake before he pulls himself together again, his face like stone.

"What do you mean? I can tell you what I saw in the news."

"No." I shake my head. "No, I want to know what

he was really like. After all, you knew him. You were friends."

He's staring at me, his eyes darting back down to the pills again.

"Chloe, you're not making any sense. I've never met that guy. Yeah, he was from home, but he was a nobody. A loner."

"A loner," I repeat, twisting the stem in my hands, the rotating glass making a rhythmic *swoosh* against the marble. "Right. Then how did he get into Riverside?"

I think back to that morning with my mother, at seeing Aaron's name on the visitor pad. I had been so angry, the prospect of them letting a stranger into her room. I had been so angry that I hadn't been listening, the words hadn't registered.

Sweetheart, we don't let people in who aren't authorized.

"God, I keep telling you to stop taking these fuckin' things," he says, reaching for the bottle. He picks it up, and I can sense the weightlessness in his hands. "Jesus, did you take all of them?"

"It's not the pills, Cooper. Fuck the pills."

He looks at me the same way he looked at me twenty years ago, when I had stared at my father on the television screen, hawked those words through my teeth like dip spit, gritty and foul. *Fucking coward.*

"You knew him, Cooper. You knew everybody."

I picture Tyler as a teenager, scrawny and awkward, almost always alone. A faceless, nameless body trailing my brother around the Crawfish Festival, following him home, waiting outside his window. Doing his bidding. After all, my brother was a friend to everyone. He made them feel warm and safe and accepted.

I think back to my conversation with Tyler on the water now, talking about Lena. How she was nice to me; how she looked after me.

That's a friend, he had said, nodding. Knowing. *The best kind, if you ask me.*

"You reached out to him," I say. "You sought him out. You brought him here."

Cooper is staring at me now, his mouth hanging open like a cabinet with a loose hinge. I can see the words lodged in his throat like an unchewed chunk of bread, and that's how I know that I'm right. Because Cooper always has something to say. He always has the words, the *right* words.

You're my baby sister, Chloe. I want the best for you.

"Chloe," he whispers, his eyes wide. I notice it now— the pulsing in his neck, the way he rubs his fingers together, slick with sweat. "What the fuck are you talking about? Why would I do that?"

I picture Daniel in my living room just this morning, that necklace tangled between his fingers. The hesitation in his voice as he started to tell me everything, the sadness in his eyes, like he was about to euthanize me— because he was, I guess. I was about to undergo a humane slaughtering right there in my living room. Put her down gently.

"When you told me about your father for the first time," Daniel had said, "about everything that happened in Breaux Bridge, everything he had done, I already knew. Or, at least, I thought I knew. But there were so many things you told me that surprised me."

I think back to that night, so early in our relationship, Daniel's fingers massaging my hair. Me, telling him everything—about my father, Lena, the way he had been watching her that day at the festival, his hands dug deep into his pockets. That figure gliding through my backyard, the jewelry box in the closet, the dancing ballerina and the chimes that I can still hear playing in my mind, haunting my dreams.

"It just struck me as odd. My entire life, I thought I

knew who your father was. Just pure evil. Killing little girls." I pictured Daniel in his bedroom, a teenaged boy with that article in his hands, trying to imagine. The news had painted us all in such black-and-whites: My mother, the enabler. Cooper, the golden boy. Me, the little girl, the constant reminder. And my father, the devil himself. One-dimensional and wicked. "But as I listened to you talk about him, I don't know. Some stuff didn't fit."

Because with Daniel, and only with Daniel, I could talk about how it wasn't all bad. I could talk about the good memories, too. I could talk about how my dad used to cover the staircase in bath towels, pushing us down in laundry bins because we had never gone sledding. How he seemed genuinely afraid when the news had broken—me, in the kitchen, twisting my mint-green blanket, that bright red bar on the screen. *LOCAL BREAUX BRIDGE GIRL GOES MISSING.* The way he had held me tight, waited for me on the porch steps, made sure my window was locked at night.

"If he did those things, if he murdered those girls, then why would he be trying to protect you?" Daniel had asked. "Why would he be concerned?"

My eyes started to sting. I didn't have an answer to that question. That was the question I had been asking myself my entire life. Those had been the very memories I had been struggling to make sense of—those memories with my father that seemed to be so conflicting with the monster he had turned out to be. Hand-washing the dishes and removing my training wheels; letting me paint his fingernails one day and teaching me how to hook a line the next. I remember crying after I had caught my first fish, its little puckered lips gasping as my father dug his fingers into its gills, trying to stop the bleeding. We were meant to eat it, but I had been so distraught, Dad threw it back. He let it live.

"So when you told me about the night he was arrested—how he didn't fight, didn't try to run," Daniel had said, leaning closer, his eyebrows raised. Hoping that I would understand, finally. That I would get it, *finally*. That he wouldn't have to say it himself. That perhaps the killing could be self-inflicted; the trigger would go off in my mind instead of on his tongue. "How instead, he just whispered those two words."

My father, in handcuffs, straining for one final moment. The way he had looked at me, then Cooper. His eyes zeroed in almost directly on my brother, as if he were the only one in the room. And that's when it hit me, a sucker punch to the stomach. He was talking to *him,* not me. He was talking to Cooper.

He was telling him, asking him, pleading with him. *Be good.*

"You killed those girls in Breaux Bridge," I say now, my eyes on my brother. The words that I had been turning over and over on my tongue, trying to make sense of their taste. "You killed Lena."

Cooper is quiet, his eyes starting to glass over. He looks down at the wine, the splash still left at the bottom of the glass, and lifts it to his lips, downing the rest.

"Daniel figured it out," I say, forcing myself to continue. "It makes sense now. The animosity between you two. Because he knew that Dad didn't kill those girls. *You* did. He knew it, he just couldn't prove it."

I think back to our engagement party, to the way Daniel had wound his arm around my waist, pulling me closer to him, away from Cooper. I had been so wrong about him. He wasn't trying to control me; he was trying to *protect* me, from my brother and from the truth. I can't imagine the balancing act he had been trying to achieve, keeping Cooper at an arm's length without revealing too much.

"And you knew, too," I continue. "You knew Daniel

was onto you. And that's why you've been trying to turn me against him."

Cooper, on my porch, reciting those words that had been chewing at my brain like cancer ever since. *You don't know him, Chloe.* That necklace, buried deep in the back of our closet. Cooper had put it there, the night of the party. He was there first, letting himself in with his key. Slipping it silently into the very place he knew it would hit the hardest before making his way outside, hiding in the shadows. After all, I had done this before. With Ethan, in college, suspecting the worst. Cooper knew that with the right memories dug up and replanted in just the right way, they would start to grow in my mind, uncontrolled like a weed. They would take over everything.

I think about Tyler Price, taking Aubrey and Lacey and Riley, re-creating Cooper's crimes in just the right way because he had told him how. I think about how broken you must have to be to let another person convince you to kill. It's no different from the way damaged women write to criminals with marriage proposals, I suppose, or how seemingly ordinary girls find themselves in the clutches of threatening men. It's all the same: lonely souls in search of some company, any company. *I'm nobody,* he had said, his eyes like empty water glasses, fragile and wet. The same way I had found myself, time and time again, tangled between the sheets with a stranger, afraid for my life, but at the same time, willing to take the risk. *You're not crazy,* Tyler had told me, his hands in my hair. Because that's the thing about danger—it heightens everything. Your heartbeat, your senses, your touch. It's a desire to feel alive, because it's impossible to feel anything *but* alive when you find yourself in its presence, the world becoming cloaked in a shadowy haze, its very existence all the proof you need—that you're here, you're breathing.

And in an instant, it could all be gone.

I can see it now, so clearly. My brother pulling Tyler under his spell again—this lost, lonely person—the way he always has. *He made me do it.* There was always something about him, after all. Something about Cooper. An aura that captured people, an attraction that was almost impossible to shake. Like magnets trying to fight iron, that gentle, natural pull. You could try, for a while, shaking under the mounting pressure. But eventually, you just gave in, the same way my anger would always melt as he pulled me into that familiar hug. The same way that swarm of people was always around him in high school, scattering with that wrist-flick of dismissal when he no longer wanted them, needed them, as if they weren't actually people, but pests. Disposable. Existing for his own pleasure and nothing more.

"You tried to frame Daniel," I say finally, the words settling over the room like soot after a fire, coating everything in ash. "Because he saw through you. He knows what you are. So you had to get rid of him."

Cooper looks at me, his teeth chewing on the inside of his cheek. I can see the wheels turning behind his eyes, the careful calculations he's trying to make—how much to say, how much not to say. Finally, he speaks.

"I don't know what to tell you, Chloe." His voice is thick like syrup, his tongue made of sand. "I have a darkness inside of me. A darkness that comes out at night."

I hear those words in the mouth of my father. The way he had regurgitated them, almost automatically, as he sat at that courtroom table, his ankles chained together, a single tear dripping onto the notepad beneath him.

"It's so strong, I couldn't fight it."

Cooper with his nose pushed to the screen, as if everything else in the room had evaporated, turning into nothing but vapor swirling around him. Watching my father, listening as he recited the same words Cooper must have recited to him when he had been caught.

"It's like this giant shadow always hovering in the corner of the room," he says. "It drew me in, it swallowed me whole."

I gulp, summoning that final sentence from the pit of my belly. That sentence that had hammered the last nail into my father's coffin, the rhetorical squeeze that drained the air from his lungs, killing him in my mind. That sentence that had angered me to my core—my father, placing the blame on this fictional thing. Crying not because he was sorry, but because he had gotten caught. But now, I know—that wasn't the case. That wasn't the case at all.

I open my mouth and let the words spill out.

"Sometimes I think it might be the devil himself."

CHAPTER FORTY-SEVEN

It's as if the answers have been in front of me all along—dancing, just out of reach. Twirling, like Lena—bottle in the air, her ripped-up shorts and double French braids, the remnants of weeds sticking to her skin, the remnants of weed heavy on her breath. Like that ballerina, chipped and pink, spinning to the rhythm of delicate chimes. But when I had reached out, tried to touch them, tried to grab them, they had turned into smoke in my grip, swirling through my fingers until I was left with nothing.

"The jewelry," I say, my eyes on Cooper's silhouette, his aging face morphing into that of my teenaged brother. He had been so young, only fifteen. "It was yours."

"Dad found it in my room. Underneath my floor-board."

The floorboard I had told him about after I found Cooper's magazines. I bow my head.

"He took the box, wiped it down, and hid it in his closet until he could figure out what to do with it," he says. "But he never had the chance. You found it first."

I found it first. A secret I had stumbled upon in my search for scarves. I had opened it up, plucked Lena's belly-button ring from the center, dead and gray. And

I knew. I knew it was hers. I had seen it that day, my face cupped against her stomach, her skin smooth and warm against my hands.

Somebody's watching.

"Dad wasn't looking at Lena," I say, thinking of my father's expression—distracted, afraid. Preoccupied by some unspoken thought tormenting his mind—that his son was sizing up his next victim, preparing to strike. "That day at the festival. He was looking at you."

"Ever since Tara," he says, the spider veins in his eyes flushing pink. Now that he's started talking, the words are flowing freely, like I knew they would. I look down at his glass, at the puddle of wine left at the bottom. "He would just watch me like that. Like he knew."

Tara King. The runaway, a year before any of this started. Tara King, the girl Theodore Gates had confronted my mother with—the outlier, the enigma. The one nobody could prove.

"She was the first," Cooper says. "I had wondered, for a while. What it would feel like."

My eyes can't help but dart to the corner, to the place where Bert Rhodes once stood.

You ever think about what it feels like? I used to keep myself up at night, wondering. Imagining.

"And then one night, there she was. Alone on the side of the road."

I can see it so vividly, like I'm watching a movie. Screaming into the void, trying to stop the impending danger. But nobody hears me, nobody listens. Cooper, in my father's car. He had just learned how to drive—the freedom, I'm sure, a breath of fresh air. I can picture him idling behind the wheel, quiet, watching. Considering. His entire life, he had been surrounded by people: the crowds around him at school, in the gym, at the festival, never leaving his side. But in that moment, alone, he saw an opportunity. Tara King.

A suitcase hanging heavy over her shoulder, a note scratched on her kitchen counter. She had been leaving, running away. Nobody had even thought to look when she vanished.

"I remember feeling surprised, how easy it was," he says, his eyes drilling into the countertop. "My hands on her throat, and the way the movement just . . . stopped." He pauses, looks at me. "Do you really want to know all this?"

"Cooper, you're my brother," I say, reaching my hand out to cover his. Right now, touching his skin, I want to vomit. I want to run away. But instead, I force myself to regurgitate the words, *his* words, that I know work so well. "Tell me what happened."

"I kept expecting to get caught," he says at last. "I kept expecting someone to show up at our house—the cops, *something*—but nobody ever did. Nobody even talked about it. And I realized . . . I could get away with it. Nobody knew, except . . ."

He stops again, swallowing hard, like he knows these next words will hit harder than any that came before them.

"Except Lena," he says finally. "Lena knew."

Lena—always out late, by herself. Picking her way out of her locked bedroom before running outside, wandering into the night. Seeing Cooper in that car, creeping slowly behind as Tara walked down the side of the road, unaware. Lena had seen him. She didn't have a crush on Cooper; she had been pushing him, testing him. She was the only one in the world who knew his secret and she was drunk with power, playing with matches the way she always did, getting closer and closer before the fire singed her skin. *You should pick me up in that car of yours sometime,* calling over her shoulder. Cooper's rigid back, hands punched into his pockets. *You don't want to be like Lena.* I picture her

lying on the grass, that ant creeping up her cheek—
her, motionless and still. Letting it crawl. Breaking into
Cooper's bedroom, the smile that twisted across her lips
when he had caught us—that knowing grin, hands on
her hips, almost as if to tell him: *Look what I can do
to you.*

Lena was invincible. We all thought it, even she herself.

"Lena was a liability," I say, trying hard to swallow
the tears crawling up the back of my throat. "You had
to get rid of her."

"And after that"—he shrugs—"there was no reason
to stop."

It wasn't the killing that my brother had craved—I
know that now, looking at him hunched over my countertop, decades of memories swirling around him. It was
the control. And somehow, I understand it. I understand
it in a way only family can. I think back to all of my
fears, the lack of control I constantly imagine. Two
hands wrapped around my neck, squeezing tight. It was
that same control I feared losing that Cooper loved to
take. It was the control he felt in the moment those girls
realized that they were in trouble—the look in their
eyes, the quiver in their voices as they pled: *Please,
anything.* The knowledge that he and he alone was the
deciding factor between life and death. He had always
been that way, really—the way he had pushed his hand
into Bert Rhodes's chest, challenging him. Walking in
circles on the wrestling mat, his fingers twitching at his
sides like a tiger circling a weaker rival, ready to sink in
its claws. I wonder if that's what he was thinking when
he had his opponents by the neck: squeezing, twisting.
Snapping. How easy it would have been, the pulsing of
their jugular beneath his fingers. And when he let them
go, he felt like God. Granting them another day.

Tara, Robin, Susan, Margaret, Carrie, Jill. That was a

part of the thrill to him—choosing, fingers outstretched the same way you would choose an ice cream flavor, perusing your options behind a glass case before making your decision, pointing, taking. But Lena had always felt different, special. She had felt like something more, and that's because she was. She wasn't random; she was taken out of necessity. Lena *knew,* and for that, she had to be killed.

My father knew, too. But Cooper had solved that problem in a different way. He had solved it with his words. Eyes wet, pleading. Talking about the shadows in the corner, the way he had tried to fight them. Cooper had always managed to find the right words, using them to his advantage—controlling people, influencing people. And they had worked. They had always worked—on my father, using him to set himself free. On Lena, letting her believe that she was invincible, that he wouldn't hurt her. And on me, *especially* on me, his fingers pulling the strings attached to my limbs, making me dance in just the right way. Feeding me just the right information at just the right time. He was the author of my life, always had been, making me believe the things he wanted me to believe, spinning a web of lies in my mind—a spider pulling in insects with his crafty tendrils, watching them fight for their lives before devouring them whole.

"When Dad found out, you convinced him not to turn you in."

"What would you do"—Cooper sighs, looking at me, skin drooping—"if your son turned out to be a monster? Would you just stop loving him?"

I think of my mother—returning to my father after our trip to the station, the rationalizations she had formed in her mind. *He won't hurt us. He won't. He won't hurt his family.* Me, looking at Daniel, the evidence I had seen stacking up, but still, didn't want to believe. Thinking, hoping: There must be good in there somewhere. And surely, that's what my father had thought, too. So I had turned him in—my father, for Cooper's crimes—and when they came to take him, he didn't resist. Instead, he looked at his son, at Cooper, and he had asked him to make a promise.

I glance at the clock. Seven thirty. Half an hour since Cooper arrived. I know that this is the moment. The moment I've been thinking about since I invited Cooper here, running through every possible scenario, thinking through every outcome. Turning them over and over in my mind like knuckles kneading dough.

"You know I have to call the police," I say. "Cooper, I have to call them. You've killed people."

My brother looks at me, his eyelids heavy.

"You don't have to do that," he says. "Tyler is dead. Daniel doesn't have any proof. We can leave the past in the past, Chloe. It can stay there."

I entertain the thought—the single scenario I haven't yet considered. I think about standing up, opening the door. Letting Cooper step outside and walk out of my life for good. Letting him get away with it, the way he's gotten away with it for the last twenty years. I wonder what a secret like this would do to me—knowing that he was out there, somewhere. A monster hidden in plain sight, walking among us. Somebody's coworker, neighbor. Friend. And then, as if I had stretched out my finger and touched static, I feel a shock run down my spine. I see my mother, the way she had been pushed against the television screen, hanging on to every moment of my father's trial, every word—until his lawyer, Theodore Gates, had come over, telling her about the deal.

Unless you have anything else I can work with. Anything at all you haven't told me.

She knew, too. My mother knew. After we got home

from the station, after turning in that box, my father must have told her, stopping her in her tracks as I ran up the stairs. But by then, it was too late. The wheels were in motion. The police were coming for him, and so she sat back, let it happen. Held out hope that maybe it wasn't enough—no murder weapon, no bodies. That maybe he would go free. I remember Cooper and I on the stairs, listening. His fingers digging into my arm, leaving bruises like grapes at the mention of Tara King. Without even realizing it, I had witnessed the moment my mother had made her choice—the moment she had chosen to lie. To live with his secret.

No, I don't. You know everything.

And that's when she changed. That slow unravel, it was because of Cooper. She had been living under the same roof as her son, watching as he got away with it. The light had been extinguished from her eyes; she had retreated from the living room to her bedroom, locking herself inside. She hadn't been able to live with the truth—what her son was, what he did. Her husband in jail, the rocks through the window, and Bert Rhodes in the yard, arms flailing, nails ripping at his own skin. I feel her fingers dancing across my wrist, tapping the blanket as I pointed to those tiles: *D* then *A*. I understand now, what she had been trying to say. She had wanted me to go to my dad. She had wanted me to visit him so he could tell me the truth. Because she had understood, listening to me talk about the missing girls, the similarities, the déjà vu—she knew, more than anyone, that the past never stays where we try to keep it, stuffing it deep into the back of a closet and hoping to forget.

I had never wanted to return to Breaux Bridge, never wanted to walk the halls of that house. Never wanted to revisit the memories I had tried to keep stranded in that tiny town. But the memories didn't stay there, I know that now. My past has been haunting me for my entire life, like a phantom that was never laid to rest, just like those girls.

"I can't do that," I say now, looking at Cooper. Shaking my head. "You know I can't."

He stares back at me, his fingers curling into a slow fist.

"Don't do this, Chloe. It doesn't have to be this way."

"It does," I say, starting to push my barstool back. But as I begin to stand, Cooper reaches out, his hand gripping my wrist. I look down, his knuckles white as he pinches my skin, hard. And now I know. I know, at last, that Cooper would have done it. He would have killed me, too. Right here, sitting at my kitchen counter. He would have stretched out his hands, clasped them around my throat. He would have looked into my eyes as he squeezed. I don't doubt that my brother loves me—to whatever extent someone like him can love—but at the end of the day, I am a liability, like Lena. A problem that needs solving.

"You can't hurt me," I spit, yanking my arm from his grip. I push my stool back, stand up, and watch as he tries to lunge at me—but instead, he stumbles forward, clumsy. His knees buckling under the sudden pressure of his weight. I watch as he trips on the leg of the barstool, his body crumbling to a heap on the floor. He looks at me, confused, before looking up at the countertop. At his empty glass of wine, that hollow orange bottle.

"Did you—?"

He starts to speak, but then stops again, the effort suddenly too much. I think back to the last time I felt that way, the way Cooper does now—it was that night in the motel room, Tyler pulling on his jeans, ducking into the bathroom. The glass of water he had pushed in my direction, forcing me to drink. The pills that were later found in those very pockets. The pills he had mixed into the water, the same way I had mixed mine into Cooper's wine, watching as his eyes had gotten so heavy so quickly. The violent yellow bile I had coughed up the next morning.

I don't bother with a response. Instead, I look up at the ceiling, at the camera in the corner, as small as a pinprick, blinking gently. Recording everything. I raise my hand and gesture for them to come inside now— Detective Thomas, sitting in his car outside with Daniel, phone in his lap. Watching everything, listening to it all.

I look down at my brother again, one last time. The last time it will ever be just us two. It's hard not to think of the memories—running through the woods behind our house, tripping on the mangled roots erupting from the soil like fossilized snakes. The way he would wipe the blood from my skinned knees, push a strip of gauze tight against my stinging skin. The way he had tied that rope to my ankle as I crawled deep into that hidden cavern, our secret spot—and suddenly, I know that's where they are. The missing girls, hidden in plain sight. Pushed deep into the darkness, somewhere only we would know.

I picture that dark figure I had seen emerging from the trees, shovel in hand: Cooper, always tall for fifteen, muscular from years of wrestling. His head ducked low, the darkness obscuring his face. The shadows swallowing him up—until, at last, he had turned into nothing.

JULY 2019

CHAPTER FORTY-EIGHT

A cool breeze whips through my open windows, sending wisps of my hair dancing into the skylight, grazing against my cheek. The glare of the setting sun feels warm on my skin, but still—it's unusually crisp today. Friday, July 26.

My wedding day.

I look down at the directions in my lap, a series of turns that end in a single address written on scrap paper. I glance through my windshield at the long driveway stretching out before me, the mailbox with four copper numbers hammered into wood. I take the turn, dust kicking up from my tires until I pull up in front of a small house—red brick, green shutters. *Hattiesburg, Mississippi.*

I step out of my car, slam the door. Then I walk up the driveway, up the steps, and reach out my hand, knocking twice on a thick slab of pinewood painted a pale green with a wreath made of straw hung squarely in the center. I hear footsteps from inside, the gentle murmur of voices. The door swings open, and a woman stands before me. She wears simple jeans and a white tank top, slippers on her feet. There's a casual smile on her face, a dish towel slung over her bare shoulder.

"Can I help you?"

She stares at me for a second, unsure of who I am, until I see the moment of understanding in her eyes. The moment her polite smile begins to fade as she recognizes my face. I inhale the familiar scent I had smelled on Daniel so many times—sickly sweet, like a honeysuckle in bloom mixed with molten sugar. I can still see the little girl I had seen in that school picture: Sophie Briggs, her frizzy blonde hair now gelled into ringlet curls, a constellation of freckles scattered across the bridge of her nose, as if somebody had taken a pinch and sprinkled them on like salt.

"Hi," I say, suddenly self-conscious. I linger on the porch, wondering what Lena would have looked like if she had been given the opportunity to grow up. I like to pretend that she's out there, somewhere, tucked away like Sophie has been, safe in her own little corner of the world.

"Daniel's inside." She twists her torso, gesturing to the door. "If you'd like—"

"No." I shake my head, my cheeks flushing hot. Daniel moved out right after Cooper was arrested, and for some reason, it hadn't dawned on me that he would have come here. "No, that's okay. I'm actually here for you."

I reach out my hand, my engagement ring pinched between my fingers. It had been returned to me by the police last week, found on the floor of Tyler Price's car. She doesn't say anything as she reaches out and grabs it, twisting it between her fingers.

"It belongs with you," I say. "With your family."

She slides it on her middle finger, fanning her hands as she admires how it looks, back in its usual spot. I look behind her, into the hallway, and see pictures displayed on an entrance table, shoes kicked off at the base of the stairs. A baseball cap resting on the corner handrail. I peel my eyes from inside and glance around her yard. The home is small but quaint, undeniably lived-in: a wooden swing attached to a tree branch with two pieces of rope, a pair of Rollerblades leaning against the garage. Then a voice erupts from inside—a man's voice. Daniel's voice.

"Soph? Who is it?"

"I should go," I say, turning around, suddenly feeling like I'm loitering. Like I'm snooping behind the door of a stranger's bathroom cabinet, trying to piece together a life. Trying to catch a glimpse into the last twenty years, from the moment she had stepped away from that dilapidated old house and started walking, never looking back. How difficult that must have been—thirteen years old, only a child. Leaving her friend's house and walking alone down that dark stretch of road. A car pulling up behind her, headlights off. Daniel, her brother, driving away slowly, dropping her at a bus stop two towns away. Pushing an envelope of money into her hand. Money he had been saving for that very moment.

I'll meet you, he had promised. *After I graduate. Then I can leave, too.*

His mother, those dirty nails scratching at tissue paper skin; watery eyes as she looked into mine. *He moved out the day after he graduated high school, and I haven't heard from him since.*

I wonder what those years had been like—the two of them, together. Daniel, taking classes online. Getting his degree. Sophie making money in any way she could—waiting tables, bagging groceries. Then one day, they looked at each other and realized that they had grown up. That the years had passed, and that the danger was gone. That they both deserved a life—a *real* life—and so Daniel had left, making his way to Baton Rouge, but always finding a way to come back.

My foot hits the top of the stairs when Sophie finally speaks again—I can hear her brother's voice in hers, assertive and strong.

"It was my idea. To give you this." I twist around and look at her, still standing there, arms crossed tight against her chest. "Daniel talked about you constantly. Still does." She smirks. "When he said he was going to propose, I guess it made me feel connected, in a way. Picturing you wearing it. Like one day, we might know each other."

I think about Daniel, those articles tucked inside a book in his bedroom. Cooper's crimes the inspiration he had needed to get Sophie out—to make her disappear. So many lives were taken because of my brother; that fact still makes me lie awake at night, their faces burned into my mind like the soot on Lena's palm. A big, black spot.

So many lives, gone. Except for Sophie Briggs. Her life was saved.

"I'm glad you did." I smile. "And now we do."

"I heard your dad's getting out." She takes a step forward, like she doesn't quite want me to leave. I nod, not really sure how to respond.

I was right about Daniel visiting my father in Angola; that was where he had been going during all those trips. He had been trying to get to the truth about Cooper. When he told him about the killings happening again—the girls going missing, offering Aubrey's necklace as proof—my father had agreed to come clean. But when you've already pled guilty to murder, you can't just change your mind. You need something more; you need a confession. And that's where I came in.

After all, it was my words that had put my father behind bars; it seemed only fitting that my conversation with Cooper, twenty years later, would be the one to free him.

I had watched my father apologize on the news last week. Apologize for lying, for protecting his son. For the additional lives that were lost because of it. I couldn't bring myself to see him in person, not yet, but I remember staring at him through the TV screen, just like before. Only this time, I was trying to reconcile his new face with the one I still saw in my mind. His thick-rimmed glasses had been replaced with wire ones, simple and thin. There was a scar on his nose from when the original ones broke, cracking as his head slammed into the cruiser, a line of blood trickling down his cheek. His hair was shorter, his face rougher, almost as if it had been buffed with sandpaper or rubbed against the concrete until it scarred. I noticed pockmarks on his arms—burns, maybe—the skin stretched and shiny, perfectly circular like the tip of a cigarette butt.

But despite it all, it was him. It was my father. Alive.

"What are you going to do?" Sophie asks.

"I'm not really sure," I say. And that's the truth. I'm not sure.

Some days, I'm still so angry. My father lied. He took the blame for Cooper's crimes. He found that box of jewelry and tucked it away, keeping his secret. Trading his freedom for Cooper's life. And because of it, two more girls are dead. But on other days, I get it. I understand. Because that's what parents do: They protect their children, no matter the cost. I think of all those mothers staring into the camera, the fathers melting into puddles by their sides. They had a child who was taken by the darkness—but what if your child *was* the darkness? Wouldn't you want to protect them, too? It's all about control, after all. The illusion that death is something we can contain, cupping it into our palms and holding it tight, never letting it escape. That Cooper, given another chance, could somehow change. That Lena, dangling herself in front of my brother, feeling the fire singe her skin, could pull away at just the right moment. Walk away unscathed.

But it's just a lie we tell ourselves. Cooper never

changed. Lena couldn't outrun the flames. Even Daniel had tried it, attempting to control the anger that was inherent inside of him. Desperate to push down those little glimpses of his father that would peek through in his weakest moments. I'm guilty of it, too. All those little bottles in my desk drawer, calling to me like a whisper in the night.

It wasn't until I found myself hovering over Cooper in my kitchen, looking down at his weakened body, that I had a taste of what it really felt like: control. Of not only having it, but taking it from somebody else. Snatching it up and claiming it as your own. And for one single moment, like a flicker in the dark, it felt good.

I smile at Sophie before turning around again, walking down the last few steps, feeling my shoes hit the pavement. I make my way toward my car, hands in my pockets, watching as dusk smears the horizon with pinks and yellows and oranges—one last moment of color before the darkness settles in again, the way it always does. And that's when I notice it: the air around me buzzing with that familiar electrical charge. I stop, stand completely still, watching. Waiting. And then I cup my hands and grab at the sky, feeling a slight fluttering in my palms as I squeeze them shut. I stare down into my clenched fingers, at the thing I have trapped inside. At the life, quite literally, that rests in my hands. Then I bring it up to my face, peering through the tiny hole between my fingers.

Inside, a single firefly glows bright, its body pulsing with life. I stare at it for a while, my forehead pressed against my clenched fingers. I watch it radiate up close, flickering in my grasp, thinking of Lena.

Then I open my hands and set her free.

ACKNOWLEDGMENTS

None of this would have been possible without my agent, Dan Conaway. You believed in this book before anyone else, signed me after reading only three chapters, and have graciously answered all of my frantic questions every day since. You took a chance on me and it changed my life. *Thank you* will never seem like enough.

To everyone at Writers House, you've been a dream. To Lauren Carsley, thank you for picking my book out of what was, I'm sure, a very large stack. To Peggy Boulos-Smith, Maja Nikolic, and Jessica Berger in the rights department, thank you for championing this story overseas.

Thank you to the entire team at Minotaur, St. Martin's Publishing Group, and Macmillan. To my wonderful editor, Kelley Ragland: your editorial eye has been invaluable, and I feel so lucky to have you in my corner. Thank you to Madeline Houpt, for keeping me organized along the way; David Rotstein, for creating the cover of my dreams; and Hector DeJean, Sarah Melnyk, Allison Ziegler, and Paul Hochman, for getting the word out. Also, a huge thanks to Jen Enderlin and Andy Martin, for your early enthusiasm and confidence in this book.

Thank you to my UK editor, Julia Wisdom, and all of the folks over at HarperCollins UK. Additional thanks must also go to all of my wonderful foreign publishing houses for translating this story into so many different languages.

To Sylvie Rabineau at WME, thank you so much for seeing the screen potential for this story. You've launched this dream of mine to completely new heights.

To my parents, Kevin and Sue. Despite what the subject matter of my books may suggest, my parents are incredibly loving and supportive people who have cheered on my passion for writing since as early as I can remember. None of this would have been possible without your love and encouragement. Thank you so much—for everything.

To my sister, Mallory. Thanks for teaching me how to read and write (seriously!), for diving headfirst into my bad first drafts, and for always giving the most valuable feedback, even when it makes me grumpy. Also, thanks for making me watch all those scary movies with you at a questionably young age. You have always been, and will always be, my very best friend.

To my husband, Britt. You never let me give up. Thank you for spending years cooking dinner while I was holed up in my office, for listening to me talk about these people I invented every single day, and for always being my loudest and proudest supporter. For that, and a million other reasons, I love you. I couldn't have done it without you.

To Brian, Laura, Alvin, Lindsey, Matt, and the rest of my wonderful family, thank you for your never-ending excitement, enthusiasm, and support. I'm lucky to have you all in my life.

To my hype squad and very first outside readers: Erin, Caitlin, Rebekah, Ashley, and Jacqueline. Whether you were screaming from the sidelines or sending quiet whispers of encouragement, I heard every word. Thank you so much for being my people. I don't know what I did to deserve friends like you.

To my wonderful friend, Kolbie. Your enthusiasm throughout this entire process has been infectious. You always cheered me on and kept me excited, even when I never had any good news to share. Also, I admire your willpower for waiting to read the book until it was actually published. I hope it was worth it!

And finally to you, wonderful reader, with this book in your hand. Whether you bought it, rented it, borrowed it, or downloaded it, the fact that you are reading these words right now means that you are also playing a large part in making my wildest dreams come true. Thank you so, so much for your support.

Turn the page for a sneak peek at
Stacy Willingham's new novel

PROLOGUE

Today is day three hundred and sixty-four.

Three hundred and sixty-four days since my last night of sleep. That's almost nine thousand hours. Five hundred and twenty-four thousand minutes. Thirty-one million seconds.

Or, if you want to go in the opposite direction, fifty-two weeks. Twelve months.

One whole year without a single night of rest.

One year of stumbling through life in a semiconscious dream state. One year of opening my eyes to find myself in another room, another building, without any recollection of when I got there or how I arrived.

One year of sleeping pills and eye drops and chugging caffeine by the quart-full. Of jittery fingers and drooping eyelids. Of becoming intimately familiar with the night.

One whole year since my Mason was taken from me, and still, I'm no closer to the truth.

CHAPTER ONE

NOW

"Isabelle, you're on in five."

My pupils are drilling into a spot in the carpet. A spot with no significance, really, other than the fact that my eyes seem to like it here. My surroundings grow fuzzy as the spot—*my* spot—gets sharper, clearer. Like tunnel vision.

"Isabelle."

I wish I could always have tunnel vision: the ability to selectively focus on one single thing at a time. Turn everything else into static. White noise.

"Isabelle."

Snap snap.

There's a hand in front of my face now, waving. Fingers clicking. It makes me blink.

"Earth to Isabelle."

"Sorry," I say, shaking my head, as if the motion could somehow clear the fog like windshield wipers swiping at rain. I blink a few more times before trying to find the spot again, but it's gone now. I know it's gone. It's melted back into the carpet, into oblivion, the way I wish I could. "Sorry, yeah. On in five."

I lift my arm and take a sip of my Styrofoam cup of coffee—strong, black, squeaky when my chapped lips stick to the rim. I used to savor the taste of that daily morning cup. I lived for the smell of it wafting through my kitchen; the warmth of a mug pushed against my fingers, cold and stiff from standing on the back porch, watching the sun come up with morning dew beading on my skin.

But it wasn't the coffee I needed, I know that now. It was the routine, the familiarity. Comfort-in-a-cup, like those dehydrated noodles you splash faucet water onto before popping them into the microwave and calling it a meal. But I don't care about that anymore: comfort, routine. Comfort is a luxury I can no longer afford, and routine . . . well. I haven't had that in a long time, either.

Now I just need the caffeine. I need to stay awake.

"On in two."

I look up at the man standing before me, clipboard resting against his hip. I nod, down the rest of the coffee, and savor the bitter pinch in my jaw. It tastes like shit, but I don't care. It's doing its job. I dig my hand into my purse and pull out a bottle of eye drops—redness relief—and squirt three beads of liquid into each eye with expert precision. I guess this is my routine now. Then I stand up, run my hands over the front of my pants, and slap my palms against my thighs, signaling that I'm ready.

"If you'll follow me."

I hold out my arm, gesturing for the man to lead the way. And then I follow. I follow him out the door and through a dim hallway, the fluorescent lights buzzing in my ear like an electric chair humming to life. I follow him through another door, the gentle roar of applause erupting as soon as it opens and we step inside. I walk past him, to the edge of the stage, and stand behind a black curtain, the audience just barely obscured from view.

This is a big one. The biggest I've done.

I look down at my hands, where I used to hold note-cards with talking points scribbled in pencil. Little bulleted instructions reminding me what to say, what not to say. How to order the story like I'm following a recipe, meticulous and careful, sprinkling the details in just right. But I don't need those anymore. I've done this too many times.

Besides, there's nothing new to say.

"And now we are ready to bring out the person I know you're all here to see."

I watch the man speaking onstage, ten feet away, his voice booming over the loudspeakers. It's every-where, it seems—in front of me, behind me. Inside me, somehow. Somewhere deep in my chest. The audi-ence cheers again, and I clear my throat, remind myself why I'm here.

"Ladies and gentlemen of TrueCrimeCon, it is my honor to present to you, our keynote speaker . . . Isa-belle Drake!"

I step into the light, walking with purpose toward the host as he signals me onstage. The crowd continues to yell, some of them standing, clapping, the beady little eyes of their iPhones pointed in my direction, taking me in, unblinking. I turn toward the audience, squinting at their silhouettes. My eyes adjust a bit, and I wave, smil-ing weakly before coming to a halt in the center.

The host hands me a microphone, and I grab it, nod-ding.

"Thank you," I say, my voice sounding like an echo. "Thank you all for coming out this weekend. What an incredible bunch of speakers."

The crowd erupts again, and I take the free seconds to scan the sea of faces the way I always do. It's women, mostly. It's always women. Older women in groups of five or ten, relishing this annual tradition—the ability to break away from their lives and their responsibilities and drown themselves in fantasy. Younger women, twenty-somethings, looking skittish and a little embarrassed, like they've just been caught looking at porn. But there are men, too. Husbands and boyfriends who were dragged along against their will; the kind with wire-rimmed glasses and peach-fuzz beards and elbows that protrude awkwardly from their arms like knobby tree branches. There are the loners in the corner, the ones whose eyes linger just long enough to make you uncomfortable, and the police officers perusing the aisles, stifling yawns.

And then I notice the clothing.

One girl wears a graphic tee that says *Red Wine and True Crime*, the *T* in the shape of a gun; another sports a white shirt sprayed with specks of red—it's supposed to mimic blood, I assume. Then I see a woman wearing a T-shirt that says *Bundy. Dahmer. Gacy. Berkowitz.* I remember walking past it earlier in the gift shop. It was clipped tight against a mannequin, being advertised in the same way they advertise overpriced band T-shirts in the merchandise tents at concerts, memorabilia for rabid fans.

I feel the familiar swell of bile in my throat, warm and sharp, and force myself to look away.

"As I'm sure you all know, my name is Isabelle Drake, and my son, Mason, was kidnapped one year ago," I say. "His case is still unsolved."

Chairs squeak; throats are cleared. A mousey woman in the front row is shaking her head gently, tears in her eyes. She is loving this right now, I know she is. It's like she's watching her favorite movie, mindlessly snacking on popcorn as her lips move gently, reciting every word. She's heard my speech already; she knows what happened. She knows, but she still can't get enough.

None of them can. The murderers on the T-shirts are the villains; the uniformed men in back, the heroes. Mason is the victim . . . and I'm not really sure where that leaves me.

The lone survivor, maybe. The one with a story to tell.

CHAPTER TWO

I settle into my seat. The aisle seat. Generally, I prefer the window. Something to lean up against and close my eyes. Not to sleep, exactly. But to drift away for a while. *Microsleeping,* is what my doctor calls it. We've all seen it before, especially on airplanes: the twitching eyelids, the bobbing head. Two to twenty seconds of unconsciousness before your neck snaps back up with astonishing force like a cocking shotgun, ready to go.

I look at the seat to my right: empty. I hope it stays open. Takeoff is in twenty minutes; the gate is about to close. And when it does, I can move over. I can close my eyes.

I can try, as I've been trying for the last year, to finally get some rest.

"Excuse me."

I jump, looking up at the flight attendant before me. She's tapping the back of my seat, disapproval in her eyes.

"We're going to need you to make sure your seat back is in the upright and locked position."

I look back down, push the little silver button on my armrest, and feel my back begin to bend forward at an acute angle, my stomach folding in on itself. The attendant begins to walk away, pushing overhead compartments closed as she goes, when I reach out my arm and stop her.

"Can I bother you for a soda water?"

"We'll begin beverage service as soon as we take off."

"Please," I add, grabbing her arm harder as she starts to step away. "If you wouldn't mind. I've been talking all day."

I touch my throat for emphasis, and she looks down the aisle at the other passengers squirming uncomfortably, adjusting their seat belts. Digging through backpacks for headphones.

"Fine," she says, her lips pinched tight. "Just a moment."

I smile, nod, and ease back into my seat before looking around the plane at the other passengers I'll be sharing circulated air with for the next four hours as we make our way from Los Angeles to Atlanta. It's a game I play, trying to imagine what they're doing here. What life circumstances brought them to this exact moment, with this exact group of strangers. I wonder what they've been doing, or what they plan to do.

Are they going somewhere, or are they making their way home?

My eyes land first on a child sitting alone, giant headphones swallowing his ears. I imagine he's a product of divorce, spending one weekend every month getting shuttled from one side of the country to the other like cargo. I feel myself starting to imagine how Mason might have looked at that age—how his green eyes could have morphed even greener, two twin emeralds twinkling like his father's, or how his baby-smooth skin might have taken on the olive tone of my own, a natural tan without having to step foot in the sun.

I swallow hard and force myself to turn away, twisting to the left and taking in the others.

There are older men on laptops and women with

books; teenagers on cell phones slouched low in their seats, gangly knees knocking into the seat backs in front of them. Some of these people are traveling to weddings or funerals; some are embarking on business trips or clandestine getaways paid for in cash. And some of these people have secrets. All of them do, really. But some of them have the real ones, the messy ones. The deep, dark, shadowy ones that lurk just beneath the skin, traveling through their veins and spreading like a sickness.

Dividing, multiplying, then dividing again.

I wonder which ones they are: the ones with the kinds of secrets that touch every organ and render them rotten. The kinds of secrets that will eat them alive from the inside out.

Nobody in here could possibly imagine what I've just spent *my* day doing: recounting the most painful moment of my life for the enjoyment of strangers. I have a speech now. A speech that I recite with absolute detachment, engineered in just the right way. Sound bites that I know will read well when ripped from my mouth and printed inside newspapers, and manufactured moments of silence when I want a point to sink in. Warm memories of Mason to break up a particularly tense scene when I'm sensing the need for some comedic relief. Just as I'm going deep into his disappearance—the open window I had discovered in his bedroom letting in a warm, damp breeze; the tiny mobile situated above his bed, little stuffed dinosaurs dancing gently in the wind—I stop, swallow. Then I recite the story of how Mason had just started talking. How he pronounced T. rex "Tyranto*snorious*"—and how, every time he pointed at the little creatures above his bed, my husband would break out into exaggerated snores, sending him into a fit of giggles before drifting off himself. And then the audience would allow themselves to smile, maybe even laugh. There would be a visible release in their shoulders; their bodies would settle into their chairs again, a collectively held breath released. Because that's the thing with the audience, the thing I learned long ago: They don't want to get *too* uncomfortable. They don't want to actually live through what I've lived through, every ugly moment. They just want a taste. They want enough for their curiosity to be satiated—but if it gets too bitter or too salty or too real, they'll smack their lips and leave dissatisfied.

And we don't want that.

The truth is, people love violence—from a distance, that is. Anyone who disagrees is either in denial or hiding something.

"Your soda water."

I look up at the flight attendant's outstretched arm. She's holding a small cup of clear liquid, little bubbles rising to the surface and bursting with a satisfying fizz.

"Thank you," I say, taking it from her and placing it in my lap.

"You'll need to keep your tray table stowed," she adds. "We'll be in the air soon."

I smile, taking a small sip to indicate that I understand. When she walks off, I lean down, digging my hand into my purse until I feel a mini bottle tucked neatly into the side pocket. I'm attempting to discreetly unscrew the cap when I feel a presence beside me, hovering close.

"This is me."

My neck snaps up, and I'm half expecting to see somebody I know. There's a familiarity in the voice above me, vague, like a casual acquaintance, but when I look up at the man standing in the aisle, I see a stranger with a TrueCrimeCon tote bag slung over one arm, the other pointing to the seat beside me.

The window seat.

He sees the mini bottle in my hand and grins. "I won't tell."

"Thanks," I say, standing up to let him pass through.

I try not to glower at the prospect of being stuck next to an attendee on the flight home—it's complicated, really, the way I feel about the fans. I hate them, but I need them. They're a necessary evil: their eyes, their ears. Their undivided attention. Because when the rest of the world forgets, they remember. They still read every article, debating their theories on amateur sleuth forums as if my life is nothing more than a fun puzzle to be solved. They still curl up on their couches with a glass of Merlot in the evenings, getting lost in the comforting drone of *Dateline*. Trying to experience it without *actually* experiencing it. And that's why events like TrueCrimeCon exist. Why people spend hundreds of dollars on airfare and hotel rooms and conference tickets: for a safe space where they can bask in the bloody glow of violence for just a few days, using another person's murder as a means of entertainment.

But what they don't understand, what they *can't* understand, is that one day, they could wake up to find the violence crawling through their television screens, latching on to their houses, their lives, like a parasite sinking in its fangs. Wriggling in deep, making itself comfortable. Sucking the blood from their bodies and calling them home.

People never think it'll happen to them.

The man glides past me and into his seat, pushing his bag beneath the chair in front of him. When I settle back in, I pick up where I left off: the gentle crack of the cap breaking, the glug of vodka as it pours into my drink. I stir it with my finger before taking a long sip.

"I saw your keynote."

I can feel my seatmate looking at me. I try to ignore

him, closing my eyes and leaning my head against the headrest. Waiting for the vodka to make my eyelids just heavy enough to stay closed for a bit.

"I'm so sorry," he adds.

"Thank you," I say, eyes still shut. Even though I can't actually sleep, I can act like I'm sleeping.

"You're good, though," he continues. I can feel his breath on my cheek, smell the spearmint gum wedged between his molars. "At telling the story, I mean."

"It's not a story," I say. "It's my life."

He's quiet for a while, and I think that did it. I usually try not to make people uncomfortable—I try to be gracious, play the role of the grieving mother. Shaking hands and nodding my head, a grateful smile plastered across my face that I immediately wipe away like lipstick the second I step away. But right now I'm not at the conference. It's over, I'm done. I'm going home. I don't want to talk about it anymore.

I hear the intercom come to life above us, a scratchy echo.

"Flight attendants, prepare doors for departure and cross-check."

"I'm Waylon," the man says, and I can feel his arm thrust in my direction. "Waylon Spencer. I have a podcast—"

I open my eyes and look in his direction. I should have known. The familiar voice. The fitted V-neck and dark-wash skinny jeans. He doesn't look like the typical attendee, with his glossy hair shaved into a sloping gradient at the neck. He's not into murder for entertainment; he's in it for business.

I'm not sure which is worse.

"Waylon," I repeat. I look down at his outstretched hand, his expectant face. Then I swivel my neck around and shut my eyes again. "I don't want to come across as rude, *Waylon*, but I'm not interested."

"It's really gaining some traction," he says, pressing on. "Number five in the app store."

"Good for you."

"We even solved a cold case."

I can't tell if it's the sudden movement of the plane—a gentle lurch that makes my stomach flip, my limbs pushing deep into the seat as we rattle down the runway, this giant metal box we're all locked inside moving faster and faster, making my eardrums swell—or if it's his words that make me feel suddenly uneasy.

I take a deep breath, dig my nails into the armrest.

"Flying make you nervous?"

"Can you stop?" I spit, my head snapping back in his direction. I watch as his eyebrows raise, my sudden meanness taking him by surprise.

"I'm sorry," he says, looking embarrassed. "It's just—I thought you might be interested. In telling the story. *Your* story. On the show."

"Thank you," I say, trying to soften my tone. We both tilt back as the plane begins to ascend, the floor rattling violently beneath our feet. "But I'll pass."

"Okay," he says, digging into his pocket and pulling out his wallet. I watch as he flips open the faded leather, pulls a business card out, and places it gently on my leg. "If you change your mind."

I close my eyes again, leaving his card untouched on my knee. We're in the air now, ripping through clouds bloated with water, a beam of sunlight occasionally finding its way through the half-drawn shade and casting a ray of bright light across my eyes.

"I guess I just thought that's why you do it," he adds softly. I try to ignore him, but curiosity gets the best of me. I can't.

"Do what?"

"You know, your talks. It can't be easy, reliving it over

and over again. But you have to if you want to keep the case alive. If you ever want it to be solved."

I squeeze my eyes harder, focusing on the little spider veins I can see in my eyelids, glowing red.

"But with a podcast, you wouldn't have to talk to all those people. Not directly, anyway. You'd just have to talk to me."

I swallow, nod my head gently to indicate that I hear but that the conversation is still over.

"Anyway, just think it over," he adds, reclining his chair.

I can hear the rustling of his jeans as he tries to get comfortable, and I know, within minutes, he'll be able to do so easily what I haven't been able to do in a year. I peek one eye open and glance in his direction. He's pushed wireless headphones into his ears, the steady thumping of bass loud enough for me to hear. Then I watch his body transform the same way it always does, predictable yet still so foreign to me: His breath begins to get deeper, steadier. His fingers begin to twitch in his lap, his mouth hanging open like a creaky cupboard door, a single bead of drool quivering in the corner of his lip. Five minutes later, a gentle snore erupts from his throat, and I feel a pinch in my jaw as I clench my teeth.

Then I close my eyes, imagining, for a fleeting moment, what it must be like.